KU-278-014

D105

# MANCHESTER
## CITY COUNCIL

Please return / renew this item.

Books can be renewed by phone,
internet or Manchester Libraries app.

**www.manchester.gov.uk/libraries**

**Tel: 0161 254 7777**

# SUNSET
# SWING

# SUNSET SWING

## RAY CELESTIN

MANTLE

First published 2021 by Mantle
an imprint of Pan Macmillan
The Smithson, 6 Briset Street, London EC1M 5NR
*EU representative:* Macmillan Publishers Ireland Ltd, 1st Floor,
The Liffey Trust Centre, 117–126 Sheriff Street Upper,
Dublin 1, D01 YC43
Associated companies throughout the world
www.panmacmillan.com

ISBN 978-1-5098-3897-4

3 5 7 9 8 6 4 2

A CIP catalogue record for this book is available from the British Library.

Typeset in Fournier by Jouve (UK), Milton Keynes
Printed and bound by CPI Group (UK) Ltd, Croydon, CR0 4YY

Visit **www.panmacmillan.com** to read more about all our books
and to buy them. You will also find features, author interviews and
news of any author events, and you can sign up for e-newsletters
so that you're always first to hear about our new releases.

*To Julia*

'In a feverish buying and selling of land, the coast has become utterly transformed and unrecognizable. Each succeeding house, bigger and grander, takes the view of its neighbors in a kind of unbridled competition . . . Developers have bulldozed the Santa Monicas beyond recovery . . . Once lost, paradise can never be regained.'

LAWRENCE CLARK POWELL,
UCLA LIBRARIAN, 1958


'This is a landscape of desire . . . More than in almost any other major population concentration, people came to Southern California to consume the environment rather than to produce from it.'

HOMER ASCHMANN, GEOGRAPHER, 1959

# PART ONE

ALONE TOGETHER

December 1967

# 𝕷𝖔𝖘 𝕬𝖓𝖌𝖊𝖑𝖊𝖘 𝕿𝖎𝖒𝖊𝖘

LARGEST CIRCULATION IN THE WEST

## Friday Final

FRIDAY MORNING, DECEMBER 15, 1967

80 PAGES, DAILY, 10c

~

## LOCAL NEWS

~

# 'NIGHT-SLAYER' CLAIMS THIRD VICTIM

*By Nick Thackery*
*Crime Correspondent*

SILVER LAKE – A man was found brutally slain yesterday afternoon in a ritualistic killing that police said may connect it to two earlier 'Night-Slayer' murders. LAPD Detectives identified the latest victim as Anthony Butterfield, 43, an engineer at Lockheed's 'Skunk Works' aviation plant. A friend discovered Mr. Butterfield's body late Thursday afternoon in the victim's house.

There were reports that the same crucifix symbol seen in the previous two murders was discovered scrawled in chalk inside the property, although police at the scene refused to confirm this. The only comment made by LAPD Detective Robert Murray on the matter was that the murder 'seems ritualistic. Like the others.' He also declined to comment on the exact nature of the death with an autopsy still pending.

3

Newly installed county coroner, Dr. Thomas T. Noguchi, arrived in the early evening. He left an hour later, but refused to answer the gathered newsmen's questions.

## Neighborhood in Shock

Local residents clustered on their lawns throughout the evening and night hours, watching the police and other officials move about the victim's house and garden. The scenes echoed those of the earlier two murders, with whole neighborhoods left fearing for their safety. Despite the fact the investigation has been underway since October, no one has been arrested, although police did state that several possible suspects are being sought.

In the previous murders, no weapons or narcotics were found at the scene, and nothing appeared to be missing, suggesting robbery was not a motive. It is unclear if this latest slaying also fits that pattern.

## Victims so far

1) Mark McNeal, 28, doctor at LA County General, murdered in his home in Manhattan Beach, on 15th October
2) Danielle Landry, 23, actress, murdered in her apartment in West Hollywood, on 22nd November
3) Anthony Butterfield, 43, engineer, murdered in his house in Silver Lake, in the early hours of Thursday morning, 14th December

## Jurisdictional Tangle

This latest murder brings the total number of law enforcement agencies involved in the case to three,

as each of the crimes was committed under a different jurisdiction – Mr. Butterfield's murder in Silver
Lake falling under the purview of the LAPD, Ms. Landry's murder in West Hollywood under the Sheriff's
Department, and Mr. McNeal's murder under the
Manhattan Beach PD. Detectives at the scene declined
to comment on the extent to which the three agencies were co-operating with each other.

Please turn to Page B, Col. 3

# 1

LA was sunshine; LA was darkness. LA was the golden dream and the broken promise. It was freeways and gridlock, canyons and smog, stars ripped out of the sky and entombed in the sidewalks. It was seven million souls dreaming the dream, drifters and grifters and corrupt politicians. LA was where the white men came and saw there was no land left. To the cops it was a battleground, to the crooks it was a playground, to the residents of Watts it was 'Lower Alabama'. Mississippi with palm trees. LA was where you could drive all day and never arrive, a city connected and dissected by freeways that writhed like serpents in the night. It was both despoiler and despoiled. LA grew fat on defense contracts and the Cold War death-drive, but fooled the world into thinking it was in the glamour biz. LA was the beautiful lie.

And maybe this was why, like millions of others, Kerry Gaudet felt as if she knew LA before she ever set foot there. But when her sixty-dollar thrift flight flew in from Spokane and she stepped off the plane she sensed something more than what she'd been told by the TV shows and magazines; she sensed some friction in the air, some knife-edge, some madness. And she could tell the other passengers felt it, too. LA was as jumpy as Saigon.

Kerry picked up her bag from the carousels, rented an Oldsmobile Cutlass from the Hertz concession and drove to the motel the travel agency had arranged. It was nestled amongst warehouses and machine shops in a bleak stretch of Culver City, just

7

off the 405. Designed with an Indian theme, the motel's concrete cabins were shaped like wigwams, so it looked as if a tribe of Sioux had set up camp right there in the shadow of the freeway.

She changed out of her jungle fatigues, worked burn cream into her neck and chest, popped two codeine to tamp down the pain. She changed into capris and pumps and a cotton T-shirt which stuck to the burn cream. Even though there was a phone in her cabin, she left the motel to use the payphone across the road, calling the man her buddies back in Vietnam had told her about. He took her order and gave her a place to meet then hung up. She put down the receiver and a weight of fear flashed through her. Only now did she pray that she could trust the man.

She crossed back to her wigwam and stopped a moment to stare at the giant billboard that loomed over the motel grounds, partially covering the roaring freeway behind. It depicted orange groves and oil derricks, idyllic beaches and gleaming freeways, the Hollywood sign and rolling green mountains. A couple rode horses through this landscape, and even though they were only shown in silhouette, Kerry got the sense that they were happy, healthy, well-adjusted. Underneath was the city's municipal slogan: *It All Comes Together in Los Angeles!*

A truck boomed past, making the billboard rattle.

Back in her room, Kerry emptied her military bag and returned with it to the Cutlass. She took the Los Angeles road map from the glovebox and found where she was supposed to be going.

She hooked north onto the 405. She watched the city flicker past, the moon bathing it in a chalky light. That frisson was in the air once more, that fever wind. She thought she could see grains of sand shooting through the night, tracing slipstreams in the dark.

She took Sepulveda Pass through the mountains, out the other side, swung east and arrived at the meeting place – the parking lot of the Big Donut Drive-In on the corner of Kester Avenue and

Sherman Way. The place was deserted, an asphalt wasteland inter-rupted only by the drive-in shack at its center, its roof adorned with a giant concrete donut. Kerry checked the time; she was early.

She parked. She waited. She fretted. Under her T-shirt, the burn cream felt gummy and pricklish, the sensation bringing back nightmare echoes of the firestorm all those weeks ago. She re-adjusted her T-shirt and her skin peeled and stung. She studied her surroundings, feeling self-conscious, wondering if she looked suspicious.

Her gaze landed on the giant concrete donut fixed into place above the shack. The hole in its center revealed a circle of night sky robbed of its stars by light pollution and actual pollution. Kerry stared at the concrete ring of nothingness and wondered what views she was missing out on. Somewhere beyond the smog the constellations were continuing their vast turn about Polaris, nebulas were shimmering, comets were journeying through the seamless dark.

She switched on the radio and skipped through the dial till a song surfaced up out of the static – 'Alone Together' by Chet Baker – a slow, doleful jazz song her father used to listen to in the old family house in Gueydan, back when Kerry and Stevie were kids, before their mother ran away and their father waded off into the bayou and blew his brains out with an Ithaca Pump. Soon after Kerry and Stevie had been forced out of the family house, onto a long, painful trek through the children's homes and orphanages of Vermilion Parish, Louisiana.

And now Stevie had gone missing. Snatched into the darkness that hung about this strange, sprawling city. Her last living rela-tive, with whom she'd been through hell.

Chet Baker ended the song in a whisper, but the brackish memories of Louisiana continued to wash through Kerry's mind, lapping with the slow relentlessness of bayou tides. Once more she thought she could see grains of sand, swirling about the asphalt now, fixing themselves for an instant into the glittering shape of a curl.

A Lincoln Continental pulled into the lot. All black and silver trim, gliding like a shark. Kerry's chest tightened. The Continental slow-rolled, turned. Its low beams swept the ground. She raised a hand warily. The car pulled into the space next to her and a man got out, hauled a duffel bag from the trunk. He walked round and got into Kerry's front passenger seat.

He was Japanese or Korean, maybe, wore a sky-blue suit with a pink carnation in his lapel, his hair side-parted and caked in styling wax that smelled something like her burn cream. His features were angular, severe, almost like they'd been carved by a scalpel.

Kerry nodded at the man, tried to hide how tense she was. He nodded back and flicked his gaze to the scars on her face, surprised by her appearance. How often did he sell his wares to disfigured women barely out of their teens?

'You found it OK?' he asked.

'Sure.'

She looked around the empty parking lot and wondered why he'd asked to meet here. They couldn't be more obvious if they tried.

'I know the owners,' he said, as if reading her thoughts. 'And the donuts are good.'

He opened up the duffel bag, took out an aluminium-framed Colt .38, a police-issue Ithaca Pump, cartons of bullets and shells. She checked the guns to make sure the serials had been removed, noticed how the sights on the front of the Colt had been filed down. She ran a hand over the pump, its barrel gleaming black. She thought briefly of her father, saw his body floating out there in the bayou still. She transferred everything to her military bag.

'You got the other stuff, too?' she asked.

The man nodded. He rummaged around and pulled out two pill bottles with enough Dilaudid in them to keep the pain in check for the duration of her stay.

'Thanks,' she said.

'You want anything else, I can get hold of it for you – pot, acid, coke, horse, ludes, benzos, meth, amyl, STP, MDA.'

'Just these, please. How much do I owe you?'

This was the moment she'd been worried about, but now she'd met the man she knew he wouldn't try to rob her, or worse.

He gave her the price. It was almost half the money she'd brought with her, but she took out her purse and paid without haggling. He nodded his thanks.

'Well, I better be going,' he said, opening the door. 'You need anything more, just call the number. And stay safe, there's a killer on the loose.'

She frowned at this, but he didn't stop to explain.

# 2

A Santa Ana was sweeping through the city that night. A desert wind. It started in the Mojave to the east of LA, picking up speed and sand particles and positive ions. It rushed over the mountains and rolled across the city's great asphalt plains, powdering them with sand and a prickly, nerve-fraying heat. The crime rate went up. The suicides, too. Los Angeles teetered on a knife-edge.

And so it was in Fox Hills, on its lonely streets, on the veranda of a house where Ida Young sat at a rickety fold-out table, hunched over a Remington typewriter, grappling with her memoirs. The going was especially tough that night, and Ida could tell it was because of the Santa Ana. She could sense its presence even before she heard it rattling down the street, before the coyotes started howling, before faraway hills began to glow, for as well as everything else, the Santa Ana set brushfires blazing.

Ida knew. She'd been in the city in '57, when the wind blew for fourteen days and reached hurricane force and people were ordered off the streets. And she'd been there in '61 and '64 when the wildfires destroyed Bel Air and Santa Barbara. And just the previous year a dozen men had died battling blazes across the San Gabriel Mountains.

Tonight the city would stew in violence. And on Ida's veranda in Fox Hills, the wind made the paper curl and the ink run dry. She thought about calling it a night and lying down to sleep, but the Santa Ana turned limbs restless, made breathing hard.

She walked back into the bungalow to pour herself a whiskey and returned to the veranda. In the distance, she spotted the lights of a car turning off toward Sepulveda Boulevard, its low beams tracing a path through the night, heading in her direction. It used to be on nights like this, when the city was sweltering under the itchy malevolence of the wind, Ida could expect to be summoned into the heart of the slaughter, to some scene of gruesome violence. But now it was for other people to pick through the gore. Now all she could do was wait it out.

She tracked the lights as they glimmered and strobed then disappeared into the darkness once more. Ida sat down on the rocking chair just by the front door, leaned over to the side table and switched on the radio. It was tuned to a jazz station and it was playing a song she knew – 'Alone Together' by Chet Baker. A mournful song, all rainy days and hotel rooms and sorrow. She turned up the volume, listened to the beautiful, haunted trumpet and wondered what had happened to the beautiful, haunted man who played it all those years ago; if he was still alive, if he'd found some solace, if he'd gone the bitter way of so many other jazzmen.

The car lights reappeared, blips on the high ground. Still a good few streets away, but still heading right for her. She thought of the revolver she had stashed in the house. She imagined the weight of it in her hand, the ridges of its diamond grip. Then she wondered why she was so nervy. Maybe it was the wind, maybe it was the killer slaughtering his way across LA, setting the entire city on edge long before the Santa Ana blew in. Ida wasn't immune to the fear, even though she'd been through it all before, decades ago in New Orleans.

Ever since she'd retired she'd been thinking more and more about the city of her birth. Maybe it was on account of writing the memoir, but these days wherever she looked she saw New Orleans – in the fields, in the alleys, in the dust by the side of the road. One city superimposed on the other. She'd even started peopling the landscape with characters from the Louisiana folk tales she'd been told as a child – the *mystère* skeletons in top hats and tails, the pirate Jean Lafitte, the Needle Men, the *loup-garou* werewolves, one-armed Bras-Coupé and his band of runaway slaves, who attacked plantations and were immune to death. She imagined them weaving through the shadows, hiding behind dumpsters, under freeways, loping across empty parking lots dappled in neon.

This was the problem with writing a memoir. Time clotted. Memories oozed. She'd thought the memoir would help her make sense of things, illuminate the path her life had taken, instead it left her wondering more strongly than ever how the hell she'd ended up where she had.

The song faded out into radio hiss. The DJ pitter-pattered in a late-night drawl. Ida searched about on the side table for her cigarette case, found it, lit up.

The low beams returned, tracing, prowling. They scythed the dark at the end of the road. Ida was about to rise and get her revolver when she saw the lights belonged to an LAPD prowler. She took another sip of whiskey, another drag on her cigarette. The prowler came to a stop right outside her house. A patrolwoman got out. Young, white, ginger, chubby round the hips. She put on her cap, straightened it, noticed Ida in the shadows of the veranda. She smiled and walked up the garden path.

'Evening, ma'am. I was looking for Ida Young.'

'You found her.'

The patrolwoman nodded.

'Ma'am, I was sent by a Detective Feinberg.'

'I know him.'

Feinberg was a Detective Third Grade with the LAPD's Homicide Division. A gifted investigator who never used pragmatism as an excuse for cutting corners. Ida had given him a job once at her agency toward the tail-end of the '40s and ever since they'd scratched each other's backs.

'There's been a homicide, ma'am. At the La Playa Motel over in San Pedro. Detective Feinberg requested you attend.'

Ida frowned. In all the years of their friendship Feinberg had never called her out to a crime scene.

'Why?' she asked.

'It's a little complicated, ma'am.'

'Who's the victim?'

'We're still waiting on an ID.'

'Well, then they can't be a known associate of mine, so why does the detective want me at the crime scene?'

'As I mentioned before, it's a little complicated, ma'am.'

Ida studied the patrolwoman. She was just a girl really, unsure of herself, unsettled by the dark, quiet neighborhood, and the crotchety old woman interrogating her. It took Ida back decades, to when she was a kid, when she read too many pulp magazines and dreamed of being a cop, not realizing that she was doubly excluded, first on account of her race, second on account of her gender. For years that naivety had embarrassed her. Only in middle age had she become proud of it. What would her life have been like if she'd had the opportunities afforded this patrol-woman? Would she have survived as long as she had?

'Stop calling me *ma'am*,' Ida said finally. 'I'm a sixty-seven-year-old retiree with a glass of Scotch in my hand. It's eight-thirty on a Tuesday night and there's a Santa Ana blowing. You're gonna have to give me something more than *it's complicated* if you want to get me off my porch.'

Ida stared at the patrolwoman. The radio played the opening bars of a bossa nova. The static of the Santa Ana crackled all around.

The patrolwoman let out a sigh, like some internal pressure had been released.

'Your name and address were found on a piece of paper at the crime scene,' she said. 'In the victim's possession.'

Ida's heart jumped. Like a stone tossed into water, sending ripples across her torso.

'Detective Feinberg was hoping you might give us a head start on ID-ing the victim,' the patrolwoman explained.

'Was the victim female?'

The patrolwoman frowned, then nodded.

'Another Night-Slayer killing?' Ida asked.

'No, ma'am. Looks like a Mob hit if anything.'

More ripples of fear. Mob hits on women were almost unheard of. Almost. Some delicate thread had wound itself maze-like across the city, from a murder in a motel room to Ida's door. Doing Feinberg the favor would mean heading out into the streets, into the violence and stewing darkness. But what really worried Ida was the prospect of getting involved in another investigation. She'd vowed never to go near one again.

'Ma'am?' the patrolwoman asked.

Ida hesitated.

Somewhere in the distance a dog barked, smoke rose, and the Santa Ana moaned, yearning for the desert once more.

# 3

LA was heroin country, a junkie's dream, a city in a pacific embrace – the endless summers, the balmy nights, the wave of lights that unfurled across the valleys at dusk and pooled about the feet of the hills like an astral tide. Even at the best of times it made Dante crave dope. But it was so much worse when the desert wind was blowing; old temptations bucked higher, the shadow of the dragon sailed by on the breeze. Dante had been clean for forty years, but on lonely, restless nights like this, it may as well as have been forty minutes.

Best to try and outrun it, on the freeways, in the Thunderbird, with its fire-red paint and quicksilver lines, its engine roaring, the city screaming by; its shadows, its grids, its rivers of light, Los Angeles gleaming with its own geometry. But in amongst the glistening all manner of ugliness lurked – knifemen stalked, grifters schemed, trash-can coyotes plotted and howled. And everyone dreamed the big dream, their fevers thickened by the desert wind swirling grains of sand and madness around.

Dante redlined the Thunderbird through it all, leaned back in his seat, watched the giant signs whispering past overhead – Beverly Hills, Mar Vista, Santa Monica. Cars glided by, the dragon rode his slipstream, weaving wraith-like between the traffic. To the north the mountains loomed, either side of him palm trees flitted by, houses with their windows illuminated by the pastel glow of TV sets, their residents smarter than Dante, riding out the maelstrom at home.

It wasn't just the Santa Ana that had summoned him onto the freeways that night. He had an appointment with Nick Licata, the newly installed head of the LA Mob. The call had come that afternoon on the warehouse phone, and Dante had been wired ever since. In the old days he would have known what the summons meant. A job. Cleaning up a crime scene, chasing product, evidence, gangsters on the lam, arbitrating beefs between hotheads in danger of starting a war. Dante had a knack for all of it, had the smarts and a calming finesse that most mobsters lacked. He was one of those rare men who could defuse a situation with a smile.

But Dante was only a few years shy of seventy now, hadn't picked up a job in months, had let it be known all over town that he was retiring. Just one week till the vineyard deal went through and he could leave the city for good. What kind of a job could Licata have for a washed-up, aging fixer like Dante?

When the old boss had died back in August, Nick Licata had taken charge against the wishes of half the men, who thought the job should have gone to Jack Dragna Junior. Now there were rumors the Mob was on the verge of splitting. And Mobs, like atoms, only ever split in a conflagration. Dante had thought he was getting out of town just in time to avoid the fallout. Now he was wondering if he'd left it just a week too late.

He lit a Lucky and roared the Thunderbird through the tunnel under the bluffs, came out the other side onto Pacific Coast Highway. The ocean stretched out on his left, its surface glassy and still, suffused with the eerie quiet that only ever descended when a Santa Ana was blowing.

At the turning for Chautauqua Boulevard he got snarled up in traffic, joining a comet stream of brake lights lining up for the Palisades. He checked his watch. He'd left the warehouse early so he could kill time driving, clearing his head with freeways and fumes. Now he just wanted to get it over with.

He switched on the car's radio, tuned it to a station playing jazz. West Coast jazz. A slow, lonesome song that he recognized from somewhere. The melody fine as a scalpel, yet still impossibly warm. He turned to look again at the ocean, and a story he'd heard years back surfaced in his mind – how in the old days, when a Santa Ana was blowing, the Indians would throw themselves off the cliffs into the water to escape its madness. Dante knew it was probably bullshit. He'd heard enough stories about the Indians to feel like most of them had been invented by white people for white people. Like the Indians were only useful now as some kind of carnival mirror, their strange reflection confirming the rightness of the people who now stood in their place. But despite this, there was something Dante liked about the story, an unnerving mix of fatalism and free will.

The song on the radio came to an end.

'And that was "Alone Together",' the disk jockey said, his voice as warm as whiskey. 'By the one and only Chet Baker.'

Now Dante remembered. Chet Baker. Jazz music's great white hope. The kid with the James Dean looks and the Miles Davis talent. Set to take over the world back in the '50s. Whatever happened to him? Was he still alive? Dante remembered newspaper stories from back then. Heroin busts, Italian jails, deportation, a scandal involving a princess. Had Baker managed to break free of the dope like Dante? Or had its riptide pulled him under?

The snarl-up unsnarled and Dante headed into the hills, the road twisting ribbon-like through the darkness. He passed by houses on stilts, thickets of eucalyptus and yucca. Now the city was laid out below him, and now, gliding round a hairpin, the city vanished, replaced by a view of the ocean, glazed in moonlight.

As he neared his destination he noticed a line of cars parked on the side of the road, fender-to-fender all the way along the cliff, half of them teetering dangerously near its edge. He found a space further down, parked, walked back toward the mansion. There was an electric eye next to the entrance, so when he approached, the gates opened automatically.

He stopped and watched them trundle backwards. Beyond the gates were the gardens, with their well-watered lawns and palms and paths leading everywhere. There were people sprawled out on the grass, already drunk and high. Not the kind you'd expect at a Mafia bash, these were young and beautiful types, fashionistas, glamor freaks. Dante wondered if he'd got the wrong address, but he couldn't have.

Beyond the gardens was the house itself, a sprawling, boxy, 1950s affair, all clean sweeping lines and giant windows and dazzling white terrazzo walls, like the architect wasn't sure if he was building an Italian villa or an art gallery. Somewhere in its pristine modernism was Nick Licata, a coterie of ruthless mobsters, Dante's fate. He tried not to think of Indians jumping into the Pacific. He lit another Lucky and headed into the fray.

# 4

The Sunset Strip jumped and writhed and seethed in the dark. Its cafés, delis and drugstores buzzed, its nightclubs blared out rock. Crowds of runaways and dropouts thronged the sidewalks, swigged from bags, laughing with eyes like UFOs. Kerry couldn't believe how young some of them were – fourteen, thirteen, twelve, eleven – and how many there were. Like every kid who'd run away west of the Mississippi had ended up here, on this same sleazy mile-and-a-half strip of unincorporated Los Angeles County.

Kerry felt overwhelmed – the life and color, the joy, the noise, the bloody haze of taillights, the illuminated billboards looming over it all. While Kerry had been in Vietnam for the last year and a half, all this had been going on back here. Like the hell she'd lived through didn't matter, maybe didn't even exist. A few of the hippies walking by were wearing thrifted army jackets along with their love beads, and all she could think of was the times she'd had to rip such jackets open to get to a wound, to stop some teen-aged soldier bleeding out before they'd even got him on the evac plane. But here those same jackets were just a fashion item. And an ironic one at that.

When she reached her destination, her spirits sank even lower. The hostel was nothing but a sign over a doorway between a liquor store and a cabaret. The doorway opened out onto grubby white walls and a greasy wooden staircase. Kerry knew the place would be seedy, shabby, depressing, and yet the reality of it still upset her. This was the hostel from which Stevie had sent his final letter, from where he'd disappeared. She ran her hand over her shoulder bag and felt the Colt inside, reassuringly heavy and real.

She ascended the stairs and came out into a reception area the size of a postage stamp. There was a window looking out onto the street, a door to another staircase, a couple of chairs, and a hole in the wall covered by wire mesh where the receptionist was supposed to be. Instead there was a piece of paper taped to the mesh – *Back in 10 minutes*. Everything was dappled in blinking green neon from a blade sign just outside the window.

Kerry sat in one of the chairs and waited, watched the neon blinking on and off, feeling the buzz of the Dilaudid pumping its way through her bloodstream, numbing the pain of the burn scars but not the memories. Questions looped around her head. The same mysteries that had been haranguing her since Stevie had disappeared, not long after Kerry had shipped out to Vietnam on her first tour of duty. She'd been trying to track him down ever since. Letters and calls across the ocean to police departments, social services, shelters.

'You know how many thousands of kids go missing each year?' a woman at a charity had told her over the phone. 'We'll add his name to the list.'

And then in November, that single letter arrived, just when Kerry was confined to a bed in the Clark Air Base Hospital, still recuperating from the fireball. She'd read the letter so many times she'd memorized it.

*I'm on to something, Kerry. Real big. To do with Louisiana and lots of other stuff. So much stuff you wouldn't believe. If you don't hear from me again, it means they got to me.*

She would have classed the letter as deranged if it had come from anyone else. Her brother was talking as if he'd discovered a conspiracy. But how could he have? He was a teenaged runaway, dirt poor, living in a hostel on the Sunset Strip. Had he uncovered something? Or had he simply gone mad?

*So I'm just writing to tell you I love you, sis. And I forgive you for what you did.*

This was another mystery. What had she done? Did he feel she'd abandoned him by going overseas?

She heard footsteps coming up the stairs. She opened her eyes and her vision blurred. Three kids staggered in. Not quite teeny-boppers, not quite hippies. The boys wore polo necks and cords. The girl was wrapped up in a Mexican shawl. None of them had shoes on their feet, just ankle bracelets and grime and cracked nails. Their eyes were red and glazed, staring at nothing and everything. They shuffled past, choosing not to notice Kerry, heading toward the stairs which led to the upper floors.

'Excuse me,' Kerry said, rising. 'You know where the receptionist is?'

They stopped and turned, a look rustled between them, secretive and suspicious. Or maybe it was just Kerry imagining it, the Dilaudid slurring her thoughts.

'Lonnie's not here?' one of the boys said. He made a show of peering at the hole in the wall, but the gesture rang fake.

'You know where he might be?' Kerry asked.

The boy shook his head, lying again.

Kerry noticed the girl was looking down, her eyes roaming the grain of the floorboards.

'Please,' Kerry said, turning to her. 'I'm looking for my little brother.'

The girl lifted up her gaze.

'He's not a good guy,' she said. 'Come back in the daytime. Speak to the other receptionist.'

'I don't have time for that. Please.'

The girl considered again, nodded. But as she began to speak, the boy cut her off.

'Megan,' he said.

They exchanged a quick stabbing look and something hardened in the girl's eyes. She turned to Kerry.

'He works out of the Crystal some nights. When he's supposed to be on shift. It's a nightclub, just down the block.'

'And what does he look like?'

'Tall. Fuzzy red hair. College student type.'

'Thank you,' Kerry said, nodding at the girl.

The girl stood there a moment, then she stepped forward. She lifted up her hand and ran a finger down the scars on Kerry's face, as if checking they were real. Kerry flinched, but the girl didn't stop. Up close Kerry could see how dilated her eyes were – glossy black disks on a sea of red veins.

'I'm sorry for your pain,' the girl said. 'I hope it stops.'

'It will. One way or the other.'

# 5

Ida sat in the back of the prowler as it sped south toward San Pedro. She was worried about what lay in store, if the victim was someone she knew, someone she loved. She searched the streets for signs of unrest, as if seeing her own inner turmoil reflected in her surroundings might make her feel better. They were passing through a shabby neighborhood of frail houses and brown lawns. Dogs chained to fences barked at the wind. A fight spilled out of a bar. There it was. City-wide angst.

'You're *the* Ida Young, right?' the patrolwoman asked.

Ida turned from the window.

'I'm *an* Ida Young.'

'You used to run the detective agency?'

Ida nodded.

The patrolwoman smiled.

'I've heard all about you,' she said. 'The Cooke murders. You're the one who found the real killers, right? And you got that kid off in the Echo Park case. And the Brandt kidnapping and the First National back in Chicago. That was all you, right?'

Ida frowned. Where the hell had she dredged up those old cases from?

'It wasn't all just me. I was part of a team.'

'And I heard, back in the twenties, you took on Capone?'

Ida frowned again.

'I never took on Capone. No one ever took on Capone except the Treasury. And syphilis.'

The patrolwoman looked confused.

'But you were in Chicago in the twenties, right? You were a Pinkerton?'

'Yeah,' Ida conceded. 'Yeah, I was. A long time ago.'

Ida fell silent, and the patrolwoman looked disappointed, another of her questions having crashed against the seawall of Ida's indifference. She wanted to hear about Ida's daring adventures, scrapes with death. Maybe even some life advice. But Ida had no wisdom to share. All she remembered were the dilemmas, the compromises, the failures. Maybe that was why the memoir was going so badly.

But none of that was the patrolwoman's fault, and it wasn't an excuse for bad manners, so Ida gave her a potted history of her life, how she'd worked with police and prosecutors, but just as often worked the other side – the miscarriages of justice. She told her about the cases that had made the papers, the ones that had made Ida's name. She talked till the patrolwoman seemed satisfied, buoyed up, confident that if Ida could do it, she could, too.

'So what are you doing these days?'

'I'm retired.'

'You miss it?'

'Yes and no.'

Ida didn't miss the brutality of the job, but she did miss being part of the world's great spin. And she rued all the unfinished business; the victims who'd never get justice, the mysteries that would never be solved. Most of all, how she'd failed to catch the worst killer she'd ever gone up against. She'd never believed in legacies. She'd always looked down on those people who strived to ensure they were remembered after they'd gone. It struck her as desperate. These fragile egos refusing to accept that all empires turned to dust.

But now she wondered if she'd got it all wrong, if maybe some legacies did have value. She felt as if she'd been duty-bound to hand on something which, in her rush to retire, she hadn't. A torch-pass she'd fumbled in the wake of Sebastián's death. But she couldn't have carried on working after that. So she'd sold up the agency and retreated to the house in Fox Hills, trying not to feel as if she was just killing time till she died.

They turned off the freeway, continued south, moving stop-light to stoplight through the industrial sprawl of San Pedro. In the distance, dock cranes slouched against the sky, signaling the location of the harbor, the largest man-made port in the world. Eventually they arrived at the La Playa Motel, a three-story rect-angle with outside walkways, and unobstructed views of the parking lot, from which a swirling red-and-blue light show was emanating. Police cruisers, cars, vans from the LAPD's Scientific Investigation Division, the County Coroner.

The patrolwoman bumped the prowler over the ramp and they entered the parking lot, pulled in behind one of the vans. They got out and a few of the officers turned to look. Ida ignored them and inspected the motel. On the side facing the street was a giant neon sign with the name on it. Just next to the neon, on the second story, police lights were illuminating the open door to one of the motel rooms, where yellow crime-scene tape glittered in the night. People milled about on the gallery outside it: forensics, uniforms, detectives.

She watched as three middle-aged white men stepped out of the room, descended the external stairs, came out into the lot. As they passed they tipped their hats. Ida caught a glimpse of their string ties, each embroidered with the words *1965 Sheriffs Rodeo*.

A gust of wind blew through the lot, making the crime-scene tape flutter, reminding Ida that this was a Santa Ana night, that there was voodoo on the wind, that it had drawn her here, to this motel, to this murder.

'Shall we?' the patrolwoman asked.

Ida nodded, and they headed for the slaughter.

# 6

Every inch of the mansion's floor space seemed to have a body occupying it, forming a continuous swirl of gilded youth that led from the hall to the lounge and out to the garden beyond. Again Dante wondered why Nick Licata had asked him to meet here, if the strange choice of location was a cause for concern.

He squeezed through the throng, past waitresses and busboys dressed up like elves, past tables decorated with mistletoe and laden with silver tureens of eggnog. He must have skirted by five different Christmas trees before he got to the lounge, which had a sunken floor, and a risqué ice sculpture of Santa and Mrs Claus dripping water all over the cut-pile carpet.

When he stepped through the sliding doors into the garden, he saw it boasted a swimming pool and a terrace with panoramic views that stretched all the way from the ocean to the city. There was a makeshift bar staffed by bartender elves and a five-piece elf band knocking out a bossa nova rendition of 'Let It Snow', the singer sultry, whispering the lyrics. Dante could never listen to the song without being reminded that it had been composed in LA, in the middle of a heatwave.

He grabbed a beer and looked out over the crowd. Mostly young, mostly half-naked. The heated pool was a swarm of bodies. Others lay about on the grass, or were sprawled across the wrought-iron garden chairs scattered around. He spotted a few celebrities – Harry Belafonte on the patio, chatting with some pals. Paul Newman holding court by the low wall that ran around the terrace, bottle of beer in hand, girls all around him.

In the distance stood a pool house the size of an actual house.

In front of it, under a beach umbrella, a group huddled around a hand mirror, snorting lines of white powder. Heroin, Dante assumed, twitching once more in the cold sweat of forty years ago. But there was something odd about the group, something that he couldn't put his finger on. As he mulled it over, an elf walked past hoicking a tray of hors d'oeuvres.

'Say, what's the party in aid of?' Dante asked.

'It's in aid of Christmas,' the elf said, nonplussed. 'It's the label's Christmas party.'

'What label?'

'Nova Records.' She smiled a plastic smile and sauntered off.

Dante surveyed the scene once more and started spotting mobsters in amongst the crowd. They were older, rougher-looking, more flashily dressed, their suits shinier, their hair shorter. Dante wondered if the glitterati were aware of the torturers and psychopathic killers in their midst.

As the band launched into 'Winter Wonderland', Dante ambled through the crowd, looking for Nick Licata. He reached the edge of the terrace and stopped to take in the view. Far below, the ocean gleamed in the moonlight, eerily smooth. Further along was the city itself, a white fire of lights rising up from the plain. Dante thought about the Santa Ana blowing through its streets, the tension, the edge. From this hilltop palace none of it seemed real – not the wind, nor the smog, nor the red mist of violence that hung about its alleys and canyons. From this high up LA looked less like a slab of cement, and more a landscape of lights, a place from which dreams, not nightmares, rose unbroken. Maybe that was why views like this cost a million dollars.

'Almost looks nice from up here,' said a voice.

Dante turned to see Vincent Zullo standing next to him. A foot soldier of the younger generation, Zullo was exactly the type of mobster Dante hated – all studied masculinity and front, probably because he knew if he ever actually tried being charming, he'd go down in flames. He was wearing a golf shirt and slacks and a thin gold crucifix on a chain around his neck. His hair was thinning and he was compensating by fixing what was left upwards and back with inordinate amounts of hairspray that gave off a cloying chemical smell.

'Don't tell me this is your new place?' Dante said, gesturing to the mansion.

A man who changed his expression more easily than Zullo might have smiled, or grimaced. Instead he grunted.

'It's a pop star's place,' he said. 'His record label and me share an accountant, so here we are.'

Dante nodded. The label was being used to launder Zullo's dirty money. A few years back, Zullo had moved from LA out to Vegas to help with the skim at some of Joey Aiuppa's casinos. Dante wondered if maybe that was where the money was coming from. Then he wondered who the unfortunate pop star was. He'd seen so many straight guys get tangled up with the Mob, screwed over, spat out. Fame and status were no guard against it.

Dante studied Zullo. His eyes were glassy and red, his nose raw, and he kept on sniffing, as if he was trying to stop something valuable falling out of his nostrils. He'd clearly come over to fish for information, to find out what Dante was doing there. Dante wondered if the fishing expedition had anything to do with the impending Mob war.

'So business is good then?' Dante asked.

'Never better,' Zullo boasted, because he'd obviously forgotten the 1950s. 'Everyone's flush on account of this Hughes thing and they're looking to expand.'

Dante nodded. Hughes was Howard Hughes, Dante's former employer at RKO. Hughes had moved to Las Vegas the previous year and had started buying up hotels from the Mob, most recently picking up the Sands. His plan was to buy up all the hotels, all the casinos, and turn the town into his own little kingdom. The Mob had started selling him whatever he wanted, but they were going to keep their men in place at the casinos – men like Zullo – to keep the skim going. The plan was to bilk Hughes out of hundreds of millions.

'Yeah, Nevada's where it's at,' Zullo said. 'No personal income tax, no corporate income tax. No warehouse, franchise or inheritance tax. Three percent sales tax. Five percent real estate tax. They know what they're doing. The only thing that costs money is buying off the Gaming Commission for a license.'

He grinned at his own joke, and Dante smiled back out of politeness. Zullo sniffed again, loudly.

'What's Joey got you doing out there?' Dante asked.

'Procurement.'

'Procurement of what?'

'Goons. Dealers. Showgirls.'

Zullo grinned again. Dante wasn't sure what effect he was going for, but it played seedy. In his mind, Dante lamented the fact that the Mob was peopled now by younger men like Zullo. Second-rate men, lesser men than those of Dante's generation. Dante had been there for the golden age of the '20s through to the '50s, meaning he had a point of reference from which he could mark the Mob's decline. It all underlined that he'd made the right decision to get out. But it made him wonder: if the Mob did eventually die a death, what would replace it?

'I heard you'd bought a vineyard and moved upstate,' Zullo said, as if remembering he was supposed to be fishing for information.

'Not just yet,' Dante said. 'Deal goes through soon, though.'

'Gonna go upstate and grow grapes like some old farmer from back in Italy?' Zullo said, his tone mocking.

'Not a *farmer*,' Dante replied. 'A *vintner*.'

It was Dante's daughter, Jeanette, who'd put him onto the vineyard. All Dante knew about Napa Valley before that was it was where mobsters went to bury corpses, mostly on Jo Dippolito's estate, where he kept sacks of lime handy in a barn. But Jeanette, who ran her own drinks distribution firm in Santa Rosa now, had driven up to the vineyard one weekend to check in on a wine supplier and had fallen in love with the place. When she heard the owner was looking to sell, she got Dante and his wife Loretta to drive up too, and they'd fallen in love with it as well. For years they'd been looking for somewhere to retire to, and they'd finally found it. They spent months arranging the deal, and now, in a week's time, they'd be the owners of a hundred and fifty acres of rolling green vineyards. It had all been going to plan until the call from Nick Licata came through that afternoon.

'I've spent my whole life dealing booze, Vinnie,' Dante said. 'From slinging bottles off boats during prohibition, to going legit and supplying every nightclub and restaurant in LA. Now I wanna try actually making the stuff.'

'You'll never beat Italian wine. Not with anything grown in California.'

'We'll see.'

There was a scream from the pool as someone threw a girl in. Dante turned to look and noticed a good-looking man joking with one of the elf waitresses by the bandstand. The man smoldered. The elf simpered. Dante tried to place him.

'Warren Beatty,' Zullo said, reading Dante's mind.

Of course, Dante thought, studying Beatty a little longer. The man was devilish even from thirty yards away. Dante turned to see Zullo lighting a cigarette, making Dante wonder if the flame might not ignite the fumes from Zullo's hairspray and incinerate half the garden. Just then he noticed someone behind Zullo, a familiar face slipping through the crowd toward him – Johnny Roselli. A gangster of Dante's own generation.

'Johnny's calling,' Dante said. 'Take care, Vinnie.'

Zullo turned and saw Roselli, and his grimace deepened.

Dante crossed the terrace. Roselli threw an arm over his shoulder, drew him in for a hug.

'Dante the Gent,' Roselli said.

Dante smiled. It was only the men of his own generation who used his old nickname.

'Nick's waiting for you in the pool house,' Roselli said. 'Come on, we got a lot to discuss.'

# 7

The Crystal Club looked like it had been converted from a Swing-era ballroom, with a cavernous dance hall, high ceilings and walls decorated with intricate moldings that were now all scuffed and broken. There was a bar along one side, thick with people, a dance floor that was also packed, and a band on stage dressed in corduroy shirts and trousers blaring out languid, hallucinatory rock. Rigs hooked to the ceiling sent shafts of colored light spinning downwards or projected swirling liquid shapes onto the dancing bodies beneath.

Kerry squeezed through the press, wondering how the hell she'd find the hostel receptionist. She made it to the bar where a bartender spotted her.

'I'm looking for Lonnie,' Kerry said. 'The receptionist at the Aspen.'

The bartender gave her a look and Kerry wondered if she'd made a mistake using the man's name so casually. Then the bartender gestured to the very end of the bar where a man was sitting on a stool. The man matched the description of the receptionist that the girl in the hostel had given Kerry – young, tall, red-haired, a college student type. He was passing a second man something, who in return passed Lonnie some cash. Even from a distance Kerry got the sense that there was something off about him. The same fear she'd experienced while waiting at the donut place resurfaced, but stronger this time.

She pushed through the fear. She had to. In six days she was due back in Vietnam. She exhaled, thanked the bartender and shouldered through the crowd.

'Lonnie?' she said.

He turned and smiled.

'What you after?'

Kerry realized he'd mistaken her for a customer.

'I need your help with something,' she said.

He frowned at her, suddenly suspicious, guarded.

'Please,' she said.

He continued to frown at her, long enough to make Kerry feel even more uncomfortable. Then he nodded and gestured to the stool next to him, allowing her to sit.

'I'm getting myself another beer,' he said. 'You want one?'

Kerry nodded. They turned so they were facing the bar and Lonnie held up a hand. A series of posters had been pasted up along the bar's back wall, cartoons and drawings and slogans which had to be ironic in this context: *Support Your Local Police – America, Love it or Leave it.*

The same bartender Kerry had spoken to got them two bottles of Schlitz. She took a sip and the beer tasted cool and hoppy, made her realize how parched she was.

'So?' Lonnie asked.

'You're the receptionist over at the hostel?'

'Sure.'

'My brother was staying there a few months back and he went missing. I'm trying to track him down.'

'Lot of kids pass through there,' he shrugged. 'It's hard to keep up.'

Kerry slipped a photo of Stevie out of her pocket, passed it over. Lonnie stared at it and appeared to recognize Stevie, and the recognition seemed to cause a shadow of sadness to pass across his features. Kerry was about to ask what the problem was when someone approached, clapped a hand on Lonnie's shoulder.

'Can I get a minute with the candy man?' the newcomer grinned.

Lonnie raked the man with a look, as if annoyed by the nick-name he'd used.

'You mind?' Lonnie asked, turning to Kerry.

She shook her head. Lonnie passed back the photo and she looked over the ballroom while Lonnie and the man huddled together to conduct what Kerry could only assume was a drug deal. On the stage, the guitars were still squealing and thundering. The speakers throbbing like they might explode. Behind the band was another of the ironic posters, blown up to giant size. It showed Mount Rushmore with speech bubbles emanating from the presidents' mouths – *I call this orgy to order* – *Live Freaky, Die Freaky* – *Do What Thou Wilt* – *Fight War, Not Wars*.

On the dance floor people swayed and Indian-danced, hands in the air. It was only then Kerry noticed their expressions, their wide eyes, their pinpoint pupils. The entire club was on LSD. Kerry had tripped a few times over in Vietnam. On one occasion some of the pilots at the base had driven her and a couple of the other nurses out to the edge of the jungle. They'd taken a tab each and smoked pot as they waited for the flash, and when the flash came, the jungle oozed, writhed in the darkness, and Kerry had felt the presence of an evil in that jungle, had visions of a serpent stretching itself all the way around the globe, clasping the world in a destructive embrace.

'Sorry about that,' Lonnie said.

Kerry turned back around. Lonnie's customer was disappearing through the throng.

'You recognized Stevie. In the photo.'

He nodded.

'He stayed a few months. Over the summer, I think, into the fall.'

'You know where he is now?'

'He skipped out. Happens a lot. Kids run up a bill they can't pay so they disappear.'

'You know where he went?'

'I'm sorry.' Lonnie shook his head. 'Like I said – happens a lot. He probably found some friends to hang with. You gone to the police? Filed a missing juvenile report?'

'I called them up. But they told me I could only file one in person.'

'So you came all the way to LA to do that? From where? Down South?'

He'd picked up on her Louisiana accent. She shook her head. 'Vietnam.'

'You came all the way from Vietnam to file a missing juve report?'

'I came to find my brother.'

Lonnie nodded, came over all somber. They both sipped their beers. Kerry stared at one of the posters on the far wall – *In deserts, all water is holy*. She turned back and looked at Lonnie, and realized he, the drug dealer, was probably the only other person in there who wasn't high.

'So what were you doing over in Vietnam?' he asked.

'I'm an Air Force nurse.'

'Is that how you got those?'

He gestured to the burn scars on the side of her face. She nodded.

'How'd it happen?'

She picked at the label on her beer bottle. In the crevice between the paper and the glass, she saw flames flicker and roar.

'Napalm.'

'Jesus.'

She shrugged.

'Fight war, not wars,' she said.

'Right on.'

They sipped their beers, looked over the dance floor. The dancers' bodies smeared across Kerry's vision. The lights seemed aqueous, like they were all underwater, a swirling rainbow of blues and greens. Kerry realized the Dilaudid she'd taken was stronger than she'd thought, and that maybe mixing it with beer wasn't a good idea.

'If you want I can give you something to calm your nerves,' Lonnie said.

'Who said I'm nervous?'

'Everyone's nervous. It's a Santa Ana night.'

She frowned. He smiled.

'It's the desert wind. When it blows – more fights, more rattlesnake bites. Out on the ocean more boats capsize. Like on full moons, but worse.'

He made a noise like a howling wind, or maybe wolves, and waved his hand through the air like it was gliding on thermals. Was that what she'd been feeling ever since she'd gotten off the plane? It sounded too fantastical to be true, yet another instance of Los Angeles self-mythologizing, turning itself into a fairyland.

'Like I told you, I can give you something to ride it out. I've got coke, horse, pot, acid, meth, amyl, MDA, STP, quaaludes, Dexedrine, Mescaline, mushrooms, peyote, benzos, black beauties and if you give me twenty-four hours, I can get you any prescription pill you want, too.'

Kerry wondered how he could have all that on him, if he was using the hostel over the road as a stash spot as well as a cover story.

'It'd help you fit in,' he continued. 'Being sober in LA's kinda like a minority approach.'

'I just want info on my brother.'

She looked at him and could see some tension in his bearing; he was holding something back.

'What is it?' she asked.

'Nothing.'

'You know something, but you don't want to tell me.'

He shook his head.

'I'm looking for my brother, please.'

He didn't meet her gaze, just carried on staring out over the dance floor.

'Tell me what you know,' Kerry said. 'Or tomorrow morning, I'll go back to the hostel and ask to speak to the manager, tell him how I couldn't check in the night before because the receptionist had abandoned his desk. Then I'll go and tell the sheriffs I heard a rumor there's a big drug stash hidden somewhere at the Aspen Hostel. You want to spend the rest of tonight finding a new stash spot? Or you want to tell me what's going on?'

Lonnie glared at her. Kerry glared back, her heart racing. Maybe she'd got it wrong about the stash spot, maybe she'd got it wrong threatening him. She prayed she hadn't messed things up already.

When he eventually replied, his tone was sour and brusque.

'I didn't wanna tell you anything because I didn't wanna upset you,' he said.

'I just got back from Vietnam. Trust me, I'm not easily upset.'

He eyed her again.

'There's a kid at the hostel your brother used to hang out with, Tom Annandale. Talk to him. He might know something.'

'Why d'you think that would upset me?'

'You'll see why when you meet Tom. He's probably out working now. But if you go back to the hostel tomorrow morning he should be sleeping it off in his room.'

'What does he look like?'

'He's your brother's age. Skinnier, though. Long hair. Pretty. Could pass for a girl if he wanted.'

Kerry frowned again, putting a thread through everything Lonnie had said – a pretty boy living in a seedy hostel, working nights, sleeping it off.

'Tom's a hustler?'

Lonnie shrugged. Kerry realized why he'd expected her to be upset – if Tom went out hustling, maybe Stevie had done so, too. A painful sadness rushed through her at the thought of her little brother working the streets. She grasped for rationalizations, for silver linings. Maybe Lonnie had gotten it wrong. Or if it was true, maybe there was even a positive there – she could talk to this Tom kid tomorrow and he'd tell her where to find Stevie and that would be it. But the possibility didn't make a dent on her sullen mood.

'Thanks,' she said.

He turned to glare at her.

'Just keep your mouth shut.'

She nodded.

He continued to glare at her for a few more seconds, then returned his gaze to the dance floor, where another customer was already approaching.

Kerry didn't bother saying anything more. She stood up and sliced through the crowd in a daze.

Outside, the Sunset Strip still writhed, like that serpent back in Vietnam.

# 8

The motel room was larger than Ida expected, with a double bed, a dresser, a bathroom en suite, a door leading out onto a balcony. The body lay at the foot of the bed, in a large pool of curdling blood. Above it, shards of skull and brain matter dripped from a section of the ceiling. Homicide detectives buzzed about, uniforms, a medical examiner, a photographer. Most of them were smoking. Ida had forgotten this about crime scenes, that mixed in with the scent of blood and death, there was always a thick fog of tobacco smoke.

Detective Feinberg had met Ida on the gallery outside, and now he led her to where the body lay. The victim was in her early thirties, Ida guessed, Mexican maybe. With dark hair and a dark complexion, high cheekbones, full lips. Beautiful until the bullet had done its work. There was an entry wound under the chin, an exit wound that had ripped through the top of her head, hence all the skull and brain matter on the ceiling.

'You recognize her?' Feinberg asked.

'I've never seen this woman before.'

Ida was relieved she didn't know the victim, but still saddened by her fate. She'd been shot under the chin. Point blank. Meaning she'd been eye-to-eye with her killer when he'd fired. There was something unnerving to how that single shot had ended her life; cold, clinical, efficient.

'What type of gun was used?' Ida asked.

'Don't know yet. We haven't found any shell casings, so we're guessing a revolver.'

'Means of entry?'

'Front door wasn't broken, but it's a cheap motel-issue lock. He could have jimmied it with a strip of celluloid if she didn't open the door herself.'

'Where's the paper with my name on it?'

Feinberg gestured to a luggage stand by the balcony door. Someone had opened up the door to air the place out, but it hadn't worked. Feinberg walked over, rummaged around the plastic evidence bags on top of the stand, picked one out, passed it over.

'We found it on the dresser,' he said. 'Under a tourist brochure.'

Ida took the bag and inspected its contents. For some reason she'd assumed her name would be on a scrap of writing paper, but it had actually been scrawled along the top of a newspaper page from the *LA Times*. Ida's full name was there, in blue biro, and next to it the address of her old agency in Bunker Hill. She tried to make out the subject of the newspaper article, but couldn't on account of how the paper was folded up inside the bag.

'That's my name all right,' she said, passing the bag back to Feinberg. 'What's the article about?'

'Let's save that for later.'

Ida nodded: later meant in private. She looked around, saw the wardrobe was open. At its foot was a suitcase filled with clothes, shoes, a valise, a handbag. The kind of things someone might take on a weekend trip.

'How'd she check in without ID?' Ida asked.

'She used an ID. But it's a fake. A good one. Name and details of somebody who died ten years back.'

'What about a car?'

'It's parked out front. A Datsun rented from Hertz five days ago on a credit card stolen in a cat-prowl in the Valley two weeks ago.'

He raised his eyebrows. Fake IDs, stolen credit cards. The victim was running from something and seemed well-equipped.

'Any eyeball wits?' Ida asked. 'Place like this there must have been people around.'

'No witnesses and no leads. There's no plane tickets, no bus tickets, no traveler's checks, receipts, nothing. Not a single scrap of anything in the whole place to tell us who she was or where she'd come from. Except for your name and address.'

He paused, came over shifty.

'How about we talk outside?' he suggested.

'Sure. The air in here's giving me a headache.'

Out on the gallery they leaned against the railing, Feinberg with his back to it, Ida looking into the parking lot below, where the carnival was still in full swing. She turned and studied her old friend. He was the hefty type, with dark hair and a bushy mustache, and eyes a drenched blue. Normally he had an easy-going manner, even in the midst of an investigation, but she'd sensed tension in him that evening, some worry straining his usual breeziness.

'So you want to tell me what other crimes this murder's linked to?' she asked.

'How do you know there's more crimes?'

'Because we're all the way down in San Pedro and you're stationed at Parker Center these days. But mainly because when I arrived I saw three men come the other way who looked like homicide detectives from the Sheriff's Department, and we're well within LAPD jurisdiction, so what the hell would they be doing here if it wasn't a courtesy call on a pre-existing investigation?'

She looked at him. He smiled.

'How'd you make them as sheriff's men?' he asked.

'They were wearing sheriff's rodeo ties. You were a little too late sending them away. You didn't have to hide them from me.'

'I wasn't. I was hiding *you* from *them*.'

'I see.'

Feinberg wanted to avoid the awkwardness of having to explain to the Sheriff's Department why he was bringing a civilian into what was clearly a case of some importance.

'So?' she asked.

Feinberg sighed.

'The newspaper article with your name on it. It's about the Night-Slayer. Some bullshit opinion piece from the *Times*, but it's a nice summary of the case.'

Ida's pulse quickened.

'It could be nothing,' she said. 'The victim wanted to write down my name and address and there was a newspaper to hand.'

'I don't think so. The article had been cut out of the paper, along its outline, like a news clipping. Looks more like she was bringing it to you. You been following the case?'

'The Night-Slayer? Just in the papers. Three killings so far. All in LA. All ritualistic. All innocent victims. No obvious motive. No evidence of robbery. The police forces involved being unusually tight-lipped about the details. I'm guessing there's a reason for the last.'

'There is.'

Ida waited for him to elaborate, but he didn't.

'That murder in there doesn't strike me as a Night-Slayer kill-ing,' Ida said, nodding back toward the motel room. 'The Night-Slayer's all residential homes, and I'm guessing he didn't use a gun. The victim in there had a fake ID, a car rented with stolen credit cards, all her paperwork's missing, a single shot to kill her and then the shooter disappearing without a trace. Quick, clean, efficient. It all screams execution, professional hit. It all screams Mob.'

'Yes, it does.'

'So, what? You think the Mob's somehow connected to the Night-Slayer killings?'

Feinberg hesitated.

'Could be.'

He took his cigarettes from his coat pocket and offered the pack to Ida. She helped herself to one and they lit up and she looked out over the parking lot, trying to keep an encroaching sense of unease in check. Just by the medical examiner's van two men in white scrubs chatted. It made her think of the Needle Men from New Orleans folklore, the white medical students from the Charity Hospital who slipped into Back o' Town at night, armed with syringes full of sleeping liquid to steal away black folks to use in experiments. She slammed the brakes on her train of thought. There she was again, turning everything into New Orleans.

'How's retirement treating you?' Feinberg asked.

The question was loaded, and they both knew it.

'Why are you asking?'

'Because I get the feeling you're not enjoying it much.'

'Not particularly.'

'You retired too early,' he said. 'If you don't mind my saying so. What happened to Sebastián fucked you up and you knee-jerked your way out of the business a decade too early.'

Ida shot him a look, making no attempt to hide her pique.

'Is this leading anywhere?' she asked, in danger of losing the cool she prided herself on.

'The Night-Slayer murders,' he said. 'The thing we kept out of the papers – it's the details of *how* they're ritualistic. The things he does to them. The way he's torturing them, butchering them. Why don't you swing by the Glass House tomorrow and have a look at the files? You're connected to the case somehow, Ida. This victim's seen to that. Come and give us your expert opinion. It'll only take a few hours.'

'Jesus, Feinberg.'

'Come on. We're stumped. And you're the best investigator I ever worked with. You made one bad call and quit when you shouldn't have and now you can make up for it.'

'I didn't make just one bad call.'

They fell into silence, watched the red-and-blue kaleidoscope show below them.

'I was up at the Training Division last month,' Feinberg said. 'Saw a whole shelf's worth of that manual you wrote.'

Ida nodded. A few years earlier she'd written a book on

investigative procedure. It had been published by an educational firm and bulk-ordered by several law-enforcement agencies.

'I should never have written it. And it's probably out of date already. Did you have a read?'

'You already taught me everything I know.'

They smiled at each other.

'Look, just come by the Glass House,' Feinberg said. 'Read the files. See what you think. That's all I'm asking.'

'I don't think so, Feinberg. I vowed I'd never work another case again and I meant it.'

'It's not working another case, Ida. It's reading a few files. Consulting. Chrissake, after all these weeks we've still not got a single plausible suspect. Not even close to one. And meanwhile the whole city's on edge. Firearm sales are up, guard dog sales are up. Suspicious persons reports, loitering reports. We're inundated. And then there's the accidental shootings and the vigilantes. Last night a bunch of bozos who'd been drinking all day in Highland Park saw a cat-prowler climbing out of a house, thought he was the Night-Slayer, chased him through the streets, beat him to a pulp with metal poles. He's still in a coma over at the Memorial Hospital.'

Feinberg threw his hands into the air, exhaled. Ida imagined the stress he was under, the pressure, the guilt. She wanted to tell him it wasn't his fault, but she knew there was no point. He was too much like her, taking responsibility for everything. It was what made him such a good detective.

'You can do this,' she said. 'I know you can. You don't need help from some old retired lady who's past her best.'

They looked at each other, the silence thicker this time. Ida could sense Feinberg's disappointment, but she couldn't get involved in a case again; the fear was too great. Eventually he realized she wouldn't budge. He sighed, shook his head.

'All right,' he said. 'I won't push it no more.'

'Thank you.'

They fell into silence again, watched the police cars' flasher bars rippling with light. Ida felt a headache coming on, the tension coagulating behind her forehead. The wind gusted, rattling the dumpsters, swaying the inkblot shadows of the palms on the asphalt.

'Santa Ana,' Feinberg said. 'In the middle of all this a goddamn Santa Ana.'

'You know in Switzerland they got something called the *föhn* wind, and the courts make special allowances for crimes committed when it's blowing through the mountains.'

Feinberg mulled this over.

'I can't see it working here,' he said. 'Not with our judges and DAs.'

They smiled at each other again.

'You want me to arrange a ride home?' he asked.

'Please.'

He nodded, pushed himself off the railings, left Ida standing alone between the light show in the parking lot, and the bloody chamber behind. The fear she'd been suppressing up till then started to flow through her on a tide of adrenaline, and in its wake, a woozy kind of despair. The victim had been running to Ida for help, and while she'd been slaughtered, Ida had been sitting on her porch writing her memoirs. How was it possible she could feel obsolete and guilty all at the same time?

She thought about the dead woman, the Mob, the Night-Slayer, the city set on edge. She got the unnerving sense that all these things were portents of the same impending doom, like they were all slouching towards somewhere, and it sure as hell wasn't Bethlehem. She looked out across the lot once more. Bats were darting about the tops of the palms, and on the rooftops further on, Ida fancied she saw a voodoo baron, perched in the shadows by the air-conditioning units, top hat black as night, skull bones gleaming.

# 9

As they headed over to the pool house, Dante studied his old pal. Roselli still lived up to his nickname of 'Handsome Johnny' despite his age. He wore a sharp, charcoal suit, a pocket square, a pair of French Tropicale sunglasses with giant blue lenses. He'd coiffed his gray hair upwards and back, much like Vincent Zullo on the terrace behind them, but Roselli managed to pull it off, didn't look like he'd just stepped out of a wind tunnel. He had natural style, a big smile, a statesman's charm. All in all, he was a magnetic bastard. With celebrity friends and connections all across the globe.

It was Capone who'd sent Roselli to LA, back in the '20s, making him one of the first Chicago gangsters to move to the city. His job had been to oversee the syndicate race wire. He'd ended up a bookie to the stars. When the Mob moved in on the film studios in the '30s, Roselli arranged the fix. When Vegas took off in the '50s, he oversaw the skim. When the Mob and the CIA were putting together separate plans to kill Fidel Castro in the '60s, Roselli put the two organizations in contact, so they could pool resources. There were rumors he'd done the same on the Kennedy assassination. He fixed fights and card games, doped racehorses, brokered deals, busted out casinos, founded offshore banks with his CIA pals. He knew everyone and everything, and he always took the largest cut.

But underlying his suave exterior, Dante could see anxiety playing around Roselli's features. He wondered if it was to do with the meeting they were about to have, or the personal problems that had been dogging him the last few months. Roselli had been caught running a card-game scam at the exclusive Beverly Hills Friars Club, where he'd gained membership via Frank Sinatra. The FBI was tailing him, bugging his houses and apartments. Worst of all, a federal grand jury had indicted him back in October for failing to register and be fingerprinted as an alien, for failing to notify Immigration of his address. Bullshit raps, technicalities. But it meant Roselli was now fighting deportation back to Italy, a country he'd left as a child.

'I heard about your recent troubles,' Dante said.

'They're blackballing me. A grand jury for the deportation bounce. Another grand jury for the card-scam bounce. I got grand juries coming out my ass,' he grinned. 'I'll deal with it. But what about you? You bought that vineyard yet?'

'We close the deal just after Christmas. Come New Year we're leaving.'

Roselli smirked, shook his head.

'What's so funny?' Dante asked.

'You never struck me as the type. Dante the Gent heaving a shovel around a field? Heaving a Martini around a nightclub, maybe.' Roselli laughed. 'Ah, I'm just fucking with you. It's a good way to retire. *Buon vino fa buon sangue.*'

Good wine makes good blood.

They smiled at each other, arrived at the pool house. Before they entered Dante gestured toward it.

'How's Nick doing?' he asked.

A shadow of anxiety passed over Roselli.

'Not good, Dante. Not good at all.'

Roselli opened the door and they stepped inside.

The place was decorated in a nautical style, with driftwood, starfish, ropes, brass sailing equipment on wooden stands. There was a bar in one corner, windows looking out onto the pool, and next to them, sitting in an armchair half-hidden in the shadows, was Nick Licata. When he saw them enter, he sent a minuscule nod their way.

'Drink?' Roselli asked.

'Sure,' Dante replied.

As Roselli went over to the bar, Dante sat opposite Licata, in an armchair facing the moonlight streaming in through the window.

'Dante. How's things?' Licata asked.

'Good, Nick. Real good.'

Licata was a slight man, balding and gray, with a mousey, accountant look to him. Normally he projected a sense of reserve, of composure. But not tonight. The Nick Licata sitting in front of Dante was pale, nervy, sweaty, preoccupied. Was he on something, maybe? Or was it just the pressure of the new job? The impending war with the rival faction inside his own Mob? Or maybe it was the rumor that out-of-towners had sensed weakness and were looking to move in? Not that the weakness was anything new; for years the LA Mob had had a reputation as the most dysfunctional in the country, had garnered itself a nickname – the Mickey Mouse Mafia – and not because its territory encompassed Disneyland.

With all that going on, maybe it was understandable that Licata was feeling the strain, that he looked the way he did.

Roselli returned with three tumblers filled with dark rum and ice. He handed them out, lifted his tumbler into the air.

'*Salute*,' he said, and they all drank.

Licata turned to Dante.

'We're glad we caught you before you left town for that vineyard,' he said. 'Not long now, hunh?'

'Not long now.'

Dante tried to stifle a growing sense of claustrophobia. Nick mentioning the vineyard was a power move, like everything was with these guys. He was letting Dante know what was on the line before negotiations began. Dante took his Luckies from his pocket and lit up. Roselli got his own cigarettes out, slipped one into a cigarette holder.

'So what did you want to see me about?' Dante asked.

Roselli and Licata shared a look.

'It's about Riccardo,' Licata said.

Dante nodded.

Riccardo was Nick Licata's son. One of those second-rate men of the younger generation, like Vincent Zullo out on the terrace. Riccardo was rash, restless, always chewing an angle, always looking for that big score that would prove once and for all he was a player in his own right. But it never happened. He made bad choices, bad plans, lacked any foresight or ability to strategize. And he never seemed to grasp it was his own deficiencies that hampered him, so he moved through life in a cloud of resentment, keeping his ego intact by blaming all his failures on other people, on bad luck, on the world at large. Licata had pretty much disowned the kid, leaving them estranged. The last Dante had heard, Riccardo was pretending to be a movie producer, running an independent that churned out turkeys and B-pictures and was probably a front for something illegal.

'What happened?' Dante asked.

'You didn't hear about him getting arrested?' Roselli asked.

Dante shook his head.

'I'm halfway to retirement,' he said. 'I'm not keeping my hand in.'

Roselli and Licata shared that look again, concerned by how out of the game Dante seemed to be.

'Riccardo got busted back in September,' Roselli explained. 'Pulled over on the Sunset Strip in a traffic stop. The pigs found forty pounds of cocaine in his trunk.'

Dante suppressed the urge to whistle through his teeth.

'Forty pounds of *coke*?'

Cocaine hadn't been popular since the 1930s. Since the golden age.

'It's back in fashion,' Roselli said. 'With the kids. The whole music industry's running on it.'

He gestured to the party outside. Dante recalled the group he'd seen in the garden huddled around the hand mirror. Now it clicked why they'd seemed odd. Dante had thought it was heroin they'd been snorting, but they didn't look like dope fiends.

'OK,' Dante said, feeling even more out of touch. 'Where's Riccardo now?'

'The cocksucker of a judge set bail at half a mill,' Roselli said. 'And they threw him into Men's Central. And then about a week ago we got a call from him asking us to bail him out. In cash, so we could get him out quicker.'

'And you did?' Dante asked, flabbergasted. 'Half a million in cash?'

'He was crying, Dante,' Licata said. 'He told me there was a jail hit out on him, he'd be lucky to survive the week. He was begging. He's my son, what was I gonna do?'

Dante nodded like he understood, but the story didn't make sense. Why had Licata left Riccardo in the jail for weeks before bailing him out? Were they so estranged that Licata had left Riccardo to rot? And surely Licata had men inside. Surely as the son of a Mob boss, Riccardo would be left alone. Who the hell had the kid pissed off so badly they were willing to go up against a whole Mob to kill him? Sure, it was the Mickey Mouse Mafia, but it was hard to believe things had got so bad.

'I know Riccardo's a liability,' Licata said, rubbing his eyes. 'But he's still my son. The only one I got. Flesh and blood.'

Dante frowned, wondered if Licata was rubbing his eyes to hide the fact he was crying, wondered if maybe that was why he'd chosen to sit in the shadows of the pool house. Was the man having a breakdown?

'So, we got the cash together,' Roselli said. 'Paid the bail, and he was released last Wednesday.'

Dante suddenly got a sense of where this was going.

'And?' he asked.

'He disappeared,' Licata said flatly. 'That same day. He got out of the jail and no one's seen him since.'

It was exactly what Dante had expected. Either Riccardo had been released and then bumped off, or he'd decided to screw over his own pops to the tune of half a million dollars and go on the run.

'Did Riccardo say who it was that wanted to kill him?'

Licata and Roselli both shook their heads.

'Who did Riccardo get the coke off?' Dante asked.

If Riccardo had been killed, the obvious suspects were whoever had supplied him with the cocaine he'd been busted for – killing Riccardo meant he couldn't inform on them.

'He wouldn't say,' Licata replied. 'He kept on saying the LAPD had set him up. Swore it wasn't a routine traffic stop. That the pigs planted it in his trunk.'

Dante frowned. When the cops set people up, they didn't do it somewhere as busy as the Sunset Strip, and they sure as hell didn't do it with an amount as large as forty pounds. The story was bullshit, surely Licata knew that.

Licata exhaled. Dante saw tears glistening on his cheeks, silver threads in the moonlight. Dante had never seen a boss cry before. Not in all his years. He looked away, so as not to embarrass Licata, to extricate them all from the shame of the moment.

'You managed to track what he did on the day he was released?' Dante asked, turning to Roselli.

If the state of Licata had perturbed Roselli as well, he didn't show it.

'It's like Nick told you,' Roselli replied smoothly. 'Riccardo left the jail and no one ever saw him again.'

Dante nodded, unsure what to say. He knew now why they'd asked him here. Dante was an expert skip-tracer, even if he was from another era. They wanted him to find Riccardo. If he'd gone on the run, they wanted Dante to bring him back. And if he'd been killed, they wanted the names of the killers and the corpse, too, because with a corpse they could get a death certificate and with a death certificate they could get the bail money returned. No death certificate or no Riccardo at the next court hearing and Licata could kiss his half a million goodbye.

'When's Riccardo's next court date?' Dante asked.

'December twenty-sixth,' Licata said.

Dante nodded. Just a week away. The same day the vineyard deal was supposed to go through. He turned to look at Licata. The man was distraught. His son had either betrayed him or been killed. And he'd called up Dante to find out which. It made Dante wonder why they'd picked him for this job. He may have been the best at one time, but surely there were better men to help them now. Surely someone in the younger generation who was closer to Riccardo, who knew the world he moved in.

They fell silent and stared out at the party. On the other side of the pool Vincent Zullo was chatting with a music industry type. From a distance it was even more glaring how fully Zullo had embraced the schlubby mobster stereotype. Like he was using the Mafia clichés he'd seen in films and TV as a life guide.

'What the fuck is he wearing,' Licata muttered.

'Makes you want to smack some dress sense into him,' Roselli said.

They smiled wearily.

'Back in my day you had Benny Siegel running Los Angeles,' Roselli continued. 'Say what you want about him, but he had style. No man wore a suit better than Benny Siegel in all America. Imagine someone going to a meeting with Siegel or Luciano dressed like that.'

Roselli threw a hand in Zullo's direction and they all went quiet, thinking old-guy thoughts, lost in a world that had itself been lost.

Licata turned to look at Dante.

'Find him for me, Dante. He's my only son. I need to know where he is, what happened to him. I can't go to my grave not knowing. You find him – dead or alive – and we get the bail money back, you can have a finder's fee. Twenty-five percent. All I want is to know what happened.'

Dante frowned. Twenty-five percent was way more than the usual ten. Suspiciously more. Dante wondered again why they'd asked him of all people to investigate. He wondered how Licata had let his own son get banged up, then disappear, all on his own turf, all with no clue as to what might have happened to him. Was the family really that third rate now? Or was something else going on?

Dante got that claustrophobia all over again. He thought of all the excuses he could use – that he was old, retired, out of touch. But he knew there was no point; Licata would find a way of coercing him. Protesting would just leave a poor impression. But there was something more than that – Dante felt genuinely sorry for him. Licata was a weak man in charge of a weak Mob, but he'd lost his son. Mob boss or not, he was flailing, and maybe Dante could help.

'I'd be happy to look into it for you, Nick. One last job before I leave town.'

'*S'abbenedica*, Dante. *S'abbenedica*.'

But even as Licata expressed his gratitude, Dante could feel he was being pulled into something against his will. He thought once more of those Indians jumping off cliffs into the Pacific's glassy realm. An act of madness to escape the madness. Fatalism and free will.

# 10

It was probably the drink and the pills and the jet lag, but this time as Kerry drove back to the motel, everything felt heightened, like she was sitting in a cinema, not a car, watching a montage of images flickering past on the other side of the glass – dance halls and palm trees, parking lots, mini-malls, gas stations, car washes, endless tract houses coated in cheap redwood siding. She had to remind herself it was all real, that in amongst this urban clutter, this sprawl, was her brother.

*I'm on to something, Kerry. Real big. To do with Louisiana and lots of other stuff. So much stuff you wouldn't believe. If you don't hear from me again, it means they got to me.*

Maybe the conspiracy was a fantasy that he'd constructed to protect himself, one that he'd come to believe in. The easiest person to fool was yourself. Or maybe it was true. Maybe he had uncovered something, and now there were killers after him, out there somewhere, lurking in the city's shadows. She had to believe she could track him down before some misfortune befell him, before her week's rest-and-relaxation leave ended and she had to return to the killing fields. She was his older sister; he was her kid brother. They'd walked over broken glass together. If she found him she could help him, soothe him, hug him. Like she used to. That's all she wanted from life now.

She turned left onto Sawtelle Boulevard and the Wigwam Motel swung into view. She parked, crossed the encampment to her cabin, let herself in, collapsed onto the bed. She desperately wanted to sleep, but the drive had woken her up. The Dilaudid had worn off and the burn scars were throbbing again, nerve endings sparked and shimmered. In her mind the fireball burned once more, people screamed.

How long had it been since she'd slept? Twenty-four hours? Thirty-six? How long since she'd left the Clark Air Base Hospital? She'd arranged a seat on a commercial airline back to the States, but when she'd heard a medical evac plane was leaving to Fairchild Air Force Base in Washington State, she hopped on that instead – it was free, and it was leaving earlier. From Fairchild it was a short taxi ride to Spokane International, and the thrift flight down to LA, the motel, the Sunset Strip, the Crystal Club. How long had all that taken?

She got up, lit a smoke, popped two more Dilaudid, knowing they'd finally knock her out. She undressed and rubbed cream into her burns, standing in front of the mirror, surveying the terrain of her injuries, a foreign landscape of red raw scars running down her face and neck and spreading out over her shoulder and the top of her chest.

As she worked in the burn cream, she found herself humming a melody. What was it? One of the songs she'd heard in the club? But it was too slow for that, too sad. Then she realized: 'Alone Together'. Despite everything else she'd heard that night, it was the Chet Baker tune that had burrowed itself into her head, the melody sleek as a bullet.

She went through her things and found the photo of Stevie and her from when they were kids, before their parents had abandoned them, each in their own way. Stevie was dressed like a cowboy, Kerry like an Indian. They were covered in dust, smiling and happy, standing in their front yard, her arm over his shoulder. Behind them was the old live oak tree they'd strewn with Milk of Magnesia bottles, hanging them by strings from its branches. The bottles chimed when the wind blew, glinted when the sun shone through their dark blue glass, casting cobalt light in dapples across the yard.

Kerry slid the photo into the frame of the dressing table's

mirror and studied it. The oak tree began to sway, the blue bottles clinked and chimed, light moved in the breeze, Kerry and Stevie squeezed each other tight and grinned. She watched all this with a smile, then when she couldn't take it anymore, she turned away, to the window, to the giant billboard with its illustrations of the city: that couple on horseback, those orange groves, those idyllic hills and beaches. Kerry had to believe Stevie was out there somewhere. She stared at the words of the municipal slogan, printed at the bottom of the billboard. Chet Baker played on. The desert wind blew. *It All Comes Together in Los Angeles!*

# PART TWO

## IDA

# 11

Ida barely slept for thinking about the motel room and the dead woman, speculating on who the victim might have been, why she'd gone on the run, why she'd been trying to find Ida. When she did doze off, the image of the woman haunted her dreams. Called to her. Ida drew parallels to Sebastián, her old colleague whose death two years before had been the catalyst for her retirement. She wondered what Walter would have told her to do. Or Michael. How she missed Michael, even after all these years. How painfully she wished he was still around. But she knew what his answer would have been. She could hear his voice telling her so clearly it was like he was standing in the room.

The next morning she got in her Caddy and drove downtown. It was one of those days that came after a Santa Ana, when the wind had swept clear the heavens, turning them a blue so deep it could have been an ocean up there. Every detail in the city was sharp, roofs glinted, freeways glimmered, swimming pools shone. And so it was at the Glass House – the block-sized glass cube headquarters of the LAPD on North Los Angeles Street.

Ida stepped inside at nine on the dot. The place was busier than usual with Santa Ana fallout. She spoke to the officer at the front desk who directed her to take an elevator to the third floor. As she waited, she looked at the bulletin boards that ran around the hall; teenaged gangs in Compton attacking people with lye, rogue tow-trucks running a parking scam, fake property investors hoicking pyramid schemes, a cult leader who'd defrauded his followers, poisoned them, then gone on the run.

Ida searched the bulletins for any reports on mutilated women or butchered prostitutes. It was something she'd been doing for the last twenty years, hunting for any signs that Faron might have come to LA. She knew he was probably dead already, but she still did it, the act having almost become a ritual by now, a way of warding him off. The worst killer she'd ever encountered, and she'd let him slip through her fingers. It was only natural his whereabouts had become an intermittent anxiety in her life. In the two decades since she'd crossed him in New York, how many more had he killed?

Ida had put out feelers over the years, to cops, informers, mobsters. She'd offered handsome rewards – if anyone ever heard anything about Faron, to let her know. Maybe she'd been foolish, broadcasting her interest in him like that. But most people had never heard of him, and those who had, thought he was a myth. In the twenty years since, she'd never had to dig into her pockets. So Faron had faded away into a background sound that followed her through life, the rustle of leaves, the moan of a house, the sound of waves in a conch shell. Always there if she chose to listen.

The elevator arrived with a bing. Its doors opened and Ida stepped inside.

When she got to the third floor she made her way to Room 318, the home of the LAPD's Homicide Division. It was a huge, rectangular space, open plan, with the detectives all working at two long tables that ran the length of it. Ida spoke to a sergeant by the door who pointed out Feinberg's desk. As she crossed the floor she saw nothing had changed in the two years since she'd last been immersed in it. Detectives typed, shouted into phones, chatted in knots, rushed about. The air was stale with cigarettes and coffee and overworked cops, and even though it was still only morning, with the scent of bourbon, too. The tension and stress of the job were plain on their faces, in their demeanor. The rawness of having no family life, no time off.

As she approached Feinberg's desk she entered the section of the floor that was dealing with the Night-Slayer case. The fever-ishness here was even more palpable, the detectives more wired. LA was a paranoid place at the best of times, but over the last couple of years it had gotten so much worse – the Watts riots, the Hippie riots, the Century City riot, the deployment of the National Guard, a curfew imposed on the Sunset Strip, the streets filling with all the country's runaways, with Vietnam vets, with revolutionaries, protests and social unrest. And right in the middle of all this, the Night-Slayer had shown up, like the distillation of all that turmoil, or the harbinger of more to come. Nowhere in the city was the stress of it felt more keenly than here, workplace of the people who were failing to keep a lid on things.

Feinberg smiled when he saw Ida approach, looking as exhausted as she felt. She wondered if he was still on shift from the previous night, if he ever went home these days.

'That didn't take long,' he said.

'I'm just here to look at the files.'

Ida had rehearsed the line, hoped it would help stave off her fear. She was only here to consult, to offer an opinion. She would *not* be getting involved in another case.

'Sure,' Feinberg said, his smile widening. 'You're just here to look at the files.' But his tone suggested they both knew it was bullshit, and that fear fluttered behind Ida's ribs once more.

He led her down the length of the room, past detectives who eyed her coldly, into a corridor, then to an interrogation cubicle. There were coffee cups on the desk, an ashtray filled with cigar-ette butts and peanut shells; dotted about the wastepaper bin were crumpled sheets of legal paper.

'This is the best I can offer you. Take a seat and I'll fetch the tubs,' Feinberg said.

Ida sat and a couple of minutes later Feinberg returned hold-ing a stack of folders.

'This is all the paperwork for the three murders,' he said. 'You've got our own reports for the murder that happened on our patch, copies of the sheriff's reports for the West Hollywood murder and three sets of files for the one in Manhattan Beach.'

'Three?'

'It happened where the jurisdictions overlap between us, the sheriffs and the Manhattan Beach PD,' Feinberg shrugged. 'Jurisdictional spaghetti.'

Ida looked at the files. They still had that same old police-file smell – that inky, fresh comic-book scent she associated with her childhood – but they looked strange, shinier than the mimeographs she was used to.

'Photocopies?' she asked, hedging a guess.

'Welcome to the future. If you need to leave the floor at any time, you come see me first and I'll escort you out. The files stay here, obviously.'

'Obviously.'

Feinberg nodded and left. Ida looked around the cramped, messy cubicle, then at the stack of files. Everything three separate LA police forces had on the Night-Slayer killings. She split them up into three piles, one for each murder. She pulled the pile for the first victim toward her and opened it.

Mark McNeal, twenty-eight, a doctor working at the Emergency Room of Los Angeles County General in Boyle Heights. On the night of his murder, McNeal had finished a shift at the hospital, gone to eat at the snack counter at a nearby Ralphs, then driven home to the apartment in Manhattan Beach where he lived alone. He called his mother in Sacramento at nine thirty and went to bed. After which the perpetrator gained access to McNeal's apartment via a fire escape and, at some point between eleven and two, stabbed him multiple times with a thin, pointed instrument similar in size and shape to a knitting needle or a carpenter's bradawl. Post-mortem the victim's body had been laid out on the bed in a coffin pose, with the legs straight and the arms folded over the chest. The killer had then scrawled a crucifix symbol onto the bedroom wall in blue chalk.

Ida took a deep breath and opened the folder of crime-scene photos. 'Stabbed multiple times' proved to be an understatement. McNeal's body had been run through. Needle-sized puncture wounds littered his torso, his limbs, his face. Savage, relentless, frenzied. The individual wounds must have run into the hundreds. How many of them did it take before he lost consciousness? Before the pain and terror stopped? She could only imagine the horror McNeal must have gone through.

She turned to the photos of the crucifix scrawled onto the wall above the bed. It was drawn in blue chalk, composed of wavering, awkward lines, like it had been scrawled by a child, or someone who'd caught the shakes. It wasn't made up of just two lines intersecting like a traditional crucifix, but four lines – two going down, two going across. The space in between each of the paired lines had been filled in with overlapping zigzags. In the four quadrants created by the crucifix were further symbols, star shapes, dots, crosses, interlocking pairs of the letter V.

Ida had a queasy sense that she had seen the image somewhere before. But she couldn't think where. Whatever parallel her mind was dimly aware of, she knew it wouldn't step into the spotlight of her consciousness right away. Decades of detective work had taught her that these kinds of leaps couldn't be forced, that they revealed themselves of their own accord, most often when the mind was occupied with something else.

She slid the folder back across the desk, brought forward the stack for the second murder. Danielle Landry, twenty-three, who'd moved to LA from Mobile, Alabama, just a year before her death. While pursuing her dream of becoming an actress she supported herself with a day job as a receptionist for a law firm in Culver City. She'd left work, popped back to her apartment in West Hollywood, gone to do her laundry down the block, returned home. At some point that night the perpetrator broke in, held her captive while he filled the bath, then drowned her in it.

Ida turned to the crime-scene photographs. There was Danielle, floating in her bath, still clothed, her body unmolested apart from bruises around her neck where she'd been held under. Her feet were sticking out of the water at one end of the tub, her face submerged at the other. Wisps of blonde hair curled in the water. But what caught Ida's attention was the money. Dollar bills floating about on the surface. Others had sunk to the bottom, where nickels, dimes, pennies glittered on the porcelain. Had the killer poured money into the bath after he'd killed her? Just like the crucifix, something tugged at Ida's thoughts as she studied the photos of the dead girl in the water, the money green and glittering all around her. Again, there was something familiar to it, like Ida had seen the image before.

She looked through the rest of the photos. There were seashells and glass beads scattered about by the front door, by the windows. Were they Landry's? Or had the killer brought them along? No usable fingerprints had been found on any of them.

At the very end of the file, Ida came to a photo of Landry before her death, an actress's headshot, full color, taken in a studio. Despite what must have been a Cajun family name, the photo showed Landry had bright blue eyes and blonde hair to go with a perfect smattering of freckles across her nose. It showed she had depth and elegant features, that she could be a commanding presence on camera. But there was something tight about the lips, something lost in her eyes. She had the air of a woman suffocating in her own life, one of the countless people who moved to LA for glamor and sunshine, but found instead just another kind of drudgery. All the things they'd dreamed about stayed just out of reach, where they always would be. But still they kept on dreaming, about doing something else, going somewhere else, being somebody else. Every one of them was in their own movie. And the unluckiest of all ended up slaughtered by some maniac who'd likewise succumbed to the city's hollow promises.

Ida closed the file, moved on to the most recent murder. Anthony Butterfield, forty-three, an engineer at 'Skunk Works', Lockheed's secretive development division in Burbank, where all manner of missiles, bombers and jets were devised for the military, for the Cold War, for the apocalypse.

Butterfield had been murdered in his house in Silver Lake. Like the earlier victims, Butterfield lived alone and was killed in the middle of the night. He'd been strangled, his body mutilated post-mortem, the right arm severed at the shoulder and placed next to his body, which again had been arranged on the bed in a coffin pose. Once more a variation on the earlier symbol had been scrawled onto the wall, this time next to the door.

On the night of the murder Butterfield had followed a similar routine to McNeal – he'd left work, picked up food at a cafeteria, gone home.

Again Ida took a deep breath before opening up the folder of crime-scene photos. Butterfield's face was swollen from the asphyxiation, eyes bulging, skin speckled red with burst blood vessels. At his shoulder was a bloody stump where the arm had been hacked off messily. The severed arm had been placed just next to the shoulder stump, bent at the elbow so the hand could be placed over the chest in the funeral pose. It had all been arranged with a delicate care that Ida found perverse.

She sighed. Closed the files. Slid them away from her. Stared out of the cubicle to the corridor beyond, its frosted windows. A detective rushed past, taking a swig from a hip flask as he went. Ida wondered what she was doing there. Had she really come to help? Or for some other reason? The fear returned, mixed in with guilt and shame for using the flimsy guise of consulting to go back on her decision to quit.

She tried to clear her thoughts, focus on what was most important – what link there might be between these murders and the dead woman in the motel room. After reviewing the files, Ida was convinced they'd been killed by different people. And yet the motel victim had that newspaper clipping with her.

Ida recalled the clipping, noted what the police hadn't passed on to the press – the severity of McNeal's stab wounds, the money in Danielle Landry's bathtub, Butterfield's amputated arm, the arrangement of the bodies. It was those same details that nagged at Ida. Not so much the details themselves, but the image of them – a man pierced through like a pincushion, a girl in a bath of money, a man with his arm cut off. Something about them felt so familiar. Where had she seen them before? It was their power as images that seemed to be important. Like the killer had made them into symbols. But why?

Ida sighed and checked her watch. It was still only eleven a.m., but she was through. She rose, sought out Feinberg, found him at his desk.

'You're done?' he asked, disappointed.

'Yeah.'

'And?'

'Aside from that newspaper article, I can't see how the motel room killing's connected to the Night-Slayer.'

'And what about the Night-Slayer killings themselves?'

'The symbolism's intriguing,' Ida shrugged. 'The way he arranged them all. Like how they're staged is the most important thing to him.'

'Like he's making art?'

Ida frowned.

'Yeah, something like that,' she said.

'I had the same feeling too.'

They looked at each other as the sound of the division bubbled away in the background.

Ida shrugged again.

'That's all I got,' she said. 'I'm sorry I can't be of more help. But like I told you last night, I'm old and rusty.'

Feinberg looked like he was going to counter her, but decided against it.

'Well, it was worth a try. I'll let you know when we get an ID for the motel victim.'

Ida nodded and was surprised to realize that she was disappointed her involvement would go no further. She'd thought ending it would assuage her fear, but it didn't.

Feinberg went back to the cubicle to scoop up the files. As Ida waited for him to return she glanced around the floor full of harried detectives. Even though they looked on the verge of cardiac arrests, liver failure, nervous breakdowns, she envied them, their sense of purpose, the meaning that shaped their days. She turned to look at the boards scattered about, the evidence lists, the giant map of LA with three red pins stuck into it. In the map she saw something more than streets and grids, she saw the arteries of the city's dark heart, the power lines strung through its neighborhoods, the forces that grouped and segregated its citizenry. In amongst them somewhere was the Night-Slayer, jostling with the film stars, the tourists, the vagrants, the hucksters, the defense contractors churning out weapons that could wipe out the planet. She imagined him stalking through it all unnoticed, head low, eyes furtive, slinking down a street, crossing an intersection.

Suddenly there was an icy knot in her chest.

She realized where she'd seen the crucifix image before.

She rushed across the floor, back toward the cubicle, saw Feinberg approaching down the corridor. He looked up at her, saw her expression.

'What is it?' he frowned.

'The crucifix he's been drawing. I know where I've seen it before. It's not a crucifix. It's a crossroads. It's a voodoo sigil.'

Feinberg's frown deepened.

'What's a voodoo sigil?' he asked.

'It's like a call sign. Every spirit in voodoo's got its own one. You want to summon a particular spirit, you draw out its sigil, in wheat flour, cornmeal, brick powder, gunpowder, chalk dust. The crossroads is part of the sigil for Baron Samedi. He's one of the voodoo barons.'

'Who are?'

'You've seen them. The skeletons with the top hats. The dolls they sell to tourists in New Orleans. Those guys.'

'So, what? The Night-Slayer's conducting ceremonies to him? Sacrifices?'

'I don't know. Maybe he's trying to, but he's getting it all wrong. The sigil I'm talking about, it's not just a crossroads, there's more to it than that. The crucifixes the Night-Slayer's been leaving, they're like a . . . kid's version of it. Like, he's trying to replicate it, but he doesn't know how. Anyone from Louisiana or Haiti or Cuba knows about this stuff. Maybe that's where the Night-Slayer's from. Or maybe he's read up on it and he's trying to copy it. It's not much, but it's a lead.'

She shrugged. Feinberg eyed her.

'You wanna go through the files again?'

# 12

Ida borrowed a pencil and pad and two minutes later she was sat once more in the interrogation cubicle. She worked with more focus this time, propelled by a pressing sense that her time with the files was limited and that maybe she was on to something.

She started by looking for the errors and omissions that inevitably crept into police reports – evidence missed, filed incorrectly, connections not made. She worked chronologically, starting with the reports from the black-and-whites first dispatched to the addresses, from the sergeants manning the backups who came after. She checked the pink DOA slips left by the ambulance units, and the paperwork re-assigning the cases to the Homicide Divisions of the LAPD and the Manhattan Beach PD, to the Homicide Bureau of the LA County Sheriff's Department. She read the reports from the Scientific Investigation Division's forensic chemists, the Los Angeles County Coroner, the County Public Administrator, Field Interrogation reports, chain-of-evidence briefs, the Sheriff's bulletins, the Teletypes from the LAPD's Valley Services Division. She read the monthly Homicide Investigation Progress Reports, of which there was only one. In it the detectives listed the MO searches they'd run through the California State Bureau of Criminal Investigation and Identification computer.

The reports from the SID's Latent Prints Section on the Butterfield crime scene contained no fingerprints that could identify the killer. Any prints lifted were those of the victims, too smudged, or too partial to be of use; a common occurrence, readable prints generally being a rarity. And it was the same story with the earlier two crime scenes.

The other reports from the SID detailed the various tests undertaken on blood samples collected from the crime scenes, Benzidine and Ouchterlony tests, blood-type and sub-type tests. There were examinations on the depths of the puncture wounds to McNeal's body, how the perpetrator had hacked off Butterfield's arm. The coroner's reports detailed fluoroscopy examinations and autopsies performed.

Ida noticed how the reports of the three police forces were different in their diligence, grammar and padding. In one of the Manhattan Beach PD reports, she noticed some passages that seemed familiar in a biography of Mark McNeal. It took her a while to realize where she'd read them before – the man's obituary in the *LA Times*. The detectives writing the report had plagiarized it wholesale to fatten out the file.

At some point Feinberg entered the cubicle holding two paper packages.

'Got you some lunch,' he said.

'Thanks.'

She checked the time – it was well into the afternoon. He sat in the chair opposite her, passed her one of the packages. She unwrapped it – a ham-and-mustard sandwich.

'So?' Feinberg asked, taking a bite of his food.

'I've been trying to find a connection between the victims,' Ida said.

The first task in such an investigation was always to establish if there was anything that linked the victims, something to explain why they'd been targeted.

'But I can't find anything,' she said. 'They're all so different from each other – different neighborhoods, jobs, genders, economic brackets. The only link is that they all lived alone, but that's hardly uncommon in LA.'

'Lonely people are the easiest to kill,' Feinberg said.

Ida agreed. There were fewer people to intervene, fewer people to report the victim missing when they were gone.

'I was thinking the link could be how different they all are,' Feinberg said. 'If the killer wants to induce as much panic as possible, he chooses victims at random, so everyone's worried they might be next.'

'Maybe. But I still feel there's something else I'm not seeing. Something under the surface. What links an actress, a medic and a defense engineer?'

'They're all pretty common occupations in LA. Only thing there's more of here than actresses is defense workers.'

'You think it might have something to do with Butterfield's work at Lockheed?' Ida asked. 'Maybe there's some espionage involved?'

She had noted how the files lacked any interviews with Butterfield's colleagues at his job at the defense plant. Had the Department of Defense stepped in to stymy things?

'Could be,' Feinberg said. 'We tried to get into Skunk Works to interview Butterfield's colleagues, but the high-ups said the situation was too delicate. Apparently they're going to send us written statements instead. Might be fishy, might just be the usual defense contractor crap. What about the other victims' jobs?'

Ida took a bite from her sandwich, sifted through the paperwork to the witness statements given by Danielle's friends and family.

'One thing bugged me,' she said. 'A couple of weeks before Danielle Landry was killed, she handed in her notice at the law firm where she worked, saying she'd found a regular gig as an actress in a series of biker movies made by a company out in Redondo Beach. What the hell are "biker movies"? Is that a euphemism for porno?'

'I don't think so. Danielle never mentioned the name of the production company, so the sheriffs have been going through the business records at the Secretary of State's Office, asking around the guilds, drawing up a list. We've got nothing so far.' He nodded at the folder of crime-scene photos from the Landry murder. 'What about all the trinkets the killer left in her apartment? The money in the tub?'

Ida flicked through the folder to photos showing the seashells by the windows in the lounge and the bathroom, the glass beads by the front door. They'd been clumped together in groups, outlined in chalk, evidence cards placed next to them for the photos.

'I've got no idea why he left them,' she said. 'It doesn't chime with the voodoo sigil, if that's what you're wondering.'

Feinberg nodded, disappointed.

'You managed to come up with any thoughts on a sketch of the killer?' he asked.

Another early task in these cases was to build up an initial profile of the perpetrator, figure out what he knew, what skills he might have, what quirks.

'Judging from the way he hacked off Butterfield's arm, he's not a surgeon,' Ida said. 'And he doesn't know much about voodoo. The choice of objects he scattered around Landry's apartment is all wrong. The drawings of the sigils are all wrong, too. But he's good at picking his victims, at breaking in, at making a getaway. Stalking, entry, stealth skills. Maybe someone with a burglary conviction? Or maybe he's ex-army? Some traumatized kid back home from Vietnam?'

'That's what we thought, too,' Feinberg said. 'We've been combing the list for crims with histories of cat-prowls involving assaults and molestations. And burglars with a military background. Nothing's panned out so far.'

He shrugged and Ida got a sense of his exasperation once more. That he'd been over these kinds of hypotheses and conjectures countless times during the last few weeks and had gotten nowhere.

'The other angle is how he picks his victims,' Feinberg said. 'We're working on the theory he's prowling the streets. Checking out properties from a parked car, seeing who's coming, who's going. Waiting till night and then striking. Suggests someone who's got a job driving around, someone who can stay parked somewhere all day without arousing suspicion. Maintenance man, gardener, utility worker.'

'I don't think so,' Ida said. 'I noticed all the victims visited public places on the nights of their deaths. McNeal grabbed a meal at a supermarket snack counter, Landry went to a laundromat, Butterfield stopped off at a cafeteria. Can't be a coincidence. They're all busy locations, people coming in and out, high turn-over of clientele. Good places to sit and watch, stalk victims, figure out who's a singleton, who lives alone, who it'd be worthwhile following home.'

Feinberg frowned.

'Maybe the laundromat and the cafeteria are good hunting grounds,' he said. 'But I don't buy he picked up McNeal at the snack counter at Ralphs. You ever been there? It's tiny. There's no way someone could hang out there waiting for victims without being noticed. He'd have to stand in the supermarket aisles and even then he'd stick out.'

Ida realized with disappointment that he was right. She took another bite of her food, sifted through the files in McNeal's folder, tracing his steps backwards through the night, the state-ments from his neighbors, from the supermarket worker who served him, from his colleagues at the hospital.

'The hospital,' Ida said, looking up at Feinberg. 'McNeal was coming home off a shift in the Emergency Room at the County Hospital. That's where the killer picked him up. The waiting room at the hospital. Open twenty-four hours, always packed, people coming and going. The pickup spots are a laundromat, a cafeteria and a *hospital*.'

Feinberg grinned at her, his weariness dropping away.

'Now that I buy,' he said.

'We need to draw up a list of other places he might be

stalking,' Ida said. 'Libraries, gyms, maybe parks and beaches – see what loitering reports there've been.'

'I'll get on to it,' Feinberg said. 'And I'll run it all as an MO search through the CII computer.'

'OK. I'll go back through the files relating to the three locations – the witness reports, ID and INS checks, the Field Interrogation Cards, see if something was missed.'

They smiled at each other, then Feinberg stood and rushed out.

When Ida turned her gaze back to the files, a chill came over her, subduing the excitement of the earlier breakthrough. Now that it had sprung into her head, she couldn't shake the image of the killer out there in the city, in his hunting grounds, in a park, on a beach, at a burger joint or a bar, sitting alone, sipping a drink, watching the crowd, looking for the next lonely Angelino to slaughter.

# PART THREE

## DANTE

# 13

The warehouse occupied the best part of a block on North Formosa Avenue in West Hollywood, not far from the old Pickford-Fairbanks lot. As Dante drove over there on the morning after his meeting at the pool party, he mulled over how he'd break the news to Loretta. She'd been asleep when he'd gotten in the previous night, and had left for work before he'd woken up. He was dreading having to tell her that there was a kink in their plans, that the retirement they'd been working on all these years might be scuppered. He found himself wishing for an obstruction to stall his progress, but everything was fine, eerily so; even the traffic was at low tide.

When he pulled into the yard, the place was already busy with orders coming in and out. He walked into the warehouse itself, past rows of giant shelving units containing all manner of drinks, past forklift trucks, past towering stacks of empty pallets. He smelled that reassuring, musty, liquor smell.

Dante had loved running the company all these years. He supplied all the best restaurants and night spots in LA. Meaning he and Loretta got free entrance everywhere, no waiting in lines, the best tables, invites to every opening for the last four decades. Loretta had dug the glamor. Dante had dug the buzz. It was a good way to spend their life together.

He reached his office in the corner of the warehouse, a messy, glass-paneled space with two desks and a sofa and a few filing cabinets. Someone had strewn tinsel about the place, stuck a plastic Christmas tree in the corner. Loretta was sitting at her desk, the phone clasped to her ear. She nodded hello as he walked in. He sat at his desk and waited for her to finish her call.

Loretta had started helping out around the place when the kids had grown up, just for something to do. But it had turned out it to be a natural fit for her as well. The bookkeeping, the strategy, dealing with the employees, all of whom preferred Loretta to Dante, even though she was the bad cop in their duo. She was professional, consummate, brusque. All fire and unstudied grace. These days, it was pretty much Loretta who ran the place.

As he studied her he felt that rush of pride that never went away, that ferocity of love. Over the years her looks had succumbed to age, just like his had. She'd wrinkled, softened, sagged. Her red hair had lost its fire and gloss, turned a papery gray. But the beauty of her eyes was undiminished. Still the deep green of mountain lakes, clear enough to wash away your sins.

She finished her call, put the phone down, looked at him and raised an eyebrow.

'Well?' she asked.

He sighed, steeled himself.

'I've been given a job.'

She didn't move, just sat there with her arms crossed, glaring at him. In the silence Dante could hear the hum of the forklifts moving about, the clank of bottles.

'You told me no more jobs,' she said.

'I know.'

'We're signing the contracts on the twenty-sixth.'

'I know. I didn't ask for this, Loretta. It was forced on me.'

'By Licata?'

'Yeah.'

She paused, taking this in.

'I couldn't say no,' Dante explained. 'His son's gone missing. He asked me to find him. It should be fine.'

Ordinarily skip-tracer jobs *were* fine. But when the missing person was the boss's son, and the boss's son was a universally recognized liability, the job had the propensity to go south fast.

'The man's son's gone missing,' Dante repeated.

'You're too soft,' Loretta said.

'There's a difference between being soft and being smart. I'll look into it for a few days, report back, and that'll be it. We'll have Christmas dinner, we'll sign the contract on the twenty-sixth and we'll be leaving LA just like we planned.'

Even to Dante it didn't sound convincing. Loretta continued to stare at him.

'You gotta stop doing this, Dante. Going off doing these jobs. The older you get, the more likely the cards won't come out right.'

'You think I chose this? You think I'm doing this for the buzz?'

It hurt that she might think he signed up to these jobs without considering the consequences, that he didn't prioritize his loved ones. Dante had lost his family once before, back in Chicago, through his own stupidity. The pain of it had shaped his life, so when he'd married Loretta he'd done everything he could to keep her safe, and he'd succeeded for decades.

She sighed and shook her head.

'If I could tell Licata to go to hell, I would,' Dante said. 'It's just a few days, Loretta. I've survived this long.'

He shrugged, but his reassurances just seemed to annoy her further.

'So you'll be taking time off,' she said, her tone halfway between a question and a condemnation.

'Just a few days.'

'Well, before you go, Mullan called and wants you to call him back, and there's a half-dozen letters and invoices that need your signature.' She gestured to a pile of paperwork she'd left amongst the snowdrifts on his desk. 'I need to talk to Jimmy and Mike,' she said, rising and leaving the office.

Dante watched her go, exhaled. It had gone as well as he could have hoped, and he felt about as guilty as he'd expected. All through their marriage, through raising their children, he'd been going off on jobs, disappearing sometimes for weeks at a time. It had left its mark. She was never quite sure she could fully rely on him, and he always felt like he had something to make up to her. The vineyard was the one real promise he had left, something they could do together, that would compensate for the shadow he'd cast over their relationship. At least, that was how he saw it.

He turned to the paperwork, rushed through it, knowing he needed to be out on the road, doing the rounds, searching for Riccardo. The longer he was missing the more tricky things would be. Dante signed all the letters and invoices and then he called back Mullan, their accountant, who was overseeing the purchase of the vineyard. It was out of their price range, but Dante had put the distribution company up for sale, taken out a loan, used his savings for the deposit. Now all that cash was sitting in an escrow account waiting for December 26th, when the sale of the company would be finalized, triggering money to be moved, which in turn would finalize the vineyard purchase. If the chain broke before that for any reason, Dante was at risk of losing his savings, being forced to sell his business, being liable for the loan. He'd been edgy about it for weeks now and being given the job last night had only made it worse.

As he waited for Mullan's secretary to put him through he noticed, in amongst his papers, a few of the brochures sent by the people selling the vineyard. He picked one up and looked at it. There were photos of lush green hills glistening with morning dew, verdant vines, grapes a rich purple, a pale yellow. It was hard not to imagine it as a paradise where he and Loretta could live out their retirement, with their daughter, Jeanette, helping them manage the place. Her house in Santa Rosa was just a stone's throw away, meaning spending more time with her and the grandkids.

The plan was for Jeanette to take over running the vineyard eventually.

So Dante had pushed ahead, had spent months mollifying the last of his clients – Mob bosses and millionaires and movie-studio executives – convincing them he really was retiring. He needed to get out of LA, he told them. He was approaching seventy and was all burned out. So he chased assurances, closed contracts, sold assets, called in markers, destroyed evidence, paid bribes and hush money, tied up loose ends. He extricated himself in a long, delicate act of contortion. He'd leave the life to make wine, while most mobsters left it riding a gurney. The plan was perfect, which worried Dante. Perfect plans were the most fragile of all.

When Mullan came on the line he explained he needed Dante's go-ahead on a few final changes with the contract. Dante gave the go-ahead, then hung up. He put a call through to a pal of his on the LAPD's Narcotics Squad, arranged a meeting for later that day. He made a last call to information to get a listing for Riccardo's company, then he rose and strode out of the warehouse.

# 14

Riccardo's office was at the eastern end of the Hollywood flats, in a five-story Spanish-style block set behind a scruffy courtyard. Dante hit the buzzers on the intercom till someone bought his spiel about a delivery and buzzed him in. He entered and looked around the hallway. The walls were grubby, the carpet threadbare. The board by the mail slots said Riccardo's company – Ocean Movies – was located on the second floor. Dante took the mail blooming out of Riccardo's slot, then went up the stairs. When he got to the office he saw there was a crack across the door. Someone had brute-forced their way in.

Dante put his ear against the door and listened. No noises. But a sickly, putrid odor was drifting out from the other side. Dante got his gun from his jacket pocket, a .38 Colt Detective Special, eased back the hammer.

He tried the door, hoping that whoever had broken in might have permanently disabled the lock. He turned the handle down, lifted it up, shoved with his shoulder and the door juddered open. When he stepped inside he expected to find Riccardo's body lying on the floor. But there was nothing to account for the smell. Venetian blinds were lowered over the windows, making the place murky, but he could see there were two desks further on, filing cabinets, an opening leading to a kitchenette. Everything had been tossed.

Dante heard a scuttling noise from the archway that led to the kitchenette. He raised the gun. He tensed his trigger-finger. The noise stopped. He approached the archway. Spun. Something moved in the shadows. Dante looked for a light switch, snapped it on. The room was empty except for a dog. A mongrel with thick brown hair. Not much older than a puppy, cowering in the corner.

Dante sighed, lowered the gun. The dog continued to cower, pushed itself further into the corner. Next to it were empty water and food bowls. Dante approached the dog, reached out to stroke it, and it flinched.

'It's OK,' he said softly. 'It's OK, boy.'

He stroked its back, felt the fear shaking through its body. The dog had been locked in here, left to starve, then some men had broken in to search the place and the dog had probably started barking and the intruders had probably hit it to shut it up, and then they'd left it to die.

'It's OK, boy. It's OK.'

Dante stroked the dog until it calmed down, even though he should have been searching the place, getting in and out as quickly as possible. Memories stirred. Loretta calling him a soft touch. How a stray dog in Chicago decades ago had saved his life.

He ran his fingers over the animal's torso, feeling for cuts and bruises. The dog yelped when Dante touched its stomach. Maybe there were broken ribs there, but there was no dried blood.

Dante rose and looked through the kitchenette, noticed the thin layer of dust on the counters, in the glasses. He found a can of dog food, filled up a bowl with water, let the dog eat and drink. How long had it been in here starving?

He walked into the main office, turned the blinds to let some light in, cracked open the windows to get the smell out. He looked around once more. There was a layer of dust in here too. Dante put it together with the amount of mail in the slot and the unfed dog, and it suggested whoever worked here had left a while ago, and wasn't coming back. Licata said Riccardo had been arrested in September. No way the dog could have survived since then. Someone had been coming in here until a few days ago. The office looked like a two-person joint with the two-desk set up. Someone was helping Riccardo run the place, had been attending to it while Riccardo had been in prison. Dante went over to the desk with the typewriter on it, opened drawers, looked for business cards, found them – *Audrey Lloyd, Office Manager*. He slipped the card into his pocket, looked around again.

On one of the walls was a large plastic panel with the company's logo on it – three blue curls representing a wave – and just next to it, the name in a curvy turquoise typeface. Across all the other walls were posters of the films the company had made: trashy surfer movies, a few hot-rod racing pics. The films had names like *Bikini Beach Party*, *The Endless Wave*, *Wild Surf*, *Summer Love*. The posters showed beautiful young women relaxing on beaches, chisel-jawed surfers, racing-car drivers, panoramic vistas of Pacific sunsets as red as glowing iron.

As Dante looked around the grubby abandoned office he wondered how the son of a Mob boss ended up somewhere so run-down. Was it on account of Riccardo's personal failings? Or was it emblematic of the Mob's general decline? Then he wondered if maybe Riccardo's disappearance wasn't anything to do with the coke he'd been busted with after all; maybe it was to do with Ocean Movies. The front door had been broken, the place ransacked, and the office manager had hightailed it in such a rush that she'd left the office dog to starve.

Dante quickly flipped through the mail he'd picked up downstairs – circulars, a rent demand, a renewal on the lease for the furniture. He dropped the mail on what must have been Riccardo's desk and sat in his chair. Maybe the intruders had left something in here that might shed some light on what Riccardo had been up to. Dante scanned the debris on the floor, noticed broken glass in amongst it, pieces of caramel corn. Riccardo must have kept a jar of candy on his desk, like a lot of Mob guys of the older generation did. Strange that Riccardo had kept up the tradition. Maybe it was the caramel corn that had been keeping the dog alive.

Dante rose, split the room into quadrants, went through the debris, the desk drawers, the filing cabinets. He searched for a safe but couldn't find one. He went through the kitchenette, under the carpets, the floorboards, the sofa, looking for hidden stashes. But most of the places he might expect to find something had already been tossed by the intruders, suggesting they knew what they were doing.

He sifted through the pile of papers on the desk and in the cabinets and was surprised by what he found – it seemed like the company actually did make films. He'd just assumed it was a paper operation, taking money from movie investors, putting it into someone else's production, receiving a percentage somehow. But all the paperwork suggested Ocean Movies was a legitimate independent film producer: contracts with equipment-rental companies and studio lots, location-scouting reports, headshots of actors and actresses. Dante sifted through the headshots. The actors looked strictly D-list, faces that people back home said were special. The actresses all looked like showgirls bussed in from Vegas because they wore their bikinis well. Dante spotted a few Italian names in amongst the company's counterparties, but none he recognized. There were no obvious connections to the underworld apart from Riccardo himself.

Dante lit a cigarette, looked over the empty office. The blinds were turned halfway, slicing the morning light, painting contours across the room. He watched the dust putting in a shift through the sunbeams, and felt like he'd stepped back into the 1930s, his old office at RKO, when he worked as a fixer for Howard Hughes. Dante had been offered the job by one of Hughes's stooges back in Chicago just when he had wanted to get out of the city, so he and Loretta had headed west.

But Dante had only lasted a few years at RKO. Being a fixer for the Mob involved moral hazards, but the studio system was something else. There was an old joke about Harry Cohn running Columbia Pictures like a concentration camp, and it was true of the other studios too. Cover-ups, casting couches, blackmail and race hate were the oil on which the system ran. Even the stars were ground down by it. Dante had seen how they had to work insane hours, play the parts they were given, date the people they were told to, take the drugs they were prescribed by shady doctors on the studio payroll. If they got pregnant they were sent to Mexico for forced abortions, if they overdosed they were sent to dry-out farms upstate. With the fame came reporters and stalkers, shakedowns and breakdowns. Then came the drugs, the booze, the fifth divorce, the weight gain and loss, the comeback flop, the unreturned calls, the suicide attempt. Dante had seen plenty go mad under the weight of it all. And he'd been a cog in the machine, helping perpetuate a system of corruption that broadcasted an image of wholesomeness around the world, a mirage. Films were a dark kind of magic.

So Dante had quit, started up the drinks distribution company, started taking on jobs for the mobsters in LA. And the days sidled into each other and the years fell away. Good years, though the argument with Loretta that morning suggested she didn't see things so rosily.

He walked back into the kitchenette, the contours of light and shade rippling over him. The dog was lying by the bowls, which were empty now. Dante went over to the cupboards, pocketed a couple more cans of dog food.

'Come on,' he said.

The dog took a second, then hopped up after him.

When Dante got back onto the street, he searched about for a pay-phone and called an old pal who worked at Ma Bell. He asked for call logs going back two weeks for Riccardo's main business line and the separate number that was listed on Audrey Lloyd's business card. His pal said he'd have something for him that night. Dante hung up and looked across the street at Riccardo's cheap, dingy office. He thought of the succession of cheap, dingy offices he himself had worked in. He thought of the warehouse, the argument with Loretta. He reminded himself again how he couldn't mess this all up.

# 15

Dante got to LAX at just gone eleven. He parked the Thunderbird in one of the short-term parking lots littered about the airport. He hopped out, and together with the dog zigzagged through the cars. He noted how the dog moved as he did, turned when he turned, stopped when he stopped, never getting under his feet, never lagging or running ahead, like they were already in synch.

As they neared the airport buildings Dante spotted a crime scene in the long-term parking lot. Yellow tape, a hearse, a medical examiner's van, a gaggle of gawkers. The action was centered on a blue Chrysler Newport parked right in the middle of the lot. A knot of cops stood next to it, chatting. Dante scanned them, looking for the one he'd arranged to meet, found him – Conor O'Shaughnessy, Dante's pal in the LAPD's Narcotics Squad. He was a short man in his forties, with a scruffy mop of brown hair and a quick smile. O'Shaughnessy saw Dante in the crowd, gestured toward the airport buildings, to the cafeteria. Dante nodded back.

Five minutes later he was sitting in the cafeteria with two coffees in front of him and the dog at his feet. The place was bright, with a cigarette stand and a counter and a raised gallery with tables and booths. Its windows looked out on the vast parking lots that surrounded the airport. The sight had always reminded Dante of the Stockyards back in Chicago, the grids of cattle pens sprawled over acres of Illinois mud, the occupants awaiting the slaughterhouse.

Every now and then a jet roared past overhead, shaking the

crockery, drowning out the sound of the Christmas tunes playing on the radio.

After a few minutes he saw O'Shaughnessy approaching through the lot. He stepped into the cafeteria, sat at the counter next to Dante.

'What happened?' Dante asked, gesturing through the windows to the crime scene.

'Dead body in a car,' O'Shaughnessy said. He had a gravelly voice that sounded like it scratched the back of his throat each time he spoke. 'Been there a while. Coroner thinks maybe a couple of days. Had his head blown to jam, but nobody heard the gun go off. Theory is the killer waited for a plane to fly past so the noise would mask the sound of the shot.'

Dante considered. 'Smart move,' he said.

'That was the consensus. And because the parking lot's the size of a goddamn cornfield and the car's parked right in the middle of it, no one spotted it for almost three days.'

'So what's the narcotics angle?'

'The homicide detectives found a couple of pounds of marijuana in the trunk. They called some of us over to see if we know the guy. We don't.'

'Seems strange the killer didn't take the pot with him,' Dante said.

'Maybe he didn't know it was there.'

Dante nodded. As the radio started playing a jazz-inflected version of 'O Little Town of Bethlehem', they stared through the window at the crime scene, at the gawkers standing around, tourists on their way home to the Corn Belt, the Deep South, the East Coast, stopping off for one last sightseeing attraction before they boarded their planes. Dante wondered if they'd had their fill of whatever it was they came to LA for – sun, surf, celebrities, pop music, a close-up view of California's counter-culture revolution. He wondered if up till now they'd managed to avoid the placid city's violent side, the pollution, the muggings, the wackos, the rot, the hookers on Sunset who got more underaged the further west you traveled.

A Mexicana jet roared past overhead, set the cafeteria shaking.

'So, what can I do you for?' O'Shaughnessy asked when the noise had subsided.

'I've been handed a skip-trace case I don't want.'

'Who's the skipper?'

'Riccardo Licata.'

O'Shaughnessy raised his eyebrows.

'I can see why you don't want it.'

'Riccardo was in the joint for a coke bust your boys made,' Dante said. 'Then out of the blue he called up his pops, begging for bail. Then the day he got out, he disappeared. You know anything about it?'

'A little. It wasn't me who caught the case, but it made waves when it happened. Nick Licata bailed the kid and now he's asked you to find him?'

'Pretty much.'

'So what's he after – his kid or his bail money?'

'A bit of both. What do you know about the bust?'

'It was a routine traffic stop. Licata's car had a busted taillight or something. When he got pulled over he was acting shifty, on the muscle, so the cops searched the car and found the mother-load of coke in the trunk. Forty pounds of pure cocaine. Weight to the T. The idiot was actually driving around town with that amount of narcotics in the car and he didn't bother to check his lights.'

'Riccardo claimed you guys set him up. Planted the coke.'

O'Shaughnessy laughed. 'Where the hell would we get that much coke from? Even if we cleared out the LAPD central evidence storage it wouldn't be enough.'

'You got any clue where Riccardo got it from?'

'That's what we've been asking ourselves ever since. No one

figured Riccardo Licata for a power player in the coke league. Last few years we're busting more and more coke distributors, but it's never anything big. Riccardo's haul was off the scale. And it happened completely by accident. We were pressuring him into revealing his source, but he wouldn't spill. And there's a footnote to all this which might interest you. It's from back in my days with the FBN.'

Dante nodded. Before O'Shaughnessy worked for the LAPD, he'd been an agent with the Federal Bureau of Narcotics – the government agency tasked with policing the illegal drug trade, both nationally and internationally. Though much smaller than its cousin, the FBI, the Narcotics Bureau was more skillful, adept and successful. With only three hundred agents and four percent of the federal law-enforcement budget, it accounted for twenty percent of the prisoners in federal prisons. But over recent years the FBN's lustre had faded with a string of corruption scandals – agents caught stealing product, stealing cash, setting up their own drug deals and import routes. O'Shaughnessy himself had been a victim of the corruption – when he'd refused to frame an innocent man on a charge that would have landed him a thirty-year stretch, paperwork started disappearing from his desk, a bundle of fake money was planted in his locker, his superiors received anonymous reports that he was on the pad. When, quite by chance, O'Shaughnessy discovered the brakes on his car had been tampered with, he realized his colleagues weren't simply trying to force him out, they were trying to kill him. So he quit and joined the LAPD.

"Bout five years back, when I was still with the Narcotics Bureau,' O'Shaughnessy said. 'We busted Riccardo in a sweep on a club in Los Feliz. It wasn't him we were after, he was just at the wrong bar at the wrong time. He had a bag of amphetamines on him – black beauties. Enough to see him go down for a couple of years. Enough to pressure him into turning snitch. Just as we were about to interview him, we got the call to let him go. Apparently he was already "an integral part of an ongoing investigation".'

O'Shaughnessy raised his eyebrows, leaving Dante to infer what had happened – Riccardo was an informant for one of the other agents in the FBN. Dante imagined having to tell Nick Licata that his son had turned rat. It would be as bad as telling him Riccardo had died. Was this why Riccardo was desperate to get out of jail? Had his cover as a FBN snitch been blown?

'Did you ever find out which agent was running him?' Dante asked.

O'Shaughnessy shook his head.

'No one ever shared their informers in the Bureau,' he said. 'That place was dog eat dog.'

Dante frowned.

'So you and your boys in the LAPD don't know anything about Riccardo – an FBN asset – disappearing without a trace?'

The question was deliberately loaded – the FBN and the LAPD had a long history of hating each other. They competed not only for busts and accolades, but for informers and detectives, too. When agents got pissed off at the FBN, they resigned and got hired by the LAPD's Narcotics Squad, taking with them all their contacts and sources. Just like O'Shaughnessy had. Some men moved in the other direction. Some men ping-ponged back and forth. Their relations hit an all-time low back in 1957, when FBN informers started turning up shot dead by the same model of revolvers that were standard issue to the LAPD. The FBN retaliated, and soon the corpses of both agencies' informers were littering the city. The story made headlines. LA's mayor convened a hasty, awkward press conference where the chief of police and the FBN district supervisor made like pals and denied the rumors.

If O'Shaughnessy was right about Riccardo being an FBN snitch, then it might not have been Riccardo's coke source that bumped him off, it might have been any one of a number of crooked cops in the LAPD.

'No one wants a repeat of what happened back in the fifties,' O'Shaughnessy said. 'And anyway, there's no point. Word is the FBN's on the way out. All the corruption scandals have got the White House gunning to have them closed down. Why would anyone on the LAPD start clipping the FBN's informers? All we got to do is wait a few months for the Bureau to be shut down and we can pick up all the best of them for free.'

It was the first Dante had heard about the FBN being closed down, but it made sense. He studied O'Shaughnessy. If his friend knew anything about the LAPD being involved in Riccardo's disappearance, he was doing a damn good job of pretending not to.

O'Shaughnessy took a sip of coffee, stared out of the windows, to the endless field of cars. A van had arrived to load up the dead man. Dante watched it with a thickening sense of gloom, like he was watching a premonition of his own fate.

'There's something else you should know,' O'Shaughnessy said, turning to Dante.

'Go on.'

'After Riccardo skipped out on bail, some of the boys on the Squad did some digging, tried to find out what happened. According to the jail's visitor log, someone came by to visit Riccardo right before he asked his pops to pay his bail – an LAPD detective named Sam Cole.'

'And what did Cole have to say about it?'

'That's the kicker,' O'Shaughnessy smiled. 'There's no one in the Police Department with that name. You ask me, if you want to know what happened to Riccardo, you need to find whoever it was that visited him in jail with the fake ID. And maybe find out what it was he told Riccardo that scared him so bad he went running to his pops for a half-million bail-out.'

Dante nodded.

'I think that sounds about right,' he said.

In the air above them another plane roared past and the cups on the counter danced.

# PART FOUR

## IDA

# 16

The traffic seemed to be against Ida on the drive home from the Glass House that night – she got caught up in a jam downtown, then on the Harbor Freeway, then on the Santa Monica. When she was closer to home she got stuck behind a clot of vehicles near the route of the extension to the 405 Freeway, where a whole stretch of suburbia was being ripped up to make room for it. Eviction notices had been issued, homes vacated, and a strip of Los Angeles, two blocks wide and four miles long, had been turned into a ghost town, empty except for vagrant wanderers breaking into the abandoned houses, teenagers turning them into party spots. Further along, the construction work had already started, with Governor Reagan arriving on the day they broke ground for a photo opportunity. Ida had seen his picture in the paper, sat behind the wheel of a bulldozer, that moronic cowboy grin on his face.

As she waited for the cars to clear, Ida peered down the street to the evacuated strip of suburbia further along. In advance of construction, entire houses were being moved. Work crews came to cut power lines, water pipes, telephone cables. Beams were driven under the foundations and the houses lifted by giant machines, so they stood a few feet above the ground, floating eerily in the sky until they were loaded onto trucks and taken away. Ida wasn't sure if the houses were to be laid back down in another neighborhood somewhere, or if they were simply driven straight to a scrapyard.

In some places there were craters where homes had once stood; grains of sand had collected, blown in from the Mojave the previous night, like the desert had arrived to claim the city, turn it back into the hinterland it had once been.

There was a metallic screeching noise and a few seconds later a flatbed truck approached the T-junction in front of Ida. As it got closer, she saw why it was moving so slowly – it had a house strapped on its bed. A complete, two-story house razed out of the ground and loaded onto the truck. Ida watched it trundle past in the moonlight with an unsettling sense of rupture. A house was supposed to be stable, fixed, the bedrock of domesticity on which the post-war dream had been built. But here was the evidence that the dream was just a dream. That the city was as illusionary as a stage set, just film scenery to be moved about. That was the nightmare in the dream. If Los Angeles was a metropolis pulled up out of the wilderness by human ingenuity, a constructed Eden, then it could also be deconstructed, and destroyed, too.

When Ida finally got home she prepared herself a quick meal and tried to eat it before Walter called her from Germany. Over the fifteen years of their marriage they'd spent many months apart, him traveling the world for the newspaper, her having to go across the country for cases. It was something they valued. They were both solitary types who needed their space, figured the time alone was the glue that held them together. Alone together. Like the Chet Baker song she'd heard the previous evening.

He called her just as she was finishing her food. It was good to hear his voice, but they had a stilted conversation. She told him about the murder, how she'd been at the Glass House all day. He fell silent, then made some non-committal remark. His reaction surprised her. It was Walter who'd tried to talk her out of it when she'd decided to retire, so she thought the news of her consulting on the case would please him. But for some reason it didn't, and that tainted the rest of their conversation. He told her briefly how his work in Germany was going, a piece about the soldiers stationed there, Christmas along the Berlin Wall.

After they said goodnight, Ida sat on the porch and wrapped herself in a shawl, even though it was a mild night. The older you get, the colder you get, Walter liked to say. She smoked, drank, sifted evidence in her head. The killer was still out there somewhere, but she tried to think of it all as an abstract puzzle, a logic problem, a formula that needed solving.

She lost herself in it, stringing variables together in countless lines of cause and effect, testing what cohered, what didn't. Just like she used to. Three murders. Three sets of evidence.

Doctor. Actress. Engineer.

Hospital. Laundromat. Cafeteria.

A punctured man. A bath of money. A severed arm.

What connection was she missing? She went back through the victims' movements the nights they were killed. They'd all left work, all stopped off somewhere to eat or wash their clothes, all gone home to empty houses. The familiar movements of lonely Angelinos through their evenings. There was such a mundanity to their routines it was almost depressing. And then Ida realized that she herself had followed a similar pattern that night. Maybe that was why she'd looked over her shoulder when she'd gotten into her car to drive home from the Glass House that evening, gripped by the same fear that was tightening around the rest of the city.

A punctured man. A bath of money. A severed arm.

Again it was their power as images that seemed important. Had the killer made his victims into symbols because it depersonalized them? Made what he was doing easier? Was it a compulsion he felt guilty about afterwards? Was that why he arranged them into those peaceful, respectful poses?

Murders were common in LA, but mostly they had some reason to them – money, love, anger, desperation. This was something else. Not just senseless, sadistic and cruel, but ritualistic, sacrificial. This was why the killings had sent a message of fear and disgust through a city that was well used to homicide. And maybe the ritualism tapped into something more, something in

LA's nature. It was a city of displaced people, exiles and refugees, built on an unstable, precarious landscape. And just like New Orleans, it dealt with the constant peril through superstition, weaving its own form of myth, a rich tapestry of cults and New Age communes. Whatever alternative worked. It was the perfect place for a new type of voodoo.

Again Ida's mind jumped to the characters from the folk tales of her youth. Maybe Bras-Coupé and his band of runaway slaves were out there, maybe the voodoo barons, the *loup-garou* were-wolves. Out there in the darkness with the Night-Slayer.

On the bookshelf in her lounge Ida had an old book titled *Gumbo Ya-Ya* where many of the Louisiana folk tales were col-lected. Maybe she should get it down, read through it, purge herself of the fantasies that were bugging her more and more. But she got back to thinking about the murders, went at it most of the night. When the tiredness was making her thoughts smear, she locked up the house, went into the bedroom and caught a few hours' sleep.

She dreamed of Los Angeles, New Orleans, the Night-Slayer, broken images of electric freeways and bayou tides, the sense of an achingly beautiful song she couldn't quite hear. Toward morn-ing her dreams coalesced around another Louisiana folk figure – the pirate Jean Lafitte, who traded slaves and fought the British at the Battle of New Orleans and killed a shipmate each time he buried treasure in the bayous, so the dead man's soul would guard the spot. The dead souls appeared as flickering blue will-o'-the-wisps, swamp lights that led travelers off the safe paths, so more souls drowned to haunt the swamps.

When Ida woke dawn was coming on, the sky pink and clean. She lay in bed and listened to the sounds of Fox Hills stirring from sleep. It was a good neighborhood; well churched, smattered with orchards and a sprinkling of farmland. Fields of corn, watermelons and avocados all grew within a stone's throw, right there in the middle of the city.

Ida went into the bathroom and washed her hands and face. The sight of the water running across the porcelain made her think again of Jean Lafitte, of those bodies left floating in the bayous to protect his treasure. She drew a parallel with Danielle Landry lying in a bath of money. Water and coins. Was that why Ida's mind kept reeling back to the image? Because it reminded her of the old folk tale?

The phone rang. She went into the kitchen and picked it up. It was her daughter-in-law, Christine, calling from San Francisco. Ida was due to go up there on the weekend, spend Christmas together with Jacob and Christine and the grandchildren. As they spoke Ida found it hard to concentrate, spending most of the conversation looking out of her kitchen window into her neighbor's garden, the grass underneath its bitter-orange tree littered with broken fruit. Ida was vaguely annoyed that her neighbor hadn't collected the fruit, and then she got annoyed with herself for being annoyed, worried that she might be turning into one of those crotchety old women driven livid by age and resentment.

They finished the call and Ida stood a moment in the silence of her kitchen, staring at the broken fruit, thinking once more about Jean Lafitte and the similarities with Danielle Landry, annoyed with her mind for making these parallels. Maybe it was a symptom of getting old. She looked across the kitchen to the bookshelf in the lounge. There was the book of folk tales, *Gumbo Ya-Ya*, cloth bound and hefty, its title embossed onto its thick spine, and underneath the title an image of Bras-Coupé, one-armed, super-strong, striding through the bayou.

Ida frowned at the image, and her heart kicked.

One-armed Bras-Coupé.

Like one-armed Anthony Butterfield.

Danielle Landry lying in a pool of money like one of Jean Lafitte's slaughtered pirates.

And Mark McNeal, punctured like a victim of the Needle Men and their hypodermics.

That was it. That was the link. Louisiana folklore.

# 17

'Louisiana folklore?' Feinberg said, not bothering to hide his skepticism.

They were at his desk in the Glass House. She risked a glance around the room and saw that the detectives nearest to them had all gone quiet, had stopped their work to watch the show, thin ribbons of smoke from their cigarettes rising into the air. Suddenly Ida felt like she was in a tension chamber, at risk of a public humiliation.

On the drive over, more pieces of evidence had dropped into place, things Ida should have realized before about Danielle Landry, those trinkets scattered about her apartment. But almost as quickly as the realizations came, so did the anxiety – that Feinberg wouldn't believe her, that she was wrong about everything. She'd been seeing New Orleans all around her since she'd started the memoir, and now she was seeing it in the Night-Slayer killings, too. Maybe she hadn't made a breakthrough, maybe she was just a doddering old woman at the far end of her life, reading her own preoccupations into the case. Good for nothing but the graveyard.

But Ida had to share her theory, whether or not she was laughed out of there. Lives were at stake.

'McNeal was a medic, worked in an ER department,' she said. 'That's where the killer saw him. And he was stabbed to death like a victim of a Needle Man. From the old New Orleans myth.'

'What myth?'

She told him about the belief in Needle Men, white doctors who slipped into the colored part of town at night to inject people with sleeping liquid and take them away to use in experiments. She explained the parallels in the other murders too, but Feinberg just sat there with the same skeptical look on his face.

'There's an old Louisiana superstition: to ward off a *loup-garou* – it's a type of werewolf – you place thirteen small objects by your windows and doors, anywhere they can gain entry. For some reason it's supposed to stop them breaking in.'

'So?'

'The trinkets in Landry's apartment – the seashells, the glass beads. They were found by the windows and doors. It wasn't the killer who left them there. It was Landry. She was trying to protect herself, and when the Night-Slayer broke in, they got scattered about. Landry's a Cajun name. She was from Mobile, just across from Louisiana. She probably knew about this kind of stuff. Maybe she realized the first murder was folklore-related somehow, and she got scared and superstitious. Go and get the photos from the crime scene, count the items, see if there's thirteen of each. The officers doing the inventory never wrote down a number, they just classed them as 'multiple items'. I bet you there's thirteen.'

Ida finished talking and in the silence she sensed that maybe she'd been doing so too loudly, because even more detectives were staring at her now, and the hush was palpable.

Feinberg sighed.

'Wait here,' he said, rising to get the files.

Ida watched him go and then turned to look around her. The men were all still staring at her. Under their scrutiny she felt a strong sense of her otherness, how she was the exact opposite to these detectives in so many respects – civilian, elderly, female, black. Throughout her life Ida had been light-skinned enough to pass as white, something which brought its own unease – she could legitimately be worried in any part of town. And in situations like this, when a few dozen unfriendly eyes were on her, she inevitably wondered what people were thinking, what race they thought she was, if they were trying to figure it out. These men were part of a police force that had a long history of race hate. It was LA's cops who enforced the city's racial curfews and segregation policies, both official and unofficial, who saw it as part of their job to keep LA safe by keeping its minorities in check, through every means at their disposal. Over the last few years the city's police had, on average, killed a black person every three weeks, half of the victims shot in the back.

But these were also the men Ida had to work with if she was ever to get justice for the people who came to her looking for help. Most of the time she could handle being around them, as long as she knew them, and there weren't too many, and they weren't all piercing her with their gazes, like they were now.

Eventually Feinberg returned with the tubs and Ida's anxiety increased. He sat, flicked through the files, stopped at a folder, opened it, skimmed.

'You were right about the inventory,' he said. 'They didn't bother to list the number of each item.' He seemed annoyed by the sheriffs' slackness, but carried on flicking through the folders. He came to the one containing the crime-scene photos from Landry's apartment and laid them out on the desk. The glass beads by the windows, the seashells by the front door. They leaned in and counted them, and Ida prayed they would prove her correct.

'Thirteen of each,' Feinberg muttered.

Landry had placed thirteen tokens by every one of the entry points to the apartment. Ida exhaled, feeling an overwhelming sense of relief.

'You were right, Ida,' Feinberg said. 'I apologize. You were right.'

'You don't have to apologize. But I appreciate it all the same.'

'So, where d'you think he's going with this? You think he's got a big list of Louisiana folk tales he's working through? He's gonna flay someone next? Turn them into one of those skeletons in top hats?'

'Maybe,' Ida frowned. In the rush of discovering the folklore link, she hadn't considered what might come next. Now that Feinberg had put it into her head, the thought of the killer working through a list of Louisiana myths chilled her, but it also gave her an idea.

'I think I can figure out what he might do next,' she said.

'What do you mean?'

'If the killer's going to work to a list, maybe we can too.'

When Ida got home she went over to her bookshelf, pulled down her copy of *Gumbo Ya-Ya*, took it out to the writing chair on the porch. The book had been published in the 1940s by the Works Public Administration during the Depression, when the government was subsidizing writers and academics as part of the New Deal. The material in the book had been gathered together and collated by members of the Louisiana Writers' Program, who'd received a grant to travel around the state interviewing people and collecting legends.

Walter had bought Ida the book as a gift after he'd seen a copy in a public library. That was the thing with WPA books – they were government made, so they were often purchased in bulk by other arms of the government, to keep everything in-house.

Ida was surprised to see, when she'd first opened it all those years ago, that her first ever case, the Axeman of New Orleans, was one of the 'legends' documented, the killer having already passed into myth when the book had been written. But if the Axeman was now a myth, what did that make her investigation of him? And what if the Axeman inspired one of the Night-Slayer's next murders? What other legends might he recreate?

The book listed numerous killers, real and mythical, who'd supposedly terrorized different Louisiana parishes over the years – the Black Bottle Man, the Gown Man, the Domino Man, the Devil Man. There were rosters of ghosts listed by plantation – the headless horseman of Lacey Branch, the Pirate Ghost of L'Isle de

Gombi, the haunted wood at Marksville. There were lists of Creole superstitions – *'The howling of a dog and the chirping of a cricket both foretell a death . . . If you sleep with the moonlight in your face, you go crazy.'* Some sections of the book focussed on different social groups – Creoles, Cajuns, street criers, chimney sweeps, prostitutes, slaves, the Sockerhause crime family. Other sections focussed on work songs and ballads, cemeteries, riverfront lore. Ida sifted through them all, compiled a list of what the Night-Slayer might try to emulate.

When she was done she made another list, of public places the Night-Slayer might be stalking. Places where people went after work, where he could loiter, where he could get a sense of their loneliness. She wondered how many potential victims he had considered, followed, lost, how many Angelinos had had lucky escapes without even realizing it.

Again something about the locations snagged in her thoughts. She thought about the first killing, Mark McNeal, the doctor, stabbed like a victim of a Needle Man. Was that why he'd been targeted? Because the killer saw McNeal in the Emergency Room, administering an injection maybe, and made a bizarre connection to the folklore? Is that what happened with the other two victims? The image of Danielle Landry in a laundromat flashed into Ida's mind. The Night-Slayer watching the girl as she slipped coins into one of the washing machines. Money and water, like Jean Lafitte's pirates. Was there a twisted logic at work after all?

Her thoughts were interrupted by the phone ringing. She went inside and picked it up. Feinberg.

'We got an ID on the motel victim,' he said. 'Audrey Lloyd. Ring any bells?'

''Fraid not,' Ida said, disappointed.

'Too bad. We ran her details through a missing persons list and they pinged against a report her room-mate made about a week ago. The room-mate's an attendant at the County Museum.

I'm going to head over there now and interview her – you want to tag along?'

A wave of something heavy coalesced in Ida's chest. She could feel herself being dragged ever further into the investigation. First she was asked to identify a body, then to review some files, now she was being asked to go to an interview.

'Ida?' Feinberg asked.

'You can talk to her. Let me know what she says.'

'Come on, Ida. Cut the bullshit. Just tag along. You don't have to say anything. I'll be interviewing. You'll be observing.'

'I know what you're doing, Feinberg. It's not going to work.'

'If you don't come with me, you're just gonna be sitting in your house fretting till I call you back.'

'I can take it.'

'Yeah, but for how long? What if I forget to call you back? What if decide it's in the department's best interest not to reveal anything to a civilian?'

'I know you wouldn't do that, Feinberg. You're a good guy.'

'I'm also under a lot of stress. Meet me there in an hour.'

# 18

The Los Angeles County Museum of Art was located on Wilshire Boulevard, just along from the La Brea Tar Pits. Recently constructed, its buildings were all sleek modernist blocks of marble, concrete and steel, arranged in a U-shape around a central plaza. Surrounding them were reflecting pools and fountains so the whole complex seemed to float dreamily on tiers of soft, glassy water.

Ida met Feinberg in the plaza and after asking around they were directed to the Lytton Gallery, where Myra Shaw – the roommate of the motel victim – was working. When they entered the gallery they saw it was all white walls and spotlights and glossy parquet floors. They passed a series of Henry Moore sculptures on a plinth, then stepped into a small exhibition of Mexican paintings. Next to a landscape stood an attendant in a gray uniform, her hair pulled back into a fussy chignon. As they approached, Ida saw that she was quietly sobbing.

'Myra Shaw?' Feinberg asked.

The woman looked up, wiped her eyes, nodded.

Feinberg flashed his badge.

'Detective Feinberg. LAPD. Are you all right, miss?'

She nodded again. Wiped her eyes again.

'You're here about Audrey, right? I was just down at the morgue, identifying her body. They said . . .'

But before she could continue she burst into tears. Ida fumbled through her purse for a tissue, passed it to her. Myra nodded her thanks. Despite her tears there was something prim and clinical about Myra Shaw, a sense of propriety which sat oddly with her youth. As Myra composed herself Ida realized she'd forgotten about this part of the job, having to question traumatized people, having to intrude on their grief, to trample all over it. She turned her gaze from Myra to the landscape next to her, a sunset over the cliffs of Acapulco, the sky a deep bloody red, the Pacific a calming blue.

'I've got a break in twenty minutes,' Myra said. 'Can I meet you out on the plaza?'

Ida and Feinberg killed the time smoking and gabbing and taking in the surroundings – the reflecting pools, the rows of gushing fountains, the clean white buildings rising into the sky. The place had a lushness to it, a brightness, part modernist dream, part Persian paradise garden. But it didn't do much to calm Ida's fears before the interview. She never used to feel this perturbed when she was working a case. Was it because there was a personal dimension to this one? Or was it just a sign of being old and rusty?

When Myra Shaw exited from the Lytton Gallery, they found a bench overlooking one of the pools and sat.

'Sorry if I seem a little shaken up,' Myra said.

'That's perfectly OK,' Feinberg said.

'When Audrey went missing I didn't think it would end like this. I mean, what was she doing in a motel in San Pedro?'

'That's what we want to find out,' Feinberg said. 'How long had you known Audrey?'

'About a year. My old room-mate moved out and I put an ad in the *Herald Examiner* and Audrey replied.'

'And before she went missing, was she acting differently at all? Worried?'

'No. Just her usual self.'

'And what happened on the day she went missing?'

'Nothing. She just didn't come home from work. She wasn't the type to stay out. She would have called to let me know. The next afternoon when I got back from work and she still wasn't home, I reported her missing.'

'So the last time you saw her was Wednesday morning? When she left for work?'

Myra nodded.

'Miss Shaw, it looks like Audrey was running away from something. You have any idea what that might be?'

'Running away?'

'She have a boyfriend? Someone she was seeing?'

'No, she was single.'

'How about an ex?'

'There was Karl,' she said. 'Karl Drazek. He was an old flame of hers, but they were still friends. He wouldn't do something like that to her.'

'I see. You know how we could get in contact with Mr Drazek?'

'He works in TV, producing stuff at Universal, I think. You could try there. Or his number might be in Audrey's address book. I can have a look for you when I get home if you want?'

'Please,' Feinberg said. 'And are there any other people we can talk to about Audrey? Friends? Parents? Family?'

'I don't know about that. She grew up in Florida. Maybe I can just give you her address book. I guess she won't be needing it now.'

Myra sniffed back a tear, stared into the reflecting pool below. Ida followed her gaze and noticed something odd. A brown, oily sludge was seeping up from between the tiles at the bottom of the pool, blooming through the water, sullying the effect of a pristine, watered paradise.

'It's oil from the tar pits,' Myra said.

She nodded in the direction of the La Brea Tar Pits, which adjoined the museum complex, where bitumen and gas leaked up out of the ground along a fault from the Salt Lake Oil Field which lay underneath the city.

'They're saying they're going to have to take out all the fountains, cement in all the pools,' Myra added. 'Crazy, huh? They only just built it all.'

She gestured to the waterscapes all around them. Ida nodded. Feinberg cleared his throat.

'Miss Shaw, are you aware of the Night-Slayer killings?'

'Yes. What's that got to do with . . .' She trailed off, coming to the wrong conclusion. 'It was the Night-Slayer who killed her?'

'No, Miss Shaw, it was *not* the Night-Slayer,' Feinberg said firmly. 'I was just wondering if you and Audrey talked about the case ever. If she expressed any interest in it?'

Myra searched her memories, frowned.

'No, I don't think so. We might have mentioned it in passing, joked about keeping the doors locked, but that's it. I don't understand – what's it got to do with Audrey if it wasn't the Night-Slayer who killed her?'

'It's just a check we have to make,' Feinberg explained smoothly. 'Did Audrey ever mention a private investigator by the name of Ida Young?'

Again Myra seemed confused and shook her head. Feinberg and Ida shared a look.

'Audrey checked into the motel with fake ID,' Feinberg said. 'And she'd rented a car with stolen credit cards. Do you know who she might have got those kinds of items from?'

'No, I don't know,' Myra replied, startled. 'You're making her sound like a criminal. I mean . . . is that what this is? She committed a crime? She stole credit cards?'

'We don't know that. We just want to know how they came into her possession.'

Myra looked at him in confusion. Feinberg glanced down at his pad, flicked through the pages.

'Can you tell us where Audrey worked?' he asked.

'At a film company. Ocean Movies. They're in Hollywood

somewhere. They make surfer pictures. It was Karl who got her the job. Her old flame.'

'And what did Audrey do at Ocean Movies?'

'Office manager.'

'She have any colleagues we could talk to?'

'I think it was just her and her boss who worked there. It's a small place. Independent. I guess she used to call herself an office manager because it sounded fancy. I mean, she did manage the office, but it was just the two of them.'

'OK,' Feinberg said. 'You know her boss's name?'

'Riccardo.'

'His full name?'

'It was an Italian surname. Ligotti. Something like that.'

'Licata?' Ida asked. 'Riccardo Licata?'

'Sure, that's it,' said Myra. 'You know him?'

Ida and Feinberg shared another look.

Riccardo Licata. Audrey Lloyd was working for the son of a Mob boss. Ida's anxiety spiked.

'We've heard of him,' Feinberg said, turning back to Myra. 'Is there anything else you think we should know about Audrey? Anything at all?'

Myra frowned.

'Well, there's the thing about her name. But you probably already know.'

'What's that?' Feinberg asked.

'About how she changed her name?'

Feinberg shook his head.

'Oh, I thought you would have known already,' Myra said. 'Lloyd wasn't her real name. She was born Lopez. A letter came for her one day, addressed to Audrey Lopez. I picked it up in the mail slot. She seemed a bit . . . *put out* about it, I guess. But then she told me how she wanted to be an actress and how maybe a Mexican name wouldn't help too much, so she changed it, like how Rita Hayworth changed hers from Rita Cansino.'

Feinberg frowned, turned from Myra to look at Ida. Ida nodded.

'Well, thank you for your time, Miss Shaw,' Feinberg said. 'We really appreciate it. As soon as we have any information we'll be in touch. And in the meantime, some men will probably come to your apartment to look through Audrey's things if that's OK?'

Myra frowned at this, surprised, but then she nodded.

They all rose. Feinberg took a business card from his wallet and passed it to her. Then they watched her walk back to the gallery in silence.

'Jesus Christ,' Feinberg said when she was out of earshot. 'Our motel victim was working for Nick Licata's son.'

'I guess that answers the question about whether or not it's Mob-related.'

Feinberg fished his cigarettes from his pocket. He shook one out of the pack for Ida and took one himself.

'She came up blank when I name-dropped you,' he said. 'And when I mentioned the Night-Slayer.'

'Yeah, but she barely knew Audrey. Audrey moved in a year ago, via a newspaper ad. Apart from the ex-boyfriend, Myra didn't know a single one of her relatives or her friends. And it took her almost two days to report her missing. And it's only because that letter turned up that she even knew Audrey's real name. They might have lived together, but they were strangers, whether Myra realized it or not.'

Feinberg considered this, nodded.

'I need to re-run all the checks. Try to find an Audrey Lopez from Florida.'

'I wouldn't be surprised if the Florida backstory was just another lie. Feels like Audrey was hiding something. Something big.'

Feinberg took a drag on his cigarette.

'This Mob link doesn't chime with your Louisiana voodoo angle.'

'Louisiana *folklore*,' Ida corrected. 'And you're right, it doesn't. Somehow we need to make folklore, the Night-Slayer, the Mob and a runaway woman in a motel room all mesh. Audrey worked for a company making surfer movies. And Danielle Landry quit her day job to star in biker movies. You think there's a link there?'

'Could be.'

They went silent, stared into the pool below them, at the brown, meandering ooze destroying the museum's spotless paradise. Ida shifted her thoughts back to the case. The more it progressed, the more complicated it became, the more Ida felt she was being dragged into something she might not survive. And yet for all its complexity, she was sure that there was a simple line connecting everything – Audrey, the Mob, the Night-Slayer, the Louisiana folklore.

She realized she needed to speak to someone Mob-connected, someone who she could trust. There was only one person in all LA who fitted the bill.

Dante the Gent.

# PART FIVE

## DANTE

# 19

Dante spent the best part of a day and a night criss-crossing LA in search of a lead. But he came up blank. Time and again. No one knew where Riccardo was. No one knew who his coke source was. The more Dante did the rounds, the more out of touch he felt, the more he succumbed to a sense of impending doom. It wouldn't be long before Licata was on the phone demanding answers. All Dante had was what O'Shaughnessy had told him – that Riccardo was probably a snitch for the FBN. The last thing Licata wanted to hear.

So Dante kept driving, interviewing, succumbing, hitting dead ends. He visited men of his own generation. Men who'd commanded fear and respect and armies of killers in their time. But their day had passed. All they gave him was old-man gossip that just confirmed what he already knew – that the LA Mob was in a state of collapse. Nick Licata had taken over from DeSimone earlier that year, and everyone agreed it was a bad move. Not that DeSimone had been much better; before he died he'd become so paranoid he didn't go out at night. Imagine that, a Mob boss too scared to go out at night. Truly it was the Mickey Mouse Mafia, the old men lamented, shaking their heads.

Then, to make matters worse, one of the first things Licata did after taking over was demote all the men in the rival Dragna clique, from *caporegimes* to *soldati*, thereby pissing off many of the Mob's best earners.

Another bad move, the old men agreed.

'So you think we're heading for a war?' Dante asked.

'We're always heading for a war,' they said.

They bemoaned Jimmy Hoffa going to prison that year, they bemoaned the racketeering bill due before Congress soon. They prophesied doom. Entire families getting pinched. It wasn't like the old days, they said. The golden days. There were no more Lucianos, Rothsteins, Costellos. The empire-builders of the past had moved on, the mantle had been handed over to a younger generation who just weren't up to the task. Now there was just an empire of dust.

In the golden age the Mob had the backing of politicians in every city. Mayors, governors, congressmen, senators. All on the payroll, all turning a blind eye. But then there were the congressional hearings, the Apalachin conference, big names started turning state's evidence, and *la cosa nostra* was all over the papers, on the TV. Suddenly those politicians were keeping their distance, and the Mob was losing its clout. Even J. Edgar Hoover had to start pretending the FBI was investigating organized crime. Of all the things to kill the Mob, it was publicity that did it in the end. Now it was just a question of how long the death spiral would last.

Once more the old men wailed, beseeched the heavens, shifted in their seats, scratched themselves. Dante drove and listened to them moan, stopping only to take the dog to the vet. The vet gave him the all-clear on broken ribs, but diagnosed it as undernourished, so Dante took the dog to a diner and ordered them each a steak.

As they ate, sunset came on. When they stepped outside again, it was already dark. Los Angeles was like that; night fell fast. Despite the cement and the irrigation systems, and the ever-expanding freeways and the galaxy of electric lights, it was still a wilderness. The sun burned hard and the nights came quick, and the desert was always encroaching, ready to snatch it all away.

Dante sat in the Thunderbird and lit a Lucky. He opened his book of contacts. He'd had enough of mobsters, so he went through it looking for the names of movie-biz folks. People who might know something about Ocean Movies. He made a list, strung freeways between addresses and started up the car.

He spent the night as he'd spent the day, roaming the city, getting nowhere, the movie men's talk matching the mobsters' talk – all doom and gloom. The film industry was dying, kids weren't going to the movies anymore, they were staying home and watching TV. Soon there wouldn't be any cinemas left. All the major studios were on the rocks. Universal was hemorrhaging cash and flops, Gulf & Western were thinking of selling off Paramount to a local cemetery, 20th Century Fox and MGM were holding public auctions of movie memorabilia just to stay afloat. Executives were jumping ship to start up their own small ventures like Ocean Movies, which were popping up like mushrooms all over LA, making turkeys on low budgets to sell to niche groups and teenagers – surfer movies, biker movies, hippie movies, hot-rod movies, mutant combinations of any of the above.

Ocean Movies was a blip in amongst all this fragmentation, producing B-movies for drive-ins and 'film clubs' up and down the country. And if Ocean Movies was a blip, Audrey Lloyd was a ghost. No one had ever heard of Riccardo's secretary, let alone knew her home address or phone number. Dante couldn't even find her in the Los Angeles Street Address and Telephone Directory.

But he carried on wading through his ever-diminishing leads, his anxiety. The Mob world was dying, the movie world was dying, Dante's world was dying. God only knew what would replace it. And in amongst all this collapse he had to find out what had happened to Riccardo, and he was getting nowhere.

He kept at it long into the night, riding the empty freeways between shakedowns and meets, the dragon on his back. He smoked and listened to late-night radio, DJs pattering and West Coast jazz, the dog sitting next to him. They watched a twilit landscape slip past: gas stations, mini-malls, dance halls, empty parking lots, low-watt bars bleating in the darkness.

They drove all the way to the city's edge, where lonely motor courts perched on cliffs above the ocean, where damp sea-fogs blew in, smothering the roads. They drove all the way to its other edge, where it petered out into the desert, an iron tumbleweed finally coming to rest amongst dust and the faintest of stars. The driving soothed Dante. The emptiness soothed him. The loneliness of the city. Its banality. The way its lights passing by reflected in the dog's eyes like a parade of pearls. He reached out a hand and stroked the dog, and it sighed contentedly.

Dante headed back to his apartment in Venice Beach, feeling weary. When he reached Windward Avenue he saw the hippies were out, lounging about in front of cafés, bars and nightclubs, half-hidden in the shadows of the long arcades that covered the sidewalks.

A long time ago, when Dante and Loretta had first moved there, Venice Beach had been chic, a moneyed haven by the sea. They'd both liked its Italianate pretensions, its piazzas and arcades and cobbled streets leading down to the beach, its houses tastefully painted in pastel shades and adorned with wrought-iron balconies.

They'd stayed when an oil boom led to a forest of rigs sprouting up amongst the canals. They'd stayed when the oil polluted the canals so badly most of them were drained and filled in. They'd stayed when the lagoon was cemented over. They'd stayed when the Beatniks arrived in the '50s, when it became LA's tackiest resort in the '60s – part tourist hell, part slum. And they were still there to witness the influx of the hippies. Dante didn't mind them. They were just the latest in the long line of outcasts to make a home in the area, outcasts like Dante and Loretta.

Now the developers were looking to move in, to get rid of the last beach neighborhood in LA that was cheap enough for poor people to live, one of the few areas in the city where different races mixed. Santa Monica just to the north had been bulldozed the year before, the old seashore houses replaced by luxury apartment blocks. Just to the south, Marina del Rey had been thrown up the year before that, destroying much of the Ballona Creek wetlands. Now Venice stood alone. There were plans to run a new freeway along the beach, bulldoze the bungalows and apartment buildings and the remaining canals, get rid of the boardwalks, the arcades, the booths, the coffeehouses, the shooting galleries, the tourist traps that hawked cheap souvenirs, cheap beachwear and cheap pornography.

Mostly the city wanted to get rid of Venice's people – the beatniks, the buskers, the bikers, the weightlifters, the nude swimmers, the communists, but above all, the hippies, the Jews and the blacks. The city officials had already got the LAPD to start a harassment campaign, a reign of terror and excess force – stopping and frisking residents without cause, arresting them without justification, beating them in the streets, breaking into homes without warrants, confiscating property, refusing to allow lawful assemblies in public places.

Dante didn't hold out much hope for the neighborhood. It was just another part of his world that was crumbling, succumbing to something ugly and new.

He parked in the square behind his apartment building. Unlike the boulevards, everything here was quiet, in total stillness except for the all-night pharmacy, its electric sign blinking wearily in the night.

Dante crossed the broken cobbles to his building, caught the elevator up to the seventh story. The apartment was too large for just him and Loretta these days, but they stayed because it was on the oceanfront, because it was where they'd lived for forty years, where they'd raised Paul and Jeanette. It'd be strange to leave it when they moved up to Napa Valley.

'I see you brought a friend home,' Loretta said on seeing the dog.

Dante gave her the backstory.

'I was thinking he could come up to the vineyard with us,' he said. 'If it's OK with you?'

'Sure. We'll have to find a name for him, though.'

'No cracks about calling him Virgil.'

Loretta smiled.

'Your pal Coombes called,' she said. 'Asked you to call him back when you got in, didn't matter how late.'

Dante's friend at Ma Bell. Maybe the search Coombes had run on the phone lines in Riccardo's office had yielded results. He got the dog some water, then called Coombes back.

'I got something for you,' Coombes said. 'Something interesting. No one's made any calls on either number since Wednesday. And those last calls are the interesting ones. First one that day was outgoing. At twelve p.m. To a payphone up in Bel Air.'

'Twelve on the dot?'

'On the dot. Very punctual. Then another at one p.m. Same payphone. Then a third at two p.m. And that's it. The first two calls lasted just a few seconds, which suggests they went un-answered. When you call a payphone and no one picks up the call gets relayed to an exchange and an automated message is played. I'm guessing those first two rang out, went to the automated mes-sage, and the caller hung up as soon as it started playing. But that third call, someone picked up. It lasted almost five minutes. After that, there's nothing on the log. Nothing outgoing, nothing in-coming. There's a few calls from the week before that. I can cour-ier the log over to you if you want, but I thought those ones on Wednesday would be the ones you're after. I'm guessing you want the location of the payphone. You got a pen?'

Dante copied down the address. Somewhere high up in the Bel Air hills. Mansion country.

'I didn't think they had payphones in Bel Air,' Dante said.

'Me neither. Looks like someone was trying to cover their tracks.'

'Looks like it. Thanks, pal.'

They arranged for Coombes's payment, then Dante hung up and sieved the info. Riccardo had been released from jail on Wednesday morning. At Wednesday lunchtime someone went to his office and started calling a payphone in Bel Air, on the hour, every hour, till someone else picked up at the other end, and presumably a meeting was arranged, with people who didn't want to be traced.

It must have been Riccardo making those calls. He'd gone straight from the jail to his office that day to arrange a meeting with whoever had picked up the payphone. Had Riccardo been calling his cocaine source? Trying to convince them he hadn't turned snitch? Surely that would have been his first priority on leaving jail.

Dante looked at the scrap of paper with the address on it. Finally he had a lead.

# 20

Dante nightcapped for a couple of hours, then caught some sleep. He dreamed of Chicago and New York, his heroin days, the bliss of being on the drug, the hell of being off it. He woke to sunshine and the dog staring at him wide-eyed. He grabbed a shower and hit the road, driving across town to the payphone Riccardo had been calling on the day of his release.

On the freeway Dante caught glimpses of family life in the cars zooming past; people heading to work, ferrying kids, couples yammering at each other between sips of Styrofoam coffee, cigarettes and sunshades. Mack trucks pounded the asphalt. Sunlight glinted off rims, signs, reflectors, flashing and vanishing, some Morse code the city was taunting him with, too complicated and subtle to ever understand.

He found the payphone on a narrow stretch of road halfway up the Bel Air hills. He parked, ambled over, looked around. The street was hilly and tree-lined, one of those lonely Los Angeles roads where the only things that moved were the sun and the sprinklers. The middle of nowhere unless you lived there. And if you lived there, you sure as hell had enough money not to use a payphone. In LA the higher the ground, the higher the income. Meaning if the person Riccardo had been calling was a local, they'd been using the payphone for secrecy. But how local? Did they live on the same road as the phone? Or ten minutes' drive away?

Dante wiped the sweat from his brow with a handkerchief. The sun was streaming down now, burning the morning mist off the hills even as the morning traffic replaced it with smog. The white walls of the houses on the slopes below shimmered yellow. Further on was the vast plain of the city itself, laden in concrete and pollution, and beyond it, the San Gabriel Mountains, pale blue against the sky.

Dante hopped back into the Thunderbird. Years ago he'd been told by a lieutenant in the coastguard that when someone fell overboard, the most efficient way to search for them was to start where the person had fallen into the water and trace a spiral around that central spot. Ever since, when the occasion demanded, Dante employed the technique on the streets of LA. Which was easier said than done, especially when those streets were cut into the side of a range of hills. Dante tossed a mental coin and drove left down the street. The first building he came to was a mansion that cascaded down the hillside in a jumble of stories, terraces and roof gardens. It was the kind of place that required an army of employees to keep it ticking over. Old money. Big money. Neither of which jived with Riccardo coming out of the Men's Central Jail.

Dante carried on going, past a series of houses all like the first, with long stretches of empty, high-walled road between them, right the way back down the hill. He turned the car and headed upwards again, tracing that spiral as closely as he could, round and round, all the time looking for something odd, incongruous, suspicious. More mansions slipped past, all of them with wires attached to the telephone poles that ran down the streets.

After almost an hour, he finally found what he was looking for. A house that was odd, incongruous, suspicious-looking. It was smaller and drabber than the others. The front lawn was brown, the plants were dying, the windows were caked in dust. To the side stood a corrugated overhang, but no car was parked under it. The house was out of place, low rent, abandoned. Dante estimated it was a five- to ten-minute drive from the payphone, depending on route and speed.

He killed the Thunderbird's engine.

All was quiet except for goldfinches in the trees, the droning of a lawnmower coming from a mansion further up the hill. And yet, despite the relative stillness, Dante had the distinct feeling he was being watched. Maybe he was so unused to peace that it came off as ominous.

He drove the car further down the street, parked, cracked the windows, slipped on a pair of leather gloves.

'Wait for me here, OK?' he told the dog.

He got out and headed back over to the house. He opened the gate, walked through the garden, stepped underneath the over-hang and examined the dust. No tire tracks, no footprints. He walked on, found a gate to the side of the house that led round to the rear garden, pushed through it.

The garden was overgrown, the lawn mostly earth, the swim-ming pool drained. Beyond it was a sunken orchard, set in front of a retaining wall. Lemon, mandarin and grapefruit trees, a kiwi vine on a rickety trellis. The ground below them was a carpet of rotting winter fruit. Dante could smell their sickly-sweet death scent even from a distance. He was reminded of crime scenes, murder victims, the wastefulness which fueled the city.

Again he got the feeling he was being watched. He spun about, taking in the surroundings. But all was still.

He crossed to the back of the house. There was a porch and doors giving on to the kitchen and the lounge. He looked through all the windows and everything seemed abandoned. He went over to the kitchen door, didn't even bother trying to pick it. He slipped a metal slider into the gap between the door and the frame, found the bolt. He pulled on the slider, yanked, and the lock clunked open.

He stepped through, quickly casing the whole place – kitchen, two lounges, three bedrooms, a bathroom, an en suite. The walls were covered in paneled plywood, the furniture old and scuffed. There was dust everywhere. A phone-line connection, but no actual phone. It looked like it was uncared for even before it had been abandoned, suggesting it was a rental place, short-term.

In the main lounge Dante noticed the rug was wonky. The armchair pointed slightly toward a wall. Next to the sofa legs were indentations in the floorboards, suggesting the sofa had been moved recently. All of which screamed struggle. And clean-up.

He kneeled and examined the rug, pulled it aside to reveal the floorboards underneath. The bloodstains were just about visible. Embedded in them were bristles from a cleaning brush. There was a faint caustic bleach smell which couldn't quite mask the scent of recently soured blood underneath.

Dante went back into the bathroom. He noticed this time the shower curtain was missing. In the cupboard under the sink were dust rings where the cleaning products should have been. On the tiles above the bath were a few tiny maroon blood spots they'd missed.

He went back into the hallway. On the wall there was a pale brown smear, undulating along the dark brown paneling. It had been scrubbed away, but not well enough.

Dante sighed. He returned to the lounge. Again he got that spied-upon feeling. He went to the windows and teased back the blind. The street out front was still empty. A plane crossed the gulf of sky to the San Gabriel Mountains, which were still a majestic blue. He let go of the blind, turned and surveyed the room.

Someone had been killed here. Probably Riccardo. He'd been kicked loose from jail and called the payphone further down the hill, repeatedly, till a meeting had been arranged. He'd come here. He'd been let in. He'd been butchered. He'd bled out. They'd gone to the bathroom and grabbed the shower curtain. They'd loaded him into it. They'd moved him to the bath. They'd waited for the blood to flow out of him, down the plughole. Maybe they'd dismembered him. They'd scrubbed down the floor in the lounge. Tried to put back the furniture as it had been. They'd wiped the stain in the hallway. They'd bleached the bath. They'd tossed the shower curtains and the cleaning products. Then they'd moved Riccardo's body out of the house and dumped him God knew where.

RIP Riccardo Licata. Son of Nick. Two-bit gangster, coke distributor, surf-movie producer and heir to the throne of the Mickey Mouse Mafia.

It had to be the people who sold him the coke. Riccardo was a glitch in their plans, so they'd un-glitched him. And yet, something didn't feel right. The house. It didn't feel like the kind of place mobsters would use. Certainly not for an execution. Why kill him in the shabbiest house in Bel Air? You couldn't pick a more conspicuous venue.

Dante wanted to check that the house really was a rental. He looked around for papers, couldn't find any. He checked the plumbing under the kitchen sink, he checked the fusebox, he checked the cisterns, he checked the air-conditioning unit in the lounge, and that's where he found it. A sticker affixed to its underside with the installation company's details – the Dyer Air-Con King Corporation. The sticker had their logo on it, a drawing of some Greek God sitting on a cloud, blowing wind through the sky. Next to it was the installation firm's address and phone number. From them Dante could get the details of who was managing the place, maybe even the owner. He jotted everything down in his pad.

He took a last look around and snuck out through the kitchen door. On his way, he noticed the garbage cans in the front yard. He had a look in them. They were empty except for a couple of cans of Clorox.

He returned to the street and walked back to his car. The house had depressed him; uncovering Riccardo's sorry fate had depressed him; so, too, did knowing he'd have to tell Nick Licata that his son had been murdered, brutally. Licata was tough, but Riccardo was his only son. Dante would be shattering the man's world. He knew. He'd been on the receiving end of similar news himself.

# 21

Dante drove up the hill to the mansion which overlooked the house, parked, got out and looked over the edge of the slope. The house where Riccardo had been killed was right there below; a perfect bird's-eye view.

He turned to the mansion. The front gates were heavy duty, either side of them stone walls stretched into the distance. Further down, however, the walls were replaced by railings, ten foot high. Dante walked over, stared at the house on their other side. It was huge and surrounded by gardens the size of parks, studded with fountains and water features, a swimming pool, lawns being sprinkled by Rain Birds. Moving to the hills and wasting water was *de rigueur* for LA's rich. The snowmelt of the Rockies and the Sierra Nevadas, stolen from rivers, diverted from farms, via aqueducts and giant, engineered watercourses paid for by the taxpayer, all so it could be tossed onto lawns in Bel Air, dumped into pools and fountains.

In the section of garden closest to Dante he could see an old Mexican man on a lawnmower, driving it back and forth across a lawn the size of a football field. Dante lit a cigarette and watched him, wondering if he might provide some info on the house further down the hill. Eventually the man turned his way and Dante waved. It took the man a moment to realize Dante wanted to talk to him. He got off the lawnmower without turning off its engine and hobbled over.

'*Hola*,' Dante said when the man approached.

He was in his sixties, Dante guessed, with a wiry frame and the leathery skin of someone who'd spent their life toiling under the sun. He wore a thin cotton shirt with the sleeves rolled up and the top four buttons undone. Dante could smell sweat on the man, the chemically fresh detergent used to clean his shirt.

'*Hola,*' the man replied.

'*It's a beautiful day,*' Dante said in Spanish.

The man eyed him warily. A white man coming to speak to him through the railings was trouble, especially one willing to speak Spanish.

'*Every day is beautiful in paradise, señor,*' the man smiled, his eyes sparkling in the sun.

In the distance, Dante saw a second gardener, a much younger man, approaching them. The older man's son, maybe? Something about the way he was striding purposefully toward them made Dante think he would cut off their conversation when he got there.

'*You know anything about the place down there?*' Dante asked, gesturing to the dilapidated house down the hill.

At the mention of it, the old man's whole bearing changed, the sparkle in his eyes extinguished by an edgy chillness.

'*I know nothing, señor.*'

Behind him, the younger man had already passed the abandoned lawnmower and was stomping toward them. Dante quickly tried to think of the right expression in Spanish.

'*Someone I know went missing there. Please. I need to find him.*'

'*I'm sorry,*' the old man said. He gestured to the house below them. '*Down there. Bad people, señor. Bad people.*'

Just then, the younger man arrived.

'*What's happening, Papa?*' he asked.

'*I was just asking your father about the house down there,*' Dante replied.

The younger man frowned, turned to the old man.

'*Papa, go back to work, I'll talk to the man.*'

The father nodded and headed back to the lawnmower without so much as a backwards glance in Dante's direction.

'What's this about?' the son asked, his English colored only by the faintest of accents.

'I'm looking for someone,' Dante said. 'A missing person. I traced him back to that house. And then, nothing.'

He shrugged and stared at the son. He was in his mid-twenties, well built, blue-collar handsome, like Dante had once been.

'You're police?' the man asked.

Dante shook his head.

'I'm a friend of the missing person's father,' he said. 'You know anything about that house? Who lives there? Your pops said there were bad people there.'

'My pops talks too much.'

Dante could feel things slipping away from him.

'Look, you've got no reason to trust me, and from what I can tell, some nasty stuff happened down there. But I'm just looking for someone who's gone missing. Please. I can pay you if you help me, and I promise I won't tell a soul we spoke.'

At this the man looked up and down the street as if to check there was no one around. Dante followed his gaze. Sunlight dappled through the trees onto the empty road, the sky was blue, the mountains hazy. Every day was beautiful in paradise.

'How much?' the man asked.

'A hundred?'

The man nodded. Dante got his wallet out. The man looked back toward the house, then put the money in his pocket. It was only then Dante noticed his father was sitting on the lawnmower once more, but hadn't set it moving, was instead staring at them both. Suddenly the railings between Dante and the gardeners felt like the bars of a prison. Him on the outside, them on the inside, trapped in an insincere Eden.

'What do you want to know?' the man asked.

'Who lives there?'

'I don't know his name. All I know is the neighbors want the house knocked down because it's so ugly. But they can't get hold of the owner because he lives in another country.'

Dante nodded. An absentee owner explained the dilapidation. Possibly the place was at the center of some long, drawn-out litigation, put into probate while family members squabbled over an inheritance. Dante wondered if he'd got it wrong about the place being a rental; maybe it was abandoned and the killers had simply broken in.

'You see anyone going in and out of there?' Dante asked.

'All the time.'

'Who d'you see?'

'Lots of people. They come and stay for a few days. Then it's empty. Then more people come,' he shrugged.

'What kind of people?'

The man paused, coming over all wary.

'You can trust me,' Dante said.

The man eyed him, evaluating.

'Cops,' he said finally.

Dante frowned.

'Cops in uniforms?' he asked.

'No. Cops in black suits driving unmarked cars like the ones the LAPD drive. I know a cop when I see one.'

'OK. So what did these cops look like?'

'Fat, white, cheap-looking. You know, cops.'

'When was the last time you saw them?'

The man wiped his hand over his chin.

'Maybe last week. Late last week.'

Dante frowned. The timing was off.

'You didn't see anyone on Wednesday?'

The man shook his head.

'OK,' Dante said. 'What did you see late last week?'

'Just the usual. A black sedan turned up and a bunch of guys in suits got out and went inside. And then later that afternoon, they were all gone. And then everything went quiet again.'

Dante nodded. 'Thanks for your help,' he said.

The man shrugged.

'It's like my pops told you,' he said. 'It's bad people down there. You take care.'

Dante tipped his hat, headed back to the Thunderbird, disturbed by what he'd learned, his thoughts orbiting around four shitty letters. LAPD.

# 22

Dante drove out of the hills and pointed the Thunderbird west, weaving through the streets with no destination in mind, the driving simply a way of focussing his thoughts. Riccardo must have met his coke source at that house up in the hills, but the gardener was saying it was an LAPD spot. The most obvious inference: they *were* his coke source. The LAPD had killed Riccardo.

Suddenly Dante was picking over the conversation he'd had with O'Shaughnessy at the airport the previous day. He had assumed it was safe to talk to him – they'd known each other for years – but now he wasn't so sure. O'Shaughnessy worked for the LAPD's Narcotics Squad. Had Dante already revealed the details of his investigation to the very people he was looking for? No matter how many times Dante spooled the conversation back through his mind, he couldn't spot anything suspicious in O'Shaughnessy's words or behavior. But did that mean O'Shaughnessy was honest? Or that Dante wasn't picking up the signals as well as he used to?

He sighed and looked around and realized his aimless driving had brought him to West Hollywood. He spotted a pastrami stand on a corner further up, pulled in to the curb, ordered sandwiches for himself and the dog.

They ate in the car and when they were done Dante used a payphone across the street to check his answering service. There was a message from Ida, asking him to call her, saying it was urgent. He knew she wasn't one for hyperbole so called her straight back.

'Where are you?' she asked.

'West Hollywood.'

'I'm at home. Let's meet in the middle.'

Half an hour later Dante turned into the parking lot of the 7-Eleven on the corner of South Fairfax Avenue and Washington Boulevard, a busy intersection just below the Santa Monica Freeway so choked with smog it was almost impossible to see the tops of the electricity pylons marching down the sidewalks.

Ida's Cadillac was already parked, its nose pointed to the traffic scooting past on Washington. Dante pulled in next to it, slipped into the passenger seat of Ida's car.

'Thanks for coming,' she said. 'Here, I got you a coffee.'

She passed him a cup and the two old friends looked each other over. Dante had first met Ida back in Chicago, but it wasn't until she moved to LA twenty years later that they got close. He was uncle to Ida's son, making Ida pretty much part of the family. Both of them were in the same line of work, but on different sides of that line, meaning they scratched each other's backs when they could, navigating the conflicts of interest because they were both conscientious in their way.

'You got yourself a dog?' She nodded at the Thunderbird, where the dog was sitting on the passenger seat, watching the traffic flit past.

'I picked him up along the way.'

'He got a name?'

'If he has, I don't know it,' he shrugged. 'So what did you want to see me about?'

He asked the question directly, knowing he wouldn't offend her by getting straight down to business. In response she told him how she'd been called out of her house a couple of nights previously to a murder in a San Pedro motel room – a young woman professionally executed, amongst her belongings a newspaper clipping about the Night-Slayer with Ida's details written on them.

137

'Now it turns out the victim's got links to the Mob,' she said. 'How so?'

'The victim's name was Audrey Lloyd. Birth name Audrey Lopez. She worked for Riccardo Licata at an outfit called Ocean Movies. Know anything about it?'

Dante stared at her as a thousand questions popped into his head.

'Audrey Lloyd's exactly who I'm looking for,' he said.

He took out the business card he'd pinched from Audrey's desk at Ocean Movies, passed it over to Ida and told her about his skip-tracer case.

'I tracked Riccardo to a house up in the hills,' Dante said. 'Someone had been killed there recently – the place was all cleaned up and abandoned.'

'So what are you thinking? The people who sold him the drugs whacked him?'

'I spoke to a local. He said it's an LAPD spot.'

'LAPD?'

'Yeah. You think from what you saw in that motel room, it could have been cops who killed Audrey?' he asked. 'Looks like they killed her boss, maybe they killed her too.'

'Could be,' Ida shrugged. 'It was professionally done and they got clean away. A whole motel and not a single eyeball witness saw them or their vehicle.'

'And you've got no idea why Audrey would have your details on her?'

'Nope. I can't draw a line between me and her, or Riccardo. What about you? You ever hear Riccardo talking about me?'

'I barely knew the man. It's his pops I know, and even then we aren't close.'

He looked at her and saw how worried she was. Her name had appeared on a newspaper clipping in a crime scene and it had dragged her out of her safe, comfortable retirement and back into the maelstrom. Ida was a couple of years younger than Dante, mid-sixties, but she'd aged well, could pass for late fifties. Yet maybe inside she felt the same as Dante did – that she was too old for all this, too out of her depth, that she might not survive it this time.

'You don't have to investigate this, Ida. You can let the cops take care of it.'

She shook her head.

'I *need* to. Not just to find out why Audrey was coming to me, but . . .' She trailed off, her eyes dark with concern. 'I feel like something's dragging me back, you know, and I need to find out what. It can't all be a coincidence. Riccardo and Audrey both wind up dead and you get asked to find Riccardo, and I get asked to identify Audrey. What are the chances? We work in the same world, Dante. And we're being pulled in the same direction. If it's not a coincidence, it means something's going on. Something big enough to be pulling everyone into it. I can't ignore it and just hope for the best.'

She shrugged and Dante got the sense there was more to her worry than she was willing to reveal, that there was something else playing on her mind. He wondered again if she felt out of her depth, in danger. But he didn't question her on it. He considered instead what she'd said about something going down. He had to admit it was plausible, and just as disturbing as the thought that they were both too old and befuddled to do anything about it.

They took sips of their coffees, watched the afternoon traffic plow through the cement tangle in front of them – the knotted-up intersection of Fairfax and Washington, the freeway overhead, the on-ramps and off-ramps, Genesee Avenue running parallel. Like tentacles all entwined, like Medusa-hair.

'Me, you, Riccardo, Audrey,' Ida said, drawing a square in the air with her finger. 'Ocean Movies, the Night-Slayer, the Mob, the LAPD,' she added, drawing another. 'There's something connecting it all.'

Dante frowned. 'You forgot the cocaine,' he said. 'And maybe the FBN, too. And the man who visited Riccardo in jail – Sam Cole – pretending to be a cop and saying something that scared Riccardo so bad he got himself bailed out and clipped.'

Ida looked at him, exasperated. 'Maybe we're seeing connections that aren't there,' she said.

'Or maybe you're right,' Dante replied. 'And it is all connected, because something big's about to happen.'

She nodded and they went quiet again, the silence freighted with a mutual sense of foreboding, of some impending upheaval, an earthquake that was beginning to make itself felt. Making Dante wonder if he might never get to leave LA. He thought of the two gardeners up in Bel Air, those railings like prison bars.

'It might be nothing,' he said. 'But let's say this is all drug-related. Then Ocean Movies isn't what's key here, so why wipe out Audrey too?'

'Because they were worried Riccardo might have told her something.'

'Maybe. But what if there's more to it than that? What did Audrey's room-mate tell you about Ocean Movies?'

Ida told him what Myra Shaw had said about Audrey's work at the production company, how it was Audrey's old flame, Karl Drazek, who'd got her the job there.

'What if it's something to do with this Drazek guy?' Dante said. 'He's the connection between Audrey and Riccardo. But the connection doesn't make sense. If you were a producer at Universal Television, why would you be getting your actress ex-girlfriend a job running the office of a two-bit mobster making surf flicks?'

Ida frowned.

'You think Audrey was planted at Ocean Movies?' she asked.

'Maybe. If Riccardo was informing for the FBN, maybe somebody placed Audrey at Ocean Movies to inform on Riccardo.'

'It'd explain why Audrey changed her name,' Ida said. 'And why she was so secretive with her room-mate.'

'If she was a plant, it was Drazek who facilitated it,' Dante said. 'It means we need to find Drazek if we want to figure out what the hell's going on.'

He turned to see Ida staring into the middle distance.

'What is it?' he asked.

'I didn't think about it till now because I didn't think Drazek was important,' she said. 'But if it's to do with film and TV, I've got a friend who might be able to help.'

# PART SIX

## LOUIS

# 23

As the plane circled through the night air above Los Angeles, the pilot came on the PA system to let the passengers know they were about to begin their descent. The announcement woke the man slumped in one of the first-class window seats. He rubbed his eyes, tilted his seat up and looked through the window.

LA was spread out underneath them. Its grids of light criss-crossing the dark plains below, broken only by the blackness of the mountains that the city had encircled, trapped in its embrace of electric light. But even those looming peaks were not entirely dark – here and there glowing taillights of lone cars trickled along hillside passes, connecting one starry grid to the next. Further on, Louis could see the vast Pacific, lit up by the full moon above. The plane banked and turned and the great ocean gyred out of view.

'Can I take that, Mr Armstrong, sir?'

Louis turned to see a stewardess standing in the aisle. She was young, pretty and white, with a white-toothed smile, and a white-gloved hand outstretched.

'Sure,' he said, picking up the empty glass on his tray and passing it to her.

She smiled her thanks and whisked herself off, revealing a man seated across the aisle, a couple of rows further up. He was white and old and staring back at Louis coldly. He had that well-heeled look to him that screamed old money – something in the haircut, the clothes, the complexion, the sneer.

Louis was used to such reactions; he was colored and famous and in first class. So he did what he'd always done in these situations, what he'd been taught by the violence of his upbringing on the streets of New Orleans – where stray glances could lead to stray bullets, stray blades, stray funeral marches – he smiled and turned the other way.

He looked out of the window once more and saw they'd descended further. Every time Louis flew into LA he studied its tracery. It was only up here that he really appreciated how much the landscape was sculpted by the automobile. It wasn't just the roads, it was everything that attended them: gas stations, parking lots, motor courts, drive-ins, garages, car washes, rental depots. All of it low rise and low density, so the city had no choice but to sprawl, spreading itself across the valleys like a flood, ending at the edge of the desert in a slow tumble of salvage yards, biker bars and lonely, isolated ranches.

The plane banked again, and the lights dimmed, and Louis closed his eyes and felt the judder of the plane as it made its final approach. He spent three hundred nights a year on tour, slipping in and out of time zones. It was a hard life that all the first-class tickets and five-star hotels in the world couldn't fully soften. But it was a life he'd chosen, a life he loved. And now, if what the doctor had told him was true, it was a life that might be coming to an end. He'd started his music career as a teenager and over fifty years later he was still plying his trade. It had been a good run. He shouldn't feel bitter about it ending, but he did.

The plane landed bumpily and taxied over to the gate. Louis rose with the rest of the passengers, stepping out into a balmy night thick with a haze of jet fuel. They were ferried over to TWA's Ambassador Room, where Louis and the other VIPs were to await their drivers. Louis went over to the bar and asked for a water and it was only then he noticed he was humming along to the elevator music being piped through the lounge's speaker system. The tune felt vaguely familiar. It was an easy-listening cover version of a song he knew – but which song? He knew it would bug him all night if he didn't figure out what it was.

The barman put his water down on the bar and Louis took a

sip, looked around. The Ambassador Room was in the new section of the airport, bright and airy, with a soaring curved ceiling made of glass and white steel beams. He spotted the old man who'd been staring at him on the plane – he was seated on a sofa further along, was staring at Louis once again, more intensely now, more irate.

'Mr Armstrong, sir?' said a voice.

Louis turned to see a kid standing next to him in a chauffeur's uniform.

'I'm your driver, sir,' he said. 'May I?' He reached down to pick up Louis' attaché case from the floor.

'It's cool, I've got it,' Louis said, and he picked the case up himself. Even after all these years he found it strange when people waited on him.

The kid smiled and Louis smiled and they headed for the exit, Louis humming the melody to the song. What the hell was it?

And then he realized. It was 'West End Blues'. The song he and Earl Hines had made famous forty years earlier, its subject the Big Easy's raucous pleasure district. Someone had turned it into elevator music, saturated in strings, stripped of its context, its meaning, gelded into mainstream respectability by some corporation so it could be pumped through LAX's shiny, new arrivals lounge where the VIPs could ignore it. So much for legacies. Louis shook his head and laughed. What else was there to do in a world where everything lost its meaning eventually, if it ever had any in the first place?

'What's the joke, sir?' the kid asked, a wary smile on his face.

What *was* the joke? Entropy? Pointlessness? Louis had been thinking about them a lot recently, experiencing a pessimism that had never afflicted him before. Maybe it was old age, maybe it was what the doctor had told him.

'Nothing, I guess,' Louis shrugged.

They stepped out of the automatic doors into the night. Taxis and limousines were parked in a line along the curb, palm trees rose high into the murk above. The boy walked him over to a Cadillac and they drove out of the airport, passing a giant billboard advertising LA to people who had already chosen to be there. It was filled with an illustrated miscellany of Los Angeles clichés – the Hollywood sign, beaches, orange groves, ranches, horse-riders – and underneath, the city's slogan: *It All Comes Together in Los Angeles!* If Louis' last few visits to the city were anything to go by, it wasn't all coming together. Like the rest of the country, Los Angeles was falling apart.

'So, what are you in town for?' the kid asked, looking at him through the rearview. 'A TV show or something?'

'Yeah. I'm doing the Christmas Special on the *Steve Allen Show*.'

'I'll be sure to tune in,' the kid said.

'You do that.'

They smiled at each other and Louis turned to look out of the window. He had other things to do while he was in town, but the most important of them was a medical appointment for the second opinion he was simultaneously dreading and pinning all his hopes on. He'd already had to cancel two tours earlier that year due to bouts of pneumonia, and when he'd gone back to work his playing had been patchy at best. Some nights were still good, some nights he had to rely on his singing. Whatever the doctor told him, he knew he'd have a decision to make. A hard one. He watched the city slip past and tried not to think about it. He'd been trying not to think about it since the last hospital appointment, but after two weeks of practice he was still no better at it.

They turned onto La Cienega, climbing north through the city. West Hollywood flitted past, the Sunset Strip, then the slow gentle rise up the hill to the Chateau Marmont, perched above the boulevard like a European castle.

The cab pulled up out front. The kid passed Louis' luggage to the bellboys, who laid it onto trolleys and pushed it up into the lobby. Louis kept hold of his attaché case. He tipped the kid, who asked him for his autograph, and Louis obliged. It felt good to be feted by youngsters – gone were the days when jazz was the music of choice among the young. Now it was rock, pop and Motown, as it had been for years. Louis was pleasantly surprised when anyone under twenty made a fuss over him.

He stepped inside the hotel and looked around. There was a Christmas tree by the fireplace, fake presents underneath, tinsel and candy canes strewn about. Not one but two receptionists came over to greet him.

The Marmont was the first of LA's white hotels to allow black guests. Duke Ellington had been a regular for years. It was a decent hotel, and it was nice to stay somewhere central where he didn't have to ride up to his room in the freight elevator.

When Louis got to his suite a bellboy gave him a tour – bedroom, bathroom, lounge, bar, study area, terrace balcony looking out over night-time LA. Louis tipped the bellboy, closed the door and surveyed his gilded cage: the fireplace with the scrub oak, the needlepoint rugs, the wet bar, the picture window, the chandelier like a cloud of teardrops.

Louis opened the door to the terrace. Lanterns were strung about, potted plants, paper Christmas decorations. The view took in a giant swathe of LA. He walked back into the bedroom, lay on the bed. He placed his hand on his heart and stared at the ceiling, feeling the room settle around him. The sound of the traffic down on Sunset leaked in, the low moan of engines, the rattle and growl of the city itself.

He noticed a couple of message cards by the phone. He sat up and flicked through them. The first was from Joe Glaser, his manager, telling him the office would call in the morning to confirm his appointments. The second was from Ida: *Called Lucille. She said you were arriving tonight. Call me when you get this. Love. Ida.*

Louis stared at the card, wondering if seeing his old friend would help him break through his ever-thickening gloom.

# 24

The next morning Ida met Louis in the Marmont lobby. They hugged and stepped outside to take a stroll. As they walked they caught up on each other's news, settled into each other's company, their conversation warm, roaming, spilling histories. As Louis spoke Ida studied his movements, his demeanor, noted some sadness about him, some anxiety. She wondered what was up, hoped he'd confide his problems without her having to push. In the meantime she told him about the case, the murders, the Night-Slayer, the possible link to a TV producer called Karl Drazek.

'Karl Drazek?' Louis repeated the name, shaking his head. 'What do you know about him?'

'Just that he works at Universal, producing TV shows.'

'I know some people who work there. I'll ask around.'

They walked westwards along the Strip, the stretch of Sunset Boulevard that lay just outside LAPD jurisdiction, in the hands of the much more laissez-faire Los Angeles County Sheriff's Department. It was something the Mob had taken advantage of back in the '20s, opening a string of nightclubs, cabarets and casinos there. Then movie business agents followed to take advantage of a tax-code loophole and soon it was home to a demi-monde of Hollywood stars, exiled writers, cocktails and glitz.

But that floating world existed no more. The mobsters and the entertainers had all been lured away to Vegas, leaving the Strip's venue owners with two choices – go younger and cater to the teenaged rock-music crowd, or go seedy and cater to the striptease-and-brothel crowd. The owners who'd gone the latter route wanted the Strip cleared of all the kids and runaways, so they pushed the county to enforce a ten p.m. juvenile curfew, getting both the sheriffs and the LAPD to harass the kids. The intimidation campaign backfired when it led to protests, and the protests led to the Sunset Strip riots, and the riots' notoriety led to the area becoming an even bigger magnet for the southland's bored, disaffected youth.

It all meant that the Sunset Strip which confronted Ida and Louis that morning was seedy, scruffy, battle-scarred, loomed over by giant billboards that glinted in the sun, packed with raggedy-looking runaways and madras-clothed hippies standing on street corners selling copies of the *Los Angeles Free Press*. As Ida took it all in, she had a sense of her city slipping away from her.

They cut south off Sunset, then west, wandering aimlessly in an arc as they talked. They walked a few blocks east to Plummer Park. They found a bench, sat, looked around. The park was full of runaways and college kids sitting around smoking joints, playing music on portable radios, the songs shimmering, competing, clashing. Ida turned to look at Louis, saw him watching the kids with a wistful expression. Louis was almost seventy, and through all his marriages he'd never managed to father a child.

'What's up?' she asked.

'Who says anything's up?'

'The person who's known you since we were twelve.'

She smiled at him, and after a moment he smiled back, but it was forced. He was mustering up the courage to tell her something.

'I've not been too good, Ida,' he said finally. 'Had to cancel a couple of tours earlier this year. I got better, went on tour again, and then I got worse again. Wheezing, tired all the time, swelling in my legs. I went up to Beth Israel Medical Center a few weeks back. The doc diagnosed me on the spot. Congestive heart failure. Told me I shouldn't be playing the trumpet no more. Told me I should retire. I ran straight out of there, tried to ignore it. Carried on playing, going out, staying up late. Had to go back two weeks later 'cos it had all gotten worse.'

She saw the pain on his face now, the bewilderment. The trumpet man told not to blow his horn.

'Louis, I'm so sorry. I don't know what to say.' She clasped his hand in hers, squeezed it. 'Did the doctor say you're going to be OK?'

'As long as I take it easy, sure. But it's just one doc's opinion,' he shrugged. 'That's another reason I'm here. I got a recommendation for a specialist in Santa Monica. The number one heart expert in the world. I'm gonna wait and see what he says before I do anything. But if he says what the other doctor said, then I got a big choice to make. The biggest one of all.'

Ida nodded, feeling his pain, reliving her own choice to retire a couple of years earlier.

'And you came here hoping I'd tell you how great retirement was,' she said. 'And instead you found me back at work.'

'Yeah,' he replied. 'Yeah, I did.'

He laughed and shook his head, and she did too.

'I didn't ask to come out of retirement,' she said. 'I don't want this case. I don't want anything to do with it.'

'But you're working it?'

'Because I have to.'

'You don't owe anyone anything, Ida. Some woman died with your name in her motel room, it don't mean you have to put your life on the line.'

'Yeah, I know. I've paid my dues. But that woman was killed while she was running to me for help, and I was sitting on my porch drinking whiskey. And then there's all those people the Night-Slayer's butchered. But there's something more than that. It feels like something's dragging me in, and . . .'

She stopped, coming to the edge of her fears, and not wanting to go any further. It was the same place she'd reached with Dante the previous day, when she'd almost revealed to him what was really upsetting her, and Dante had had the politesse not to press her on it.

'What is it?' Louis asked. 'You wanna talk about it, you can talk to me.'

She nodded, looked out over the park.

'When I retired, everyone thought it was because I felt guilty over Sebastián dying. And I let people think that. Truth is, I was scared into retiring. It wasn't guilt. It was fear. It was a coin toss between me and him about who'd go into that building that night. He went in and died, but if the coin had landed the other side up, it would have been me. I feel like I should already be dead, you know. It was blind luck that saved me. And now an even bigger case has come along, and I'm already feeling out of my depth, and I just can't shake the feeling this'll be my last-ever case, this'll be the one I won't survive.'

She trailed off and looked out over the park, her emotions bubbling up, reaching a brimming point, making her scared that if she made any movement, talked anymore, they'd all spill over. She felt Louis' eyes on her. He was wise enough to know she wasn't looking for soothing words, for that kind of reassurance, so he reached over and hugged her and she could have cried at his embrace.

She hugged him back and they stayed like that for a while, holding each other in the low winter sun. She realized with a sharp sadness that they were both in the same boat. Normally when they met, if one of them was in a bad way, the other pepped them up. Over the years of their friendship, they'd learned the knack of lifting each other's spirits. But now, as they sat on that park bench, it didn't seem like either of them could buoy up the other. All they could offer each other was consolation. Maybe that was enough.

They disengaged from the embrace, took in their surroundings, the sun pouring light across the park. It felt like one of those bright days where the weather was completely inappropriate, insincere, idiotic.

Louis grabbed his attaché case from the bench next to him, opened it up, and Ida saw, as she expected, that it was full of pot. He took out some cigarette papers, rolled a joint.

'You sure you should be smoking that stuff with your heart the way it is?' she asked.

'I hardly smoke it at all these days,' he said. 'Maybe one joint a day, if that. If this doc in Santa Monica says I should quit, I'll quit. It's not the joints I'll have a problem giving up, Ida, it's the music. We are what we do. If we stop doing it, then what's left?'

He slanted a meaningful look in her direction.

'You telling me I should put my fears aside?' she said. 'Carry on going?'

'You've always been sharp, Ida. Sharpest person I ever met. It ain't your brains that you've lost, it's your confidence.'

She considered this and was annoyed by how something so simple could be so true and how she hadn't seen it herself.

Louis lit the joint, took a toke, passed it to her. She waved it away. She only ever got high when Louis was around, and the older she got, the more it seemed to affect her.

'I'm too old to be smoking that stuff,' she said. 'And so are you.'

'You've been saying that since the nineteen forties. C'mon. You're still a few years on the sunny side of seventy.'

She smiled, continued shaking her head, but took the joint anyway, took a toke. It tickled the back of her throat, tingled in her lungs. They smoked and looked out across the park, the two elderly friends sitting on a bench who were also the two kids running through the mud of New Orleans fifty years ago.

'Ever since I started working on those damn memoirs, I've been thinking about New Orleans more and more,' Ida said. 'The things we used to get up to, places we used to go. Collecting dandelions and peppergrass from the railway tracks, following funeral parades, watching the banana boats on New Basin Canal, sneaking round the back of the honky-tonks to listen to the bands.'

She smiled at Louis and he echoed it back. There was something warming to the fact that half a century later, the two of them could still relive those moments together, cracking the rust of nostalgia that coated their memories, allowing them to come alive again. For all the tricks time pulled on them, bringing those memories to life was their own special trick.

'You been back to New Orleans recently?' Louis asked, his tone less wistful, more serious.

'No, not for years,' she said, shaking her head.

'It's all changed. Jane Alley's been torn down, South Rampart, the honky-tonks, all of 'em gone so they can drive roads through the city. It's where we created jazz, Ida, and they've ripped it all up for six-lane freeways and parking lots. Not even the Waifs Home's there anymore.'

They'd met through the Waifs Home, a juvenile detention facility that Louis had been sent to after shooting a gun in the street in celebration of New Year's. Ida's father had been the music teacher at the home and had recognized some talent in the boy, brought him back to their house to practice, with Ida accompanying him on the piano. She'd been a lonely child, and through those practice sessions, she and Louis had become friends, despite the class difference. She'd often thought it strange how from those beginnings it was she who'd ended up living amongst the criminal world, and he who'd gone on to live the high life.

They settled into a rich silence, smoked the rest of the joint. It made Ida's thoughts swim and swirl, coming sluggish and quick all at the same time. Her mind kept drifting back to the Waifs Home, like it was important somehow, like there was a connection to the Night-Slayer buried somewhere in the emotional charge that joined her to her hometown, a connection that she was missing.

'What is it?' Louis asked.

'Talking about the Waifs Home,' she said. 'I've got this feeling it's related to the Night-Slayer case.'

'You think he used to be an inmate?' Louis grinned.

'No,' she said, shaking her head. 'Maybe it's just the joint that's confusing me. But one thing that's bugged me since the start is the places he picked up his victims – a hospital, a cafeteria and a laundromat. I always got the feeling there was a connection between them that I was missing. And now I feel like there's a connection to the Waifs Home, too. But I just can't figure it out.'

Louis looked at her blankly.

'Isn't it obvious?' he said.

'You know what it is?'

'Sure. A hospital, a cafeteria and a laundromat? Change the names, Ida. Infirmary, mess hall, laundry room. They're all locations you get in places like the Waifs Home. They're all prison locations.'

Ida stared at him.

'Of course,' she said. 'A prison.'

Suddenly her thoughts were accelerating through the fug of the joint.

'What is it?' Louis asked.

'I think I know how to catch the Night-Slayer.'

# PART SEVEN

## DANTE

# 25

After Dante's meeting with Ida he spent what was left of the day trying to get more details on Riccardo, Audrey Lloyd, Karl Drazek, Ocean Movies. But it all amounted to nothing. He looked into Mob connections to the Night-Slayer. Nothing again. He asked around if anyone knew about cops moving coke, or with access to a house in Bel Air. Nothing again.

Day turned to night and Dante exhausted the last of his contacts. Night turned to day and he awoke to a cloud of stress, to anxiety tying a knot through his gut. He'd been doing his damnedest shaking down people, chasing down leads, hustling, running, on the clock. But it had all amounted to nothing. Like he wasn't good enough anymore.

When he called his answering service, the operator told him he had a message from Nick Licata.

'He asked you to call him,' she said. 'He left a number.'

Dante scribbled it down, hung up and sighed. Licata clearly wanted an update. It was three days till Christmas and after that it would be Riccardo's court date. But what did Dante have to tell Licata? That the LAPD had probably chopped up his son in a slaughterhouse in the hills? That Riccardo had probably turned snitch for the FBN? That Dante had a feeling something big was happening, but he had no clue exactly what?

The conversation with Ida flashed back into his mind, her suggestion that whatever it was, it was big enough to be dragging them all in. It had been strange to see her looking so fearful. He regretted now not asking her about it. It had seemed like she was projecting the same worry he'd been feeling, that sense of being too old, too out of synch with the city, with the world they had to navigate.

Dante briefly considered calling Licata back, decided against it. He'd chase down his last couple of leads before he made the call, praying they would pan out.

He left his apartment building and crossed the square. As he approached the Thunderbird he noticed a black sedan parked on the corner further along, on a spot where one of the beatnik stores selling candles and sandals usually put out a stand packed with independent newspapers and small-press magazines. When his first glance fell on the car he thought he saw the silhouettes of two men sitting in the front seats, but when he looked a second time, the car seemed empty. Was his eyesight playing up? Or had the two men ducked down behind the dashboard?

He got into the Thunderbird, angled the rearview so he could look at the sedan. It still seemed empty. He tried to get its license-plate number, but it was too far away. He waited to see if the two silhouettes reappeared, but they didn't. He put it down to paranoia. He started up the Thunderbird.

He drove downtown, to the Los Angeles County Hall of Admin-istration. Dante normally hired a lawyer to do real-estate searches, but the man and his family had already headed off to Palm Springs for Christmas, meaning Dante had to sift the files in the County Recorder's Office himself, combing through them for the title deeds of the ramshackle slaughterhouse up in the hills.

It didn't take long to find what he was looking for. The owner of the property was listed as Belknap Holdings LLC, registered to a business address in Delaware. Dante sighed. No way to get any more details except by writing to the Delaware State Division of Corporations and waiting six to eight weeks for a response, and even then he might just get the address of the company's regis-tered agent, still no way of finding out who actually owned it.

A complete dead end. That was the point of incorporating in Delaware.

Dante left the Recorder's Office even more downbeat and edgy. He walked over to the Thunderbird, opened the door, let the dog jump out. He looked around for somewhere to get them some food and spotted a hotdog seller further up the street, on the steps leading to the Civic Center Mall. He bought two hotdogs for himself, two for the dog. They sat on a bench and ate, watched the giant fountains tumbling water in the plaza, the lawns, the palms, the art-deco tower of City Hall in the distance.

When they were done Dante found a payphone. He couldn't stall Licata any longer. He steeled himself, made the call.

'Dante, where've you been?'

Licata's tone was flat, emotionless. It sounded like he was somewhere busy, a hubbub reverberating in the background.

'Working, Nick. Chasing Riccardo's trail.'

'And?'

Dante knew he shouldn't over-promise, but Licata unsettled him.

'I might have a lead.' Dante regretted it as soon as he'd said it.

Licata didn't reply for a moment, so all Dante could hear was that background hubbub, metallic, clattering, brimming with reverb. Where the hell was he?

'Can you talk about it now?' Licata asked eventually, meaning over the phone.

'Best not.'

'Come see me.'

'Sure. How about tomorrow?'

'How about now?'

For the first time Licata's tone wasn't flat. It was annoyed, and menacing.

Even so, Dante couldn't meet right away. He didn't have it in him to be making up bullshit cover stories on the fly.

'Tomorrow, Nick,' Dante said, doubling down. 'I need to confirm something first.'

'Tomorrow's the twenty-third already.'

'I know. And the court date's on the twenty-sixth. I know. Just let me confirm this thing first. OK? I don't wanna waste your time.'

There was the hubbub again as Licata considered.

'All right, Dante. Tomorrow,' he said, his tone flat once more. 'Call me in the morning to arrange.'

And with that, he hung up.

Dante put the receiver down, rubbed his temples. He'd hoped the real-estate search would have given him something, but it had only deepened the mystery. He was down to his last lead. He rummaged around his pockets for the number of the maintenance company he'd found stuck onto the air-conditioning unit in the house where Riccardo had been whacked. He called it.

'Dyer Air-Con King Corp,' said a girl on the other end, her voice young and bright.

'Morning. My air-con's broke, and I saw your sticker on the machine.'

'OK. We can certainly help you get it fixed.'

'Thing is, I'm subletting the place so I don't know who the account's with.'

'I can check our records for you.'

'Great.'

'What's the address?'

He gave her the address, and the girl went to check the books. Dante lit a cigarette while he waited.

'So, we've got the address on file,' the girl said. 'But there's no account. It was a one-off call-out charged to Chevalier Real Estate. Would you like us to come out and fix it, anyway?'

'Let me talk to the landlord first. Thanks for all your help.'

He called directory assistance and asked for an address for the real-estate company. As the operator fetched it for him, Dante looked around. Parked further up the street was a black sedan with two silhouettes in front. Dante felt his paranoia return. He swept his gaze past the sedan, like he hadn't noticed anything, stared at some building across the road, watched the sedan out of the corner of his eye. He waited a few seconds, glanced back at it. The silhouettes were gone again.

'Motherfuckers,' he muttered.

The operator came back on the line and gave him the address for Chevalier Real Estate. Dante jotted it down, hung up, wondered what he should do. He had his Detective Special in his pocket, and the element of surprise. He calculated the distance between the payphone and the sedan, how quickly he could cross it at his old man's speed. How busy the road was.

'Fuck it,' he said, filling with resolve.

He turned and bounded as fast as he could up the sidewalk, pulling the gun from his pocket, heading straight for the sedan. The two silhouettes reappeared in the front seats – middle-aged men in suits. The sedan roared into life, swerving out of its parking spot. Dante raised his gun. The man in the passenger seat wound down his window, lifted up a shotgun.

'Shit,' Dante muttered. He threw himself behind a parked car, cracking his elbow on the sidewalk. He listened to the sedan roaring off down the road. He heavy-breathed. He composed himself. He looked over the hood of the car. The sedan had disappeared. He pocketed his gun, tried to pull himself up off the ground.

'You need help, sir?'

He looked up to see a young couple staring at him.

'I'm fine.'

He smiled back at them, rose unsteadily, rubbed his elbow. He felt like an absolute fool for deciding to confront the men. It was the kind of idiot move he'd never have made in the past. He'd given up his advantage, put himself in danger, and hadn't even got the sedan's license plate. Worst of all, he'd alerted whoever was trailing him that he was on to them.

Half an hour later he was walking down Hollywood Boulevard, still smarting, still feeling like an old fool, with a sharp thudding pain in his elbow. He slipped through the sightseers who flocked to the Boulevard and ambled about its tourists traps: souvenir shops, stands selling maps, postcards, overpriced sodas, tours of movie stars' homes.

Dante found the real-estate company's office further up from the tourist trail, tucked between a travel agency and a legal firm. Its windows were covered in blue cellophane to keep out the glare of the sun, but through the cellophane, Dante could see signs and photos of the various properties they had for rent. It was all tastefully done, upmarket. It looked like a regular office, in a regular building. Not a Mob place, or a money-laundering operation. At least from the outside. And yet, this was the company that managed the house on behalf of Belknap Holdings LLC, the house where the cops had lured Riccardo to clip him.

Dante pretended to look at the cards in the window while he cased the building's security – a deadbolt lock on the front doors that he could open in a couple of minutes, no alarm systems. He walked around the block, checked the alley that ran along the back of the office, made plans, the entire time edgy that the men in the sedan would return, would point that shotgun at him again.

He drove back to his apartment, tried to catch some sleep, but couldn't for thinking about the men in the sedan. He wondered who'd sent them – the cops, the coke source, the FBN, maybe even Licata himself. When Loretta came home from the warehouse he ordered Chinese food. As they ate, she eyed the dog.

'I hate to say it,' she said. 'But he looks like a Virgil.'

After they'd eaten Loretta made them nightcaps of Benedictine and brandy and they drank them on the balcony, watched the moon casting silver nets across the ocean. Normally Dante enjoyed sitting like this, turned away from the city, staring at the ocean, the ships like stars on the horizon. Normally the view calmed him, made him feel insignificant, and thereby made his problems seem insignificant, too. But not this time. The episode with the sedan was still needling him. It wasn't so much the gun that was pointed at him; it was his own bad decision-making. His terrible choice to confront the men, letting his jitters get the better of him. It underlined his fear that he wasn't up to the task anymore.

'You look worried,' Loretta said.

He considered confiding in her, telling her about what had happened, decided against it.

'I need to go out tonight.'

'Where?'

He told her instead about the slaughterhouse, the real-estate company that managed it.

'Aren't you a little old to be breaking into places?' she said. 'You get caught they might lock you up for good.'

'Yeah, I know.'

At his age, any sentence was a life sentence. He thought about what she'd said at the warehouse, when he'd first told her about the job. And here he was again, putting everything on the line, proving her right.

'There's no other way?' she asked.

He shook his head.

'Licata's called me in tomorrow and I've got nothing.'

She nodded and they settled into silence, looked out across the dark Pacific, listened to the snap of the waves below.

After a few seconds, she reached out and took hold of his hand.

# 26

Dante left the apartment just after midnight, taking with him his lock-picking kit, gloves, a rag, a flashlight, a blackjack. He drove up to Hollywood again, meandering, doubling back on himself, taking quiet roads, all to make sure no one was tailing him, that there was no sign of the black sedan. When he finally reached the real-estate office, he saw there was still too much traffic on the street to break in through the front.

He drove past, parked just off Vine. He slipped his tools into his pockets, and walked around the block, to the alley that ran behind the buildings. It was empty here, quiet enough that he could hear anyone coming.

He found the rear of the real-estate office. There was a window on the first floor, at head height, small, frosted glass, an extractor fan next to it. All of which suggested it opened on to a restroom. Dante looked around, saw a garbage can further down the alley where some dogs were scratching through trash. He hauled it over, stood on it, smashed the window with the blackjack, then walked straight back round to his car, got in and waited.

Years ago he'd known a patrolman who'd told him that when he worked the night watch, him and his partner spent most of their shift in their cruiser, prowling alleys, windows down, lights out. That they caught most of their criminals that way. And sometimes, late at night, they'd just stop, turn off the engine and listen.

So Dante listened, too, waiting to see if the noise brought any cops to the scene, cops like the patrolman from all those years ago. He smoked, watched the empty, moonlit street. A disorientating sense of exposure descended on him, aftershocks of the encounter with the men in the sedan. A quiet street in the middle of the night was a good spot for them to return and gun him down. Dante switched the radio on low, tuned it to KPFK. Alan Watts's *Way Beyond the West* show was broadcasting from Berkeley, a weekly talk show that Dante tuned into now and again when he couldn't sleep. Watts was discussing the way of Zen, as he always did. How the self, the universe and time were all an illusion, how the past and the future were ephemera, how it was possible to live in the eternal moment.

Dante thought the last thing he needed was to live even more in the eternal moment. His home was a city that was already drowning in it; LA was a place that had no proper seasons, where nothing stopped on the weekends, or at night, where you could have anything, anywhere, anytime, where you could grow old looking young, where it was summer all winter long. In LA everyone was crushed under the weight of it always being now. It was one of the things Dante couldn't wait to leave behind.

He listened to Watts for another ten minutes. When there was no sign that anyone had been alerted by the sound of the window breaking, Dante returned to the alley. He put on his gloves, used the blackjack and the rag to remove the shards of glass from the frame, and hopped through into the building.

He dropped down into a bathroom stall. His foot landed in the bowl of a toilet. His ankle twisted. His shoe got wet.

'Shit,' he muttered.

He took his shoe out and wiped the sole so he didn't leave footprints all over the place. He rotated his ankle, winced with the pain, hobbled out of the stall and into a corridor, headed to the front of the building.

The office itself was open-plan, two rows of desks taking up most of the space. There was a small reception area just by the door, a line of filing cabinets. All the lights were off, the only illumination coming from the sheet-glass windows that gave out onto the street. Beyond them a few people strolled along the sidewalk, cars cruised past. Dante headed over to the filing cabinets. He switched on the flashlight, cupping his hand around it, and started scouring them, looking for client contracts. All he found were brochures. Halfway along he came across an entire cabinet that was locked. He took out his lock-picking kit, slipped a flat piece of metal from it, then slipped the metal into the gap above the topmost drawer. He shoved, brute-forcing it. The bolt clunked back.

Outside the windows, the whoop of a police siren pierced the silence. Dante killed the flashlight. He turned to look. A cop car slow-rolled past the windows. Disappeared. Dante waited for it to come back, his pulse quick, adrenaline pooling in his chest. The cop car didn't return.

He switched the flashlight on again and got back to the job at hand with a growing sense of unease, working faster now. He slid the drawer back. Contracts ordered by date. He checked the other drawers. The contracts were cross-filed by name and location. The County Recorder's records had said the owner of the property was the Delaware corporation – Belknap Holdings LLC – but Dante couldn't find it in the naming system, so he checked by location. After a couple of minutes he found the file. But as he expected, Belknap wasn't the name on it; instead the property's owner was listed as 'Reginald Eisner'. Eisner had a contract with the realtor going back eleven years. His correspondence address was listed as Rue du Rhône, Geneva, Switzerland. Dante remembered the gardener he'd spoken to saying the owner lived abroad. The paperwork confirmed the story. Maybe Eisner used the Delaware corp as a holding company for the property. He'd left LA, hired the realtor to look after the house.

Now Dante needed to find out to whom the property had been rented. He went back to the files and checked the cross-references. He found the rental contract, signed in July 1965. The realtor had brokered an agreement to rent the property out to the Miraflores Pharmaceuticals Corp, who were still the registered tenant.

Dante didn't like where this was going.

He needed to check more cross-references. He popped open more cabinets. Bank records. He found the details for Miraflores. Its address was listed as Lima, Peru. It paid its initial deposit and quarterly installment via the Castle Holdings Banking Corporation, registered in the Cayman Islands.

Dante really didn't like where this was going.

What the hell had Riccardo got himself mixed up in? A front corporation in Latin America. Payments made untraceable through an offshore bank. Dante's heart sank, the adrenaline sluiced higher. The gardener hadn't seen LAPD going in and out of the house.

This had CIA written all over it.

# PART EIGHT

## IDA

# 27

Ida killed the time driving through the night, stopping at pay-phones every half-hour to check her answering service, to see if Feinberg had called her back, hoping her hunch about the prison locations paid off. She'd met him in a deli near the Glass House earlier that day, outlined her theory about how they could catch the Night-Slayer. He didn't seem to buy it until she mentioned the book – *Gumbo Ya-Ya*. And then he'd bought it, had run out of there without even finishing his food to chase the lead. Now all she could do was wait for his call.

At some point she spotted the Richfield Tower in the distance, its art-deco facade detailed in black and gold to simulate the oil gushers that had made the company's fortune. It made her realize she was driving toward Bunker Hill. Without even noticing it she was heading to her old neighborhood, where her agency used to be, summoned to LA's historic center, her favorite part of the city.

Ida was saddened to see the area's redevelopment was continuing apace. In a neighborhood once filled with genteel wooden architecture – with Queen Anne mansions, craftsman homes, delis, pharmacies, hotels, bars – hardly anything was left. It was all being ripped up to make room for a steel rain of skyscrapers. Even the hill itself had been reduced, great diggers lopping a hundred feet off its height, so more buildings could be put up on the flattened ground. Here and there plots had been cleared but not yet built on, leaving entire fields of open space.

The Bunker Hill of Ida's time had been seedy, dirty, crime-ridden. A soup-kitchen neighborhood of winos and desperadoes and cow-town refugees, people brought low by poverty and madness, scarred by disease. But it was also a place that teemed with life, where community and history flourished. The streets bustled with panhandlers and hotdog sellers, sailors and whores, two-bit shills, the saloons roared with jazz musicians and jukebox balladeers. It was where a thousand film noirs had been shot in the 1940s and '50s, a living movie set. Perversely it was the area's slum-on-a-hill depiction in those same films that gave the area such a bad reputation, which then gave the Community Redevelopment Agency the excuse it needed to raze it to the ground. Condemnation and eviction notices had been issued, the area's poor shunted off to Skid Row and MacArthur Park. And all that history and community was being destroyed now to line the pockets of a few corrupt property developers and politicians. Just like it was being destroyed in New Orleans. Once more Ida had the saddening sense of the city slipping away from her, of time slipping away from her.

She zigzagged through the neighborhood, taking in what was still there, what had gone. She drove past the gaping mouth of the 3rd Street Tunnel, the Angel's Flight Pharmacy, the Nugent Deli and Grand Hotel. She was pained to see the wreckers had already moved in on the Sunshine Apartments.

Further along there used to be a Queen Anne mansion, home to some long-gone water baron or railroad prince, long-since converted into a flophouse. Old folks used to sit on the benches next to it, shooting the breeze, feeding the pigeons. Now the benches were gone, and the mansion had been torn down, but the debris had yet to be taken away, so all that remained was a wrecked jumble behind a wire construction fence. Here and there the remnants of intricate fretwork poked up out of the dust: snapped balustrades, wooden screens that craftsmen must have spent months carving and painting. All ripped up, left in the dirt for bulldozers to crush.

Ida pulled up on Hill Street, stayed there smoking, watching the orange funicular cars navigating the steep tracks of Angel's

Flight, going up and down the hill with the clanking relentlessness of oil derricks.

Despite the redevelopment, a few of the old neighborhoods' residents were still about – the drifters, the drunks, the whores, the loons. Ida could have added herself – the private detective – to that list of ghosts, floating through a city that no longer had a place for them, drifting like the Night-Slayer.

A hospital, a cafeteria, a laundromat.

The Night-Slayer hadn't picked those locations because they were good hunting grounds. He'd been drawn to them because he'd been institutionalized, damaged, driven mad. Just like these ghosts on the streets of Bunker Hill.

Infirmary, mess hall, laundry room.

She put herself in the Night-Slayer's shoes, saw the world through his eyes, through a mind fractured by psychosis, or schizophrenia, or delusions, or paranoia. Ida was sure he'd spent time in a prison, or a mental facility, and then he'd been released and had come to LA. He wandered the streets, drifted, zombie-like, clinging to whatever coping mechanisms he had to keep past traumas in place. And then he stumbled into an environment with negative associations, somewhere that reminded him of his incarceration. An infirmary, a mess hall, a laundry room. Suddenly those coping mechanisms were overwhelmed, he experienced a psychotic break and it triggered him to kill.

None of it was pre-planned. Ida had got that all wrong. It was random. Spur of the moment. Which fitted much better with the childish, sloppy way he'd committed the murders. She thought back to the very first killing – Mark McNeal, working in the Emergency Room at LA County General. She imagined the Night-Slayer stumbling in, taking a seat in the waiting room. Maybe he saw McNeal injecting a patient, and it brought to mind the old story of the Needle Men in New Orleans. It triggered him, some mental voodoo taking hold. He followed McNeal home, killed him by stabbing him with something that resembled a hypodermic needle, recreating the folk tale in the here and now. Trying to mesh the fantasy world of his delusions, and the real world he was wandering through, maybe in the mistaken belief that by connecting the two, he might join together the pieces of his fractured mind, and find some respite.

'OK. But we already figured he was probably an ex-con,' Feinberg had said when she'd outlined her theory. 'And it's been pretty clear from the start that he's a nut job, so where does this get us?'

That was when she'd pulled out her copy of *Gumbo Ya-Ya*, laid it on the deli counter.

'This is a compendium of Louisiana folklore, probably the most widely distributed one there is, because it's a WPA publication. A government publication. Walter bought me a copy after he saw it in a library. All these WPA books were bought up by other government institutions, like libraries, and schools, and . . .'

She'd looked at him, raising her eyebrows, waiting for him to complete the thought.

'Prisons,' he'd muttered.

'My bet is our Night-Slayer was in a prison or a mental facility when he came across a copy of *Gumbo Ya-Ya*,' Ida had said. 'He read it, obsessed over it, and in his mind it got jumbled up with being incarcerated. And then he was released. He came to LA, drifted, stumbled into that Emergency Room and saw McNeal injecting a patient and suddenly he was back in prison, reading about Needle Men, seeing one right there in front of him. And that's how it all started.'

She'd looked at him, had seen he was starting to buy it. She'd pressed on.

'We go through all the prisons in-state, all the mental facilities, we find out which ones have got a copy of the book registered in their library. Maybe we find out which inmates checked it out, when they were released, if they've got histories of violent psychotic episodes, connections to Louisiana. Suddenly we don't have to check every inmate in the whole of California, we whittle down the numbers, hone in on a tiny subset.' Ida had tapped the book on the counter. 'This is how we find him.'

It wasn't till gone ten p.m. that she got a message from Feinberg, telling her to meet him in a bar on the edge of Little Tokyo. She got suspicious when the operator read out the address – why not just meet her at the Glass House? She drove over there and got even more suspicious when she saw it was a piano bar, with a baby grand in the corner and bartenders in white shirts and bow ties and everyone sipping cocktails.

She sat at the bar and ordered a whiskey and tried not to feel out of place. At the baby grand, a middle-aged white guy was knocking out sleepy piano versions of jazz standards, the occasional Christmas tune thrown in. Ida's mind flashed back to the honky-tonks of New Orleans, the stride piano players at the rent parties in Chicago. How raucously those musicians played their instruments, the exuberance, the energy, the sheer force of what they did. How this jazz paled in comparison.

Feinberg arrived a quarter of an hour after she did, looking just as out of place. He had a paper folder in his hand, a harried look on his face. He sat on the stool next to her.

'You want to tell me why you arranged to meet me in a bar no cop would ever be seen dead in?' she asked.

'The answer's in the question, Ida. I don't want anyone from the Glass House seeing us.'

He raised a finger to the bartender, gestured to Ida's whiskey, asking for another.

'I shared your prison-triggered *Gumbo Ya-Ya* theory with Walker, my section lieutenant,' Feinberg said. 'He didn't buy it.'

'So you didn't follow it up?'

'No, I followed it up. On the hush-hush. I got a pal of mine to help me call all the prisons in-state. Took us all afternoon and most of the evening. If Walker finds out, I'm screwed, and if he finds out I passed information to you, you're screwed. Hence meeting in a piano bar in Little Tokyo.'

'Thank you,' Ida said, understanding fully the risk he was running.

Feinberg nodded. The bartender deposited a whiskey in front of him. Feinberg downed it and ordered another. The pianist launched into a rendition of 'Stardust', filling it with a deluge of glissandos.

'There's thirty prisons we had to check. We got through to someone at all of them. Eleven of them have the book in their library. Only six of them keep records of which prisoners check out which books. We got a list from each one, cross-referenced them with prisoners who've been kicked loose in the last six months. We got twelve matches in total.'

'And?'

Feinberg shook his head.

'No luck. None of them have got a Louisiana link, none of them with psychosis, no rap-sheets or MOs that come close to the Night-Slayer. No hot prowlers, no assault jackets. Who's in prison checking out books on folklore, Ida? It's not violent offenders. Here.'

He took a sheet of paper from the folder he'd brought with him, passed it over to her. Ida perused it – a list of prisoner names, crimes, dates of release, Department of Corrections parole addresses. With a sinking sensation she saw Feinberg was right. The handful of inmates who'd checked out the book had all committed non-violent crimes – grand theft auto, grand theft money, bail forfeiture, fraud, transportation of a controlled substance.

She sighed, looked up.

Feinberg was smiling at her.

'However,' he said, 'we also called through to the state ding-a-ling farms. Turns out the California Medical Facility in Vacaville has a copy in their library, and they keep strict records on who loans out what.'

He handed her another sheet of paper.

'It's a list of every inmate at the Vacaville facility who's loaned out the book in the last six months. There's twelve in total. Crimes range from jaywalking to public intoxication to arson. But none of them have got an MO to match the Night-Slayer. Although one of them does have a link to Louisiana.' He pointed to a name on the sheet. 'Stephen Gaudet. A runaway from an orphanage in Vermilion Parish, Louisiana. Looks like he hauled up in California last year sometime. A few busts for the usual run-away crap. Shoplifting in June last year, six months' probation. Then in October last year, possession of a controlled substance, sent to Terminal Island, where he stayed for a month before being moved on to Vacaville after his "mental state deteriorated".'

Ida read between the lines. The kid was a runaway and a petty criminal and he'd been sent to an adult prison where he didn't belong, thus his 'mental state deteriorated', meaning he tried to kill himself rather than endure the brutal prison conditions any longer. Someone in the California Department of Corrections had thankfully seen sense, and after a psychological review Gaudet had been moved to Vacaville.

'That could be him,' Ida said.

Feinberg shook his head.

'No violent assaults in his rap sheet, Ida. And he's only eighteen. Five foot eight. A hundred and twenty pounds. I don't see him having the physique to subdue McNeal or Butterfield. Hell, I don't see him subduing Danielle Landry.'

He gave her the last few sheets of paper – a telex from Vacaville with the same details he'd read out. And clipped to it, psychological progress reports from the doctors there.

'Is there an address for him on file?' Ida asked.

'That's the other thing. He's disappeared. No wants or warrants but a few days ago his sister turned up from out-of-state to file a missing person's report with the Sheriff's Department.'

'You got contact details for her?'

'They're in the folder with everything else.'

'Are you going to talk to her?'

'No, Ida. I've already spent most of a day on this. I keep following unauthorized lines of investigation, Walker's going to find out and I'll get disciplined.'

'So what are you going to do?'

'I'm going to finish my whiskey and then I'm going home.'

'But—'

He held up a finger to silence her, drained his glass in a single gulp. Then he rose and headed for the door.

'The drinks are on you,' he said, without looking back.

It was only when he was gone that Ida smiled. He'd left the folder on the bar for her.

# 28

Ida headed over to the Wigwam Motel. She'd seen it from the freeway a million times and had always wondered what kind of person would ever choose to stay there. When she arrived she saw it looked even worse up close than it did from a distance.

She drove further down the street, turned the car around, killed the engine. She walked back up to the motel and took a turn around the forecourt. Just to the side of the parking spots was a small hut which looked like the motel's reception, where an attendant sat behind a desk, watching a TV set. Ida stared at him from a distance and wondered if he was the type to accept a bribe. She'd called the motel before she'd driven over and asked to speak to Kerry Gaudet, but when the receptionist put the call through to Gaudet's cabin, no one had picked up, which gave Ida an opportunity. She went to a payphone across the street and called the motel again.

'Wigwam Motel,' said a gruff voice on the other end.

Ida could hear a TV in the background and guessed it was the man she'd seen in the reception hut.

'Hello, sir. I'm looking for Kerry Gaudet. She's a guest at the motel. I called earlier but she wasn't in. I was wondering if you'd give me her cabin number, please?'

'We don't give out cabin numbers.'

'Well, would you connect me to her room, then? Maybe she's returned since my last call.'

'Just a sec.'

Ida heard a click down the line and then she was put through to Kerry's room and again the phone rang without being picked up. Ida laid the receiver down on the top ledge of the phone box, settling it gently so it didn't slide off. Then she crossed back over to the motel and walked through the shadows of the parking lot so the receptionist didn't see her.

When she reached the cabins she stopped and listened and could just make out the dull sound of a phone ringing over the rumble of cars. She followed the ringing to the far end, to Cabin 14. She looked around, checking sight-lines. The cabin was secluded enough. She kneeled and inspected the lock. Cheapo motel issue for cheapo motel owners. She got a couple of hairpins from her bag, bent one into the shape of a torque wrench, the other into a pick. She slid both into the lock, moved the pick about to get a sense of the lock's springs and pins. She applied pressure with the torque, she scrubbed the pick back and forth over the pins, adjusted the pressure, setting the pins, sliding the pick out. She managed it on the fifth try, turning her hand so the lock opened with a satisfying click.

She must have worked faster than she'd imagined because the phone was still ringing when she stepped inside. She picked up the receiver and put it back down again, killing the noise. She switched on a reading lamp and a pale gloom filled the space.

She looked around, then quickly tossed the room. There wasn't much in there. A military bag and a few clothes, among them jungle fatigues. There were rental papers from Hertz, showing Gaudet had rented an Oldsmobile Cutlass from the LAX concession on the same night Audrey Lloyd had been attacked in the La Playa Motel. Ida copied down the details of the car. In a duffel bag slid into the air vent Ida found a police-issue Ithaca shotgun with the serial numbers removed, a carton of shells, another of bullets. Ida returned everything to the air vent. She stopped at the dressing table, where a photo had been stuck to the mirror. Two children standing in the dusty outdoors, dressed up as a cowboy and an Indian, a live oak strung with medicine bottles in the background. Ida guessed it was Gaudet and her brother back in the good old days.

She let herself out of the room, returned to her car, waited. To kill the time she read through the psychological reports on Stephen Gaudet from Vacaville:

*Tests administered: the Minnesota Multiphasic Personality Index, the Rorschach, the Thematic Apperception, the Grassi Block Substitution, the Zulliger Individual and Group.*

The tests were administered repeatedly, on rotation, over the course of a few months. They charted Stephen Gaudet's arrival, psychological deterioration, return to health, and release. Ida skimmed through them then flicked back to the start and read them in more detail:

*Zulliger Individual and Group Test – date administered 11-14-1966. Initial observations: subject anxious, careful, self-conscious, shy. Superior intelligence. Affectivity is partially adaptable. Introversive qualities; which persistently press toward realization. Subject has experienced abandonment and disappointment in other people: first, the mother deserting the family; then the father's suicide; last, the sister's decision to join the military. This shock has led to an unwillingness to enter into strong relationships. Subject finds friends easily, but gives them up just as easily. Inability to establish profound and long-lasting friendships results in a deep loneliness and sense of social isolation.*

As Ida read, she looked up sporadically to check the parking lot and see if an Oldsmobile Cutlass had turned up. By midnight, there was still no sign of it.

*Thematic Apperception Test – date administered 12–12-1966. Subject continues to deteriorate. Defense and coping mechanisms continue to fail at controlling underlying psychotic encroachment. World view turning notedly more pessimistic and depressive, expressed in increasingly derisive and sardonic language.*

*Previously noted distrust of authority and institution, linked to shock experiences during the subject's time growing up in orphanages (physical and mental abuse, possibly sexual), continues to interfere with the subject's ability to mediate reality and cope with his situation. Distrust of authority shows signs of morphing into resentment and anger, with possibility of violence. Segregation from main facility population should be considered.*

Ida continued reading, wondering if this was a psychiatric evaluation of the Night-Slayer. She tried to picture the young man these reports described, tried to reconcile that image with the photo she'd seen in Gaudet's sister's cabin – the young boy dressed as a cowboy standing in the Louisiana dust, his sister's arm over his shoulder.

*Rorschach Test – date administered 01-09-1967. Subject complains of anxiety, panic, helplessness, hopelessness, fear of death, lack of motivation. Though he showed some interest in the test, responses became ill-humored and morose. When he did speak at any length, it was to doubt the reason for the test. When pushed his obstinacy converted into aggression. Test aborted.*

Ida finished the reports and put them on the passenger seat, feeling a deep sadness. Words strung themselves through the blackness of her mind – *superior intelligence – abandonment – deep loneliness – coping mechanisms continue to fail – underlying psychotic encroachment – possibility of violence.*

She imagined a kid running away from an orphanage in

Louisiana, pitching up in LA, drifting into petty theft and drugs, drifting into a prison sentence, into the State Medical Facility, all the while his psychological state fragmenting. She imagined him taking out a book from the Medical Facility's library and finding in it the folk tales from his home state, finding some kind of solace in their grisly nature, their voodoo. She imagined him leaving the Medical Facility, drifting back to LA, lonely, cut loose, his psychosis coalescing around the folk tales. Louisiana and Los Angeles meshing together in his mind, just like they had for Ida. She imagined him stalking the streets at night, ending up in the Emergency Room at the hospital, seeing McNeal, following him home, murdering him. More drifting, more stalking, more murders.

It seemed plausible. It seemed real. If Gaudet was the Night-Slayer, then he was still on the loose, alone, ready to be triggered at any point by a random interaction that connected in his mind to *Gumbo Ya-Ya*, to his incarceration, to some other unknown trauma in his past.

And yet, Ida just couldn't make the psycho-history she'd constructed tally with the other links that spread out from the case – links to Audrey Lloyd, to the Mob, to the LAPD. How did that connect with poor, lonely Stephen Gaudet? The Night-Slayer felt like a loner, which chimed with Gaudet, but it didn't chime with the wider conspiracy, if there even was one.

Ida sighed, lit a cigarette. She switched on the radio, found a late-night station playing a Miles Davis score. Haunting brass and desolate piano, the notes laced with the sleekest melancholy. She studied the empty, scruffy street, the closed stores, the freeway, the moonlight bounding down, the occasional car crawling through the crossroads in the distance.

Despite its reputation for sunshine, it was in these dark hours that Los Angeles truly revealed itself, long after the suburbs had pulled their shades against the sun, after the tidal wave of lights had pooled across the plains at dusk, after egrets and night herons had settled down in Ballona Wetlands. It was when the traffic had eased and the intersections no longer hemorrhaged brake lights, when neon theater signs had blinked on and coyotes stalked the alleys, when lonely cars drifted up dark roads through hills, when heated swimming pools released steam silently into the night. This was when you could know LA. If you knew how to look.

By two a.m. there was still no Cutlass, so Ida drove home and caught some sleep. She dreamed of starless skies, knives flashing, houses on the backs of trucks driven through the moonlight. She stood on a hill and watched the construction of the freeway extension, its elevated section unfurling itself across the skyline, pointing at her through the darkness, accusing her of something.

She awoke in a panic, heart racing, looking around. But her room was empty, silent, dark. She checked the clock on the bedside table. Still another couple of hours till dawn. She lay back down, closed her eyes, but couldn't sleep. Her thoughts drifted, landed on Faron, as they always did in moments like this. She wondered if he was out there still. Stalking. Slaughtering. How many had he killed since she'd failed to catch him all those years ago? Where was he now? In amongst the canyons and alleys of Los Angeles, moving to its dark pulse? Or maybe over in Vietnam, where the killing was these days. Or any of those revolutions in Latin America.

After their encounter in New York Ida had done some digging, trying to unearth every scrap of information she could about him. But most of the people she spoke to said he was just a rumor, a myth, a spook. No one knew where he was from. There were stories he was a preacher's son, others that he was an orphan, that he ran liquor through the Appalachians during prohibition, that he was muscle for hire. The first time he really made a mark was during the Depression when he worked for Murder Inc., traveling the East Coast killing men for money and women for pleasure. There was a pattern to it. He'd arrive in a city on a job, shack up in a derelict or industrial area, a place he could come and go unseen, a place that emptied out at night so there was no one to hear the screams. Anywhere there was poverty and violence and crime. He'd work his contracts, fulfill his other desires on the side. But he'd always go a step too far, do something too violent, too sickening even for the mobsters who hired him, so he'd move on to the next city, the next mob, the next victims.

That was how Ida had run into him back in the '40s, and then he'd moved on again, vanished, and she was left with an intermittent background fear. Sometimes it resurfaced randomly, like remembering out of nowhere a long-forgotten sadness. Sometimes it had a clear catalyst – a news report about a woman knifed, a prostitute murdered. Most often, though, it happened in these quiet moments, moonlit moments, in silences rich with time.

In the morning Ida returned to the motel. At a little after eight a Cutlass with a broken passenger-side window turned into the lot. Ida waited fifteen minutes, then got out of her car and crossed to Cabin 14. She knocked on the door. There was no answer. She tried again, kept knocking until she heard someone moving about in the cabin. A few seconds later the door opened to reveal a young white woman in jeans and an olive-green T-shirt. She had brown hair that was wet from the shower, recent-looking burn scars down the side of her face. There was anguish playing around her eyes, giving Ida the feeling she was looking at someone who'd just been through a trauma. She wanted to ask her if she was all right. Instead, she asked her name.

'Kerry Gaudet?'

'Who wants to know?' Kerry replied in a Louisiana accent that reminded Ida of home.

'My name's Ida Young. I'm a private investigator. I was wondering if we could talk.'

'About?'

'Your missing brother.'

Kerry frowned. Ida studied her face once more, thought about the shotgun she'd found in her cabin, the jungle fatigues, the photo of the two kids. She tried to reconcile it all with the woman standing before her.

'You know where my brother is?' Kerry asked. There was a hopefulness in her voice that surprised Ida.

'No, but I'd like to find out.'

'Why?'

'It's a long story, but I'd be happy to explain.'

Kerry eyed her suspiciously once more.

'You got ID or something?'

Ida pulled the photostat of her ID out of her pocket, passed it over. Kerry inspected it. Ida noted how well built she was. The taut muscles in her arms, the leanness in her torso.

'This is two years out of date,' Kerry said, looking up at Ida.

'I've been retired two years.'

'And you came out of retirement to talk to me about my brother?'

'Something like that.'

Kerry continued to eye her. She passed her back the ID.

'I guess you better come on in, then.'

She moved to the side to let Ida through, stepping into the sunlight as she did so, allowing Ida to get a clearer look at her. Again she had the sense the girl was anguished. There was a puffiness around her eyes, the ashes of a recent fear haunting her appearance. Ida was sure now that something terrible had happened to her, something shocking. Had she maybe discovered already that her brother was the Night-Slayer? Had she had a brush with death? What could have traumatized the girl so much in the three days since she'd arrived in LA?

# PART NINE

## KERRY

# 29

*Three days earlier*

Kerry woke to spasms in her neck and a headache jackhammering her skull. It took her a few moments to remember where she was. A dingy motel under a freeway in LA. In hallucinatory flashes the previous evening came back to her – flying in, picking up the guns and painkillers from the armorer, going to the Sunset Strip, talking to the hostel receptionist. She recalled what he'd said about her brother, that he'd run away from the hostel after running up a bill, that maybe he'd turned to prostitution to keep himself fed. Kerry felt the same sickness she'd felt back at the club. The same sadness.

She rose and popped an aspirin to take the edge off the night before's beer. As the aspirin fizzed through her headache she showered and straightened out her plans for the day.

The West Hollywood sheriff's station was on San Vicente Boulevard, not far from Stevie's hostel. The deputy who took down Kerry's missing person's report seemed bored by the process, yawning and staring over her shoulder as she gave him the details of Stevie's disappearance.

'And is your title *Miss* Gaudet or *Mrs* Gaudet?' he asked, yawning once more, not even bothering to cover his mouth.

'It's *First Lieutenant* Kerry Gaudet, Nine Hundred and Third Aeromedical Evacuation Squadron, United States Air Force.'

The deputy looked flummoxed. Kerry smiled. He nodded, scribbled something on the form.

'And your address?'

'I'm stationed at the Cam Ranh Bay Air Force base in Khánh Hòa Province, Vietnam. You want me to spell it?'

Again the deputy looked puzzled, again Kerry smiled.

'You came all the way from Vietnam?' he asked. 'Why didn't you just call it in?'

'I was told that wasn't possible.'

He went to say something, maybe tell her it *was* possible, but he thought better of it.

'You got an address in LA?' he asked.

She gave him the details of the motel. He nodded, filled in the last few boxes on the form.

'OK, is there's anything further you'd like to add?' he asked.

Kerry considered telling him about the contents of Stevie's letter.

*I'm on to something, Kerry. Real big. To do with Louisiana and lots of other stuff. So much stuff you wouldn't believe. If you don't hear from me again, it means they got to me.*

'No, nothing to add,' she replied.

'OK. This'll get passed on to the Missing Persons Unit. They'll be in touch with any news.'

He nodded at her, the gesture a dismissal, telling her to go.

'That's it?' she asked.

'Did you want something more?'

'Maybe to speak to a detective. Find out what they're going to do.'

The deputy sighed.

'The detectives are busy with their current cases. Lot of kids go missing here. West Hollywood's a real hotspot. If you'd like, I could put a note on the file to have the detective assigned to the case call you.'

'Please.'

He scribbled something along the top of the form, then they both rose. As Kerry turned to walk out of the doors she saw the deputy throw her report onto a stack of similar files a foot high.

\*

Ten minutes later she was back at the hostel, which somehow looked even seedier in the daylight. There was a middle-aged woman in a Peck & Peck dress behind the reception desk this time. Kerry asked after Tom Annandale, the boy the night receptionist had told her was a friend of Stevie's.

'I don't know where he is. But you can wait here till he comes through.'

Kerry sat on the same row of chairs where she'd sat the previous night. She felt groggy and half-asleep. Maybe jet lag, maybe the Dilaudid pills she'd bought from the armorer, maybe just a generalized weakness from her injuries. She pulled the bottle of Dilaudid from her pocket, read the warnings on the back. *Can cause dizziness and severe drowsiness.* She sighed, closed her eyes, drifted in and out of sleep.

After forty minutes or so a young man entered from the doorway leading to the dorms.

'Tom, you got a visitor,' the receptionist said, gesturing to Kerry.

Tom turned and squinted at her blearily, like he'd only just woken. He was tall and skinny, with long sandy hair and a deathly pallor that was quite the achievement considering the climate. He wore jeans and a long-sleeved Henley shirt, sported a bead necklace and a well-worn anxiety that suggested he was no stranger to grief.

'Hello. My name's Kerry Gaudet,' Kerry said, rising.

The name clearly meant nothing to Tom.

'I'm Stevie's sister.'

'Oh,' he said, wakening.

'I wanted to talk to you. Maybe I can buy you breakfast?'

They went to a joint down the block called the Polar Bear Icecream Parlor. It was dazzlingly lit and painted moon blue, with aluminum fittings and a display counter filled with a million different colors of ice cream. There were runaways everywhere, neon lighting, a radio blaring rock, a stack of newspapers on the counter with Night-Slayer headlines splashed across them.

They sat in a fake leather booth. The counter man approached.

'What can I get you?' he asked. He was old and stooped and couldn't have looked more out of place amongst the teenaged clientele.

'I'll have a strawberry sundae and an orange soda,' Tom said.

Kerry eyed him.

'That's your breakfast?' she asked.

Tom shrugged.

'I'll just have a coffee,' she said, hoping the caffeine might chase away her grogginess.

The counter man nodded and headed off. Kerry studied Tom. In the cotton-candy colors of the parlor's neon lights Kerry could see even more clearly how pale his skin was, translucent almost.

'Stevie said you were in Vietnam,' Tom said, lighting a cigarette.

Kerry nodded, pleasantly surprised to hear that Stevie had talked about her.

'Is that where you got those?' he asked, nodding at the burn scars on the side of her face.

She nodded again. She'd have to get used to this. The doctors back at the Clark Air Base Hospital had said the scars would become less noticeable over time, but not by much.

'I came all this way to find Stevie,' Kerry said. 'You know where he is?'

Tom made a gesture that was halfway between a shrug and a flinch.

'I don't know. I haven't seen him since he moved out of the hostel.'

'The receptionist I spoke to last night said he ran up a bill then ran away.'

'Something like that.'

'You know where he ran to?'

Tom stayed silent.

Just then the counter man returned and laid a coffee cup on the table, filled it up. Tom seemed glad of the interruption. Kerry waited for the counter man to leave.

'Tom, do you know where he ran to?'

'No.' Tom looked shifty, clearly lying.

Kerry eyed him, wondering how to get him to talk. If she pressed him, he might clam up. If she eased off, he might settle into his lies. What other tactics could she use?

'Please,' she said. 'I've traveled from the other side of the world. I just got done at the sheriff's station, filing a missing person's report. They couldn't care less.'

'They're cops,' he shrugged. 'What did you expect? You think they've got time to look for Stevie when they're so busy ragging on us? Driving us off the Strip, breaking up our love-ins in Griffith Park. They see a kid selling copies of the *LA Free Press* and they snatch 'em up and haul 'em off to the Glass House, the downtown police sty. You think they've actually got time to do any actual police work?'

He shrugged, turned to stare out of the window, took a drag on his cigarette. For the first time Kerry got the feeling his insouciance was all for show.

'Tom, my point is if the police aren't interested then you're the only person in this whole city who can help me track down Stevie. He's my little brother, my only relative. I need to find him. Please. I don't have much time. I'm on a week's rest-and-relaxation leave and I spent the first day of it just getting here.'

He turned from the window to stare at her.

'Stevie said you abandoned him.'

Kerry's breath caught.

'He told me all about it,' Tom continued. 'How you both grew up in an orphanage and when you turned eighteen you left him to join the army. And now you're looking for him? What happened, you get a guilty conscience?'

He smiled at her, relishing his vindictiveness.

Just then the counter man returned with Tom's order. Tom thanked him brightly, then dipped his spoon into his strawberry sundae, hoisted out a lump of ice cream, and without taking his eyes off Kerry, put it into his mouth, clamped his lips around the spoon, and slowly pulled it back out, its metal wiped clean.

Kerry felt a sharp rage surge through her, but she knew she needed to stay calm, stem the roar of blood through her head, keep Tom on side. Maybe she was angry because his account was so inaccurate, or maybe because it was true, because it explained that line in Stevie's letter.

*So I'm just writing to tell you I love you, sis. And I forgive you for what you did.*

Kerry recalibrated her plan of attack.

'You've got it all wrong, Tom. I didn't abandon him. They kick you out of the orphanage when you turn eighteen. I'm five years older than Stevie, so we made a deal. I'd join the Air Force so I could get my nursing degree. He'd stay in the orphanage. When he turned eighteen I'd come back and we'd leave together, head to California. Start a new life. Together. But he didn't wait for me. He ran off while I was deployed. See? You got it all wrong. I didn't abandon him. *He* ran away from *me*.'

She eyed Tom, studying his face for a sign that her words were turning him around. But no expression moved across his features, not even a twitch.

'Prove it,' he said.

Stevie's letter. She took it from her pocket, slid it over the table.

'Stevie sent me that in November. I didn't get it till December because I'd been evacuated to the recovery room of the Clark Air Base Hospital in the Philippines. I should still be there recuperating. But first chance I got, I flew over here. Maybe he thought I abandoned him. But we had a deal. Either way, I'm here to make up for it.'

Tom read the letter, frowned, slid it back across the table, sighed.

'Stevie left the hostel to move in with someone,' he said. 'A guy he'd met.'

Kerry remembered what the receptionist had said – that Tom turned tricks, and maybe Stevie had, too.

'You mean like a friend?' Kerry asked. 'A client?' She said it matter-of-factly, to show she wouldn't be shocked if it turned out that way.

Tom smirked, shook his head. He spooned another lump of sundae out of his glass, did the same trick of staring at her and licking the spoon clean.

'Stevie's not like that,' Tom said. 'He likes girls. And he always turned his nose up at hustling. How much do you even know about him?'

Kerry felt an immense relief that Stevie hadn't ended up where Tom had, though it was tempered by his suggestion she didn't really know her brother.

'The guy . . .' Kerry prompted.

'I don't know what their deal was. I could never figure it out.'

'Who was the guy, Tom?'

'He was a Fed.'

'A Fed? You mean like an FBI agent?'

Tom nodded.

A dozen different questions popped into Kerry's head, a confusing barrage that wrong-footed her.

'How did Stevie meet a Fed?' she asked.

'I don't know. I think it was something to do with Vacaville.'

'What's Vacaville?'

'You don't know?' He frowned. 'It's the state loony bin. Stevie was in there for, like, six months earlier this year.'

Kerry's stomach lurched. Her fears about Stevie's mental state reasserted themselves with depressing force. And then she realized something else: all those months she hadn't heard from him – was it because he was locked up?

'What happened?' she asked.

'Back in October last year we both got busted in a bar roust. Stevie had some STP on him, some pot. He got sent to the Terminal Island prison and while he was there he tried to kill himself. After that they moved him to Vacaville. It's a hell of a lot nicer up there. He got released back in June, I think, came back to the hostel. We started hanging out again, but, like . . .' Tom shook his head. 'He wasn't the same after he came out. Mentally, you know. Something happened to him while he was inside. But he never wanted to talk about it.'

Kerry swallowed down a bitter sadness at the thought of Stevie trying to kill himself. How much pain had he been in? Why hadn't he reached out to her? She tried her best to put the feelings to one side, focus on getting what she needed from Tom.

'So how does the Fed play into it?' she asked.

'Stevie said the Fed approached him after he came out of Vacaville, said he needed his help with a case, like they were going into business together. I don't know. Stevie skipped out of the hostel and I never saw him again.'

'What about the Fed? Does he have a name? An address?'

'Stevie never told me his name. But he lives over in the Valley. Sherman Oaks. Nice part of town.'

'You know where exactly?'

'Kinda. Stevie took me there once, when the Fed was away. This giant pink house. Looked like it'd been dumped in a vat of Pepto-Bismol.'

'You think you might remember it if we went for a ride?'

'Sure, but Sherman Oaks is pretty big. And I charge by the hour.'

# 30

Sherman Oaks was one of those picture-perfect LA suburbs Kerry had seen photos of in magazine features. Wide streets and greenery and a mismatch of houses flitted by on either side of the car – Spanish haciendas, English cottages, French chateaus, Italian villas, Swiss chalets. Each one cased in stucco and painted in nursery-room colors: pistachio green, lemon yellow, ice-cream pink, like wedding cakes rolling by on a conveyer belt.

'It's Disneyland but you never have to leave,' Tom said.

He was sitting in the passenger seat of the Cutlass, smoking, watching the passing scenery with disdain and that same grating insouciance.

The Disneyland gag echoed a sentiment that Kerry had also seen in those same magazine features – California's suburbanism as a type of dropping out, a nihilism. People moved to these types of neighborhoods to insulate themselves, to turn their backs on the world's problems. Everything was so picture-perfect it slipped your mind that there was poverty just down the block, race hate, pollution, nuclear missiles being built in your own backyard. Ironic then that these same suburbanites so looked down on the hippies, who were just more honest about their dropping out.

'You from around here?' Kerry asked.

'Nah. Sacramento. Ever been?'

'No.'

'Don't bother. Not even the governor spends any time there.'

He smiled at her, then turned back to watch the houses spin by. Kerry wondered if the neighborhood he'd run away from in Sacramento – because she was certain he'd run away – was like this one: stifling, suburban, hollow, a place you tried to leave behind but couldn't because it was the springboard for every rebellion that came after.

They carried on snaking randomly through the neighborhood. Kerry had wanted Tom to hold the map as they drove, do things systematically, grid-search the area. But Tom had complained, insisted they 'wing it', making Kerry wonder if this was just a way to pad out his hourly rate.

They stopped at a red light, and the sound of pop music floated toward them, coming from the driveway of a house where a group of teens were clustered around a hot rod, its bodywork painted with flames, its engine sticking up out of the hood. It had been raised up on a jack, and two teens were working on it while their friends lounged about, smoked, drank Cokes.

Kerry turned to Tom and saw him staring at the young men with a mixture of aloofness and envy. A couple of them saw him staring and frowned. They nudged each other, rose, chests puffed out with teenaged testosterone.

'Fuck are you looking at, you hippie faggot?' one of them shouted.

Tom looked away and they burst out laughing.

The traffic light changed and Kerry drove off.

When they'd crossed the intersection she turned to Tom again. He was staring at the footwell, shaken, the world beyond the car no longer a safe place to rest his gaze. Kerry wondered if this was the type of thing he'd run away from in Sacramento. These people, these streets, these picture-perfect houses distilling a picture-perfect kind of hate.

'They're just assholes,' Kerry said. 'Forget about it.'

'Assholes like that keep ragging on us, there's gonna be a war,' he said, shaking his head.

'A war?'

'A revolution. An uprising. Whatever you want to call it. The shit is coming down, man. You can't feel it in the air?'

'I've been overseas.'

'Yeah, right,' he said, remembering she was military. 'I'm telling you, all this is gonna go up in flames.'

He spoke with bitter conviction, with self-righteousness tilting his tone, but it rang false. His apocalyptic spiel had come too late, had been directed at the wrong person. He was simply hurting and trying to hide it.

'You see those Night-Slayer killings?' he continued. 'They're only the start.'

'What's the Night-Slayer got to do with it?'

'He's a symbol. Of the breakdown. The way we're going. The bloodbath that's coming. And he's just the start.'

Tom shook his head and they fell into silence, carried on driving. The more they scoured the area the more it inspired in Kerry a pastel-colored dread – especially after the encounter with the kids, Tom's visions of societal collapse. Kerry tried to imagine Stevie hanging out with Tom, living in Sherman Oaks, but she couldn't. If she'd been put off by the neighborhood, and the boy sitting next to her, surely Stevie had been, too?

'It was round here,' Tom said, out of nowhere. 'Slow down.'

'You sure?' Kerry asked. They'd already been down this road twice.

'That's it,' he said, pointing to a house on the corner.

Tom's description in the ice-cream parlor had been right – it was a large house painted flamingo pink. She pulled up to the curb and switched off the engine, inspected the house more closely. The drive was empty, the lawn uncut, there was a pile of newspapers on the porch. It all suggested no one had been living there for a while.

'You sure this is it?' she asked.

'Yeah, this is it. You don't believe me, you can check. When I came here last time the Fed had left the keys under one of the plant pots over there.'

He gestured to a line of glazed pots that ran along the porch, behind a row of jacaranda trees.

'Which one?' Kerry asked.

'How am I supposed to remember which one?'

He gave her a withering look. She ignored it, checked the street. Nothing was stirring, but still she got the feeling that someone was watching them.

She got out of the Cutlass, taking her keys in case this was all a ruse so Tom could steal the car. She walked over to the house and looked under the pots. There was a key under the third one she tried. She returned to the Cutlass. In the bay window of a house opposite, a curtain twitched.

'Thanks,' she said to Tom, getting in, starting the engine.

She'd be back after dark.

# 31

Kerry drove back to Sherman Oaks at around ten p.m. Through the Cutlass's windows she watched the city slip past, its concrete dyed a deep blue by the moonlight. Out there somewhere in amongst the maelstrom of suburbs and freeways was her little brother. She tried not to think of him losing his mind, going to prison, attempting suicide. He was still the kid from her memories. He could still be saved.

When she arrived at the Fed's house the lights were off, no cars in the drive. She cruised the neighborhood, which was somehow even more dead at night.

She went to a diner, killed time drinking coffee. She popped two Dilaudid, hoping the drowsiness they caused would be tamed by the caffeine. She leaned her head against the wall to her side, closed her eyes, told herself it would just be for a couple of minutes. But before she knew it she was asleep, dreaming of the fireball, like she always did now.

It started with the rumble of a C-130 Air Force plane, lumbering out to Quảng Trị that morning, where the South Vietnamese had miscalculated some coordinates and dropped mortars on a couple of American platoons by mistake. By the time Kerry's evac team got there, it was carnage. They triaged, seeing who was alive, who was dead, who could walk, who needed a litter. One of the wounded was still strapped into his flamethrower. Kerry was still unsure how it happened, but suddenly the flamethrower was going off, spraying everyone with napalm.

Kerry had seen victims of napalm before, knew what it did to them, that it stuck to whatever it touched. If you tried to wipe it off, you just smeared it over more of your skin. So when some of it landed on her face, dripped down her shirt, she knew she needed to stop herself trying to wipe it off, despite the excruciating pain. Water boiled at two hundred degrees, napalm burned at two thousand.

Somehow she managed to run back to the plane, grab bandages, tamp out the burning on herself. She grabbed more bandages, Sulfamylon cream, turned around to help the others, and that's when she finally yielded to the pain, blacking out, collapsing.

Weeks later she could still feel the heat in her body, in her scarred skin, tingling through her nerves. Maybe she'd feel that heat for the rest of her life.

'Miss? Miss?'

Kerry opened her eyes, looked around groggily, realized she was in a diner in Sherman Oaks, with the counter man standing by her table, glaring.

'Miss, this is not a hotel. I think it's time you left.'

She returned to the Fed's house, got there just past midnight. She parked on the street behind it. She walked back down the road, one eye on the house where the curtain had twitched earlier that day. She went around the block, trying to pump herself up. She'd never broken into anywhere before, had no clue what she was doing. She had the .38 she'd bought from the armorer in her jacket pocket, prayed she wouldn't have to use it. She'd had weapons training in Vietnam. M-16 rifles and the Smith & Wesson Model 10 she'd been issued as a sidearm. Legally she was in a non-combatant role, but that didn't mean much in Vietnam. Despite the training, she'd never shot a gun in anger, and never wanted to.

She came back, her heart thumping. She walked up the garden path and grabbed the key from where it had been earlier. She slid the key into the lock, turned it, and it worked. She gently opened the door. When she was inside, she took the gun from her pocket, and looked through the gloom. The hallway was big, filled with perfectly chosen furniture and decorations. Kerry wondered if this really was the house of an FBI Agent. It was more the kind of place a family lived.

She tiptoed down the hall, her heart jumping at each creaking floorboard. She stepped through into a kitchen, Early American style, with copper pots and pans hanging from rails above a traditional stove. It was all too perfect, as if the whole thing had been pulled from a catalogue.

She quickly went through the rest of the house to make sure there was no one home. It was all empty and silent and covered in a layer of dust that was weeks old.

Kerry started her search back in the kitchen. In a drawer she found bills from the power and phone companies addressed to a George Hennessy. In the study she found a two-month-old copy of the *LA Times*, its front-page story a report on the first Night-Slayer attack. In the bottom drawer of a writing bureau there was a box file. Kerry tried to open it, but it was locked. She went to the kitchen, found a knife, used it to pry open the lock. It popped easy. She opened the file, flicked through the pouches inside, pulled the papers out. Payslips, employment contracts, pensions contributions; all related to the employment of one George Hennessy as an agent of the Federal Bureau of Narcotics, stationed at the FBN office here in Los Angeles. Tom was right – this was the house of a federal agent, but not an FBI man; Hennessy was a Federal Narcotics Agent.

It made her think Stevie might have been right about a conspiracy. Maybe he'd teamed up with Hennessy to uncover it. Kerry went through the documents but couldn't find anything related. She put the box file back and moved through the rest of the house.

In the lounge she found a photo album. A bunch of pics looked like they'd been taken at an FBN shindig, a New Year's Eve party at a Tiki bar. Drunk poses, the men with their ties askew, arms over each other's shoulders as they sat at tables covered in Mai Tais and rumaki sticks while torches burned in the background.

Kerry wondered if she should follow up with the FBN, but dismissed the idea. Agent Hennessy and Stevie had both gone missing. Maybe it was the FBN itself they were running away from.

She carried on flicking through the album, found a few head-shots taken in a studio, the kind that were used for ID. Surely these were of Hennessy. The photos showed a middle-aged man with small eyes and a strong jaw, a ruddy, outdoorsman's complexion.

Kerry pocketed one of the photos. She rose to check the rest of the house and froze. Through the window she could see the house opposite, where the curtain had twitched that morning – the light was on in the very same window. Kerry stayed still, coming over woozy with fear. She looked at her wristwatch. It was past one o'clock. What was the neighbor doing? Getting a drink of water? Or calling the cops?

She knew she should run, get the hell out of there, but she still didn't have any proof that Stevie had been in the house, that she was on the right track.

After what felt like an eternity, the light went out, but Kerry's anxiety didn't dim. She worked as quickly as she could, panic pulsing through her the whole time.

She found nothing of Stevie's in the house, but in the master bedroom, on the bedside cabinet, amongst a pile of possessions that looked like they'd been emptied out of someone's pockets before they went to bed, she found a couple of receipts, one for a hotel, one for a diner, both of them in Vacaville, site of the Medical Facility where Stevie had been incarcerated.

Tom's words came back to her – something had happened to Stevie in Vacaville, he was a changed person when he'd been released. And that's when Hennessy had approached him. And then they'd both disappeared.

Vacaville.

Kerry was certain that was where the answers lay.

# 32

The next morning Kerry got in the Cutlass and drove to the first gas station she saw. She bought a California Freeway map, unfurled it on the counter and the attendant pointed out Vacaville; a dot on the map far to the north of the state. She was surprised to see it was just a stone's throw from Travis Air Force Base, from where she'd flown out to Vietnam for both her deployments. The attendant estimated the drive at seven hours. Kerry asked him to fill up the Cutlass, then she paid, hopped in and headed north.

Seven hours there, seven hours back. In a car with no air-conditioning, no muffler, and no power-assist. Seven hours of staring at macadam and distant landscapes. And once she got there, no clue how she'd find what she was looking for, that piece of information that would help her track down Stevie.

She took Pacific Coast Highway out of the city, caught her first glimpse of Malibu, wondered what all the fuss was about. There was the beach on one side of the road, and the hills rising up on the other with a few houses dotted around. There didn't seem to be any restaurants or bars or shops, no center to the place, just the long beach and the long highway, and the lonely-looking houses. Maybe that was the allure – a place where your only immediate neighbors were the highway and the gas stations. Even the beach wasn't up to much – the sea was gray, the sand brown and strewn with sinewy cables of seaweed and kelp.

Just after Bakersfield, LA radio cut out and it was alternating local stations and static. Not that Kerry could hear it much over the roar of the engine. The sun dazzled. The Freeway rolled. The road markings flickered past, those white lines strobing, humming, hypnotizing. She passed Union 76 stations, Mobil stations, Standard Oils. She passed roadside diners and billboards on metal stilts. Mountains loomed, and as they grew closer, their single masses broke into sections, with passes and gaps and valleys materializing between them, as if the mountains had drawn all that emptiness inside themselves, cradled it.

Between the industrial works and the suburban sprawls, she caught glimpses of what California looked like underneath all the concrete and metal. There were still orange groves and orchards, green valleys, blue hills. Just like the billboard that hovered over the Wigwam Motel.

She stopped for a Coke and a burger and a refuel at a Flying A joint just after the turnoffs for Fresno. She popped a couple of Dilaudid for the pain, downed three coffees for the drowsiness. She started to form a plan of what she'd do when she got to Vacaville. She started picking up San Jose and San Francisco on the radio.

She reached Vacaville just after sunset. The roads all around were littered with the same sign: *Warning! Hitch-hikers may be escaped lunatics.*

She found the Medical Facility cum prison. She parked. She waited. Strange to think she wasn't more than five miles from Travis Air Force Base. She remembered the flight out from it to Vietnam that first time, her first tour of duty. The plane was packed with grunts, but there was another woman on the flight too, an older woman from the Army Nurse Corps who'd served in the Pacific, Korea, had already done a tour in Vietnam.

'The thing about Vietnam that's different to Korea and all the other wars,' the older woman said, 'is there's no front line. The war's everywhere. Not just in the jungle. You can come under fire on the streets of Saigon, or in the most secure army hospital. Absolutely anywhere.'

It was a twenty-four-hour flight, cramped and sleepless, the food inedible. The soldiers were raucous, many of them going back for a second tour. But when the coast of Vietnam came into view, glittering in the moonlight, an eerie hush descended on the plane. Everything turned solemn. Then the clanking started up — the men wordlessly assembling their guns.

Shift change at Vacaville happened a couple of hours later. The doors opened and a dozen guards trudged across the Medical Facility's parking lot, disappearing into cars. Kerry scanned their faces, trying to figure out which one might spill. Toward the rear of the group she saw a single guard walking with a slight limp. He was a few years either side of forty, she guessed. His build and crewcut screamed ex-army, his slumped shoulders screamed wage-slave, the kind of guy for whom the weekly payslip was never quite enough, and never would be. He was Kerry's servicemen pals in twenty years' time, if they were lucky.

The guard got into a beaten-up Oldsmobile and drove north-northeast, heading for Sacramento. Kerry followed him; sidling close on account of the heavy traffic, hopping lanes, swerving. She'd never tailed someone before, but she managed it, following him all the way to a bar in downtown Sacramento. Perfect.

Kerry waited five minutes, till he had a beer in front of him, till the sludge of the working day had oozed off him. She thought of Tom telling her not to bother visiting Sacramento, and here she was, just a day later.

She crossed the street, stepped inside. It was one of those bars that was dingy as hell despite the presence of fifty different neon beer advertisements and a TV showing a football game. The clientele was a mix of barflies, juicers, working girls, men you'd peg as ex-cons from half a mile away.

The guard was sitting on a stool halfway along the bar, hunkered over a Coors. Kerry sat next to him, ordered a beer. She grabbed a handful of peanuts from the bowl between her and the guard. She tried to think of a clever opening gambit, realized she was too tired for it.

'You work over at the Medical Facility in Vacaville?' she asked.

The guard turned and frowned at her, and she realized she'd got it all wrong. He wasn't anywhere close to forty, he was late twenties at most. He hadn't fought in Korea or World War Two, he'd just got back from Vietnam.

'Yeah, I work at Vacaville. What's it to you?'

Kerry shrugged, thrown, clueless as to how to proceed.

He continued to frown at her, only faintly suspicious. He had a look of someone lost in the midst of a great sorrow, a look she recognized from the patients she tended to back in the war – hurt, confused, as if they'd been betrayed by a world which up till their injuries, they'd assumed was beneficent.

'Where'd you get the limp and the crewcut?' she asked.

'What's it to you?'

'I'm just wondering if it's the same place I got these,' she said, turning her face so he could see the scars running down the side of it.

'You were out there?' he asked.

'Just got back a few days ago.'

'Army nurse?'

'Air Force.'

'You nurses saved my life,' he said. 'I got back a year ago.'

For the first time since she'd been back, she'd met someone who wasn't surprised people like her existed. He took a pack of cigarettes from his pocket, shook them at her. She took one, and they lit up.

'Now, you going to tell me how you knew I worked at Vacaville?'

'I followed you.'

'Why?'

'Because I need a favor.'

'Oh, yeah? And why should I help you? Because we were both out in Vietnam?'

'Sure, why not?' she shrugged. 'Anyone else out here going to help me?'

She studied him as he considered, his face full of sorrow, the lights of the beer advertisements floating across the curve of his eyes. Despite what he'd been through, he was still attractive, the school quarter-back only just going to seed.

'What do you want?' he asked.

'Information.'

He frowned. Took a drag on his cigarette.

'What's the scoop?'

'My little brother was an inmate a while back. When he came out, he wasn't the same. Then he disappeared. I think his disappearance is something to do with the Medical Facility. I thought if I could learn about his time there, maybe who his buddies were, who was visiting him, I might be able to find out where he is now. I'm just looking for anything that'd help.'

She shrugged, told him the details of Stevie's disappearance, how no one gave a shit but her. She told him about the letter that had arrived while she'd been recuperating from the fireball, and before she knew it, she was telling him about the fireball itself, the napalm, everything that had happened that day at Quảng Trị, realizing as she did so that it was the first time she'd ever spoken to anyone about her ordeal.

'I woke up in the Ninety-third Evacuation Hospital at Long Binh Post,' she said. 'You ever been in a burns ward?'

He shook his head.

'I knew where I was before I even opened my eyes,' she said. 'Burn wards got their own smell. Pungent. Queasy. Like smoke and rotting flesh. It gets into everything. It follows you around, in your nose, in your hair. I stayed there a while, then got flown out to Clark in the Philippines for the rest of my recuperation.'

She fell silent as she remembered the flight. The plane was a C-130, the same type she'd flown her missions in. As they were leaving, the airstrip came under attack, forcing the pilot into a combat climb, a hair-raising forty-five-degree take-off procedure that got planes out of range faster.

'That was the last I saw of the place,' she added. 'But ever since it happened, all I dream about is fire. When I'm asleep, when I'm awake. When I'm driving and the light glints off windows. I see it in shadows. I close my eyes and it's burning away in the darkness.'

He mulled this over.

'I hear a car backfiring,' he said. 'A radio screech. And I'm right back there in the jungle. Can't breathe for the humidity. I drink to steady my head, pop Nembutal to steady the drink, down coffee to smooth off the Nembutal. I heard talking helps. I mean, I've heard people say that, but I don't have no one to talk to. At least, no one who'd understand.'

'Me neither.'

They sipped their beers, glanced at the game on the TV, then she sensed a change in the guard, his posture tightening, as if he was steeling himself up for something. He tapped his leg, the one he limped on.

'Three bullets went through it,' he said. 'We were camped out in Bình Định Province when our company got surrounded, wiped out. I hid under my dead buddies for a day and a night, while the gooks mutilated anyone they found alive. When a platoon rescued us the next day, there were only eight of us left. They flew us out to the Sixty-seventh Evac Hospital in Qui Nhơn. My sergeant was one of the survivors. He refused any treatment till the nurses and doctors had looked after all the other men in the company, me included. Even though he had a cracked skull. Sat there bolt upright in a chair in a corner of the treatment room with a damn hole in his head. Didn't say a word, didn't move a muscle till he knew we were all safe.' The guard shrugged. 'How d'you go back to working a nine-to-five after you been through something like that?'

He shrugged. There was that confusion in his eyes again, as if he'd just woken up in this world of civilians, and was wondering how long it would take to feel at home.

They turned back to the TV, pretending once more to take an interest in the game, in the world around them.

'Listen, I don't have much money,' Kerry said. 'But you can have it, all of it, if you just tell me something about my brother. Who his pals were, who was visiting him. Anything. Please.'

'What's your brother's name?'

'Gaudet. Stevie Gaudet. Here.'

She rummaged around her purse and pulled out the same photo of Stevie that she'd shown Lonnie in the nightclub. The guard took it, stared at it.

'Yeah, I remember him. He was with us a few months earlier this year.'

He passed the photo back, quickly, coldly, as if he didn't want to hold onto it for too long in case it overwhelmed him.

'You know something,' she said.

He shook his head, lying.

'I don't know who his pals were inside,' he said. 'But I can look in the log and see who was visiting him.'

'No. You know something more than that. You know what happened to him.'

He exhaled.

'Maybe,' he said.

'What does that mean?'

'It means maybe I know why he came out different, but I'm not going to say till I'm sure, and to do that I'd need to go back to the facility and check.'

'You'd do that?'

'I'm back on shift tomorrow – eight through till six p.m. Meet me after my shift and I'll tell you what I found out. And you can keep your money.'

'Thank you,' Kerry said, returning the bills to her purse. 'But it's too late. I need it now. Tonight.'

'You want me to just waltz back into work in the middle of the evening? It's not happening.'

'I can't wait twenty-four hours. I'm over here on my rest-and-relaxation leave.'

'You came all the way home for your R-and-R?'

He knew how crazy it was. Most troops in Vietnam spent their R-and-R in Bangkok, Hong Kong, Sydney. Flying to the States and back wasted two of their seven days off.

She nodded. 'And I've only got four days left. That's including the day it's going to take me to get back to my squadron. One day might not mean a lot to you, but it means a hell of a lot to me. Please. How about you go back there now and say you forgot something? I need to find my brother. Please. I'll wait for you here.'

He frowned at her, exhaled.

'All right,' he said finally. 'But don't wait for me here. This ain't the right kinda bar for that. And let me finish my beer first. This is supposed to be the high point of my day.'

An hour later Kerry was parked in the lot of an apartment building just opposite the bar. The sky had turned dark, what moonlight there was blanketed everything in a cool blue hue. She had the radio tuned to a San Francisco station playing Stan Getz, which seemed appropriate enough. She tapped her fingers along in six-eight time to the bossa nova, to the tambourines and jaunty guitar. She looked up at the stars, figured she should make the most of them while she was out of LA.

She thought once more of that flight over to Vietnam, remembering something else that older nurse had said to her. It was when they'd landed and had stepped outside the plane, and Kerry had felt that suffocating blast of heat and humidity for the first time. Like nothing she'd ever known. The other nurse had explained something to Kerry as they'd said their goodbyes.

'Every nurse, over the course of her career, sees a certain amount of death and tragedy and sorrow. But when you're a nurse in a war zone, you see that lifetime of pain in just a single year.

It's only the ones who accept they need help with the burden that make it through.'

Five minutes later Kerry saw headlights approaching through the rearview. The guard's beaten-up Oldsmobile. He pulled in, got out of his own car and into hers.

'Got lucky,' he said. 'Friend of mine was pulling the night shift on the entry box, so I got to look through the visitor logs. Your brother only had one visitor the whole time he was inside. Same guy visited four times. Sam Cole. Ring any bells?'

'Nope.'

'He signed in with LAPD credentials. I checked who else he visited. Another five inmates.'

He handed Kerry a sheet of paper. She looked at it. A list of names and dates and details. He took his cigarettes out and they each lit one up.

'Remember in the bar I said I might know what happened to your brother? I wanted to be sure before I told you. The fact this cop was visiting him confirms it.'

'Confirms what?'

'Months ago, when your brother was at the facility, these people came down – university types – wanted to run some tests on the inmates. Drug tests. Experiments, you know. It was voluntary, but the facility authorities dangled early release as a carrot. Maybe twenty, thirty inmates signed up. Your brother was one of them. The other people the cop visited, they were volunteers too. He was visiting inmates who'd all taken part in the drug tests. You ask me, it looks like he was trying to build a case.'

'I don't understand,' Kerry said. 'Building a case against who? What were the tests?'

'Drug tests. I told you. I don't know what drug they were testing, or who was doing it. Like I said, they looked like college types. All I know is, after those tests, those volunteers were never the same again. It screwed them up. Made 'em even crazier than when they were admitted.'

The guard shrugged, and Kerry could feel his remorse. His guilt. This was why he'd been willing to help her. It wasn't just that he was being nice, that he felt sorry for her, that they were two Vietnam vets cast adrift. It was also this. Something horrible had happened in the facility that he was guilty about. Tests on inmates who were in no position to consent to taking part in a medical trial.

Kerry had a million questions – what the hell were they testing? Who was in charge of the tests? How did the cop fit into it? Mostly she was wondering if this was Stevie's big conspiracy. And if so, what the hell did it have to do with Louisiana and an FBN agent called George Hennessy?

'There's something else,' the guard said. 'All these inmates the cop visited. They're all from LA, and except for your brother, they're all Negro. And none of them are at the facility no more. They either got early release or they escaped.'

'Escaped? How? It's supposed to be a secure facility.'

'It's supposed to be, but it ain't. Last couple of years we've had a whole bunch of escapes. Like someone's letting them out, and someone higher up's not too fussed about it. The fact this cop's only been visiting guys who ended up flying the coop, well, one way or the other, feels kinda suspicious if you ask me.'

'When did they escape?' she asked.

'The last ones back in October. It's all written down there.'

The guard nodded at the paper.

'Thanks,' Kerry said.

She took a drag on her cigarette, hoping it might help her swallow down the dread that was constricting her throat.

'You look like you could use a drink,' he said. 'We could go back to the bar if you want, or my apartment's just up there.'

He gestured to the crummy apartment block whose lot they were parked in. She looked at him, the way he was staring at her. There was a pain they both shared, and they didn't have to speak to acknowledge it.

'Not the bar,' she said.

# 33

Kerry rose as quietly as she could, put on her clothes, checked the time. Not even midnight. She could be back in LA for dawn, chasing down the names the guard had given her. She left him sleeping in his bed and went into the kitchenette, found his coffee, made the strongest cup she could. As she waited for it to brew she looked around the pokey, dimly lit kitchenette and realized she'd never even asked his name.

The coffee brewed and she poured herself a cup, loaded it with sugar, downed it. She stepped into the hallway. She peeked into the bedroom for one last look at the sleeping guard and saw that he'd woken.

'Hey. I need to go,' she said.

'I know. Just a sec.'

He leaned over, grabbed a pencil and a receipt from the bedside table, scribbled something onto the receipt and held it out for her. 'My number. Gimme a call if you're ever back in Sacramento.'

She crossed the room and took the receipt, went back to the doorway. She stopped just as she was about to pass through into the hall.

'What happened to your sergeant?' she asked. 'The one who refused treatment till you and your buddies were all fixed up?'

He seemed confused by the question.

'He caught sepsis from that wound in his head. Died a little while later.'

She fought sleep all the way back to LA. She stayed off the Dilaudid so she didn't get drowsy, so the pain kept her awake. She stopped off at service stations and hopped herself up on yet more strong coffee, thick and treacly sweet. As she drove she thought about the guard. She'd slept with a few boys in Louisiana and in Vietnam, but they'd been fleeting encounters, ways of passing the time. Like drinking a beer, smoking a joint, going to the movies because the night was there, and you needed to fill it with something.

But with the guard it was different, it felt as if they'd done each other a kindness. She thought about what he'd said – a car backfiring and he was back there in that jungle. She got the sense that they'd both left a part of themselves over there, and no matter how many more days they spent on this earth, they'd never feel whole again. And they both knew it. The only way to stop that empty feeling was not to feel at all.

She made it back to LA just as the sky was turning pearly rose with the first gentle light of dawn, the sun finding purchase on cornerstones and windows, hauling itself up over the city. On the street corners kids were catching stacks of morning editions thrown at them from newspaper vans, smog was beginning to settle.

When Kerry got back to the motel she popped a couple of Dilaudid, slept a couple of hours. She woke and went through the list the guard had given her:

*Paxton, Julius – admitted 09-13-64, released 09-27-67*
*Henderson, William – admitted 04-23-62, released 09-14-67*
*Rawls, Anton – admitted 11-27-66, released 09-03-67*
*Cooper, Peter – admitted 05-05-65, escaped 10-01-67*
*Mouzon, Ronald – admitted 07-30-66, escaped 10-01-67*

Five men who'd been involved in the Vacaville drug trials, five men who'd been visited by Sam Cole there. The same cop who'd visited Stevie. There was no hope of finding the two men who'd escaped, but she might track down the other three. And maybe even the cop.

She left the cabin, walked over to the reception hut. The man behind the desk looked up from his TV.

'You got a phone book in here?' she asked.

He gave her a look, nodded toward the waiting area, where there was a coffee table with a copy of the Los Angeles Street Address and Telephone Directory on it.

'You mind if I take it to my room?' she asked.

'Nope,' the man said without looking away from the TV. 'Just make sure you bring it back.'

She returned to her cabin. She found every Sam Cole, Julius Paxton, William Henderson and Anton Rawls in LA. She called them up, whittling down the list. She ripped out directory pages. She hit the streets.

She spent all day on it. Two dozen addresses scattered across LA. A day of driving, of car fumes, burn cream, cigarettes and Dilaudid. Pulling up at diners to mainline coffee to ward off sleep. She forced herself to stay awake, to not give up. It was hard on account of the doors slammed in her face, the dead ends.

The sun carved its way across the sky, and night came on hard and fast. Traffic patterns shifted like tides. When she got caught up in jams she stared at her reflection in the windshield, superimposed on cars, taillights, off-ramps, moonlit snapshots of the hardscrabble city, its freeways like serpents in Eden, whispering hidden truths.

Maybe it was on account of all the coffee, but she caught the jitters, a shaky paranoia that she was being stalked. But each time she checked the rearview, she couldn't see any tails. Along with the paranoia came something more disturbing – hopelessness. She started giving in to the thought that she was wasting her time, that she'd reached a dead end, that she'd never find Stevie on her own, and this whole endeavor was a vain, ridiculous waste of time.

She swallowed down her desperation, succumbed to the temptation of just one more hit of Dilaudid-and-caffeine before she drove back to the motel. She pulled into the parking lot behind a Mobil station, went in and ordered a coffee to go. When she returned to her car to drink it, she heard a baby screaming. Further down the street, a man had stepped out of his house, holding the baby in his arms, shushing it, rocking it gently back to sleep.

As the man moved, Kerry saw he was dancing the steps to a rhumba, up and down his driveway, in the darkness, the baby cooing now, rhumba-ed back toward sleep. Kerry remembered all the times she'd comforted Stevie when they were kids. All the times he'd run to her after being picked on by the bullies and predators who stalked the orphanage. All the times he'd asked when their mother would be coming back, as if the bewilderment would never leave him. He'd come to her because she was all he'd had. And then she'd left him there.

# 34

Kerry woke to sunshine and knocking on the car window.

'Miss? Miss? Are you all right?'

A kid in a Mobil uniform was peering in.

Shit. She'd fallen asleep in the car, in the gas station's parking lot. The Dilaudid must have knocked her out, and she'd slept through the night. How late was it? How much time had she wasted?

'I'm fine, thanks,' she said to the kid.

He gave her a look, unconvinced. Kerry checked the clock on the dash, started up the engine and tore out of there, racing back to the motel, ruing the lost hours.

It wasn't until she pulled into the motel that she realized she hadn't eaten. She flipped the car round and headed up the block to a twenty-four-hour supermarket. The place was empty on account of the early hour, silent except for the buzz of the refrigerators, the sickly elevator music. The quiet unnerved Kerry. She had that sense that someone was following her again. She looked around, couldn't see anyone. She picked up a bag of potato chips, peanuts, chocolate bars, a few mandarins.

When she stepped back outside into the lot, she froze. There were three men standing by her car, the door was open, one of them was rifling through it. Even from a distance she could tell these men were federal agents. The black suits, the white shirts, the patent-leather shoes buffed to a shine, the sense of superiority.

She thought of going back into the supermarket, waiting it out, but one of them spotted her, glared, gestured her over. With a rising panic, she crossed the lot. She saw they'd smashed one of the car's windows to get inside. It was only then she remembered she'd left the .38 in the glovebox.

'Kerry Gaudet?' one of them asked.

She could tell he was the leader. He was a giant of a man; tall, broad-shouldered, with a colossal belly. His head was completely bald, his eyebrows just wisps of blond-gray hair.

Kerry nodded.

He held up his badge. The same eagle crest she'd seen on the paperwork at George Hennessy's house.

'My name is Agent Henry White, of the Federal Bureau of Narcotics. We're here about your brother. You want to get in our car and we'll go somewhere to talk?'

He gestured to a black Ford Galaxie parked just along from Kerry's Cutlass.

'I'm not getting in your car,' Kerry said, clutching the bag of groceries to her chest.

The man who'd been rifling through her car stepped out of it, slammed the door shut, showering shattered glass everywhere. He looked to Agent White, shook his head.

White turned to Kerry.

'Get in the car,' he repeated, gesturing once more to the Ford.

'I'm not getting in the car.' Kerry tried to stop herself from shaking.

White nodded at his two men. They rushed forward, grabbed Kerry, threw her into the back of the Ford. She felt a knee on her spine, hands running all over her, frisking her, grabbing at her.

They drove up Culver Boulevard, heading northeast. Kerry tried to catch the name of every cross street they went past. She focussed on that because it was the only task she could think of, because she needed something to keep her mind from falling down a spiral of panic and fear. Wherever they were taking her, she knew it would be somewhere they could do whatever they wanted.

One of the goons was in the driver's seat, Agent White sitting next to him. The second goon sat opposite Kerry in the back, glaring at her. None of them said anything the whole way. Occasionally White would turn around, run his eye up and down her, grin. She was shocked by how red his skin was, how glazed his eyes. He was drunk or high or both, had been up all night with his goons, waiting for her. To scare her, to watch her reaction with bent eyes and a malicious smile twisting his lips.

After five minutes they turned off the road near the junction with Washington Boulevard, stopped at a set of unmanned security gates. The goon in the driver's seat got out, unlocked a padlock, opened the gates, returned to the car. They drove into a sprawling lot of warehouses, completely silent, empty, abandoned. But as they passed the last of the warehouses, Kerry saw what looked like a New York tenement building, then a lake, a Dickensian street, a cowboy ranch, a pioneer's homestead. Suddenly she realized where she was – a film-studio back lot. One that had long since fallen into disuse, the sets all weather-damaged and falling apart.

They skirted round a Norman Rockwell-style Main Street, came to a stop at the edge of the lake. The driver killed the engine. White turned to look at Kerry, signaled for her to get out, and they all exited the car. White walked around and sat on the hood, gazed out over the water. The goons gestured for Kerry to go and stand next to him.

She walked over. He carried on staring across the lake. Kerry noticed blackened, charred remains on its far bank, like a fire had burned through a few of the abandoned sets.

'This is MGM's Lot Number Two,' White smiled. 'This is where Gene Kelly danced in *Singin' in the Rain*. It's where Judy Garland sang "Have Yourself a Merry Little Christmas". *Meet Me in St. Louis*, *An American in Paris*, *Some Like It Hot*, *North By Northwest*. All of them filmed here. But MGM's having money troubles – all the studios are – so it's all getting bulldozed, sold off, destroyed. A fire started over there a few months back.' He gestured to the other side of the lake. 'Suspicious, if you ask me. Anyway, MGM thinks if they can sell this all off to property developers they can use the money to build a casino in Las Vegas. They're taking a bet on Vegas becoming a family-friendly holiday destination. Same bet Howard Hughes is making. It's some gamble. You ever been to Vegas?'

Kerry stared at White, shook her head.

'Horrible town. Corrupt. Seedy. It's all Mafia-run casinos and prostitutes. I can't see it ever being a family town. Can you?'

He looked at Kerry, waiting for an answer. But she didn't want to play his games. She wanted to know how they'd tracked her down. The missing person's report? Tom Annandale? Maybe Lonnie at the hostel? More importantly, she wanted to know why they'd driven her out here, what lay in store.

'What do you want with me?' she asked.

A confused look crossed White's face, like he was surprised at the abrupt change of topic. Again Kerry got that sense that he was high and drunk and wild. He turned to his two goons, shrugged, showing he was game to let Kerry ask a few questions.

'You're in town looking for your brother, yes?'

She nodded.

'And how has your search been going?'

'Well, I haven't found him yet. What's it to you?'

White raised his eyebrows.

'Your brother's disappearance is related to an ongoing Narcotics Bureau investigation, which brings it into our sphere of jurisdiction.'

'I see.'

White took a pack of Marlboros from his pocket, popped one in his mouth. He offered her the pack. She refused. He lit his cigarette with a gold lighter.

'Miss Gaudet,' he said. 'You seem like an intelligent woman, so I'm not going to try and fool you with any bluster. At roughly the same time your brother went missing, an agent of ours, George Hennessy, also disappeared. It looks like Hennessy had taken your brother in as a witness to the ongoing investigation I just mentioned. The investigation is highly sensitive. When you filed your missing person's report with the Sheriff's Department you inadvertently put it into jeopardy. A case that's been going on for years, costing tens of thousands of taxpayer dollars. Furthermore, you jeopardized the safety of Agent Hennessy, and your brother. You understand?'

Kerry frowned. It must have been the sheriff who'd informed the FBN about the missing person's report. There must have been a flag on the system next to her brother's name. How else would they have got to her so quickly?

She stared at the three men, trying to remember if they'd appeared in the photographs she'd seen at Hennessy's house. Wondering if they really were Hennessy's allies in the Bureau, or his foes. They had to be his foes. They'd broken into her car, abducted her, driven her out to an abandoned studio lot.

'I understand if all that's true,' she said. 'Then you probably had the Sheriff's Department quash my missing person's report.'

'We don't have that kind of jurisdiction over the Sheriff's Department.'

'Not officially.'

She didn't want to come across as petulant, bratty, but she also didn't want to look like a pushover, because he'd clearly brought her here to push her over, or worse.

'Miss Gaudet, in such an instance, it's better for us to investigate. We're trained in these kinds of investigations. We have expertise that you don't have. We know much more about the case than the Sheriff's Department, and we can investigate without putting anyone in harm's way. I'm sure you came here with the best of intentions, but you need to realize your actions might endanger innocent people.'

'So I should stop looking for my brother?'

'Well, by your own admission you're not getting anywhere. And if you're waiting around to see what the sheriff comes back with, well, you're going to be waiting a very long time.'

He smiled at her, letting her know they *did* have that kind of jurisdiction after all.

Kerry eyed him, not believing his story for a second. They hadn't shit-canned the missing person's report to investigate it themselves, they'd shit-canned it to protect themselves. And just for good measure, they'd taken her here to scare her off.

'How long have Agent Hennessy and my brother been missing?' she asked.

'Excuse me?'

'Because it seems to me they've been missing for weeks. At least since October, meaning your investigation's making about as much progress as mine. So maybe you're not as shit-hot as you think you are. This whole thing stinks. Why not ask me to come down to FBN headquarters with you? Make this an official interview? Why are you doing this all off the books? Go peddle your bullshit somewhere else.'

White grabbed her neck with a speed that belied his size. He pulled her toward him, so her face was right up to his, right up to those eyes, devil-red and drug-glazed. His grip made her scars burn. She could feel the wounds opening up, scar tissue that had taken weeks to form ripped apart. She knew the consequences of that happening, the risk of infection, of permanent damage. Pain pulsed through her torso. Fear, too. She could barely breathe.

He lifted his free hand to her face, ran the back of it over the scars, caressing them. Kerry turned her head. White chuckled.

'We've been looking into your history, Miss Gaudet. We know everything there is to know. You're the orphan child of a disgraced cop. A man who dragged his family into poverty, then shot himself. You're the product of the American nightmare, Miss Gaudet. Riches to rags. It doesn't matter how many noble stands you make, you'll always be bayou trash. Worthless, good-for-nothing bayou trash. So who do you think you are that you can impinge on my good name? On the Federal Bureau of Narcotics' good name?'

He squeezed her neck tighter. Her scars burned. She struggled for breath.

'I'm no one,' she wheezed.

'You're who?'

'I'm no one.'

He removed his hand from her neck. She crashed onto the ground. Her burns still pulsed from his touch. He kneeled down next to her, stared her in the eye.

'You're just a girl,' White said. 'On your own. In a city you don't know. A dangerous city. A sick city. Corrupt and rotten and sinful. Worse even than Las Vegas. All that glamor and shine, it's all as fake as these film sets.' He swept his hand across the vista in front of them: the lake, the Norman Rockwell-style Main Street, the cowboy ranch, the pioneer's homestead, fabricated pieces of an America that never was.

'Don't be fooled,' he warned. 'Underneath it all Los Angeles is just puppet masters and blood money. You can't see it because you're an outsider. But we know. We see. That picturesque suburb with the candy-paint houses? It was built by Mexicans earning ten cents on the dollar compared to whites, and the ones who complained ended up in the foundations. That beautiful mansion downtown where the mayor lives? Stolen from Japs who got sent to concentration camps during the war and never came back. Those cops driving around, waving at kids, joking and smiling? For a fee they will abduct, torture and murder anyone you want, anytime, no questions asked. That child star everyone loves? They get her through filming with pep pills in the morning and barbiturates at night. She's been passed around every studio head in town and her parents were in on it. There's people here who can look at any make and model of car and know exactly how many bodies you can fit in the trunk. That's LA, Miss Gaudet. They lure you here with promises of heaven and they take your soul. That's what this city runs on, its very own brand of voodoo. So you let the system take care of your brother, OK? And you can get out of here before it corrupts you too.'

Kerry looked up at him. Again she saw that glazed, wild-man stare that could only ever be interpreted as a prelude to violence.

She nodded, terrified.

He smiled.

'Now, my friends at TWA tell me the ticket you purchased has a return date of Christmas Day,' he said. 'Flying back to Washington State, and from there, I guess, to Fairchild Air Force Base and the battlefields of Southeast Asia.'

Kerry nodded again.

'So, to help keep your ever-living soul pure, we'll bump that return departure forward, shall we? Get you away from this Gomorrah as soon as we can.'

He took a chunky wallet out of his pocket and peeled off a hundred dollars.

'For a new ticket,' he said.

He leaned forward and slipped the bills into the pocket of her shirt, left his hand there a few seconds, maybe to feel her breast, maybe to feel the terror thumping through her heart.

Ten minutes later they tossed her out of the Ford back into the supermarket parking lot from where they'd snatched her, threw her bag of groceries onto the asphalt after her. As she picked them up, White wound down his window and grinned.

'You have yourself a merry little Christmas of your own, Miss Gaudet.'

The goon driving smirked. They peeled out of there.

Kerry watched them go, collapsed onto the asphalt, panic racing through her, all the emotion and adrenaline she'd been trying to keep in check choking her up now, forcing itself up through her body, out through tears and sobs. But she pushed them back down. The most important thing was to hide her fear, her shame. She rose and stumbled toward her car, and the emotions coursing through her seemed to catch alight, powering her on.

When she got back to her cabin, she locked the door and went to the bathroom. She emptied her pockets, turned on the shower and stepped into it fully clothed. She collapsed onto the tiles, scrunched herself up fetally, and cried through the darkness.

She wasn't sure how long she stayed like that, but at some point she heard knocking, insistent, heavy, making itself known through the sound of the shower. Someone was at the door. New waves of fear pulsed through her. Maybe they'd come back.

She switched off the shower, stepped out of the bathroom, only now becoming aware of the pain in her neck where White had grabbed her. She changed into dry clothes. She picked up her .38, held it behind her back and stepped up to the door. She looked through the peephole. It wasn't Agent White or his goons, but a woman. She was slight, with gray hair pulled back into a bun, wore a navy skirt, a white blouse.

Kerry opened the door.

'Kerry Gaudet?' the woman enquired.

'Who's asking?' Kerry tensed, tightening her grip on the gun behind her back.

'My name's Ida Young,' the woman said. 'I'm a private investigator. I was wondering if we could talk.'

# PART TEN

## IDA & KERRY

# 35

Kerry sat perched on the cabin's windowsill while Ida took a seat on the chair by the dresser. Kerry noticed Ida had a certain ease to her movements, a natural poise. She wondered how old Ida was. She looked too young to have retired already.

'You mind if I smoke?' Ida asked.

Kerry shook her head.

Ida took a battered old silver cigarette case from her pocket and lit up.

Kerry turned and tossed a quick glance out of the window behind her, to make sure Ida didn't have any accomplices waiting. It was quiet outside the cabin. The rows of wigwams glinted in the sun, fumes wafted down from the freeway. When Ida had entered, Kerry had slipped her .38 into the waistband of her jeans, nestled it against the small of her back, so Ida wouldn't realize she was packing. But even though she had the gun so close by, Kerry was still scared, still trembling with the aftershocks of the encounter with White.

She turned back to see Ida staring at her.

'Gaudet's a Cajun name, no?' Ida asked in her muted Louisiana accent.

Kerry nodded.

'Where are you from?' she asked.

'New Orleans,' Ida replied. 'A long, long time ago.'

Kerry nodded again. Ida's thin face and high cheekbones made Kerry wonder what she'd looked like in her youth, back in that New Orleans of long ago.

'How did you find me?'

'You filed a missing person's report on your brother. It was passed on to me.'

Kerry felt that same pang of stupidity she'd felt with White. First the report had brought White and his goons to her door, now it had brought Ida.

'So why are you looking for my brother?' she asked.

Ida considered her response. 'You hear about the Night-Slayer killings?'

Kerry nodded.

'I'm trying to find him,' Ida said.

'For the police?'

'In a way.'

'So what's Stevie got to do with it?'

Ida sighed. 'Well, this is the hard part. We've come up with a theory about who the killer is. A sketch. Your brother matches it. I want to find him, to see if I can eliminate him from the pool of suspects.'

'You think my brother's the Night-Slayer?'

'No. I think he fits the sketch.'

'What's the sketch?'

Ida paused, debating what she should reveal to Kerry.

'Male,' Ida said eventually. 'Louisiana background, spent some time in a California correctional institution, history of psychological problems, access to a car, knows something about breaking and entering.'

'Stevie doesn't drive,' Kerry said. 'And he doesn't know anything about breaking and entering. And he damned sure isn't a murderer.'

'I see.'

It seemed bizarre to Kerry that she was having this conversation, that anyone could suspect Stevie of being a murderer. And then she realized. Maybe it was bizarre because it was a lie. A cover story. Maybe this woman had come here for some other reason. Maybe she'd been sent by Agent White. But then Kerry's thoughts jumped back to Stevie's letter – *I'm on to something, Kerry. Real big. To do with Louisiana.*

'Why do you think the Night-Slayer's from Louisiana?' she asked.

'It's just a working theory. The Night-Slayer looks like he's been inspired by Louisiana folklore.'

'You mean old stories and stuff?'

'You're from Vermilion Parish, right? You must have heard all those old bayou tales growing up.'

Kerry frowned, trying to match up what she knew of the Night-Slayer murders with the bedtime stories of her childhood.

'I don't understand,' Kerry said. 'Stevie wouldn't be killing people because of old stories.'

'Miss Gaudet, you ever hear of book called *Gumbo Ya-Ya*? It's a collection of Louisiana folklore.'

'I know what it is. My father had a copy at our house back in Gueydan.'

'That's the book the killer's been copying the murders from. There's an edition in the Medical Facility at Vacaville. While he was there, your brother checked it out.'

Kerry's heart sank. With a speeding panic her mind raced to reassess everything. Maybe Stevie wasn't a runaway who'd stumbled on a conspiracy, maybe Stevie *was* the conspiracy. Maybe he'd sent that letter because he thought he was in danger of being caught.

'Miss Gaudet, are you OK?'

'It can't be him,' she said. But her voice was weak; she could hear the lack of conviction in it.

'Then help me prove it's not.'

Kerry frowned.

'Why are you so interested in this?'

'Because in a way, I feel responsible. Earlier this week a woman was murdered in a motel room. It looks like she had information on the Night-Slayer, and she was running to me for help. Except I wasn't there to help her.'

'Why was she running to you?'

'I used to operate a detective agency. Women used to come to me for help. Abused women. Sometimes it almost felt like I was running a refuge. But then I stopped being there for them. I can help you, too, Miss Gaudet. Help you find your brother.'

'But if you do find him and you think he's the killer, you'll have him locked up.'

'Yes, because if he is a killer he *needs* to be locked up, and nothing either of us can do will change that. But if he's *not* the killer, then I'll have helped you find him. You've been looking for him, haven't you?'

'What makes you say that?'

'Because you seem like an intelligent young woman. Too intelligent to be putting your trust in the Sheriff's Department. What have you been doing since you filed that missing person's report? Seeing the sights, twirling your hair while you wait for a deputy to call you back? You don't seem the type. How long were you planning on staying in LA?'

Kerry went to answer, then hesitated, remembering in a spark of panic how Agent White had tried to strong-arm her into leaving early.

'I'm here on a week's rest-and-relaxation leave from Vietnam,' she said. 'I'm supposed to be flying back Christmas Day.'

Ida frowned at her, as if sensing her panic, but she didn't comment on it.

'Then you've only got two days left,' she said. 'The clock's ticking for both of us, Miss Gaudet. I understand why you might not trust me. If you'd like you can call Detective Feinberg at the LAPD, he's working on the Night-Slayer case. He'll vouch for me.'

Ida took a pen and paper from her pocket, wrote something down. As she did so, Kerry checked out of the window. Everything was still quiet.

She turned back, and Ida passed her the paper – it had the detective's name and phone number on it.

'In the meantime, I was wondering,' Ida said. 'While you've been in town, have you contacted anyone who knows Stevie? Friends, associates, anyone? It'd be a real help if I could talk to someone who knows him here.'

Kerry wasn't so stupid as to give up information to a complete stranger, even though she desperately wanted to tell someone everything. Share her pain, her trauma, her theories. Agent White's words floated back to her – *you're just a girl. On your own. In a city you don't know.* Kerry needed a friend. Someone she could trust. But an old woman who might have been sent by White, who wanted to pin a series of murders on her brother, was not that person.

'There's nothing I can tell you,' she said finally.

Ida didn't flinch.

'I understand,' she smiled. 'I know what it's like trying to make your way in a strange city, amongst the kind of people this work entails. If you decide to talk to me, I can offer you help in return. I've been an investigator for almost fifty years. I can't count the number of missing person's cases I've been involved in. I've got experience in this. I know the city. I know people on both sides of the criminal line. You're new in town, you're young, you're inexperienced. I can get a lot further a lot quicker than you can.'

Kerry nodded, noted how Ida's assessment of her so closely resembled Agent White's.

'Here are my details,' Ida said, rising. 'I know you've got no reason to trust me, but maybe have a think about it, OK?'

Kerry took Ida's card and showed her to the door.

'Miss Gaudet, can I offer you one last piece of advice?'

'Sure.'

'Never stash your gun in the top of your pants.'

Kerry watched Ida get in her car and drive off, and only then did she close the cabin door. She pulled the gun from her jeans, tossed it on the bed, sat, gazed at the carpet, feeling more alone than ever. It was only then she realized that Ida hadn't asked her about her scars. And not just that, Kerry hadn't even caught Ida casting surreptitious looks at them, like everyone else she'd encountered.

Kerry rose and went over to the dresser, checked the mirror, saw how terrible she looked. She inspected the scars where Agent White had grabbed her, a few drops of blood speckling her skin where tissue had torn. She went into the bathroom and cleaned herself up as best she could, then returned to the bedroom and stared at the note from Vacaville. The names of the five inmates. It had been in her pocket when White and his goons had taken her. Thankfully they'd just patted her down for weapons, not searched through her clothes. If they had, she would've lost her only actual lead, a lead she'd made a mess of following up.

Suddenly a thought struck her. What if Stevie wasn't the Night-Slayer, but one of these other inmates was? Maybe one of them fitted Ida's sketch of the killer – from Louisiana, with burglary convictions, had checked out *Gumbo Ya-Ya* whilst in Vacaville? She thought about Ida's offer, that she knew people on both sides of the criminal line. But could Kerry trust her? She picked up the paper Ida had given her with the name of the police detective and his phone number. It could be anyone's number, a residential address with an accomplice waiting to answer.

Kerry walked over to the dresser. She hadn't bothered taking the telephone directory back to reception yet. She flipped it open, flicked to the emergency numbers, checked the number for the LAPD. It was different from the one Ida had given her. Kerry called the number from the directory, asked to be put through to the Homicide Division, to Detective Feinberg. After five minutes of being shunted around the switchboard, she was finally connected.

'Homicide, Feinberg,' said a gruff, gravelly voice at the other end.

# 36

A couple of hours after their meeting in Kerry's cabin, Ida met the girl for a second time in a Pup'n'Taco just down from the Wigwam Motel. The place was decked out with red tables and chairs, red carpets, red-tiled walls, red cellophane across the windows, making Ida feel as if she'd stepped into a sunset. There were a couple of children's parties in there and the kids were blowing up red balloons and volley-balling them about, running around, screaming.

Ida ordered a meal, Kerry just a bowl of fries.

'You don't want a hotdog or some tacos?' Ida asked.

'I've not been able to eat meat since my first week in Vietnam.'

The server put their orders on a tray with a sealed pack of complimentary red balloons. They found a window table as far away from the kids as possible. Kerry laid out the extent of her investigation, and Ida was impressed. Kerry pulled out evidence and leads, a photo of her brother, a photo of Agent Hennessy she'd stolen from his house. She even told Ida about an encounter with another FBN agent that morning – Henry White – who'd strong-armed her, tried to pressure her into leaving town early. Was this the trauma Ida had seen on the girl when they'd first met at the motel? Ida asked her about the incident, if she was all right, but Kerry shrugged it off, claimed it hadn't bothered her. Ida could tell she was lying, but decided not to press her on it.

'They didn't manage to get this off me,' Kerry said, passing Ida a scrap of paper. 'It's the list the guard at Vacaville snuck out for me. The list of drug-trial participants who were visited by the same cop who visited my brother – Sam Cole.'

'Sam Cole?' Ida repeated, her heart kicking with surprise.

Kerry nodded.

Ida's mind raced. Sam Cole. The same fake cop who'd visited Riccardo, scared him so badly he went begging to Nick Licata to be bailed out of the Men's Central Jail. With that one name everything folded together, the facts from one case gliding into the gaps of the other.

'You know what's going on?' Kerry asked.

'I think so.'

Ida told her about Sam Cole's visit to Riccardo, how it spooked Riccardo into getting bailed out, and probably killed.

'So the same cop visited my brother in Vacaville and this Mob guy, too?' Kerry frowned. 'So it's to do with this cop somehow?'

'Yeah. And the thing is, Sam Cole isn't even a cop. He's doing this all on a fake ID. With what you've told me about Vacaville and the drug trials, I think I've finally figured out what he's been up to.'

'What?'

'You said your brother teamed up with Agent Hennessy as a witness to a case he was working on, right?'

'Right.'

'Let's say, as a starting assumption, the case they were working on had something to do with the drug trials in Vacaville. Maybe they were being run illegally and Hennessy heard about it. He's a Federal Bureau of Narcotics agent. It's his job to investigate stuff like that. Maybe he went down there to look into it. Undercover. With a fake ID because he doesn't want his name appearing on any prison visitor logs.'

Ida paused, stared at Kerry, waited for her to fill in the blanks.

'Sam Cole and Agent Hennessy are the same person,' Kerry said.

'I'd say so. Sam Cole's just a fake ID that Hennessy's been

using to cover his tracks. He recruited your brother to help him look into the drug trials, because your brother was a participant. He also visited Riccardo Licata in jail. For reasons as yet unknown. But what we can say is Agent Hennessy is what links everything together. He's at the heart of it all. My guess is, we find Hennessy, we find your brother, we find out what the hell's going on.'

They smiled at each other just as two kids dressed as astronauts ran up to their table.

'Ma'am, are you using those balloons?' the older of the two asked, pointing to the complimentary balloons on Ida's tray.

'Knock yourself out, kid,' Ida said.

The kids scooped up the balloons and ran off, screaming thanks over their shoulders. Ida watched them go, turned to look at Kerry, saw her expression was clouded with worry.

'This proves it's all a conspiracy,' Kerry said.

'Why d'you say that?'

Kerry considered. She took a piece of paper from her pocket, passed it over.

'It's the last one he ever sent me,' she said.

Ida unfolded the paper. It was a letter from Stevie. Ida read it. Noted the date. Noted the reference to Louisiana. To a conspiracy. She started drawing lines from the breakthrough they'd just made to the Night-Slayer, solving yet more mysteries.

Ida looked up at Kerry, saw by her expression that the girl had joined the dots in the exact same manner.

'You think one of the other drug-trial participants is the Night-Slayer?' Kerry asked. 'That's how it's all related to Louisiana? That's what Stevie meant in his letter?'

Ida nodded.

'A Vacaville inmate volunteers for an illegal drug trial,' she said. 'It sends him off the edge. He gets released and starts killing people. Your brother and Hennessy are investigating the trials, and they stumble on to the fact. Your brother gets so worried about what he's fallen into he sends you this letter in case anything happens to him.'

They stared at each other. All around them children screamed.

'Damn,' Ida muttered.

'What is it?'

'I got a bad feeling about something. You mind if I take this list over to the phone there? Make some calls?'

'Sure,' Kerry said.

Ida rose, crossed to the payphone in the alcove by the entrance. She called Feinberg at the Glass House. She gave him the names, the context.

'Shit,' he said, animated by the same worry. 'I'll get on it now. Call me back in ten minutes.'

Ida hung up, put a call through to Dante at the warehouse. Loretta picked up, told her that Dante was still running about on his skip-tracer case. Ida left a message for him to call her. She hung up, waited by the phone till it was time to call Feinberg back. She prayed she'd got it all wrong.

She took her cigarettes out and lit one up. She looked across the floor, at the kids, at the sea of red balloons being batted about, at Kerry, who was staring across to the two girls serving at the counter. Ida sensed a longing in her gaze. The two servers were Kerry's age. While they were selling tacos and hotdogs in California to make a living, Kerry was flying in and out of combat zones, seeing so much mutilated flesh she couldn't stand to eat meat any more. Ida studied Kerry's bearing, her scars, her forthright demeanor. Everything about her reminded Ida of Michael. It was uncanny. Or maybe it was just her mind playing tricks.

She called Feinberg back, and it was exactly as she had feared. They arranged a meet for an hour's time. She hung up, returned to the table.

'I just called Detective Feinberg, my friend at the LAPD,' she said. 'He called a friend of his at the Department of Corrections. He's got files on all five of the names on your list. We can head on over to him and pick them up. In the meantime, he gave me a quick rundown on the inmates. It explains why you couldn't find any of them when you were searching for them yesterday.'

'Why?'

'The three inmates on this list who were released. They've all been murdered. Someone's killing them off as soon as they're out. One by one.'

# PART ELEVEN

## DANTE

# 37

Dante sat in the Thunderbird staring across Ocean Avenue at the upmarket Santa Monica apartment buildings. It was the same coast as Venice, but a whole different world: rich and well-heeled and home to the man who could answer all the questions Dante needed answering. So he sat in the Thunderbird and waited. Smoked Luckies. Stroked the dog. Took in the view, kept an eye out for the black sedan or any other tails. He tried not to let his anxiety get the better of him. He had the meeting with Licata later on and he desperately needed answers before that.

The door to one of the apartment buildings opened and Johnny Roselli stepped out. He walked his old-man walk up Ocean Avenue, moving parallel to the beach. Giant gray hair swept back. French Tropicale sunglasses. A wool sweater tucked into his belt.

Roselli had made a career out of being the middleman between the Mob and the government. He'd teamed up the Mob and the CIA on the plan to assassinate Castro. He'd done legwork on the Kennedy hit. He'd helped finance their offshore banks. If the CIA had killed Riccardo in that house in the hills, Roselli would know about it. Which made it interesting that when Dante had been given the job, Roselli had been there, sitting next to Licata in the pool house, filling in the details, consoling, coaxing, lying through his teeth.

Dante got out of the Thunderbird and trotted toward him. The sand on the asphalt dulled his footsteps, allowing him to creep up on Roselli without the man realizing. When Dante was just behind Roselli, he spoke.

'Morning, Johnny.'

Roselli jumped.

'Jesus!' he said. 'You scared the shit out of me.'

'Good.'

Dante glared at him and Roselli realized he'd been rumbled.

'What is it?' Roselli asked, dissembling.

'You weren't on the up-and-up the last time we met.'

'Oh, yeah? How so?'

'Because I tracked Riccardo to a CIA safe house up in the hills. Where he was butchered. I've got a meeting with Nick Licata in a few hours. I tell him the CIA killed his son, he's gonna come straight for you. You think anyone's going to believe the Agency whacked a boss's son without you knowing about it?'

Roselli didn't seem to know where to put this information, tried to find a way through his befuddlement.

'I didn't know they were going to whack him,' he said eventually.

'But you knew something.'

'I had an idea. Look, let's sit down at least. I haven't even had my breakfast yet.'

Five minutes later they were sitting in the prime seats on the terrace of the Georgian, a towering art-deco hotel with orange railings and a teal-and-gold facade that somehow managed to straddle the divide between classy and kitsch. The Georgian was where celebrities and statesmen stayed when they came to Santa Monica, where Roselli drank his breakfast every morning.

Roselli and Dante both took out their cigarettes. Roselli loaded his into a holder. They lit up. They took in the view, neither wanting to be the first to speak. The hotel was just across from the beach, a palm-lined strip of soft sand, blue Pacific, benevolent sun. This was the Southern California of postcards and movies and magazine articles. It was what people in rainy cities across the country daydreamed of when their thoughts turned to running away to the golden state; the California of teenagers and suburbanites, of optimistic pop songs, of surfboards and Corvettes.

A waiter approached and Roselli ordered them both breakfast coffees with double cognacs on the side. As the waiter was leaving to get their drinks, he stopped and frowned at the dog, which was lying by Dante's feet.

'Sir, I'm sorry. We don't allow dogs in the restaurant.'

Dante and Roselli looked at each other.

'It's just a dog,' Roselli said.

'It's the rules, sir.'

Roselli grimaced with the confusion of a man whose life was seldom affected by 'the rules'. He swept his gaze from the waiter to Dante and back again.

'It's just a dog. We're not even in the restaurant, we're on the terrace.'

'The terrace is part of the restaurant, sir.'

'Oh, it's part of the restaurant, hunh?' Roselli mocked. 'Well, thanks for clearing that up for me, you little prick.'

'Johnny, cool it,' Dante said.

'No, fuck that. We're the only ones here,' Roselli said, gesturing to the empty terrace. He turned back to the waiter. 'The dog stays. You go inside, find out who the fuck I am, and then you come back out here and apologize, OK?'

Realization sparked on the waiter's face. He turned and walked back into the restaurant. Roselli sighed, shook his head in exasperation. But something rang false. It was all too theatrical. A performance for Dante's benefit, a power play to remind him of Roselli's clout. Dante had caught him on the back foot, and now Roselli was countering.

Dante turned to look into the restaurant. The waiter was conferring with someone behind the bar, who peered over at Roselli and said something to the waiter which made him blanch. Dante could see it even from a distance, even with his old man's eyesight, the way the color drained from the waiter's face. He inhaled, rushed back out onto the terrace.

'Mr Roselli, sir. I am deeply sorry. I didn't know it was you. Of course the dog can stay. And your drinks are on the house.'

'Good,' Roselli said. 'Now apologize.'

The waiter frowned.

'I did apologize, sir. I am very sorry for my rudeness.'

'I don't want you to apologize to me. I want you to apologize to the dog.'

'Sir?'

'Apologize to the fucking dog.'

'Johnny, lay off, OK?' Dante said.

Roselli ignored him, stared daggers at the waiter, who looked bewildered, embarrassed.

'You want me to apologize to the dog?'

'Yeah, I want you to apologize to the dog. What, are you deaf?'

The waiter looked from Roselli to Dante, back to Roselli. Eventually he swallowed, looked down at the dog.

'I apologize,' he muttered, directing the comment to the dog.

'Say it louder. I apologize for being a faggot asshole.'

The waiter swallowed again.

'I apologize for being a faggot asshole.'

'Good,' Roselli said. 'Now fuck off and get our drinks.'

The waiter turned, humiliated, and walked back into the restaurant.

'Jesus,' Roselli said. 'What a way to start the fucking day.'

Dante eyed him, considered calling him out on the way he'd just belittled the waiter. But there wasn't any point. The whole thing had been a pantomime. The more he dwelled on it, the more it would get Roselli's back up.

'So you gonna tell me what's going on?' Dante asked. 'And I don't want no con job this time. I'm on the clock. I need answers.'

Roselli sighed.

'About a year ago, one of the guys from the Agency who I've worked with in the past came to talk to me.'

'I want names. Details.'

'Big Jim O'Connell. He was the go-between on Operation Mongoose, when we were training up the Cubans down in Florida for the raids on Castro. He came to ask me about Riccardo. Vague shit. What he was up to, if he was moving product, if I knew who he was getting it from. O'Connell was asking questions and trying to hide why he was asking them. The usual CIA spook shit.'

'But you got a feel for what he was after?'

'Yeah, I got a feel. It was like he'd heard Riccardo was moving coke from south of the border, and he wanted to know who he was getting it from. I got the feeling he was more interested in the source than Riccardo.'

Roselli raised his eyebrows, pecked at his cigarette holder, challenging Dante to join the dots. Dante knew the CIA moved cocaine from Latin America through Mexico, using Mexican cartels as drug runners.

'O'Connell wanted to know if Riccardo was getting his coke from CIA-backed smugglers in Mexico?' Dante ventured.

Roselli nodded, suggesting he'd come to the same conclusion.

'Looks to me like the triangle sprung a leak.'

Dante frowned. The triangle was 'the triangle of death', a drug route the CIA and a group of Corsican drug smugglers had set up years ago as a way of funding the CIA's anti-Communist wars in Latin America. Dante had heard about it in the past from Roselli, from a few of the other bosses. It was the kind of thing even the most hardened of them were impressed by. Cocaine was produced in Latin America and shipped to Europe for sale, because there wasn't much of a market for it in the States. With the proceeds heroin was bought in Europe and shipped back to the States, because there definitely *was* a market for heroin in the States. With the profits from selling the heroin stateside, American weapons were purchased and sent to Latin America to aid the anti-Communist smugglers who'd produced the cocaine at the apex of the triangle.

Latin America, Europe, the States.

Cocaine, heroin, guns.

It had a perfect, gleaming geometry.

The triangle meant the CIA assets fighting the Communists in Latin America could swap cocaine for American weapons in a way that the Agency could deny all knowledge of. All they had to do was help set up the smuggling routes, the offshore banks, and turn a blind eye. And best of all, the whole thing financed itself. The CIA never had to dip into its pockets to fund its anti-Communist guerrilla wars, insurgencies, counter-revolutions.

Roselli's talk of a leak meant a CIA asset working in the triangle had started diverting product, sending cocaine to the States instead of Europe, and thus upsetting the triangle's perfect geometry.

'So Riccardo started buying coke off some CIA-backed smuggler who'd gone rogue,' Dante said. 'And then he was dumb enough to get busted by the LAPD. The spooks realized what was happening, and they whacked him before he could reveal anything.'

'Seems right.'

'Except Riccardo wasn't big-time. He was two-bit at best. If you're smuggling coke for the Agency, it means you've got clout, so why not hook up with someone big in the States? Why not move it through Florida? Or New Orleans?'

'Maybe the cocaine was being stolen by someone just as two-bit as Riccardo in the operation down south?' Roselli suggested. 'O'Connell came to me looking for leaks, for someone in the triangle that had gone on the skim.'

The waiter returned, set down their drinks, his head hung low. Roselli eyed him the whole time. The waiter didn't meet his gaze, left quickly. Dante took a sip of cognac, warming and sweet.

What Roselli had said about the CIA made logical sense, but

it didn't fit in with the rumor that Riccardo was an informer for the Federal Bureau of Narcotics. Roselli had said nothing about the FBN, which was interesting as the two super-agencies hated each other, even more than the FBN and the LAPD hated each other. While the CIA used drug smugglers to promote America's interests around the world, the Narcotics Bureau was tasked with taking down those very same drug smugglers. Also to promote America's interests around the world. The CIA set up drug routes, the FBN tore them down. Two different arms of the US government with directly clashing remits, fighting each other like Mafia families at war. The whole thing was a disjointed, colossal waste of government resources and taxpayer dollars. Was this what Riccardo had been caught up in? Was he a pawn in the battle between the two super-agencies? Was this an extra facet to the situation that Roselli didn't know about? Or was Roselli deliberately hiding it from him?

'How much of this have you shared with Licata?' Dante asked.

'How much do you think?' Roselli said. 'Nothing. I'm not ratting out O'Connell. I tell you, if I'm scared of anyone, it's those CIA guys. Crooked cops you can reason with. They're shady, but they got a code. Politicians, too. All they want is money, pussy and power. But those CIA guys? They make everyone else look like school kids. I'm telling you, Dante, they ain't human. It ain't just me that's scared of them. There's whole fucking countries that are scared of them.'

Dante looked at Roselli and in the harsh light of the morning sun he seemed old, frail, edgy. He was afraid of the people he'd wound up working with, fallen prey to the specter of the CIA, the fear they could instill, the same voodoo the Mob had used for decades. And just like the Mob their power came from the fact that they only existed in the shadows, on the edges of people's imagination.

'Or maybe you didn't say anything to Licata because you've

got those two grand jury indictments coming your way,' Dante suggested. 'And you're hoping O'Connell might pull some strings.'

Roselli paused. Dante tried to make out what he was thinking, but it was hard with those big sunglasses the old man always wore, their lenses like voids.

'Yeah, maybe that too,' Roselli said eventually. 'But here's a third possibility. Riccardo and Nick hated each other. I mean, they really fucking hated each other. Deep down. Nick hated what an embarrassment Riccardo was. And Riccardo hated how his pops didn't think he was boss material. They'd go months without talking. When Riccardo got arrested he didn't even call Nick for a lawyer, for bail, for a phone call to set the judge straight. And Nick just cut the kid loose, let him fend for himself. That's how great their relationship was. Riccardo lasted all of two months in jail before he was calling up his pops for bail, scared shitless. Why d'you think Riccardo didn't tell his pop he was moving jumbo-sized quantities of coke, Dante?'

'You tell me.'

'My theory – Riccardo was so pissed at Nick he was planning a coup. Wrestle the Mob away from the old man. Show him he really *was* boss material. Use this cocaine money, the spooks, to help him take over the whole of LA. It's exactly the kind of idiot move Riccardo would have thought was smart. So put yourself in my shoes, Dante. Why would I go and tell Licata what his son was up to, when it would put me in the shit with the Agency *and* destroy Licata too? You saw him that night at the party, hiding in the pool house so no one would see him crying. A fucking Mob boss, Dante, crying like a woman.'

'Come on, Johnny. He's lost his only son. Cut him a break.'

'Nah, fuck that. You don't cry, Dante. Ever. You think Luciano or Siegel or Genovese would ever be caught crying? It's pathetic, Dante. It disgusted me. And what's he crying about?

Riccardo? If it was me I'd be saying that five hundred gees bail money was the best I ever spent if it meant I got rid of the clown.'

Roselli took off his sunglasses, looked directly at Dante.

'So you think I'm going to tell Nick that his son probably got killed by the CIA? While he was plotting an attack on his own pop? I kept my mouth shut, Dante. And I kept it shut when Licata said he wanted to bring you in to find Riccardo, and I kept it shut when we had that get-together in the pool house. You're the only person I've told about this. 'Cos you're old school, Dante. You're a pro. You're one of the only ones left who's up to the task. So the real question is – what are *you* going to tell Nick when you meet him later today? You tell him the truth, and all hell breaks loose, just a few days before you're supposed to be heading off to that vineyard of yours. Maybe you end with the CIA on your back. You *don't* tell Licata the truth, maybe you end up with the Mob on your back. You're in exactly the same ass-backwards predicament as me. So ask yourself – who d'you want breathing down your neck for the rest of your life? The Mob? Or the CIA? I know who I'm pitching in with, Dante, because it's like I told you – those CIA guys ain't fucking human.'

# 38

As Dante drove crosstown to his meeting with Nick Licata he mulled over everything Roselli had told him, tried to decide if he should lie, or tell the truth. Could he really tell Licata that his own son died trying to usurp him? Should he mention Riccardo was possibly an informer? That he had probably been killed by the CIA? Was there any way of surviving the shitstorm that would be unleashed? The Mob and the cops were big. The FBI and FBN were bigger. The CIA was bigger still. It was like a pantheon, each god more powerful than the next. All of them warring and vengeful. All of them specters and spooks.

*Those guys ain't human, Dante.*

He rubbed his temples, still couldn't figure out what he should say to Licata. Roselli had been dismissive of the threat Licata posed, as if Licata crying meant he was weak. But Roselli was wrong. Licata having a breakdown meant he was dangerous. High emotions did that to people, turned them into live wires, loose cannons. Maybe Licata had wanted to patch things up with Riccardo, but he'd lost his chance. So Riccardo had died hating his pops, and now Nick was realizing that would haunt him for the rest of his days.

After a half-hour drive Dante arrived at the meet spot – a vast drive-in movie theater in East LA. He pulled up to the gates and saw they'd been left open. He looked around to make sure he hadn't been tailed, then he drove through into a giant field with a movie screen on one side, and a small building on the other where food and drinks were sold. As Dante slow-rolled the Thunderbird over the bumpy field, he was surprised to see the place was empty, save for a couple of cars parked near the building. At night it was normally packed, a pointless B-movie on the screen, dealers moving car-to-car selling kids dope, pills, booze, guns, whatever they wanted under the cover of dark.

But in the daytime the drive-in was busy as well, even though no films were screened, because it was the venue for what could only be described as a criminal swap meet, filled with boosters, burglars, muggers, looking to offload their goods to fences. Junkies turned up with stuff they'd stolen from warehouses and mansions, antique furniture, paintings worth a hundred grand they'd sell for a twenty-spot. Dante had been there once when an actor-turned-junkie was trying to hawk his Oscars for a hit. It felt so strange for no one to be there in that giant, empty field. Eerie. Like one of those TV shows about what the world would be like if the bomb ever went off. For the place to be deserted meant Licata must have shut up shop for the day. Like he wanted Dante alone in that desolate, grassy field. Suddenly Dante got the chilling feeling that he was about to get whacked. The drive-in had been used for executions in the past; it was a perfect spot for it.

He pulled up outside the building, killed the Thunderbird's engine, grabbed his Detective Special and slipped it into his jacket. He told the dog to stay in the car. He got out, walked around to the entrance and knocked. It was opened a few seconds later by Pete Toscano, a bear-sized, low-level schlub, with prison-inked forearms and a tan bowling shirt that didn't do his blotchy skin any favors.

'Dante the Gent,' Toscano grinned. 'How you doing? Come in. Nick's in the kitchen.'

Toscano led Dante down a corridor, through the dining area where the stolen goods were normally purveyed, on through to the kitchen. When Dante stepped inside he was blasted by a wave of heat. The kitchen was small, with a traditional brick-made pizza oven, and next to it, a rack of electric ovens, all of which were switched on full blast, their doors open, making the place feel like a sauna.

'Jesus,' Dante said, squinting.

In front of the oven doors two goons sat in chairs, wrapped up in blankets, bathing in the heat, bottles of vodka in their hands. Licata was sitting by the door to the storeroom, reading a racing form, not a drop of sweat on him. He gestured Dante over to a chair opposite. Dante sat and realized there was a cool breeze coming in from the storeroom door behind Licata.

'What the hell's going on?' Dante asked, gesturing to the two goons.

'Paolo and Marco,' Licata said. 'They've both got a Nalline test coming up. Normally they go to the sauna up the street, but it's closed. We said they could use this place.'

'What the hell's a Nalline test?'

'Department of Corrections use 'em to check parolees with dope convictions haven't fallen off the wagon. They measure your eye dilation, give you Nalline, measure your dilation again. But you can fool the test with severe dehydration. Hence Paolo and Marco trying to give themselves heatstroke.'

Licata shrugged – it was all in a day's work. One of the goons took a long swig of his vodka bottle.

'So?' Licata asked.

Dante took out his Luckies as a way to buy a few seconds, because he still wasn't sure which way to play it.

'I don't know what to say, Nick. I'm coming up short. It looks like Riccardo went to his office after he got released, made a bunch of calls to a payphone up in Bel Air, on the hour, every hour, like he was arranging a meet with someone he was expecting to be at the payphone. After that, the trail disappears. My guess is whoever answered that payphone knows what happened to him. Who that is – no one knows. I thought if I could find out who was supplying Riccardo with his coke, maybe I could find out what happened to him. But no one knows anything. I spoke to everyone I can think of. I spoke to a pal on the Narcotics Squad and they're as stumped as we are. No one's talking, Nick, because no one knows.'

Dante shrugged, looked over at the sweating goons.

'Then I thought maybe I'm looking at this all wrong,' he continued. 'Maybe it's not to do with the coke, maybe it's to do with the company he was running – Ocean Movies – but I looked into that too, and I came up short again. You ask me – Riccardo got involved with some out-of-towners bringing in coke and they're the ones who know what happened to him. Aside from all that, I don't know what to say, Nick. This one's too much for me.'

Dante finished his spiel, looked Licata in the eye. He'd just lied to the man. He could have told him the truth and it would have offered Nick some consolation, he could have started grieving for his son. But Dante hadn't. He'd lied, like a coward.

'You sure that's all you've learned?' Licata asked, eyes narrow.

Dante suppressed the urge to swallow, to look away, to twitch. Licata knew he was lying, knew he was holding back.

'That's all I've learned,' Dante said, managing to keep his tone even. 'But I'll keep digging, Nick. Someone out there must know something.'

Licata continued to stare at him and Dante saw a coldness in the man's eyes, could almost see it frosting over his whole being. Dante was sweating in the heat, Licata didn't have a drop on him.

'When did you say you were signing those vineyard contracts?' Licata asked.

'If all goes well, the twenty-sixth.' Dante tried to speak as nonchalantly as he could, but the mention of his retirement plan was a threat, and they both knew it.

'And you think you'll get this job wrapped up for me before that?' Licata asked. 'Because Riccardo's next court date is also on the twenty-sixth.'

'Sure.'

Licata continued making small eyes at Dante, tapping the racing form against the edge of the table.

'You know how all these junkies come here selling shit they've jacked,' Licata said. 'Shit you wouldn't believe. Last week, a pair came in. Real fucking bozos. Had a pallet of smokes they'd boosted from one of our own trucks. Pete tells me what's going on. So I come down, check out the merch. We know for sure they've stolen it from us. And now they're here, trying to sell it back to us. It wasn't a power move or nothing, they were just too stupid to know who they'd pinched 'em from. So we're asking 'em – did you boost these from such-and-such a truck, on such-and-such a night? And you see it in their eyes, they realize what they've done. But instead of admitting it, they start lying. Lying right to my face. In front of everyone. *Nah, nah. It was another truck, another night.* Now, we didn't give a shit about them jacking some smokes. I mean, it's funny if you think about it, being so fucking stupid they tried to sell 'em back to us. We'd probably slap 'em around a bit. Maybe bump one of 'em off real quick for the look of the thing. But it was the lying I couldn't take. The disrespect. So me and Pete fire up the ovens. That traditional brick-built one goes up to nine hundred degrees. We hold 'em down, stick their hands inside, one by one. You should have heard 'em scream. Crying for their mothers. And the way their skin turned black. Looked like niggers from the elbow down.' Licata paused, remembering the incident. 'It was because they lied, Dante.'

Dante felt a chill ripple through him.

'So, with that unfortunate episode in mind,' Licata said, 'I'll ask you again. You sure you've told me everything you know?'

Again Dante tried not to make any moves which would reveal to Nick he was lying, not even the tiniest twitch. And he knew when he spoke his voice had to be level, couldn't falter.

'I've told you everything, Nick.'

Dante could hardly breathe as he waited for Licata to reply.

'Then keep searching,' he said. 'I want this wrapped up by the twenty-sixth.'

# PART TWELVE

## LOUIS

# 39

The Luau was located at 421 North Rodeo Drive. Built as part of the Tiki craze in the 1950s, it was packed with waterfalls, totem poles, reed screens and secluded alcoves. There was even a moat around the place and a bridge to get over it. 'Hawaii without the volcanoes,' the owner liked to joke.

Yet despite its kitschiness, it was one of the trendiest eateries in LA. The Hollywood elite hung out there, Steve McQueen and his bikers pals hung out there, Johnny Roselli and his mobster crowd hung out there, and because of its location opposite Joe Glaser's ABC offices, most of the agents and artists connected to Louis' management agency hung out there, too. Although that particular lunchtime, as Louis waited for his manager to cross the road, traverse the moat and join him at a booth, the clientele seemed to be mostly high-school girls from Beverly Hills, movie-brat children of the city's richest and most powerful men.

Louis stared out of the windows onto the intersection of Rodeo and Brighton Way. The winter sun shone, traffic rumbled past, rich women took their migraines for a walk, touting trophy dogs and facelifts. Glaser had picked a good spot when he'd moved the talent management agency out to LA in the '40s. Even though back then the agency had specialized in managing only black artists, Glaser located the office here, in the heart of white Los Angeles, to reassure his customers that even though they were booking black talent, it was white people who'd be handling the business end. It was a play for legitimacy, Louis supposed. Maybe that was something Glaser craved. Being a Chicago Jew he was hardly on the inside himself.

Since the move Glaser had diversified, which meant attracting white stars onto the books – from Louis and Billie Holiday in the early days on to the likes of Barbra Streisand, Noël Coward and Bob Hope. When the State Department organized international music tours as part of its cultural diplomacy against the Soviets, Joe Glaser helped arrange them. It was quite the rise from his gangland beginnings back in the 1920s, running a prostitution ring and a nightclub for Al Capone – the Sunset Café – where Louis and his pals had been the house band.

A few years after Louis and Glaser had met there, Louis was damaged goods, with gangsters, record companies and an ex-wife hounding him. He had spent months hiding out from them in Paris and New York before calling up Glaser and making him an offer – get the mobsters and lawyers off my back and we go into business together. A strange offer considering the closest Glaser had ever been to a talent manager before that was promoting fixed boxing matches back in Chicago. But Louis knew even then that the music industry was a shark tank, which meant you needed your own shark. And Glaser was it.

The partnership spun them meteorically through the century, from poverty and crime on the streets of Depression-era Chicago, to controlling the third-largest theatrical agency in the country and traveling the world as government-endorsed 'cultural ambassadors'. It was a long history the two men shared, and now Louis had to summon up the courage to tell the man that he might retire, that maybe his career was over. It probably wouldn't affect Glaser that much – he had all those white stars on the books now. But Louis still felt he'd be letting him down.

A couple of minutes passed and Joe Glaser entered, walking his old-man walk, head stooped these days, like it was weighed down with too many memories.

He spotted Louis, came over and sat.

'How are you doing? Flight in OK?' Glaser asked in his serrated Chicago tones.

'Sure, boss. All good.'

Glaser smiled. 'I had one of the girls update the itinerary for your stay.'

He pulled out a sheet of paper, passed it over. Louis appreciated this about Glaser. No preamble, no bullshit. Just business. Louis scanned the itinerary. Rehearsals for the *Steve Allen Christmas Special*, then doing the show itself, flying out to Vegas for a week of dates at the Tropicana, one of the Mob casinos out there, where Lucille would join him, then studio time to record a new song, then back to LA, then back to NY. A grueling couple of weeks even for a man half Louis' age.

'What's this recording time you've booked in for Bill Porter's place?' Louis asked.

'It's a new song Bob Thiele sent over. I think it'll be good for you.'

Louis nodded. He knew what the sessions would entail – he'd finish his midnight show at the Tropicana, then head over to Bill Porter's United Recording studio to record through the night and into the morning. The place was near a freight line, meaning the whistles of the trains going past ended up being captured on the tapes, meaning the sessions were stop–start at best.

Glaser must have sensed Louis wasn't relishing the prospect.

'It'll be a hit, Louis,' he said. 'Trust me. The biggest of your career. It'll be "Hello, Dolly" all over. I wasn't wrong then, and I'm not wrong now. I'll have a copy of the sheets sent over to you.'

Louis nodded again. 'Hello, Dolly'. Back in '63 he hadn't recorded anything for a couple of years when a music publisher convinced Glaser that Louis should record the title song to a new Broadway show by an up-and-coming songsmith called Jerry Herman. Even though it was just done as a favor, Louis and the band were glad to be back in the studio. But they didn't think much of the tune when they read the sheet music. Louis had shaken his head in dismay. They all preferred the B-side. They recorded it in a day and went back on tour.

It was only Glaser who liked the recording. 'It'll be a fucking hit,' he exclaimed when he heard the acetate. Optimistic considering the charts had been dominated by rock and Motown for years already.

But Glaser had been right. The song started getting heavy airplay, coast to coast. Copies flew off the shelves. Glaser called up Louis on tour and told him he had the biggest hit of his career on his hands, that he should add the song to his nightly repertoire. But weeks had passed since they'd recorded it, and neither Louis nor anyone else in the band could remember how the song went. They failed to find a copy in the local record stores, so had one sent out to them from New York. When they finally listened to it again they still didn't think much of it. After the recording session the engineer had added a heavier rhythm section to it, strings, and a banjo of all things, so the released version sounded even quainter. But when they played it at their concert that night they had to take eight curtain calls, and it was only then that they realized.

'Hello, Dolly' kept on getting radio play, kept on selling. It knocked the Beatles off the top of the charts, sold three million copies, became the biggest hit of Louis' career by a mile. And it wasn't even close to being a jazz tune. Louis became a regular on TV – the *Tonight Show*, the *Dick Cavett Show*, the *Ed Sullivan Show*, the *Dean Martin Show*. He was everywhere.

That was four years ago now, and nothing could ever top it. Louis was sixty-seven years old, he'd been working as a musician since he was twelve. He was lucky to have scored his biggest hit at the tail-end of his fifty-year career, the oldest act ever to have a number one. There wouldn't be another, not now he was even further into his sunset days. Why jeopardize his health for just another tune?

'Everything all right?' Glaser asked. 'You don't seem your usual self.'

Now was the time to tell him about the doctor's appointment. The doctor's secretary had called the Marmont that morning to confirm it for the next day.

'Yeah, just a bit of jet lag,' Louis said.

Glaser frowned. 'You sure that's all it is?'

It was remarkable the way Glaser did it, how he could make his voice both threatening and cajoling at the same time. It reminded Louis of their old boss, Capone, who also had a threatening gentleness that left you unsure if you were his best friend, or if he was about to put a knife in your back.

Louis nodded, felt like a chickenshit yet again, wondered why it was such an effort just to tell people. It wasn't as if his manager didn't know he'd had to cancel those tours earlier that year on health grounds. He looked Glaser over and was reminded that they were similar in age. If Louis was falling apart, Glaser probably was too, no matter how much he persisted with the Chicago tough-guy act.

A waiter arrived, handed them menus. Glaser ordered steak Bora Bora, Louis Tahiti shrimp. Neither of them ordered alcohol because Glaser was teetotal and Louis didn't feel comfortable drinking around him.

The front doors opened and two men stepped in who Louis pegged straight away as security goons. Their gunslinger walks, the way their gazes swept the room like scythes. They turned to the doors behind them, ushering in two other men, both vaguely familiar. When the maître d' spotted them, he rushed over, fawned, ushered them to one of the prime tables.

As they sat, Louis realized who the first one was – Governor Reagan. Dressed in a tan suit and burgundy necktie. And then he finally realized who the governor's lunch companion was – Sidney Korshak. Ostensibly a corporate lawyer, Korshak was the legal counsel for Glaser's management company, with his own office on the top floor of the building, and a private elevator behind a gold curtain on the second floor to get to it.

But Korshak was also the legal counsel for some of the country's biggest corporations, biggest labor unions, and most of its mobsters. A combo that made him the *éminence grise* of the entertainment world, able to shut down both Hollywood and Vegas if he ever felt like it. As the legitimate face of organized crime he brokered deals between the underworld, the unions and the conglomerates, especially the ones who ran the entertainment industry. Just like Korshak had a hand in Glaser's agency, he also had a hand in MCA, the biggest management agency of them all until it moved into production a few years before. MCA was run by some of Glaser and Capone's mobster pals from back in Chicago and was responsible for Governor Reagan's career, both in the movies, and afterwards in politics; it was MCA and its mobsters who'd bankrolled Reagan's successful bid for president of the Screen Actors Guild and then the California governorship.

'Korshak and the governor are pals, hunh?' Louis said.

He turned to look at Glaser, who was studying the men with an annoyed expression.

'Korshak helped Reagan out on a land deal last year.'

'What land deal?' Louis asked, lighting a cigarette.

'Reagan used to own a ranch up in Malibu,' Glaser said. 'Acres of hill land good for nothing but riding horses. After he got elected governor last year, he decided to sell it. Twentieth Century Fox made a bid because their lot adjoins the land. The idea was they were going to expand and build new studio space on it. Except it turns out the land isn't suitable – too rocky and hilly, like anyone with a pair of eyes could have told them before they bought it. So they've never bothered developing it. And then it turns out that Fox paid more than double the going rate – eight thousand dollars an acre. The county appraised it at less than four thousand. And then it turns out a bunch of the executives at Fox helped bankroll Reagan's bid to run for governor. And then it turns out one of the first things Reagan does when he's governor is institute the biggest tax cut in California history specifically to benefit the studios. Somewhere in amongst all the paperwork Sid Korshak was involved, like he always is. Using a dummy corp in Delaware, an offshore bank.'

Glaser shrugged. Louis got the sense that he disapproved of Korshak, or his political dealings, at least. Strange to be so disapproving of your company's own legal counsel. Louis wondered if there was something else going on between them. He turned from his manager to study the man sitting with the governor. Korshak was tall and handsome, with sleepy eyes that belied what must have been a predatory character; his hair was thinning and gray and brushed back from a receding hairline. As Glaser and Louis stared, Korshak looked up and spotted them both. He nodded at Glaser, lifting a finger to tip an imaginary hat.

Glaser nodded in return then he and Louis turned their attention back to their own table. They chatted their way through the bottle of water and the entrees, talking about everything except their health. The whole time they chatted, Louis couldn't stop thinking about the men sitting a few tables further along. Louis had been planning to ask Glaser if he knew anything about Karl Drazek, the TV producer Ida was looking for. Louis had been asking around but had kept on coming up blank. Drazek had disappeared off the face of the earth. But now that Louis had seen Korshak and Reagan, he thought better of asking Glaser. Drazek worked for Universal Television, which was owned by MCA, the same gangster-run conglomerate that Korshak and Reagan were connected to.

Maybe it was just his old man's mind seeing things that weren't there, or maybe there was a conspiracy at work, one that took them all in. Either way, something about the manner in which everything in LA was linked made Louis wary, sent a wave of chilling fear right through him. He drew a mental line from himself to Glaser to Korshak to Reagan – from the jazz musician to the ex-Capone stooge to the gangland lawyer to the governor of California. This lashing together of entertainment, organized crime, politics, the bilking of the taxpayer, all done so brazenly, so openly. If Louis' impending appointment with the doctor wasn't enough to fuel his burgeoning pessimism, this mesh in which he'd been ensnared would have done it just fine on its own.

# PART THIRTEEN

## IDA & KERRY

# 40

Ida and Kerry drove in convoy to a store so Kerry could buy cellophane and tape to fix up the car window that White and his men had broken. Then they drove over to a bar downtown to meet Ida's cop friend. Ida went in and Kerry sat in her car and waited, looking around for any sign of White and his goons. On top of the incident with them that morning, Ida's revelations about the Night-Slayer had further set Kerry on edge. If the Vacaville inmates who'd taken part in the drug trial were on a kill list, then surely Stevie must be on it, too.

After about ten minutes Ida stepped back out with a folder in her hand, got into the Cutlass next to Kerry.

'All right,' Ida said, skimming through the paperwork. 'I got some more info on the three inmates who died. Henderson and Rawls were both killed in hit-and-runs. Paxton was knifed to death in a suspected burglary. All not long after their release. All of it suspicious as hell. Someone's definitely trying to cover up the Night-Slayer's connection to those drug tests. Paxton's room-mate told the cops that a few days before he was killed someone claiming to be a policeman visited him and after the visit he was nervy as hell. The policeman matches Hennessy's description. Looks like Hennessy turned up there with his fake police ID to warn Paxton he was in danger. After that, Paxton was too scared to leave the house, which is probably why they killed him in a staged burglary rather than a hit-and-run like the other two. Anyway, the room-mate also said Hennessy had someone with him in his car. Someone younger who matches Stevie's description. If we can trust the room-mate, it means Hennessy and Stevie are definitely working together. Which means Stevie's under Hennessy's protection.'

Kerry mulled this over, feeling some reassurance that Stevie wasn't alone.

'It also means it's less likely Stevie's the Night-Slayer,' she said. 'Hennessy wouldn't be working with him if he was a killer.'

Ida nodded. 'It's leaning that way.'

'So what do we do?'

'We go after the two inmates who escaped from Vacaville – Ronnie Mouzon and Pete Cooper – they're assumed to be at large somewhere in the state. The police have issued BOLOs for them, that's *be on the lookout for*. They were visited by Hennessy in Vacaville. They managed to hightail it before they were bumped off. If we find one of them they might point us in Hennessy and Stevie's direction. Maybe they can point us to the Night-Slayer, too. You never know, one of these two escapees might actually *be* the Night-Slayer. That's if we can find them, and if you want us to work together?'

The question surprised Kerry, she'd assumed they already were.

'Sure I do,' she replied.

'Good.'

Ida smiled at her, then looked down to skim through more paperwork.

'So, the two escapees. Mouzon was caught dope dealing in sixty-two and sixty-seven. Picked up in street stings by the Narc Squad both times. Two stretches in Folsom. Don't know how he ended up in Vacaville. Cooper had a string of juvenile misdemeanors; assaults and petty thefts mainly, and then a few public-order offenses up in San Francisco. Then he got sent to Salinas Valley after getting high on STP and trying to set fire to a police station. From there he was transferred to Vacaville. Also in the file are both men's KAs, that's *known associates*. There's nine of them.

Add in next-of-kin and previous addresses, we're looking at six-teen different locations to visit.'

Ida passed Kerry the papers. She flicked through Cooper and Mouzon's rap sheets, their long criminal histories. Then she flicked through the details of their KAs. They were all underbelly and just as bad as Cooper and Mouzon themselves, with histories of dealing and rape, barroom brawling, knife-fighting, street rob-bery, assault. Somehow none of them were currently in prison. A stroke of luck for Kerry and Ida, misfortune for society at large.

'One last thing,' Ida said. 'We're going to visit these addresses in convoy. I want you to park a little way back from each one and stay in your car while I do the talking. That's so they don't spot you or your car. If I feel anyone I'm talking to might know where Cooper and Mouzon are, that maybe they're going to try and con-tact them, warn them, I'll give you a signal. The signal means you stay where you are and follow them, see where they go.'

'What's the signal?'

'I'll drop my keys on the ground when I'm getting back into my car. All right?'

'Sure.'

Two minutes later they were on the move. Cooper and Mouzon's known associates were spread all over the city – the freight depot at Hobart Yard, the kitchens of the Riviera Country Club, hotel rooms on Skid Row, salvage yards where packs of slobbering Dobermanns were kept in wire cages in the full glare of the sun. From the hills to the flats to the canyons to the coast. The day filled itself once more with freeways and streets, traffic and smog, cigarettes and radio stations playing jazz, pop, blues, Motown. A disjointed soundtrack to a disjointed city. The cellophane Kerry had taped over the broken window shuddered, rattled, and tapped. The sun bounced off road signs and cars, each reflection glinting briefly as Kerry drove past, like the city was tracing out her route in fragmentary flashes, signaling something in those echoes.

At one point they drove past the giant concrete donut on the roof of the Big Donut Drive-In, and Kerry smiled when she saw the landmark. After that she started spotting other roofs likewise adorned: a milk bar sporting a giant cow; a Mexican joint, a giant sombrero. Elsewhere other blown-up ephemera littered the skyline – cowboy boots, TV dinners, Saran Wrap, packs of Marlboro Red, steaming cups of coffee. Like the city was lifting them heavenwards, offerings to a consumer sky-god.

It wasn't till late in the afternoon they hit gold – an address in Watts listed as the home of Paul Brockhalt, a known associate of both Cooper and Mouzon. Kerry parked a way back; Ida right opposite.

Kerry watched as Ida crossed the street toward a large wooden house with a banner over the garage reading: *Home of the 'Watts Free Press'*. The garage door was open and a half-dozen black men were moving boxes from the shadows of the garage and loading them up into a van that was parked on the driveway.

Ida spoke to some of the men, who pointed her toward another man – Brockhalt, presumably – further back, near the mouth of the garage. He was young and mousey, dressed in a T-shirt and jeans with big hair and a bigger scowl. Kerry tried to square the man with his rap sheet – spells in Folsom for drug busts and a knife-fight. But he looked more like a student than a thug.

Ida spoke to Brockhalt, and Kerry saw how his posture turned taut and guarded. But after a few seconds he held up a hand and he and Ida disappeared into the shadows of the garage. Kerry got her cigarettes out and smoked and watched the men filling up the van with the boxes. They all sported a similar look to Brockhalt; their hair left to grow long, their T-shirts a garish splash of colors. She could have pegged them as hippies if it wasn't for their purposeful air. Despite the casual clothing, there was something pointed to the way they moved: motivated, focussed, drilled. They reminded her of the black servicemen she'd nursed over in Vietnam, making her wonder if any of them had been in the war.

If they'd taken the skills and discipline they'd learned in the army and brought them back home, using them to organize enterprises like the *Watts Free Press*, whatever that was.

The men finished filling up the van. One of them hopped into the cab and drove it off while the rest of them returned to the garage. Kerry looked about the neighborhood. Further along was a row of shuttered-up shops, blackened by fire damage, their roofs partially collapsed. She wondered if they'd been destroyed during the race riots a couple of years previously. She'd watched the riots on TV back in Louisiana, not long before she'd joined the Air Force. Running battles across the neighborhood, entire streets set ablaze, the National Guard called in. She'd seen talking heads on news programs blame the riot on the heatwave, the full moon, the tides, a passing meteor. Hardly any discussion of the poverty, despair and racism prevalent in Watts. Only once did she see it mentioned that the residents of the neighborhood were denied insurance on commercial properties, so they couldn't start their own businesses; were denied mortgages, so they couldn't even own their own homes.

It had shocked Kerry at the time, but now race riots were commonplace. That summer just gone had been dubbed 'The Long Hot Summer' because of the riots — over a hundred and fifty of them — that had taken place in cities across the country, though not, for some reason, in Watts. By then Kerry was in Vietnam and the racial strife was even being felt over there, with black and white servicemen segregating themselves, antagonizing each other, fighting. Increasingly she was transporting servicemen who'd been injured by their fellow soldiers in racial brawls.

But 'The Long Hot Summer' had also been dubbed 'The Summer of Love' on account of the hippie revolution in California. How could the single same summer go down in history with two such opposite nicknames? Which would win out in the end?

About ten minutes later Ida re-emerged under the watchful eye of Brockhalt and a few of the others. As she approached her

Cadillac, she lifted her keys to the door and fumbled them. They dropped and she scooped to pick them up. It only took a couple of seconds and looked completely natural. She got in her car and drove off, and Kerry was surprised to feel a spike of panic as she was left alone.

The men went back inside, and Kerry waited, suddenly feeling incredibly exposed, conspicuous, white. She slumped down in her seat. She waited the rest of the afternoon, the entire time praying someone didn't walk past and ask what the hell a white girl was doing there. She chained cigarettes, tried to contain her edginess. She wondered why Ida had found Brockhalt suspicious enough to signal that Kerry needed to follow him. Was Brockhalt harboring the Night-Slayer? Would he lead Kerry right to him? Or to Stevie?

Kerry watched a blood-orange sunset daub the sky, then the blue of night came on, smothering the street. More time passed. Eventually people began leaving the house, among them Brockhalt. He scanned his surroundings, looking for potential tails perhaps, then headed off toward his car, a beaten-up Dodge Dart. He got in and hauled south, then east, then north, driving in a hook till he hit the Harbor Freeway. It was only then that Kerry realized how cut off Watts was from the rest of the city. Los Angeles was lashed together by freeways, but in Watts it was as if the road network was being used to enclosed the neighborhood, to wall it off, let it stew, foment, distill. No wonder there'd been a race riot.

On the freeway the traffic was thick. Rain started to fall. Tiny drops that turned the city slick. Kerry felt their coolness on the side of her face and realized the rain was making its way into the car, through the cellophane she'd stretched over the broken window.

They hooked north for ten miles then Brockhalt turned off the freeway and zigzagged through side streets until he approached a night market on a cobbled street. He parked and hopped out.

Kerry pulled in just further on and followed him. It was like they were in a Mexican village from the old Wild West, with stalls lining the streets selling tourist souvenirs – Mexican dresses, serapes, ponchos, pottery, glass dolls.

They walked up the street, past bearded vagrants in baggy clothes sheltering under awnings. They came out onto a square with a fountain and a statue and an old Spanish Mission church. Brockhalt walked over to a stall selling Mexican food and greeted the man behind it. The stallholder filled a paper bag with food, then slipped something into it from somewhere underneath the stall, something too small to be a gun. Brockhalt paid the man and filtered back through the crowd, and Kerry fell in behind him.

Back into their cars, driving through the city once more. Through Chinatown, onto the Pasadena Freeway, Chavez Ravine, the Golden State Freeway, the Glendale Freeway, with raindrops at sixty miles an hour flinging themselves at Kerry through the now completely compromised cellophane window.

They drove another six or seven miles. They hit Glendale and it seemed nice enough. They hit the back streets and it plummeted downmarket. Brockhalt turned on to a decrepit-looking street in the foothills, pulled up outside a decrepit-looking house. Kerry drove past and stopped a block and a half further up. She walked back down the street, over sidewalks padded with yellow leaves loosened from the trees by the rain. She passed the house. She noted the number, the street name. She noted the car in the drive, its license plate.

The house was on a corner, and from a window on its side, light spilled out. Net curtains were drawn across the window, but not completely. In the gap Kerry could make out a stove, a refrigerator, a slice of kitchen table. She could see Brockhalt pacing around. After a minute or two she caught a glimpse of two other men, who till that point had kept well away from the windows. One of them matched Ronnie Mouzon's description. The man Agent Hennessy had visited in Vacaville before his escape.

Kerry walked back to her car, wondering if the man she'd seen was the Night-Slayer. She sat in the Cutlass and waited. The night rain drenched her. She listened to its cutlery sound on the roof of the car. She watched it mist against the hills, the lightning splash against the mountains.

She imagined the rain filling the landscape till it was flooded, till a bayou formed, lapping against the houses, with road signs and telephone poles rising up out of the water, with street lights refracting off its surface, and further on, in the shadows, her father's body, floating face down. On the day they'd found him, she'd put her arms around Stevie, clasping him tight, keeping her own tears in check by wiping away his, promising that she'd never let him go.

An hour or so later the front door opened and tossed a fan of yellow light across the unkempt lawn. Brockhalt stepped out and drove off in his Dodge. The rain stopped shortly thereafter. Kerry found a payphone, called Ida and told her what had happened.

'You sure you're in Glendale?' Ida asked.

'Yeah, I'm sure. Why?'

'Glendale's a sundown town. No black people allowed on the streets after seven.'

Kerry frowned, wondering why Mouzon and his pal had hidden out somewhere like that.

'I'll be there in half an hour,' Ida said, putting down the phone.

Kerry walked back to the car, smoked her last cigarette. She stared at the puddles the rain had formed on the dash, their surfaces cradling reflections of the clouds scudding by overhead, the foothills looming over the street. She watched drops trickle down the curve of the steering wheel. She felt that same despairing loneliness come over her, the fear she'd never see Stevie again. It loomed like the foothills. It passed like the clouds.

\*

Half an hour later Ida pulled up and Kerry got out and went over to her car.

'Good work,' Ida said.

Kerry smiled.

'Are we going in there to talk to them?' she asked.

Ida nodded, but in a guarded way.

'Ideally I wouldn't go in there at night with just the two of us,' she said. 'But the clock's against us. They could be getting ready to move hide-outs, and then we'd lose them. I'm willing to risk it if you are?'

'Sure.'

'Good. I don't want to be hanging around on these streets too long. This is the most racist place in LA. It's where the American Nazi Party's headquartered. You got your gun on you?'

'Yeah.'

'You know how to use it?'

'I had weapons training in Vietnam.'

'Then let's go.'

# 41

Ida and Kerry approached Mouzon's hide-out and Ida got a look at it for the first time: a tumbledown bungalow with chipped paint, a brown lawn and a half-collapsed fence. The neighboring houses were maintained to a similar standard. Running behind them, parallel to the street, was an earthen bank studded with bushes that rose up to support a section of elevated road.

They walked up to the front door and knocked. There was no answer, only the noise of the cars roaring past on the elevated road behind the house. They waited, knocked again, waited again.

'Who that?' a voice called eventually from the other side of the door.

Ida imagined Mouzon and maybe the other man Kerry had told her about standing behind the door, both holding guns. She stepped to the side, gestured for Kerry to do the same.

'Sir, my name's Ida Young. I'm a private investigator. I spoke to your pal Paul Brockhalt earlier today. I'm trying to find a killer who attacked someone I know.'

She waited for Mouzon to respond. He didn't. She decided to take a chance on the possibility that he might already know there was a killer after him and his fellow inmates.

'This killer's looking for you, too, Ronnie,' she said. 'And I think you know that. If you let me talk to you, I can offer you help, advice, money, a safer place to stay. All I'm asking is to come in and talk. Think about it. If I found you so easy, you think the man who killed all those other inmates from Vacaville won't find you so easy, too?'

She waited. About twenty seconds passed in silence before the voice from behind the door spoke again.

'Why don't you get the fuck off my property?'

Ida considered.

'We both know it's not your property, Ronnie,' she said. 'Black people can't own property in Glendale. And even if they could, I still wouldn't go anywhere because I've got all the advantages here. I can stay where I am and send my friend over to the payphone down the street to call the cops. Which would leave you with two choices. You come out shooting, or you jump out the back window and disappear, but this time with no hide-out and no car. Just think of the hassle. But you let me in and we talk, I can leave you the two hundred bucks I got in my purse and then I'm gone.'

Again there was silence, although this time Ida thought she could hear whispering on the other side of the door, the two voices conferring.

'How about you slide that two hundred bucks under the door and then we talk?'

'Sure. I trust you.'

Ida took the money from her purse, kneeled, and slid it under the door. She looked at Kerry and shrugged. They waited. The door opened a sliver. Mouzon looked at her through the gap. He matched his description – tall, light-skinned, green-eyed. But his eyes were glazed, his face puffy. Over his slight frame he wore a beige terrycloth dressing gown. Ida wondered if this was the Night-Slayer. When he saw the guns Ida and Kerry were holding, he came over suspicious.

'You'd have them too if you were in our position,' Ida said. 'We're just two women, Ronnie. And we just want to talk.'

He considered. He shrugged. He opened the door. He had a .38 in his hand, down by his side. Standing next to him was a tall black man in a T-shirt and jeans, the same age as Mouzon, same type of gun in his hand.

Mouzon gestured for Ida and Kerry to follow him. They walked through a dingy hallway into a lounge at the rear of the house that was scattered with beer cans and fast-food wrappers. There was a faint metallic tang of car fumes in the room – probably coming in from the elevated road that ran behind the house. On the coffee table, in amongst the ashtrays and cigarette butts, was dope paraphernalia. Ida looked at Mouzon again, realized he was high, had probably shot up not too long before she'd arrived. Hence his eventual acquiescence. You could rely on junkies opting for the path of least resistance.

'Take a seat if you can find one,' he said, slumping down into an armchair.

Kerry cleared a space for them on the sofa and they sat. Ida kept her gun in her hand, resting it on her lap. Mouzon put his .38 on the coffee table in front of him. His associate went over to the window and perched himself on the sill, slipped his gun into his belt, crossed his arms and glared at them.

It was only then Ida noticed the shotgun in the corner, stood upright on its butt, leaning against the wall. An Ithaca 12-gauge. Police issue. A carton of shells on the carpet next to it. Four people in the room, five guns. She turned back to Mouzon. He eyed her, and then out of nowhere, his face jerked, like he was winking, but more extreme, involuntary, painful. He grabbed a can of beer from a side table and chugged it, like the alcohol would keep the tic at bay. When he put the can down he stared at Ida the way junkies did, slant-eyed, so it was impossible to tell what they were thinking.

After a moment he turned to look at Kerry, studied her.

'What the fuck happened to your face?'

Kerry's eyes narrowed.

'Napalm.'

'No shit,' Mouzon muttered, his surprise leaking out through the haze of dope and booze that hung between him and the world. 'You been out in Vietnam?'

Kerry nodded.

Mouzon raised his beer in mock salute, took a sip. His associate continued to sit by the window, but was peering out of it now, looking across the rear garden, keeping sentry, or maybe waiting for someone to arrive. Ida wondered again why these black men had holed up in Glendale, where they could be arrested just for being on the street after dark. There was a black neighborhood in Pasadena, just ten minutes away. Was the associate looking out for racist neighbors? Or were they waiting for more associates? People to come in and help them kill Ida and Kerry. They'd brought them to a room at the back of the house, which would be the best place for it.

'So what did you come here to ask?' Mouzon said.

Ida turned, studied him, tried to think of the best way to ease into things.

'When you were up in Vacaville, you had a visit from a cop called Sam Cole,' she began, using the fake name Hennessy employed.

She passed him the photo of Hennessy.

'Yeah, that's him,' Mouzon said. 'He came up to see me a couple of times.'

'What did he come to talk to you about?'

'The drug trials they were running up there.'

'You took part in them?'

Mouzon nodded. He took a sip of beer, grabbed a pack of cigarettes and lit up. It made Ida crave a smoke, but she couldn't, not while she had a hand on her gun.

'What did Cole ask you exactly?'

'He wanted me to talk him through what happened when they gave me the drug. He showed me some paperwork, carbon copies of the forms I filled out when I signed up. Asked me to check my signature on them. That kinda shit.'

Hennessy had taken documentary evidence up to Vacaville that he wanted confirmed. He was definitely building a case.

'You know what drug they were testing?' Ida asked.

'They called it a truth drug, but we all knew what it was – LSD. Acid. High-strength shit.'

Ida frowned. The idea of using LSD as a truth drug had been abandoned years ago, and just the previous year the government had passed the Drug Abuse Control Amendments, banning anyone from producing it. Even government agencies that had previously produced it for research purposes. It confirmed the drug trials were illegal, and why Hennessy, an FBN Agent, would look into them.

'Tell me more about the trials,' Ida said.

'The deal was you signed up and you got time off your sentence. 'Cos the drug was supposed to help your recovery. But we all knew it was bullshit. Half the people who went into the trial came out bat-shit crazy on account of how goddamn powerful the acid was, and the shit they did to you while you were on it. And it weren't no coincidence it was mostly blacks who got recruited for the trials.'

Ida's mind jumped back to *Gumbo Ya-Ya*. The Needle Men who whisked off black people to perform experiments on them. The myth was happening for real, in the California Medical Facility. And as soon as the Night-Slayer got out of there and saw McNeal that night in the Emergency Room, he must have thought it was happening there, too, and his murderous spree began.

She looked at Mouzon, wondering again if he was the Night-Slayer. Something told her he wasn't. He had that tic, but he didn't seem damaged enough by the drug trials, traumatized enough. And she couldn't peg the Night-Slayer as a junkie. Junkies were too busy scraping together money to get high. If a junkie had killed those Night-Slayer victims, he would have robbed their houses while he was at it. Mouzon seemed too broke and too in touch with reality to miss an opportunity like that. And he certainly didn't seem to be suffering from psychosis or hallucinations.

'You sure it was mostly blacks who got recruited to take part in the trials?' she asked.

'Yeah, I'm sure. Except for a couple of crackers they threw in. Trust me.'

Ida nodded. Did the test have a racial element to it they needed to control for, with a few white inmates as well? Or had they simply picked the most expendable inmates, black people like Mouzon, poor whites like Stevie?

'What did they do to you when you'd taken the drug?' she asked.

'They showed us these movies when we were all dosed up, like slideshows. Black power shit, news footage about Vietnam, about Communist revolutions. Shit about Castro and Cuba. On a loop. Over and over. For hours. Even if you weren't tripping on acid, it would have drove you crazy.'

'Propaganda? They were showing you propaganda?'

'Yeah, you could call it that.'

Ida stared at him. The people running the tests weren't interested in LSD as a truth drug, they were trying to see how susceptible it made people to propaganda, how useful it might be as a brainwashing tool. She realized now why Hennessy had been investigating the tests, why he'd run his case *sub rosa*. But more importantly, she realized exactly who was behind the tests.

'And that's what happened to Cooper,' Mouzon said. 'Lost his damn mind.'

Ida looked up at him.

'Pete Cooper?' she asked. 'The inmate you escaped with?'

'Yeah. After Coop finished his sessions, all he did was talk crazy, saying he could see demons coming after him. He never came down from the acid they gave him. Imagine that, your whole life a permanent bad trip.'

Ida frowned. Was Cooper the Night-Slayer? He'd been given acid in high doses, fed propaganda, driven mad, then he and Mouzon had escaped a couple of weeks before the first killing. Ida was sure now that Mouzon wasn't the Night-Slayer, but could Cooper be?

'You know where Cooper is now?' she asked.

'What's it to you?'

'I wanna talk to him. Like I'm talking to you.'

'I don't think Coop would appreciate me giving out his whereabouts.'

'He will when I pay him. Just like I paid you.'

Mouzon eyed her.

'How about you lay down some more of your money and then I tell you where Coop is?'

There was menace to the way he said it. To the way he was eying her.

'Sure,' she said.

She got her purse, pulled out what bills remained in it.

'All I've got is another fifty,' she said.

She looked up at Mouzon, saw him glaring. She suddenly got the feeling things might be heading south, that he and his pal might try to rob them after all. Put a bullet through their heads to make it easier. Ida flicked her gaze to Mouzon's pal. He was still sitting on the windowsill. But he'd taken his gun out, had it in his hand now, tensed. She turned back to Mouzon, and she could tell he was contemplating it.

She saw the gunfight play out in her head. If she had any chance of surviving, she'd have to take out the man by the window first, because he already had his gun in hand. Then dive, spin, hope to take out Mouzon before he got to his gun on the coffee table. Hope Kerry didn't get shot in the meantime. But Ida was too old to be diving and spinning. Too frail. Too slow. She'd have to talk them down. She turned to Mouzon, about to launch into a speech, when she saw there'd been a change in his expression, that whatever thoughts of violence had fluttered into his mind had just as quickly left.

'All right,' he said, nodding at the money in her hand.

Ida relaxed a touch. The man by the window relaxed a touch. She passed the money over and Mouzon pocketed it. Ida felt some of the tension pulse out of her.

'Coop used to hang out in San Fran before he ended up in Vacaville, with all these Haight-Ashbury hippie motherfuckers. Some of 'em moved to a ranch just out of town. Coop figured he'd be safer up there, so he split.'

'Where's the ranch?'

'Agua Dulce. It's just off the road between Santa Clarita and Palmdale.'

Ida nodded. She'd go and check the ranch as soon as she could.

'Ronnie, this is really important – is there anyone else you know that took part in the drug test and then came here to LA? Someone who hasn't been bumped off yet?'

Mouzon frowned. A tic convulsed his face. He chugged on his beer to chase it away

'I dunno. There were maybe two dozen guys who signed up for the tests,' he said. 'I dunno who came back to LA.'

'What about this one?' Kerry said, fumbling through her pockets, pulling out her photo of Stevie. She passed it over to Mouzon. He looked at it, nodded.

'Yeah, I remember him,' he said, eyeing her differently now. 'He related to you or something?'

'He's my brother. Have you seen him since you came out?'

'Why would I have seen him? We didn't mix.'

'You know anyone from Vacaville he was close to?' Kerry asked. 'That might know where he is?'

'Nope. You lost him or something?'

Kerry nodded. Mouzon handed her back the photo.

'How about Sam Cole?' Ida asked. 'He get in contact with you since you came back to LA?'

'You think I'd let a cop get in contact with me?' Mouzon sneered.

'All right. Did Cole maybe give you a card when he visited you in Vacaville, some way of getting in contact with him, telling you where he might be, where you might find him?'

Mouzon shrugged, shook his head.

'Thanks, Ronnie. You've been really useful,' she said, wrapping things up. 'Just by way of a tip – I don't think you should stay here much longer. There are people out there looking for you. I found you this easily, they can, too.'

Mouzon laughed, a quick snort of a laugh, and then there was the tic again, like an aftershock.

'I'll be all right,' he said. 'All I got to do is hold out till Christmas.'

'Why Christmas?'

'Coop said this trigger that's been going around clipping us all – he's only going to be in town till then. That once Christmas came, he'd be leaving. So all we had to do was stay alive till then, and we'd be fine.'

Ida frowned.

'How did Coop know he was only going to be in town till then?'

'Shit, Coop got fixated. After we got out, me and Coop started hearing about how all these other cats from Vacaville were being bumped off after they'd been released. Everyone who'd been involved in that acid trial. It flipped Coop's lid. He started asking around, found out about this killer who'd been sent after us. Heard all these rumors about him, how he'd worked for the Mob going back decades. How he had a kill count in triple figures. Boogeyman shit. Spook shit. It all made that bad trip Coop was having even worse. I don't know how he did it, but he tracked the guy down, followed him around, even found out where he lived.'

'Cooper found out where the trigger was living?' Ida asked, incredulous. 'Where?'

'I dunno.' Mouzon shrugged. 'He never gave me an address or nothing. But you can head up to that ranch Coop's staying at and ask him if you want. Flash your cash and maybe he'll even tell you about that Christmas deadline. You can trust him on all that. Coop went nuts off those drug trials, but he was real meticulous when he came to learning about this trigger.'

Ida inhaled sharply, steeled herself to ask the question she was dreading hearing the answer to.

'Did Coop find out what the trigger's name was?' she asked. 'Or what he looked like? Anything like that?'

'Yeah. Coop said he was a big old hayseed-looking white guy called Faron.'

Ida heard the words as if they were floating over her head.

It was Faron on the Night-Slayer's trail. The worst killer she'd ever encountered. The name that had haunted her for decades.

Suddenly she was gasping for breath.

# PART FOURTEEN

## DANTE

# 42

Dante drove long into the night trying to figure out a way to get Licata what he wanted – Riccardo or a death certificate in the next three days. He'd have to settle for a death certificate, but to get one Dante would have to find Riccardo's body first. If there still was a body. They could have thrown it in the ocean, chopped it up, burned it, dissolved it in acid or lime, crushed it at a junkyard, dropped it into a cement pour, driven it up to Napa Valley and buried it under a vineyard. Dante hit the streets on the trail once more, chasing CIA and FBN leads, Mexican smuggler leads. But once more no one knew anything. Dante drove back to Riccardo's office, went through his paperwork looking for anything CIA or FBN or Mexico-related. But the cops had been, had messed the place up even more. The CIA–Mexico link remained a specter, a shadow, a mirage.

He waded through dwindling leads and strengthening anxiety. He listened to jazz on the car radio. At some point rain started falling, smearing the world beyond the glass. The hypnotic free-way was everything now, the city either side just a carousel of shadows and shapes. He fell into nostalgia once more, his life in LA coming to mind in snapshots and feelings, landscapes of fear and desire. The alleys and nightclubs, the devil winds, the flood-lights blazing at Chavez Ravine, the oil well that used to stand in the middle of La Cienega Boulevard, gone now except in the memories of Angelinos like Dante who'd maybe lived too long. He started to get that night-terror feeling he got sometimes, star-tled awake at three a.m., panicked, worried the world was spinning out of control and there was nothing that could be done.

Around four a.m., he found himself near his warehouse. How long had he been away from it? Three days? Four days? But it felt like an age. At this time of night the place would be empty. He could sneak in, check what had piled up on his desk without having to talk to anyone. He could lie on the sofa in his office, try to think his way through the mess.

He pulled into the lot, killed the engine. He sent the warehouse's roll-shutter clanging upwards, stepped inside. He snapped on the lights, and long rows of tubes high up near the rafters blinked and clicked into life. He walked past the giant shelving units, his footsteps echoing and rebounding, the dog's feet pattering along in quickstep.

He sat at his desk, lit a cigarette. On the wall the clock hands ticked round to 4.30 a.m. and he could feel something was wrong. Something about the warehouse was different. Someone was watching him.

He stared through the office's glass partition, at the dust motes floating through the vast emptiness of the warehouse, the darkness where the lights didn't reach. All was still and silent. Only the ticking of the clock, the buzz and hiss of the tube lights. He second-guessed himself. He was just an old man jumping at shadows, succumbing to that night-terror feeling again, that vague sense of impending doom. He hadn't slept, he was stressed, he was giving himself the jitters. He turned back to his paperwork. He saw a note from Loretta saying Ida had called, decided to give it an hour or two till the sun rose to return her call. He checked a couple of letters and then out of nowhere the dog was barking. Dante looked up. It was barking at the same shadows where he had felt a presence. He rose, squinting into the darkness. He reached into his pocket for his gun. He stepped out of the office. He scanned the space. The dog was still barking, angrier now.

Seconds ticked by.

Then he heard a noise, movement, the dog jumping. He felt something cool and thin, then a burning sensation.

There was a garrote wire around his neck.

He gasped, yanked back. Shock and fear roared through him.
There was a man behind him, lifting him up. He could smell his
scent – stale sweat, the chemical tang of hairspray.

Dante swung his hand back to shoot his attacker, but he didn't
have his gun in hand anymore. He tried to grab the man's face,
but he was too far back. He tried to pull the wire off his neck, but
there was no way to get purchase on a wire. He flung his legs back
to catch the man in the groin, and he did. But the man didn't even
flinch. It was only then Dante realized his feet weren't touching
the ground. His attacker had lifted him up so Dante was perched
with his back on the man's chest. Professional. He was compress-
ing Dante's lungs so he blacked out faster.

They must have swung around because now Dante could see
his reflection in the mirrored panel that ran down the office partition. His face was turning a horrific shade of red. And behind him
was his attacker: a young man with a rhinocerine nose, his eyes
glazed, great black bags under them. His arms were all muscles
and needle-marks, suggesting he was juiced up on something
strong. The dog was biting him, its teeth at his leg. But the dog
was too small, the man too big.

Dante felt the crush on his windpipe like a vice, pain bolting
into his chest. He heaved for breath and couldn't do it.

This was how it was going to end.

His vision rolled, woozy now. He needed to stay conscious or
that was it. He needed something to fight back with. But all he had
was his wallet and his cigarettes and lighter.

He grabbed for his pocket. Pulled his lighter out, lit it, waited
for the flame to catch, then launched his hand backwards into his
attacker's face.

There was a whooshing sound as the man's hairspray went up
in flames, and then his hair, and then the man screamed. He let go
of the wire and Dante stumbled forward, collapsed onto the floor.
He pulled the wire from his neck, gasped for sweet air, drank it

in. He spun around. His attacker was stumbling, hyperventilating, smashing his palms against his eyes.

Dante turned and looked for his gun, saw it glinting further along the floor. He scrabbled over, picked it up, whirled around.

But the man was gone.

There was just the dog barking still, Dante's own labored breaths rasping their way out of his crushed windpipe. The smell of burned hair hanging heavy in the air.

Dante fanned his gun around, looking for movement amongst the rows of storage shelves disappearing into the shadows.

Pain exploded across the back of his head. He fell forwards, crashed into the floor, rolled over to see the man above him, his face a mess of melted skin. The man barrelled his fist toward Dante's head. Dante jerked out of the way. The fist cracked into the cement floor, but the man didn't even scream. He pulled it back to try again.

Dante pulled the trigger. The gun snapped three times, cold and hard. Two of the shots missed their mark, ricocheting off the metal shelving above, smashing bottles, but the third was a charm. It burrowed diagonally through the man's neck, took a chunk off the back of his head. He collapsed onto Dante, knocking out what little breath he still had in him. Dante pushed the man off so he rolled onto his side, stared at him. His eyes were open, gazing into another world now.

Dante shuddered. His rasping breaths echoed through the warehouse. He needed to check the rest of the building for accomplices. He needed to check the streets outside for cars with backups and getaway drivers. He needed to do a lot of things, but all he could do was stare into the eyes of the man he'd killed not half a foot away.

The dog came over and only now did Dante register it was barking still. Then he heard a rustling on the shelves above. The crash of an explosion. He looked up. A few crates of gin were on fire. Had the stray bullets sparked against metal and set fire to the booze? To the wooden crates? Surely that wasn't possible? Did the attacker have an accomplice inside the warehouse setting off fires?

'Shit.'

More explosions as more bottles burst. A splash of burning liquid barreled downwards through the air. Dante rolled away just in time.

He got to his feet. He looked about for the extinguishers but then realized there was no point. The fire was already heading toward the ceiling; the only way he could reach it now was with a cherry-picker. But by the time he'd found one, moved it into place, it would be too late.

He stumbled into the office, called the fire service, keeping his eyes on the warehouse beyond for more attackers. He put the phone down and ran back out of the office. The whole ceiling was ablaze. It would cave in at any minute.

He turned his attention back to his attacker. He searched his pockets. Came up with a wallet. Cash, receipts, a gym membership card, a driver's license. It identified the man as Wayne Bach, twenty-seven years old, an address in El Segundo. Dante slipped the wallet into his pocket. He kept searching, found a set of house keys. He slipped them into his pocket, too.

He picked up the dog and ran as best he could for the exit. When he got to the yard he scanned it and the lot beyond. No suspicious cars parked anywhere.

Soon there were sirens in the distance. He turned back to look at the warehouse and saw the roof ablaze, lighting up the neighborhood like the dawn had come early. It wouldn't last long. The roof would collapse and crush the thousands of gallons of booze underneath it. It would all go up. Every single drop. He watched as the fire trucks roared into the yard and footsteps rushed around him. He remembered he still had his gun in his hand. He slipped it into his pocket and watched as the flames engulfed his life's work.

# 43

Dante and the dog sat on the asphalt at the edge of the yard and watched the warehouse burn. They sat there as the firemen arrived, the patrolmen, the detectives, the local TV news crews. They sat there as dawn spread across the sky, as the pain from Dante's injuries pulsed through him, making him woozy. When the cops came to talk to him, he made sure he pulled his shirt collar up to hide the garrote wounds. They ordered him to stay put, so he had to get their permission to go to a payphone and call Loretta.

'What's wrong with your voice?' she asked.

It was still rough and croaky from the garrote.

'Smoke inhalation,' he lied.

She hung up before he'd even finished telling her about the fire, turned up within a half-hour and burst into tears. They sat and hugged and watched the carnage. When the first wave of shock had passed, she asked what had happened and Dante said he didn't know and they both knew he was lying. She nodded, her eyes narrowing, but for whatever reason, she let it pass.

They watched the smoke drifting into the sky, the red and blue lights of the response vehicles, the people moving about. A little after seven o'clock employees started arriving, hustling over to ask what was going on, if they still had jobs. Dante calmed them as best he could. Told them to take the day off, not to worry, they'd be paid in full till they figured out what could be done. It seemed to placate them. They stayed to watch the fire, they drifted away.

'We can't pay the whole staff without money coming in,' Loretta said. 'We'll go bust.'

'I think we've already gone bust,' Dante croaked.

'Insurance'll pay out, won't it?'

'I hope so.'

She glared at him, and something seemed to snap, the tension she'd been keeping inside her bursting out.

'You *hope* so? Dante, we've got everything on the line here. How the hell are we going to sell the business without the fixed assets? Without the stock? If we don't get the price we agreed and the insurance doesn't pay out, then we don't have the collateral for the loan anymore. The bank can pull the plug. We lose everything, Dante. The warehouse, the business, the money, the vineyard. Everything. You need to tell me what happened.'

She went to say something further, then paused, some realization stopping her.

'What is it?' he asked.

'All our insurance documentation was in the building. I'm going to have to dig their number out of a phone book. Give them a call. Mullan, too. The lawyers. The bank.'

She shook her head, looked at him as the lights of the police cars' flasher bars washed over her.

'Soon as I call the insurance company, they're going to send people down here,' she said. 'Those guys don't mess about. It means we need to get our story straight. Right now. You need to tell me what happened. No bullshit this time. You tell me the truth or I swear I'm going to walk away and let you deal with all this on your own.'

Dante felt a rising dread at the prospect of reliving the attack with her, but knew he had to. He swallowed and the garrote wounds seared across his throat. He felt the bruise on the back of his head pulse. Then he told her everything. Arriving at the warehouse, the dog barking, the sudden, brutal fight, making angels in the floor dust, his attacker's lifeless eyes.

'Jesus,' she said.

Her tone was softer now, realizing that he'd almost been

murdered. She reached out, and they hugged again, fell silent again. They watched the scene some more.

'I'm a mobster whose business just caught fire,' Dante said. 'You realize how this all looks, right?'

'Yeah, I know.'

Setting fire to your own business to claim on the insurance was a Mob scam as old as the Mob itself. The insurance company would do everything it could to prove Dante had started the fire, and if the fire inspection report backed them up, Dante and Loretta would lose everything, and Dante would probably be on the hook for arson. If it turned out the dead man had a criminal history, they might even think Dante and the man were starting the fire deliberately, meaning Dante would be on the hook for manslaughter as well.

'What did you tell the cops?' Loretta asked.

He'd given his story to the patrolmen who'd first arrived, telling them he'd stumbled on a burglar, had shot him in self-defense. He'd made no mention of the garrote. The patrolman had noted down what he'd said, didn't seem too bothered about poking holes in his story; he'd let the detectives do that.

'I told them I came in to do some work and stumbled into a burglary,' he said. 'Shot the guy in self-defense.'

'How the hell does that explain a fire starting, Dante?'

'What else could I say?'

She exhaled lengthily, eyed him.

'Was it related to the job Licata gave you?'

'It has to be. It's the only side work I've done in months.'

She gave him an icy look, and he felt as if she was gearing up to say something big.

'I want in,' she said.

'In on what?'

'On this job Licata's given you. This isn't just about you anymore. Our business is torched. My job's gone. Maybe all the work and money I put into the vineyard deal too. Forty years of our hard work is gone, Dante. And now I want in. I want oversight. I'm fed up of being palmed off.'

He looked at her, frowned. He'd expected her anger, but not like this.

'It's too dangerous,' he said.

'Don't give me that shit, Dante. I've had a lifetime of it. Never saying anything so you could *protect* us. It doesn't cut it anymore. Not when you're this old and shit like this happens. I wanna protect my investment. I'm going to make those phone calls, and then me and you are going to see this through to the end. And if you say no, it's already ended.'

She turned and left him sitting there forlorn amongst the smoke and ashes and the notion that there was a reckoning in the works, a painful one.

He sighed, looked up to see a detective approaching.

'Sir, I'm Detective Chavis. LAPD.'

The detective smiled and they shook hands. He was young and had a buoyant air about him, like he hadn't yet been weighed down with that resentment that seemed particular to the LAPD.

'Helluva thing to wake up to on Christmas Eve,' the detective commiserated.

Dante nodded, gestured to the warehouse.

'Have they recovered the body yet?' he asked.

'It's going to be a while before that happens. There's a fair few tons of roof on top of the man.'

Dante nodded again. It meant he had a head start on the cops. He still had the dead man's wallet in his pocket. He could start looking into the name that was written on the driver's license – Wayne Bach. The man who'd failed to kill Dante, but might still have wrecked his life.

'You said you'd only just arrived when he attacked you?' the detective asked.

'That's right.'

'You were coming to work from your apartment?'

'Yeah.'

'You often come to work at half four in the morning?'

Here it was. The hole-poking had begun.

'I'm old. I don't sleep. I have my lunch at nine thirty.'

Dante smiled. The cop smiled back. The confused old man routine. Dante wondered how much longer he could play it before it stopped being a routine. The detective checked his notepad, but Dante could see it was just for show.

'Dante Sanfelippo,' the detective said. 'That's an Italian name, right?'

'Sure.'

'Dante the Gent?'

The detective eyed him again. Dante knew what he was getting at. A mobster setting fire to his own business; it was so obvious it was a cliché. And Dante was a cliché too; he even had his own Mafia nickname, one the detective had already dredged out of the past.

'That was a long time ago,' he said.

The detective nodded.

'So, you turned up to your place of work at gone four in the morning, and just happened to stumble across a burglar. Who you shot. And then a fire started, you're not sure how.'

Dante shrugged and the two men stared at each other silently, because what was there to say? They both knew how it would go. The detective would wait till the body was recovered and autopsied. He'd wait till the body was identified to see if it was that of a known mobster. He'd wait till the fire investigators provided their report. Until then there was no point interrogating Dante. If Dante was guilty, the evidence would convict him; all the detective had to do was wait.

'We'd like you to stay here until we say otherwise, Mr Sanfelippo. And when you are free to go, not to leave town.'

*

The insurance men arrived within the hour. Dante got the detective's permission to take them to the Formosa Café just up the street. Before they sat down he went to the restroom to check his throat in the mirror. He expected to see a thin, red line across his neck, but instead there was a bumpy ring of purple bruises and burst blood vessels.

He went back out. They ordered coffee and went through the paperwork the insurance men had brought with them. Every time Dante swallowed, the bruises on his neck throbbed, his vocal cords felt like they were being ripped apart. The insurance men said they'd be in touch, gave him the number of a company that could clear the site once the cops okayed it.

They said their goodbyes. Dante called his cop pal, O'Shaughnessy, and asked him to run a check on Wayne Bach. Then he and Loretta walked back over to the warehouse.

'So?' she said.

He tried to peg recent events to a line and string it through his mind – he'd shown his face at a pool party cum Mob convention, he'd gone looking for Riccardo, he'd spoken to O'Shaughnessy, he'd been tailed by two men in a sedan, he'd stumbled onto a CIA safe house. Then someone had tried to whack him, the very same day he'd pressured Roselli and been called in by Licata. He told all this to Loretta as they returned to the warehouse, stood in the yard.

'It could have been anyone who sent the guy to kill me,' he said. 'The LAPD, the FBN, the CIA, Roselli, Licata. It's the first time I've been to the warehouse in days. Maybe they'd been laying in wait for me here. Maybe they'd been following me and thought this was the right moment to take me out.'

'And the fire starting?' she asked. 'It can't have been the stray bullets, Dante. You sure he didn't have someone with him?'

'There were no cars parked outside when I came out. But maybe the accomplice drove away before that. Maybe the attacker was supposed to kill me, and his accomplice was supposed to start a fire, you know, burn away the bruises on my neck so it looked accidental. Maybe that's why they used a garrote instead of a gun.'

'But the dog barked and alerted you and you killed the attacker.'

'If the accomplice was as high as the one I killed then maybe he wasn't thinking straight, maybe instead of helping his pal he got spooked, started the fire and hightailed it. The whole thing was sloppy, panicked, unprofessional.'

Loretta frowned at him.

'What is it?' he asked.

'You told me it could have been LAPD, FBN, CIA. Pick a goddamn alphabet agency. Do any of them sound like the kind of people who'd send two unprofessional junkies on a job like this?'

Dante shook his head and they looked at each other in mutual confusion. They turned to look at the smoldering ruins of the warehouse, took in the sight of their life's work reduced to smoking rubble.

'Feels like a cremation,' Loretta said.

Dante nodded, noticed how the smoke was slanting as it rose, diagonally, east to west.

'Wind's blowing in from the desert again,' he said.

She looked at him.

'Well?' she asked.

She was an impressive woman, and he didn't think that just because she was his wife. She'd saved his life in Chicago, she'd seen him through bad times in LA. And here she was, standing in the ruins of their business still lucid enough to be strategizing, picking up snags in the story, while most people would have been lost in a cloud of shock. Was there really any question about accepting her help?

'We use the dead man's driver's license,' Dante said. 'It's got his address on it. We go to the address and look for clues, maybe figure out who the man was working for, maybe who the accomplice was. We find the accomplice, pressure him, he tells us what the hell's going on. Whoever did this is probably going to try again. We need to find them before we really do lose everything.'

'*We* need to find them?'

'Yeah. We.'

# PART FIFTEEN

## IDA & KERRY

# 44

After leaving Mouzon's hide-out Ida and Kerry drove in convoy to the Wigwam Motel. Kerry grabbed her things and checked out while Ida hovered, looking over her shoulder, gun at the ready, still edgy and unsettled after hearing Faron was in town. As they dumped Kerry's bags into the trunk of her car, Kerry turned to look back at the motel.

'I'm sure as hell not going to miss this place,' she said.

'Yeah, I never understood the appeal of all this wigwam stuff.'

'They're not even wigwams. They're teepees. They got the name of the whole motel chain wrong.'

They drove over to Fox Hills under night skies still swollen with rain. When they arrived at Ida's house they cased it for a few minutes before going in. Kerry stayed in the living room while Ida grabbed her stuff, throwing things into a laundry bag. When she returned to the living room, she saw Kerry had pulled down a copy of the manual Ida had written from the bookshelf, was flicking through it.

'You wrote a book?'

'Yeah. Take a copy. I've got four boxes of them in the garage.'

Ida called her phone operator and instructed them to divert all her calls to her answering service. They stepped outside and Ida looked up at the house with a strong disquiet, wondering if she'd ever see the place again. She had a sense of a darkness closing in on her, a despair she needed to outrun. Then she noticed another cause for concern.

'What is it?' Kerry asked.

'The wind's changed. It's blowing in from the desert again.'

They took La Cienega north, Santa Monica west. They hooked onto the Harbor Freeway then turned off, snaked through Bunker Hill. They parked not far from Ida's old agency, on a gray, characterless street, the kind of place two strangers could hide out without anyone noticing them. They crossed to an apartment block equally nondescript, stepped into a dusty hallway, caught an elevator up seven flights, entered an apartment that smelled of disuse. There was a lounge-kitchenette, two bedrooms, a bathroom, and that was it. Sparse furniture. Windows looked onto a few cordoned-off buildings scheduled for demolition, a few of the sterile-looking office blocks that were popping up all over the old neighborhood.

'You own this place?' Kerry asked.

'Unofficially. It wouldn't be much of a hide-out if my name was on the deed, but, yeah, it's mine. I've got a couple of them for situations like this. Funny, I was thinking of letting the lease lapse. Dump your things and then we'll grab some breakfast.'

They went to an old Jewish deli that had somehow escaped the bulldozers. There was a counter piled high with bottles of kosher dills and baskets of rye bread. There was a reassuring smell of soup being cooked, bagels being baked.

They took a table by the window, ordered eggs and toast and coffees. Ida went to use the payphone. She called Feinberg and got through to him at the Glass House, where he was pulling a night shift. She gave him Faron's name.

'You serious?' Feinberg asked. 'Faron's a myth. He's the boogeyman that gangsters use to scare their kids.'

'He's not a myth, Feinberg. I've looked him in the eye. If what I heard is right, then he's in LA, and he's hunting. Put a BOLO out for him.'

There was a pause as Feinberg considered Ida's story, realized she was being serious.

'All right,' he said. 'I'll ask around about Faron, but for a BOLO I need a description.'

Ida gave him one as best she could, then she gave him the phone number of her hide-out. Feinberg jotted it down and they hung up.

Next she called Dante to let him know what was going on, that he was in danger, but no one picked up at his apartment and when she tried the warehouse the line appeared to be dead. She hung up with a sense of trepidation. Maybe it was nothing, just her state of mind. Faron was back. Slaughtering again. And Ida was jumping at whispers.

When she walked back to the table, the food had already arrived. She sat down, stared at her plate, smoked a cigarette instead.

'I just called Feinberg,' Ida said. 'I told him about Faron. He said he'd look into it. In the meantime, we need to stay alert, keep safe. Faron knows we're after him, which means he'll be coming after us, sooner or later.'

'How are you so sure he's on to us?'

'Because of what Mouzon said.'

A shadow of fear passed through Ida again. The interview had gone as well as she could have hoped. And then Mouzon had mentioned the name of the hired killer and everything had turned, scars had ruptured, demons resurrected, Ida's poise had crumbled. She wondered how she must have looked, stumbling out of there like she was having a heart attack. How fragile and breathless she'd sounded when she'd explained to Kerry they were in danger, that they needed to move out, that time was of the essence. Even twenty years later, Faron's name was enough to set her heart racing.

'Mouzon told us they were testing LSD at Vacaville,' Ida said.

313

'But LSD's illegal, so where did the people running the tests get it from?'

Kerry frowned, shrugged.

'Put yourself in Agent Hennessy's shoes,' Ida said. 'Why did he conduct his investigation in secret? Use a fake name when he visited Vacaville? Disappear to carry on the case? Why did Agent White trash your missing person's report? Why did he meet you off the books and try to run you out of town?'

Ida looked at Kerry, wondering if she'd overwhelmed her, or if she'd see through the confusion of possibilities to the most elegant answer, to the one that had to be true because it was the simplest.

'Agent White was supplying the LSD to Vacaville?' Kerry's tone was unsure, worried she might have got it wrong. Something about that lack of confidence pleased Ida. She nodded.

'That would explain Hennessy's actions. And White's. The FBN's got stores of illegal drugs confiscated from the dealers they bust. My guess is Hennessy found out some of it was going missing. That Agent White was taking it, passing it on to Vacaville illegally. That's how Hennessy found out about the tests. And that's why he ran his investigation in secret – he was investigating his own agency, or at least, the corrupt agents within it. That's why White tried to warn you off. So you see now why we're compromised?'

Kerry nodded. 'White and Faron are on the same team. White knows about me, which means Faron probably knows, too.'

'Exactly. White's first attempt was to warn you off. When he sees that hasn't worked, he'll send Faron after you. This is getting more dangerous by the minute, Kerry. It's why when we've eaten, we're going to go back to the apartment, book you on a flight out of LA.'

Kerry stared at Ida, her expression going from surprise to annoyance.

'I thought we were working together?'

'We were. And then we found out Faron was involved. I'm sorry, but you need to let me handle things from here. I promise you I'll do everything I can to find Stevie.'

'I'm not leaving,' Kerry said. 'I came here to find my brother, and I'm going to find him.'

'I'll find him for you. On my own.'

Kerry's eyes narrowed.

'I'm not leaving,' she repeated. 'No matter how dangerous it gets. If Faron's looking for all of us, I say we stick together.'

'You're only saying that because you don't really know what you're up against.'

'Faron's that bad?'

Ida began to speak but the memories overwhelmed her. As she tried to compose herself, she turned to look out of the window and caught sight of their reflections in the glass, like there were four of them there, like they'd been tailed by two shadows. She turned back to Kerry, told her Faron's entire history, all the details she'd cobbled together over the years, all her attempts at trying to keep track of him.

'I've worked as a detective since I was nineteen years old. I've gone up against plenty of killers, but he's the one that's haunted me. Maybe because I failed to catch him twenty years ago and since then he's gone on to kill so many more. Or maybe because I looked him in the eye, saw his true nature. And now he's here, in LA, after all these years.'

Ida stopped speaking, shrugged, tried to fight off the implications of his return. She stared at the blackness of her coffee, the swirl of brown bubbles floating across its surface. She and Dante had both been right about something big happening, a powerful conspiracy sweeping through the city. And Faron was at the center of it, the boogeyman, pulling along in his wake everyone who worked in their world. That was how Ida's details must have ended up on that newspaper in Audrey Lloyd's motel room. Audrey Lloyd worked for a mobster, part of the same Mob Ida had asked to keep an eye out for Faron. Audrey had found out he was in town, was linked to the Night-Slayer, and she was bringing that information to Ida. Maybe not to ask Ida for help, but to *warn* her.

The dread Ida had been experiencing suddenly coalesced into a single, pointed certainty – that this would be her last-ever case, that if she was to go up against Faron once more, she wouldn't survive the onslaught this time. And yet she had to go up against him, she had no choice. But that didn't mean Kerry had to go down too.

She looked up to see Kerry staring at her.

'If Faron's as bad as all that, then it's all the more reason to stick around.'

'I can't let you put yourself in danger like that.'

Kerry shook her head.

'Ida, if you put me on a plane you're not sending me home, because I don't have a home to go to – you're sending me straight back to a war zone. It ain't exactly putting me out of harm's way. You're so busy trying to protect me, but maybe you're the one that needs protecting. I'm younger than you. I can run faster, see further, push stronger. You never know, Ida. You let me stick around, maybe I end up saving your life.'

Kerry raised her eyebrows, continued to stare at Ida, not letting her gaze waver. Whether or not it was deliberate, she had tapped directly into Ida's fear that she might not survive the case. Ida realized then that maybe her fear about taking on Faron wasn't based on her age, but on the fact she was taking him on alone. Maybe between her and Kerry they could make it through, just like she and Michael had made it through last time. She studied Kerry, noted again how similar she was to Michael. It wasn't just the scars on her face, or her gangly physique, it was something in her look, her bearing, in the strength she projected without even meaning to.

'All right,' Ida said. 'Let's stick together.'

Kerry smiled.

'So what do we do now?' she asked.

'We go up to that ranch where Pete Cooper's hiding out. Mouzon said Cooper had found out where Faron was based. Maybe Cooper gives us Faron's address. Maybe it turns out Cooper's the Night-Slayer, so we've killed two birds with one stone. Either way, I want to find out why Cooper would think there's a deadline. That this is all going to be over by Christmas.'

Kerry frowned. 'It's Christmas Eve already.'

'Exactly.'

Kerry's eyes narrowed as she mulled this over. She peered down at the plates of food in front of them, neither of which had been touched. It seemed like she was about to pick up her fork, start eating, when she frowned again, looked up at Ida.

'One thing I don't get is who was in charge of the tests,' she said. 'The guard I spoke to said it was outside people who came to Vacaville to run them. Mouzon said the same. So White's been supplying them, and they hired Faron to clean everything up. But we still don't know who they are.'

'Isn't it obvious?' Ida said.

'Not to me.'

'Whoever was running those tests had high-level authorization. They hired a Mob-connected contract killer to clean up after them when it all went wrong. Think about it – LSD, brainwashing, propaganda, Mob connections, contract killers. There's only one organization that fits the bill.'

'Which one?'

'The CIA. The Night-Slayer's government made. That's why they're trying so damn hard to keep it secret.'

# 45

Kerry and Ida took the Golden State Freeway north, crossed the river, sliced past Elysian Park, Griffith Park, and into Burbank. As they were approaching Sun Valley, Kerry turned to her left and looked out over the last haze of night still clinging to the city. Not more than five hundred yards from the freeway, the lights of a plane shot into the sky. And then another set, a few seconds after. And then a third. There was something eerie at the sight of them darting up into the orange pollution above, and it wasn't just on account of their proximity. It took Kerry a moment to realize what it was – they were making hardly any noise. Compared to most airplanes, their engines were practically silent.

'Skunk Works,' Ida said. 'It's Lockheed's development plant. They're testing military planes.'

'Over Los Angeles?'

'Sure. Lockheed built their plant here back in the twenties, before there was even much of a city in Burbank. Then they set up Skunk Works in the thirties. It's where Anthony Butterfield was employed, the Night-Slayer victim. They make bombers, fighter jets. All kinds of technology for the Cold War. For Vietnam. But I guess you already know about that.'

Kerry nodded.

'And it's not just Lockheed,' Ida continued. 'Rocketdyne, RCA, Packard Bell. Nine of the Valley's ten biggest employers are defense-related. And yet when the world sees Los Angeles, they only see the film biz.'

Kerry nodded again. Was it a coincidence that the movie and defense industries had found a home in the same city? The one

weaving dreams of paradise, the other nightmares of the apocalypse? Hope and dread, side by side. Even their worksites were
similar – the studio lots with their giant sound-stages, the defense
companies with their giant hangars.

She looked in the side mirror, caught a final glimpse of the
defense plant, of the lights shooting through the murk. It reminded
her of those nights back at the air base in Cam Ranh Bay, when she
and the technicians and pilots in her crew were off duty and they'd
find a roof to climb onto, drink beer and smoke joints and watch
the battles in the distance, the firefights, the tracers and mortars
arcing, illuminating the dark like fireworks on the Fourth of July.
Then the helicopters would start flying toward them with the cas-
ualties, and the whole thing would turn horribly real.

Kerry turned to Ida, studied her as she plowed the Cadillac
through the dulling dawn.

'You mind me asking you a question?' she asked.

'No. What do you want to know?'

'How'd you get started? Being a detective, I mean.'

'It's a long story. You sure you want to know?'

Kerry smiled and nodded and Ida gave her an outline of her
beginnings in New Orleans, working for the Pinkertons, transfer-
ring out to Chicago just in time for the start of prohibition, then
setting up her own agency and moving out to LA. Even though
Kerry got the sense Ida was skating over large parts of her history
it seemed like she'd had a long career. And yet she didn't seem
that old – early sixties, maybe. With a sprightliness that suggested
she could keep working for a few years yet.

'So how come you retired?' Kerry asked.

Ida paused.

'An investigator I worked with was killed. It was partly my
fault. We got given bad information, and we didn't verify it and
he was the one who paid the price. But it could just as easily have
been me. It didn't feel right carrying on after that. Truth is, I got
scared. So I put my agency up for sale. I had two people make

offers – the Pinkertons, and a guy running another independent outfit – Al Clarke. I sold it to him 'cos there was no way in hell I was selling to the Pinkertons.'

'Why not?'

'The Pinkertons are a bunch of strike-breaking thugs for hire. They beat up the little guy so the big guy can get even richer. That's why I quit working for them all those years ago, started up my own agency. So I could look myself in the mirror again. And in all the decades since they still haven't changed. There's a Hearst newspaper here in LA called the *Herald Examiner*. Last week the workers went on strike. Can you guess who Randolph Hearst Junior hired to break the strike, harass the strikers, attack the pickets?'

'The Pinkertons.'

Ida nodded. 'The whole reason I started my agency was to fight against them. Everything they stood for. Anyway, six months after I sold up to Clarke, I found out he was selling out himself. To the Pinkertons.'

'Damn. I'm sorry.'

Ida shrugged.

'No fool like an old fool,' she said. 'I still don't know what the story was. If the Pinkertons just made Clarke a good offer or if Clarke was acting as their proxy all along to scam me out of the agency. And truth be told, it doesn't matter. The agency I spent nearly forty years building as an alternative to the big guys, ended up getting eaten by the very same big guys. And now it doesn't exist anymore.'

She shrugged again and Kerry sensed she still hadn't come to terms with what had happened, the betrayal, the loss.

'What about you?' Ida asked. 'Your family's always been in Vermilion Parish?'

Kerry looked out of the window.

'No,' she said. 'My pop was from New Orleans. Like you. He was a cop with NOPD. But he moved us out to Vermilion Parish to work a case at some point. After a couple of years, my mom up and left. Then a few months after that, my pop killed himself with a shotgun. I was nine, Stevie was four.'

Kerry told her the whole story. The years of jumping between orphanages and foster homes that never worked out. Kerry playing the protector role to Stevie, though looking back, it probably protected her more than it did him. Gave her purpose and distraction, while it just gave him a sense of helplessness. She told Ida about the deal she and Stevie made when she turned eighteen and was kicked out of the orphanage. She'd do two years of community college, get her nursing diploma, get it paid for via the military's Student Nurse Program. Then she'd enlist, serve out her time, come back to the orphanage to pick up Stevie when it was his turn to get kicked out, and they'd head out to California together. But it didn't work out that way.

She should have known. Stevie had always lashed out at the institutions that kept them trapped in Louisiana. When she'd joined the Air Force, she'd known she was just stepping into a new institution, an even more hierarchical one – twelve-hour shifts, six days a week, waking up to loudspeakers playing the 'Star-Spangled Banner' at six o'clock every morning.

Stevie on the other hand had left the orphanage looking for freedom, for California, for the adult happiness he was so desperate for. But he'd ended up in correctional facilities, swapping one institution for another, just like her.

Ida considered all this, nodded.

'We've got a lot in common,' she said.

'How so?'

'We both grew up in Louisiana, and we both left it looking for something better. Me with the Pinkertons, you with the Air Force. And now here we are.'

They carried on up the freeway. They turned off just before Santa Clarita and headed east. They passed dusty scrubland, arroyos, rickety wire fences faltering through the emptiness. Signs appeared for the Agua Dulce Canyon Road. They turned up it and left the safety of the freeway behind, passing by a few dilapidated, long-forgotten construction sheds onto a narrow, meandering road. The wind howled as it blew in from the ever-nearing desert, rattling through mountain passes on its way to the city, to the coast, searching for that faraway ocean.

Eventually they arrived at Agua Dulce. It wasn't a town, wasn't even a village. From what they could see it was a gas station and a general store on opposite sides of the road. Further on, in the shadows of the hills, sunlight glinted off distant houses and ranches.

They pulled up at the gas station and Ida asked the attendant if there was a ranch around there where hippies hung out. The attendant gave her a sour look and mumbled directions.

They turned off the road a mile further down and made their way up an uneven dirt track. They passed a thicket of juniper trees, and arrived at the ranch. On the other side of its gates were two stone ranch houses, the yard lights on their roofs blazing, a row of stables, a couple of trucks, a Ford Falcon parked between a barn and the shade of a live oak. Further up the brush-covered hill were a few outlying shacks, and bizarrely, a swimming pool. It all looked dilapidated and abandoned, like a ghost-town in a cowboy movie.

'Something's wrong,' Ida said. 'The yard lights are on even though the sun's up, and there's no noise, no movement. This is supposed to be a commune. Where the hell is everyone?'

Ida killed the engine and they sat there listening. All was silent except for the sound of mockingbirds, the rustle of the wind, dogs barking in the distance.

After what felt like an age, Ida finally moved, opening her handbag, taking out her .38.

'Get your gun and come with me,' she said.

They stepped out of the car and Kerry followed Ida across to the yard.

'Try not to touch anything,' Ida said. 'And maybe walk in my trail if you can. The less we disturb the better.'

Kerry nodded and they continued on. Up close the ranch looked even more dilapidated. Sage bushes and sumac sprouted everywhere, the two trucks were blanketed in rust, the stables mostly collapsed.

Near to the closest ranch house they found the first body, hidden from view by the truck further along, so they smelled it before they saw it, its rich odor mixing with the pharmacy scent of the eucalyptus trees further on. It was a man, dust-covered and crawling with insects, lying in a wide stain of dried blood, face down, limbs contorted, as if he'd been tossed there. His clothes were shredded, his flesh ripped to the bone. What little skin hadn't been torn off was littered with cuts, bruises, welts, sun damage. His remaining fingers and toes had turned black.

'Try not to get too close to the body,' Ida said. 'You squeamish?'

'I've seen worse in Vietnam.'

Ida nodded, kneeled, inspected the body.

'What are you looking for?' Kerry asked.

'Clues as to how he died. And when. I'd say it's been a week maybe. Which is good – means we don't have to worry that Faron's still on the property. These are stab marks across his torso, they're probably Faron's work. All this flesh that's been ripped off was coyotes in the days since. You can see their bite marks, their paw prints in the dust. Plus, the way his body's contorted, that's from them dragging him around. I'm surprised his intestines are still inside him. Come on, let's check the rest of the place.'

The lights had been left on in the first of the two ranch houses, revealing a long space with wooden walls, and folding beds set up in rows, like a cabin in a summer camp. There were sheets

323

hanging from the walls with crude paintings and messages on them about peace and love. There were two bodies on the floor. Girls younger than Kerry. Even though no coyotes had entered the room, the injuries on these girls were just as horrific as those on the man outside. The bodies had been punctured by countless knife-wounds. A roll of slashes, slices, and gashes etched into their flesh like the letters of some frenetic language. Kerry remembered what Ida had said about Faron slicing his way across the century, and she felt a leaden weight of sorrow. One of the girl's hands still clasped a blanket, curling it in her fist, even now, days after the attack.

In the silence Kerry noticed the sound of dogs barking again, but closer this time, louder.

Ida sighed, rose up from the corpses, mulled something over.

'What are you thinking?' Kerry asked.

'Just wondering where these kids came from, how they ended up here. Did they run away from good homes in good neighbor-hoods? Or were they kids from the margins?'

Ida shrugged. Kerry looked at the two dead girls again, asked herself the same questions. Had they run away from stable homes, rebelling against nothing more than the hollowness of their sub-urban lives? Or were they forced onto the road by bad circumstances? Like Stevie. Drifting hardscrabble to California across the country's nameless, violent plains?

In the second house they found another three bodies. Two men and another girl.

'Looks like this is all of them,' Ida said. 'Strange. I always imagined these hippie crash pads to be teeming with people. All these buildings and land, but there's only six bodies.'

'Maybe the rest of them hightailed it.'

'Maybe.'

The bodies in this second house weren't as badly mutilated. One of the men was black, matched the description of Pete

Cooper. He'd been slashed across the throat and his hands were still clasped against the wound, pressing wads of newspaper to it.

'He was trying to stop himself bleeding to death,' Ida said. 'Means Faron cut his throat and left him to die. Not sure why he used newspaper though. There's bed sheets right there.'

'Newspapers are antiseptic,' Kerry said. 'The chemicals in the ink. Is that definitely Pete Cooper?'

'Looks like it. So much for finding out where Faron's holed up, and about that Christmas deadline.'

They fell silent, studied Cooper's body some more.

'You think we're looking at the Night-Slayer?' Kerry asked.

'Could be. Last Night-Slayer killing was twelve days ago. Cooper looks like he's only been dead a week.' Ida sighed. 'We're in a race against Faron, and he's got a week's head start.'

'This was all definitely Faron?'

'Yeah. He's massacred like this before. At least twice that I know of. All his markers are here. The women are more savagely attacked than the men, their wounds are sexual. And then there's the biggest marker of all, that he hasn't left a single clue or piece of evidence for us to chase. He's meticulous, I'll give him that.'

Ida looked around the room once more.

'If Cooper really had uncovered where Faron was hiding out,' she said, 'maybe he left some evidence lying around that can tell us where. Let's see if we can find it before we call the cops.'

Kerry nodded. Once more she could hear the dogs, closer yet again.

'You hear that?' Kerry asked.

'Yeah. Could be they're getting closer. Could just be the wind's changed direction. Either way, let's work quick.'

They went through the two houses, the long-disused stables, the outlying shacks, the broken-down trucks; they even checked the swimming pool, but it was bone dry and empty except for leaves and algae and the corpses of unfortunate animals that had fallen in and couldn't get back out.

In a storage box at the back of the sleeping quarters they found yellow pills and a few plastic bags with white powder in them, credit cards, maps, knives, a gun, a bottle of eye drops – the 'anti-smog' type that were sold in LA. They found a room that looked like an explosion in a thrift store, filled by a flea-infested mound of clothes, like the people who lived there shared a communal set of clothing.

They tossed the Ford Falcon that was parked just to the side of the barn. There was nothing in the side pouches, nothing in the footwells or glovebox, nothing hidden above the sun visors. In the cup-holders were a few packs of chewing gum, a few receipts, a ticket stub for a diner out in Chino Hills.

'Nowheresville,' Ida muttered.

She popped the trunk and again there was nothing much – a spare tire, a crowbar, a pair of boots.

'Maybe Faron took the evidence with him,' Kerry said.

'Maybe.'

They fell silent, looking around the desolate, eerie ranch. Kerry strained her ears, couldn't hear the dogs barking anymore. The entire time they'd been tossing the place she'd been worried about their approach. And now, all was silence, which unnerved her even more.

She turned to look at Ida and saw she was studying the surroundings, her eyes narrow. Kerry had noticed Ida doing this throughout the search, evaluating, and sometimes muttering, but not to herself exactly. It felt more like she was in a dialogue with someone who wasn't there. That she was discussing things with some old partner maybe, some old fellow detective long since gone.

Kerry watched her a moment as she surveyed the landscape.

'You looking for those dogs?' she asked.

'No, just looking,' Ida said. 'Trying to reconstruct how it might have played out the night he came here.'

'You sure he did it at night?'

'Why else would all the lights still be on? I'm guessing he entered the compound from the rear. He went to the second building first, because he could see the light was on, knew there were people in there. He dispatched those three quickly, then he went to the other building, where the two girls were hiding, and took his time with them. I'm guessing the body out front found a hidey-hole somewhere and tried to run away when he thought Faron was distracted, but didn't get very far.'

'How can you tell all that?'

Ida shrugged. 'From the distribution of bodies around the compound, from the marks in the dust, from the blood spatter, from the stains. You can reconstruct the whole thing. Not with complete certainty, but you can hazard a guess if you've seen enough crime scenes. It also helps if you look at it from Faron's point of view. If you had to come here and kill people, how would you do it? You'd stake the place out. You'd come at night. You'd sneak in from the rear.'

'Yeah, but I wouldn't use a knife,' Kerry said. 'I'd use a gun.'

'The sound of a gun carries a long way in a landscape like this, carries further than screams. Plus, Faron prefers knives. Lot of killers do.'

They drove back to Agua Dulce and called in the police, drove back to the ranch and waited. Kerry lit a smoke, stared through the car window at the ranch, which felt even more eerie now. She wondered if Pete Cooper was the Night-Slayer, if this was where he'd been based. There was something fitting about the desolate location, something that chimed with *Gumbo Ya-Ya*, with folklore, with people living outside the system. Kerry could see people like this creating their own mythology, their own voodoo, and killing for it.

Kerry's gaze landed on the Ford parked between the side of the barn and the shade of the oak tree further on, and something about it struck her as strange. She frowned, trying to figure it out.

'What is it?' Ida asked.

'Something about where the Ford's parked. Why park it right there? Why not park it *in* the barn? Or under the shade of the oak? Why park it out in the sun on the far side of the yard?'

As they considered this, Kerry could hear cop cars in the distance, their sirens soft on the wind.

Ida narrowed her eyes, staring at the Ford.

'Dammit,' she said, reaching for the door handle.

She was out of the car in a second, striding across the yard, Kerry on her heels. When they got to the Ford, Ida bent down to look underneath it.

'There's something here,' she said.

She put her gloves on, opened up the driver's side door, released the handbrake, put it into neutral.

'Push,' she said.

Kerry pushed the car and it eased back, revealing a wooden pallet inset into the earth of the yard. Kerry lifted the pallet, revealing a footlocker in a shallow ditch.

As they stared at it, Kerry could hear the sirens getting louder.

'Come on, we don't have long till they get here,' Ida said.

Kerry kneeled and hauled the footlocker out of the ditch. It had a padlock on it.

'I'll get the crowbar in the trunk,' Ida said.

She popped the trunk, grabbed the crowbar they'd seen earlier, handed it to Kerry. Kerry used it to prise open the footlocker's flimsy padlock. Inside were possessions which presumably belonged to Pete Cooper. Some money, a *Green Book* turning yellow, an ancient-looking .38 snub-nose revolver. They rifled through them all as the sound of the cop cars got louder. The *Green Book* was unmarked, offering no clues as to Cooper's itinerary before he was killed. But folded into the back page was a sheet of paper torn out of a legal pad, and scrawled on it were addresses: among them was Hennessy's house in Sherman Oaks, the addresses of the three inmates who'd been killed after they'd been released, and another address in Pacoima, with a name above it – Bud Williams.

'I know that name,' Ida said, frowning. 'Where the hell have I seen that name before?'

She looked at Kerry, confused. And then her face lit up.

'Feinberg gave me a list of Vacaville inmates who'd checked out *Gumbo Ya-Ya*,' she said. 'The name Bud Williams was on the list. Why would Cooper have the address of an inmate who checked out *Gumbo Ya-Ya*?'

Ida and Kerry looked at each other, the sense of an important discovery rustling along the line of their gaze. Ida slipped the paper into her pocket just as the ranch filled with the noise and flashing lights of police cars.

# PART SIXTEEN

## LOUIS

# 46

Louis stood in the lobby of the Steve Allen Playhouse at 1228 Vine Street and stared at the wall of black-and-white photos in front of him. John Coltrane was there, Nat King Cole, Sammy Davis Junior, Dave Brubeck, Chet Baker, Louis himself. All the celebrities who had appeared on Steve Allen's late-night talk show over the years. Louis noticed how many of the people in the photos had passed away; John Coltrane had died that summer, Nat King Cole a couple of years earlier. How soon till Louis was just a photo too? Maybe the doctor would let him know at his appointment that afternoon.

Despite Louis' grueling schedule and the pot he'd been smoking heavily since he was in his twenties, he'd outlived most of his contemporaries – Jelly Roll Morton, Bunk Johnson, Sidney Bechet, Johnny and Baby Dodds. Musicians Louis had known since he was a kid back in New Orleans, had played with throughout his career. All of them gone.

He'd even outlived many in the generation of jazz musicians that had come after him: Charlie Parker, Billie Holiday, Lester Young, Bud Powell. All of them dying much too young. An entire generation stalked by poverty, drugs and madness. Now here Louis was, alone in a theater lobby, feeling like the last man standing, clutching his trumpet case like he was holding on for dear life.

The door to the auditorium opened and a gawky white kid popped his head in.

'We'll take you through now, Mr Armstrong.'

They walked along a corridor to the auditorium. The Playhouse was an old vaudeville theater from where the *Steve Allen*

*Show* was broadcast five nights a week, Allen preferring its old-fashioned feel to that of NBC's Color City Studios in Burbank. When they stepped inside, the audience seats were all empty. A skeleton crew of cameramen and sound technicians were on the stage, a clutch of producers, and Steve Allen himself.

'Satch,' he said, crossing over. 'How was your flight in?'

'All good, yeah. All good.'

They shook hands warmly. Steve was his usual buoyant self, full of the manic energy that worked so well on screen.

'Excellent,' he said. 'We got your picks for the songs. "Cool Yule" for the Christmas number and then "Mack the Knife" for the classic.'

'They OK?'

'Sure. Sure. "Mack the Knife". The happiest song about a murderer I ever heard. And "Cool Yule" is the greatest Christmas song of all time,' Steve joked.

The song had been written by Steve himself, who was an accomplished composer as well as a TV personality and comic. Louis had recorded and released a version back in the '50s.

'Come on over and say hello to the band,' Steve said.

They walked over to the music stage, where Steve's house band – the Donn Trenner Orchestra – were setting up their instruments. A round of hellos ricocheted around Louis and the band. Louis knew Donn and his guitarist Herb Ellis, the trombonist Frank Rosolino, all of them established jazz musicians in their own right.

After some catch-up talk, Steve wandered off. Louis watched him go, ruing a missing opportunity. He'd wanted to ask him about Karl Drazek, the TV producer that Ida was interested in, the man who'd got Audrey Lloyd her job at Ocean Movies. Louis was still having no luck finding him and was hoping Steve might know something – Steve had worked at Universal, where Drazek had also been employed.

Louis decided to track down Steve later and he and the band started practicing. They had to read from sheets for 'Cool Yule', but they knew 'Mack the Knife'. Louis ran them through his preferred arrangement of it. He sang the vocal parts but made excuses when it came to playing the horn sections, choosing to scat his way through them to save his lungs for the doctor's appointment later on.

After an hour or so they took a break and as the band and the technicians slunk off, Louis stood on the stage alone for a moment. Without the rehearsal to distract him, the same fog of doom that had been enveloping him since he'd woken up that morning drifted back, clouding his thoughts. He stared at the rows of empty seats in front of him in the darkness, the cameras, the microphones, the lights, the thick cables creeping across the floor into the shadows, all the way back to New Orleans, the Suburban Gardens some time in the 1930s. Louis and his band were scheduled to play a set which was to be broadcast on the local WSMB radio station. At the start of the set, the radio announcer who was supposed to introduce them shook his head, declaring to his producer, 'I just haven't the heart to announce that nigger on the radio.' So Louis had grabbed the microphone and introduced himself and his band, and thus became the first black voice ever to speak, not just sing, on American radio.

Louis blinked, and the fog dispersed and he was back in the Playhouse, standing alone on the stage, staring at nothing. He recalled Ida telling him that her mind these days was constantly drifting homeward, to memories of their youth in New Orleans, and now here was Louis falling prey to it, too.

'Sir? Mr Armstrong, sir?'

Louis turned to see a kid standing a few feet away at the edge of the stage.

'Sorry to bother you, sir,' the kid said. 'I work over at ABC. For Joe Glaser.'

'Sure.'

'Mr Glaser asked me to bring you over the sheet music for the Bob Thiele number he wants you to record.'

The kid held out a manilla envelope, walked over and passed it to Louis.

'Thanks, kid.'

'You're welcome, sir. Is there's anything else I can help you with?'

The kid smiled. He was in the same mold as Joe Glaser – Jewish and Midwestern, with a toughness he was trying to hide behind good manners. But Louis could see he was just as much a gangster as his boss at the Agency.

'I'm all good,' Louis said.

'Well, if you need anything while you're in LA, you can call on me as well as Mr Glaser.'

The kid held out a business card and Louis took it – *Jerry Heller, Talent Agent. Associated Booking Corporation.*

'Sure, will do,' he said.

The kid smiled and headed off into the shadows. Louis pocketed the card and went looking for Steve Allen.

Ten minutes later, after getting directions, Louis stepped into a room in one of the Playhouse's upper stories. The place had been refitted into an editing suite cum screening room, with a projector, tape player, editing console, chairs and sofas dotted around. Steve was seated at the console, talking with a few suits sitting on the sofas. He waved Louis in.

'Let me introduce you,' he said.

The suits turned out to be executives from NBC. They talked jazz to Louis, the type of West Coast jazz that rich old white guys listened to now that the music was mainstream, freed from the social and racial stigma that had dogged it for much of Louis' career. As the youth migrated to rock, rhythm and blues, or the soul music pumped out of Motown's womb-to-tomb hit factory, jazz had become the preserve of well-heeled types, the cocktail party crowd, the college campus crowd, the rich, white TV executive crowd. While Louis made small talk he had that same feeling he'd had staring at the photos of all his dead pals in the lobby, that something had been lost with jazz music's acceptance into the mainstream, something essential, that the New Orleans of his youth was being washed away.

After a while the suits said their goodbyes and left the editing suite.

'Thank God for that,' Steve said. 'The worst kind of exec is a network TV exec. They don't have the talent to be creative, or the smarts to work for a proper business, so they end up in TV, where they can fuck two things up at once. They've been dogging me since the Lenny Bruce thing, coming down here for surprise visits to spot-check all the pre-recorded skits we're putting out.'

Louis nodded. A while back Steve had invited a young comedian called Lenny Bruce onto the show to do a few stand-up routines. They'd caused such a scandal the show's sponsors had threatened to pull the plug, and now the network was keeping Steve under close supervision.

He hit a button on the console and pre-recorded footage started playing on the screen. Steve standing on a sidewalk, interviewing a glassy-eyed white guy dressed in a poncho.

'All I know,' the man in the poncho said, 'the weekend Jimmy Hoffa disappeared, there was a lot of UFO activity.'

It was one of the skits that Steve's show was famous for – Steve prowling the streets around the Playhouse late at night, filming impromptu vox-pop interviews with members of the public. Just over the road from the Playhouse was the Hollywood Ranch Market, a supermarket popular with both hippies and Hollywood celebrities. The market had no doors, was open twenty-four hours, seven days a week, with a sign above it proclaiming: *We Never Close*, and to underscore the point, a giant clock fixed onto its roof whose hands ran backwards. Steve and his camera crew would pitch up at the Ranch Market at three, four o'clock in the morning and interview the hippies, wackos and weirdos who were there at that time of night, the types of nut jobs Los Angeles was famous for.

'What did you want to see me about?' Steve asked as he scrubbed through the footage.

Louis told him he wanted to track down Karl Drazek. As soon as Louis mentioned the name, Steve frowned, paused the footage, turned to look at him.

'Drazek?' Steve said. 'Why d'you want to know about Drazek?'

'For a friend. You know him?'

'Yeah, I know him. We worked on a few shows together when we were over at Universal.'

'He's not there anymore?'

Steve shook his head. 'He quit a few years ago, after Korshak and MCA took over Universal and merged the film and TV units together.'

Louis frowned, thought back to his lunch with Glaser, how Korshak and Reagan had been sitting a few tables away. The Mob lawyer seemed to be everywhere. Was Korshak connected to Drazek's exit from Universal? Was he connected to Ida's case? Was there really a link between the Night-Slayer and the men who ran the city? Once more Louis had the gloomy sense that they were all caught in a dark net that was too vast and intricate to ever be seen in its entirety.

'I heard he went to work at an independent film-production company,' Steve said. 'Strange move.'

'How so?'

'Everyone else is moving the other way – from film to TV, because that's where the action is these days. All the big film studios are getting killed. Why go out to a movie theater when you can watch TV at home? They're hemorrhaging money. MGM's holding movie memorabilia auctions just to stay afloat. They sold Dorothy's slippers from *The Wizard of Oz* not long back. Fifteen grand. It's ain't a good sign, Satch, so the talent's all jumping ship.'

'But Drazek went the other way.'

Steve nodded.

'He's shady, Louis.'

'Shady how?'

'He's one of those rich, powerful, successful types who isn't happy being rich, powerful and successful, feels like he's got to spice things up, live life on the edge. Slums it with the freaks on the Sunset Strip, the junkies up in Laurel Canyon, mobsters, cultists, bikers. Anyone dangerous and exciting.'

Louis nodded, getting the measure of the man.

'Say I wanted to get hold of Drazek, where'd I find him?'

'I haven't heard from him in months, but I can ask around if you want.'

'Thanks, pops.'

They smiled at each other. Steve turned back to the console, hit play, and the skit started up again. Footage of the clock above the Ranch Market, its hands flying backwards, time reversing with beautiful elegance. Louis stared at the image, thinking of his dead pals on the lobby wall, the doctor's appointment that afternoon.

The footage cut back to the man in the poncho.

'It's a whole different world, baby,' he said. 'A whole different world.'

# PART SEVENTEEN

## DANTE

# 47

Dante and Loretta found Wayne Bach's apartment building easily enough – a crumbling stucco affair painted dollhouse pink on a busy, smog-choked street in El Segundo. Even though he hadn't slept, Dante was wide awake, wired on adrenaline, desperate to find out everything he could about the man who'd attacked him and why.

'How are we going to get in?' Loretta asked.

'I took some keys from his corpse. I'm guessing they're for this place. We need to make sure it's empty first. Maybe his accomplice was also his room-mate.'

They approached the intercom next to the front door and Dante buzzed the number for the apartment. They waited. No one responded.

He turned to Loretta.

'You got gloves?' he asked.

'Sure, in my handbag.'

'Put them on.'

After they both put their gloves on Dante slid the dead man's keys into the lock. They worked. He and Loretta stepped into a cool, shady entrance lobby. They took the stairs to the third floor. They found the door to Bach's apartment.

'Stand behind me,' Dante whispered. 'Just in case.'

He took his gun from his pocket, held it in one hand, put his ear against the door and waited. Heard nothing.

He rang the bell, stepped back, waited once more.

Again nothing.

With his free hand he slipped the keys into the lock and

pushed open the door. It swung back, revealing the apartment's lounge, a roomy place with big windows looking out over an oil rig in the building's backyard. Dante stayed in the doorway, looked about for signs of a room-mate or a girlfriend, didn't find any. It all screamed bachelor pad and rarely used. He entered, checked the rooms at triple speed to confirm no one was home. He went back to the front door, ushered Loretta in, locked the door behind her, leaving the keys in the lock.

'OK,' he said. 'Now we toss the place.'

In the living-room sideboard they found cocaine and marijuana, stacks of *National Geographic* from the Second World War. In the bedroom they found a box under the bed; inside were a handgun, a garrote wire, a machete and porno mags, all blonde women in leather. In a storage trunk in the bottom of the wardrobe they found Nazi paraphernalia – a Luger, military medals, badges from the Berlin Olympics.

'Wayne Bach isn't exactly endearing himself to me,' Loretta said.

Dante suppressed a smile, carried on working. In the bedside cabinet was a tobacco tin with a hypodermic in it, a vial full of a clear liquid.

'Steroids?' Loretta asked.

'Maybe. He was juiced up on something when he attacked me.'

Also inside the cabinet was a Kodak envelope containing photos. Most of them were of two couples on a trip to the beach.

'Is one of them the guy who tried to kill you?' Loretta asked.

'Yeah, that's him,' Dante said, pointing to a shot of Bach.

The woman accompanying him in the photos was blonde and statuesque and fitted the Nazi ideal of the porno mags. The other man was in his thirties, with brown, windswept hair and an easy smile. He wore a polo shirt with a logo embroidered onto it: an illustration of a hamburger and underneath it the words *Benny's Burger Shack*. He had a muscled build, tree-trunk arms.

'Looks like he worked out as much as Bach did,' Loretta said.

'You think he could have been the accomplice who came to the warehouse?'

'Let's hope so,' Dante said. 'It'll make for an easy lead.'

They flipped through the rest of the photos, but they showed nothing more than the day out at the beach, a few pics of the sunset, the two couples lounging around their car before the drive back home.

In one of the drawers in the kitchen, they hit gold. A travel wallet filled with documents: the rental lease on the apartment, the paperwork for a Chevrolet, a receipt from a garage, an earnings statement in Bach's name from Universal City Studios. Dante paused.

'Universal,' he said. 'It's the same studio where Karl Drazek worked.'

'Who's Drazek?'

'Riccardo had a girl working for him at Ocean Movies, Audrey Lloyd, she was killed in a motel room hit just after Riccardo disappeared. Lloyd got the job through Drazek.'

'Could be a coincidence,' Loretta said. 'Universal must employ a few thousand people.'

'Could be. But if it's not, it brings us one step closer to finding out what happened to Riccardo.'

Dante flicked through more documents, found Bach's letter of employment. It listed his position as 'security'.

'Same job you used to have,' Loretta smiled ruefully.

The job title was deliberately ambiguous. It could mean Bach was manning a gate or patrolling the lot at night. It could mean he was a hired goon. Or that he worked as a studio fixer, like Dante had.

'It's dated three months ago,' Loretta said, scanning the employment letter. 'The apartment lease and the Chevrolet paperwork are dated three months ago, too.'

Dante frowned. He took Bach's driving license from his

pocket, showed it to Loretta. It too had been issued at the same time.

'Bach's life in LA only starts to exist three months ago,' Dante said. 'Rented a room, rented a car, got a driver's license and a job, all within a few weeks.'

'He must have only arrived here then. Either from out of town, or from a prison somewhere in-state.'

'I don't see Universal giving out security jobs to fresh ex-cons. He's an out-of-towner.'

'He strike you as the kind of guy the FBN or CIA might hire?' Loretta asked.

'I dunno. It's like you said back at the warehouse – the whole thing feels too sloppy for a government agency. And all the weapons in here. The Nazi crap. Bach was a psychopath. Who hires someone like that? Maybe when O'Shaughnessy has run his name we might find out. Either way, I don't like where this is going.'

Dante returned the paperwork to the drawer and they went back to the photos in the Kodak envelope, the ones showing Bach's pal in his polo shirt with the *Benny's Burger Shack* logo.

'I can't see him flipping burgers or slinging plates,' Loretta said.

'Maybe it's a cover job. Or a parole gig. Either way, all it'll take to find him is a look through the phonebook for Benny's Burger Shack.'

'You're making it sound like it's going to be easy.'

'One thing I've realized all the years I've been doing this job – if it's going easy, it's probably because it's going wrong and you haven't realized.'

They looked at the photos a moment longer. In the silence they could hear the low wheezing of the oil rig in the backyard, like a series of breaths that always seemed on the point of dying, but never did. They turned to look out of the window. Half-hidden behind a row of Mexican fan palms, it was the type of small-scale horse-head pumpjack that used to exist in yards and gardens and empty lots all over LA. It was rusted and ancient-looking and would probably be tapped out soon. They watched the pump move up and down, dipping its head to the earth, pumping out oil. The oil that financed the state even as it destroyed it.

'How the hell did he put up with the noise?' Loretta said.

'Maybe that's what drove him crazy.'

# 48

Dante called directory assistance and got an address for Benny's Burger Shack, which turned out to be in Huntington Beach. An hour later Dante and Loretta were there, cruising the beachfront, which was teeming, cars parked fender to fender all the way down, glinting in the sun. The sidewalks were filled with people heading toward the ocean despite the cold. Half of them had portable radios with them, switched on already, so songs clashed over the roar of the traffic.

Towering behind all of this was a steep ridge that ran parallel to the beach, the high ground atop it cordoned off by wire fences and studded with dozens of oil derricks pumping away, great iron structures that resembled telephone pylons, Eiffel towers, looming over the beach like a rusting metal forest, nightmarish and apocalyptic. And yet the sand was full of people, families, teens, couples, unperturbed by the mechanized landscape, happy to spend their Christmas Eve relaxing in the shadow of heavy, noxious industry.

Dante and Loretta found the Burger Shack in amongst the stores and eateries that lined the beachfront road. Dante was surprised to see rows of Harleys parked outside of it. He thought back to the Nazi trash in Bach's apartment; the medals, the Luger, the porno mags full of Aryan beauties.

'I get the feeling we're on the right track,' Loretta said.

Dante moved the Thunderbird a little further down the street. Then he and Loretta and the dog walked back, cast a few glances through the window and clocked the clientele – ex-cons, knifers, meat heads, brawlers. Like a casting call of punch-clock villains.

All of them white, smash-nosed, dressed in denim and leather, many of them prison-inked in swastikas, eagles, iron crosses.

'Guess it's more of a biker bar than a burger shack,' Loretta said.

'We walk in there asking questions we probably don't come out alive.'

'So what are our options?'

Dante considered.

'Let me call O'Shaughnessy back to get Wayne Bach's rap sheet. Maybe it'll give us a lead.'

They found a payphone further down the strip and Dante put a call through to O'Shaughnessy at the Glass House. As he waited to be connected he looked up at the giant oil derricks looming over him on the ridge behind the beach. Christmas trees had been affixed to one of them, running all the way up to its top, four or five stories high, their fuzz of pine needles adding to the sense that the headland was covered by a spindly metal forest.

'Where you been, pal?' O'Shaughnessy's voice boomed down the phone. 'I got Wayne Bach's rap sheet for you. Reads like a railroad schedule, most of it courtesy of the Vegas PD.'

Vegas. Dante's mind jumped back to Ocean Movies, to the actresses that looked like Vegas showgirls Riccardo had been hiring for his films. Was Bach an accomplice of Riccardo's?

'What are the details?' Dante asked.

'Like I said, Vegas PD stuff mainly, some Highway Patrol arrests in there too – DUIs and grand theft auto. A few bar fights and assault charges that were dropped on insufficient evidence. Nevada State convictions for drug possession and distribution: LSD, barbiturates, and the motherload of black beauties back in December sixty-one. Got four years in Carson City. Released this January. Parole ended in September.'

Dante nodded. Black beauties – the same form of high-strength Mexican amphetamines Riccardo had been busted for years before. Maybe Bach had a line to the same Mexican drug runners Riccardo used. And the timeline fitted. Bach's parole had ended three months back, the same time the paperwork in his apartment started. As soon as his parole was over and he was free to leave the State of Nevada, he'd upped sticks and moved to California.

'He got any KAs in the file?' Dante asked.

'He's got a whole football team of 'em, all in Vegas except for three with Los Angeles addresses.'

Dante pulled the photos he'd taken from Bach's out of his pocket, gave O'Shaughnessy a description of the man in the Burger Shack shirt.

'That match to any of the three in LA?' he asked.

The line went silent as O'Shaughnessy checked the files.

'Uh-hunh. Kyle DeVeaux. Twenty-eight. No current address on file. He's on parole for possession of dangerous drugs, released from Folsom six months ago.'

Dante considered this. He thanked O'Shaughnessy, hung up, and stood there a second, his mind jumping to Wayne Bach's body buried under the rubble of the warehouse. When the cops uncovered it and found out he was a criminal, they'd add two and two together and come up with five, figuring Bach was Dante's accomplice in an arson job gone wrong, or worse, that Dante had murdered Bach and set the fire to cover it up.

'Everything OK?' Loretta asked.

He laid it on her and she looked at him with deepening worry. When he finished, she mulled it over.

'We'll get through this,' she said.

'Sure.'

'So what do we do now?'

'We check if the guy in the Burger Shack shirt is Kyle DeVeaux, the guy whose name O'Shaughnessy just gave me. He matches the description and he's on parole, and working in a burger joint's a parole-type job.'

Dante picked up the phone, called directory assistance again, got the number for the Burger Shack and called it. After a few rings someone picked up. Dante could hear the roar of rock music playing in the background, rough and distorted by the phone line.

'Yeah?' shouted a voice over the roar.

'Is Kyle on shift? I need to talk to him,' Dante said, trying to keep it as vague as possible.

'Yeah, he's on shift, which means he ain't got time to talk. Who is this?'

'You know when he's getting off?'

'Who is this?'

'It's a pal of his from Folsom.'

The line went quiet except for the distorted pounding rock music.

'He finishes at seven, call back then.'

And with that, the man hung up.

Dante put down the phone.

'Well?' Loretta asked.

'It's him. And he's on shift. But I got a bad feeling I just tipped him off.'

Dante moved the Thunderbird again, to a spot at the edge of the beach with a view of the Burger Shack's entrance and the yard to the side where the kitchen door was. He got his gun from his pocket, laid it on his lap, thought about the imminent confrontation with DeVeaux, the violence it would entail, the way having Loretta there would complicate things.

'Maybe you should let me take it from here,' he said.

'Screw you, Dante. I'm not going anywhere. And it'd be nice if you told me what the plan is.'

He considered, and realized he didn't have it in him to break yet another promise.

'We wait till his shift's over, we follow him, we find the right opportunity and we surprise him. Exactly what they did to me. In the meantime, we hope my phone call doesn't make him skip out of there early, guns blazing.'

She nodded and they fell silent. Dante tried to take his mind off his jitters, stared out over the sea. Despite the winter chill, the water was peppered with surfers, riding their way back to shore, or out into the distance to pick up waves.

'This happen a lot when you're on a job?' Loretta asked.

'What?'

'Waiting around? Just sitting in a car waiting around.'

'Yeah, more often than not it's a waiting game.'

Loretta mulled this over.

'Huh,' she said.

'What?'

'When you were out on jobs all those years and I was at home, lying in bed, wondering what you were up to, I always imagined you were out there doing something exciting. If I'd have known you were just sitting in your car looking at storefronts, it wouldn't have been so bad. I guess we were both just waiting around.'

She shrugged. Dante looked at her and frowned, saddened by this picture she'd painted of their marriage.

'Why didn't you say anything?' he asked.

'I did. You think I kept my mouth shut? You kept your ears shut.'

Had it really been like that? A panic rose inside him that he was somehow a stranger in his own life. Why had it taken the warehouse turning to ash, and Loretta coming out on a job, for him to realize?

'You were right about what you said that day at the warehouse,' he said.

'What day?'

'When I told you I got the job from Licata. You said it was a last fling. You said all this time I'd been putting us in danger 'cos I got off on the thrill off all the side jobs. You were right. I was an asshole, Loretta. I should have brought you in, or not done it at all. Looking back on it now, it was like someone else was making all those choices. Not that that's an excuse.'

'You weren't an asshole, Dante. That's the last thing you were. I saw how the other wiseguys treated their wives. Not an ounce of respect. You were never like that. And what I said at the warehouse, you got it all wrong. If I thought you were putting yourself in danger just for kicks, I would have left you years ago. You put yourself in these situations because you still feel guilty over what happened in Chicago. How everyone else died, but you survived. It's always made you feel like you didn't deserve this life you got to lead. So you put it all on the line. But it's just your guilt, Dante. Which is good. Imagine if you went through all that trauma and *didn't* feel any guilt.'

He let her words soak through him, unsure what to feel. Maybe he *had* always felt unworthy of his family, of his life, because of what had happened to his previous family. Was that why he put it all to the test? To see if he really did deserve it? To have some certainty?

'Don't start re-evaluating everything while you're in a slump,' Loretta said. 'We had a good life together and we'll have an even better one when we fix this all up and get the hell out of LA.'

She smiled at him through the gloom and he smiled back. Whatever lay in store, the fact Loretta was by his side gave him strength, a sense of purpose he hadn't felt in years.

'Why are you looking at me like that?' she frowned.

'Because I can't tell if you and me working together is a reckoning for past sins, or just a way to create a whole bunch of new ones.'

She looked at him slant-eyed and smiled.

'Why not both?'

# PART EIGHTEEN

## IDA & KERRY

# 49

Kerry dreamed of the house back in Gueydan, the bayou, the pecans. She stood in the yard with Stevie and both her parents, smiling, the live oak with the blue medicine bottles swaying in the breeze. But then in the distance, a buzzing, a swarm of locusts approached, metallic, their rotor-blades chopping the air, whining, dropping napalm across the bayou, setting it alight. The trees caught fire, the bushes, even the surface of the water. And then the flames were on top of the house, burning up her parents and Stevie, but they just stood there in the yard, smiling at her.

She awoke with a jolt, in a sweat, heart racing, disorientated. She could still smell the napalm of her dream, in her nose, on her hair.

'Shit,' she muttered to herself.

She looked around, her vision tinted with sleep. She was in the passenger seat of Ida's car, which was still parked outside the slaughter ranch. The light was different now, later in the day. How long had she been asleep? She could see Ida outside, leaning on the hood, arms folded, watching the goings-on.

The whole scene had changed since the cops had screeched up. The ranch was abuzz with men and equipment, flooded with high beams and red-and-blues, a mix of county cops and LAPD detectives. The county cops had come first, had treated Ida and Kerry like criminals until Ida told them the murders were related to an ongoing LAPD homicide investigation. The county cops had told them to stay put till everything had been verified, and that was when Kerry had gone back to the car to rest her eyes.

She opened the door and stepped out, perched herself on the hood next to Ida.

'How long was I asleep?' Kerry asked.

'Couple of hours.'

'They haven't said we can go yet?'

'No, they said we can go. I asked to stick around. I want to see if they come up with any evidence, any IDs for the victims, confirm it really is Cooper we found.'

Kerry nodded, looked over to the ranch house. Two men were entering the building, carrying bulky cases of medical equipment. Kerry thought about Cooper running to this ranch for safety and being slaughtered by Faron. She tried not to draw parallels with Stevie, who was also on Faron's list of targets.

'Did you speak to them about that name we found in the book underneath the Ford?' Kerry asked.

'Bud Williams? Yeah. First thing I did when the LAPD detectives turned up was ask them to radio the name through to Feinberg. It's another reason we're waiting around – for Feinberg to show up. I remembered I still had those files he gave me in the car – the list of Vacaville inmates who checked out *Gumbo Ya-Ya*. Bud Williams is on the list. If it turns out Cooper isn't the Night-Slayer, I'd say Bud Williams is our next-best suspect. I know you're flying back tomorrow, but I got a feeling this is all coming to a head before then.'

Kerry nodded again. She had the same feeling they were closing in on the Night-Slayer, but she still wasn't sure there was enough time to find Stevie.

Ida smiled at her.

'Good work with figuring out there was something suspicious about where the Ford was parked,' she said.

'It just looked odd,' Kerry shrugged.

'It was still a good spot. I should have noticed it myself, but I guess I'm getting old. It shows you've got a talent for this kind of thing.'

Kerry shrugged again. They settled into silence, watched the crime scene once more. Just further on, by the gates to the ranch, a few of the local county cops were shooting the breeze. The same local cops that had given Ida and Kerry a hard time, had sauntered about the ranch contaminating the scene while they waited for the LAPD to show up. They noticed Kerry staring at them and stared back. Beneath their thin veneer of professionalism, the county cops seemed pleased that it might all be the LAPD's problem soon, pleased that their prejudices about the dropouts who'd lived at the ranch had been well-founded. The hippies had arrived from Los Angeles, bringing the taint of that Gomorra to their doorstep, and now they were no more.

Just then a young man in a suit stepped through the gates of the ranch, passed the local cops, approached Ida and Kerry.

'Ma'am,' he said, addressing Ida.

'Detective Ericksson,' Ida said. 'This is my colleague Kerry Gaudet.'

Ericksson tipped his hat at Kerry. Kerry nodded back, surprised that Ida had referred to her as a colleague.

'The detective's with the LAPD,' Ida explained to Kerry.

'We managed to get a few IDs,' Ericksson said, turning back to Ida. 'The young girl in the sleeping quarters was Jennifer Stevens, fourteen, from Colorado Springs. We checked with missing persons when we saw her age. Her mother reported her missing eight months ago. No one's seen her since. No arrests or convictions.'

Ida nodded. Kerry's mind jumped to Colorado Springs, where a police car was probably slicing through whatever suburb the girl had skipped out on; officers were knocking on a door, shattering someone's world.

'And the men?' Ida asked.

'Your pal there in the dust,' the detective said, pointing to the first body they'd come across. 'Adrian Morris. Twenty-five. Washington State driver's license. Conviction for statch rape three years ago back in Seattle, then last year a California conviction for forging Dexedrine prescriptions. And finally, the Negro male in the lounge quarters, or whatever they are. Peter Cooper. Twenty-five. This one's a doozy. Stints in juvenile detention as a teenager. Long list of assaults and thefts, all in LA. Then some public-order stuff in San Fran. After that, he did a stint in Salinas Valley after he got high and launched an arson attack on a police station. He was declared insane and moved to Vacaville, from where he escaped back in October.'

Ida nodded, pretending this was new information.

'We also ran a search on that Ford Falcon,' Ericksson said. 'It was registered stolen two months ago down in San Clemente, was seen at a string of break-ins of abandoned houses near Westchester and Inglewood. It's where the freeway extension's being built, pretty much a ghost town now, so lots of kids are breaking in, squatting, starting fires. Then it was clocked at another break-in at a doctor's office in Torrance, stealing prescription pads. Looks like they were keeping busy.'

'OK. Thanks for letting me know,' Ida said. 'Any news on when Feinberg'll be getting here?'

'I don't think he'll be getting here for a while,' he frowned. 'He's at the other crime scene.'

'What other crime scene?'

'You didn't hear? There's been another Night-Slayer killing.'

# 50

It felt strange to be rushing from one crime scene to another, from Faron's killing field to the Night-Slayer's. Ida had a sense of the two killers stalking each other, playing a gruesome game, unleashing upheaval through the city like an earthquake.

On the drive over, Ida got Kerry to tune the car radio to an all-news station that was giving rolling updates. As they listened Ida got annoyed that none of the reports mentioned the manner of the latest victim's death. She wanted to know which Louisiana folk tale the killer had emulated this time. But it wasn't until they'd reached Baldwin Hills that the reporters started mentioning a forensic seen leaving the crime scene with a bloody axe in a plastic evidence bag.

'The Axeman?' Kerry said, turning to Ida.

Ida batted back waves of panic.

'You know about the Axeman?'

'Sure. He was one of the local boogeymen. One of the ghost stories the older kids at the orphanage used to tell after lights-out.'

Ida nodded.

'The Axeman was my first-ever case in New Orleans,' she said.

'I thought it was folklore,' Kerry frowned.

'It is now. Apparently.'

Ida must have said it bitterly because when Kerry next spoke, her tone was consoling.

'I mean, it's not the actual Axeman,' Kerry said. 'It's the Night-Slayer. It's a copycat. It doesn't mean anything.'

'Maybe. But it still feels like old wounds opening up.'

It was unsettling to think that her first-ever case had gone down into folklore, from where the Night-Slayer had retrieved it, re-enacted it, here in Los Angeles, fifty years later. A familiar sense of despondency filled Ida. She'd never caught Faron, the Pinkertons had taken over her agency, and now, the first case she'd ever solved had been mimicked by a copycat, and a poor one at that. It felt as if her entire life's work was being undone, turning to dust, and she was still alive to watch it happen.

Suddenly she was back in New Orleans fifty years ago, just a girl again, standing on a cold, foggy street, waiting for a funeral march to go past. Strange to think it had all started at a funeral. She'd gone down there looking for Louis, to ask for his help as she began her investigation into the Axeman. She'd found Louis, and he'd offered his help, and the funeral had marched off into the fog. But it was as if she was still standing on that street, still alone, still feeling the chill of that morning, like it had been clinging to her through all the years since.

'You ever hear of Jake Bird?' Ida asked. 'The Tacoma Axe-Killer?'

Kerry shook her head.

'He got sentenced back in forty-nine for killing a mother and a daughter with an axe. Went to the gallows claiming he'd killed another forty people, all of them with axes, most of them women, right across the country, Florida to Washington State.'

'So?'

'So history repeats itself. I read about this Christian sect once, believed there wasn't just one Jesus. That in each generation a Jesus was born, a Judas, a Pilate. Different names, different faces, but the same drama played out, over and again, down through the centuries. I'm wondering if maybe as well as a Jesus and a Pilate there's a Devil born into every generation, a Faron, a Night-Slayer, an Axeman, someone the rest of us have a duty to stop.'

Kerry kept her eyes on the road. Ida got the feeling she'd made the girl uncomfortable with her pessimistic mysticism.

'Every house with a woodpile and a fireplace has got an axe,' Kerry said. 'They're easy to find, easy to pick up, easy to swing at someone when the red mist's come down. If there's axe killings every few years, it's just because axes are everywhere.'

'Sure, but that doesn't change history. New Orleans in nineteen nineteen. Tacoma in nineteen forty-nine. LA now. Who's to say in twenty years there won't be another Axeman coming down the line?'

'Then there'll be another detective there to stop him.'

The scene outside the victim's house in Baldwin Hills was even more frenzied than that at the ranch. Neighbors had come out, reporters, camera crews; a TV news helicopter was circling, getting aerial shots, pissing everyone off.

When Ida and Kerry had squeezed through the scrum, Ida signaled over a uniform, who went to fetch Feinberg. He came to meet them a couple of minutes later.

'This Stevie Gaudet's sister?' he asked.

'This is her,' Ida said.

Feinberg and Kerry nodded at each other.

'Let's talk out back,' he said.

He let them through the cordon and they walked around the side of the victim's home, a well-maintained bungalow set in a well-maintained garden. They stepped into the backyard, which had been turned into an operations hub, with cases of equipment strewn across the lawn, cops and forensics coming and going. Feinberg led them over to a low retaining wall at the very end of the garden. They sat on the wall, lit cigarettes.

'They said on the radio he killed her with an axe,' Ida said.

'Yeah. You wanna step inside, have a look?'

Ida turned to the victim's bungalow, to the open kitchen door.

But she'd had enough of butchery for one day, of picking over corpses.

'No,' she said. 'You can tell us.'

Feinberg nodded.

'Victim was Barbara Martinez, thirty-seven. Worked in a library over on La Brea Avenue. She didn't turn up for work two days running, wasn't answering the phone, so her colleagues came round this morning. Broke in, found her. It's the same as the previous ones – she lived alone, was butchered in the night. Same crossroads sigil on the wall. Only difference is this one's worse than the others . . . He hacked her up so bad she's just pieces now.'

He gave them a quick rundown on the crime scene, sparing nothing in describing the extent of the savagery, the severed limbs, a head cleaved through.

'It's the Axeman myth, right?' Feinberg asked.

'Yeah,' Ida said flatly, too weary to correct him about it being a myth. 'Was the victim working at the library the afternoon before she was killed?'

'She was. I know what you're thinking – it's another prison location. We've got men interviewing all the staff there, seeing if they've spotted anyone loitering the last few days. Anyway, it was the icing on the cake. Now everyone in the division believes your folklore prison-triggered theory. We're pursuing it as the primary line of inquiry. Hence me being able to consult with you out in the open again.'

And all it took them was one more brutal murder, Ida thought.

'We're also following up Bud Williams as our lead suspect,' Feinberg continued. 'As soon as you sent his name through I had someone at the Glass House dig out his file, got some more telexes from Vacaville. I also sent down his mugshot to the library. Any of the victim's colleagues recognize him, then we know we've got our man.'

He passed Ida a folder of papers he'd been carrying with him.

'Williams is twenty-four. He was admitted to the Medical

Facility at Vacaville three years back after going for a jaywalk along the Golden State Freeway. Caused a pile-up. He had a long history of psychiatric problems before that. He was released back in August. Moved out to his grandmother's house in Pacoima. I had some uniforms head down there to interview her. There's notes in the folder. She says he disappeared around the start of October.'

'That's a couple of weeks before the first Night-Slayer killing.'

Feinberg nodded.

'The grandmother says when Williams came out of Vacaville he was a mess. Like he'd regressed. She also said just before he ran off, a cop came to visit him. Or at least someone pretending to be a cop. He matches Hennessy's description.'

'She have any idea where Bud is now?' Ida asked.

Feinberg shook his head.

'She says the last time she saw him was maybe three, four weeks ago. He turned up out of the blue at her church one Sunday. She said he looked ragged, like a vagrant. He told her he'd been staying with friends from Vacaville at a horse-riding ranch out of town somewhere.'

'The ranch we've just been at,' Ida said. 'He'd been there with Pete Cooper.'

'Looks like it. Ericksson said on the radio the slaughter-job there happened at least a week ago, though.'

'Means Bud Williams was there, and he left before Faron arrived and killed everyone.'

'Lucky escape for Bud, not so lucky for Barbara Martinez,' Feinberg said, nodding at the bungalow. 'Last thing he told his grandmother was he'd be back home by Christmas. That once Christmas had come, everything was going to be all right. That make any sense to you?'

Ida frowned. Bud had set a deadline, the same one Cooper had mentioned to Mouzon. She told Feinberg about it. He took in the information, frowned.

'Maybe we'll find out what they mean come Christmas Day,' he said.

'Maybe.'

He gestured toward the paperwork in Ida's hand.

'Anyway, read the file,' he said. 'There's details in there of the connection Williams has to Louisiana. It explains how we missed it when we did our initial trawl through all the inmates in Vacaville. There's also a photo courtesy of grandma.'

Ida opened the folder. The photo was clipped to the cover sheet. It showed Bud Williams standing in a front yard somewhere, smiling uncertainly at the camera. He was of average height, chubby, young-looking. He was dressed in jeans and a check shirt and his hair was unkempt. He looked completely unremarkable. Although there was something hollow in his eyes, something withdrawn. Ida could see how he might have stumbled onto folklore, mythology, voodoo, to fill that emptiness.

'Oh, there's something else,' Feinberg said. 'Remember I told you we'd run checks on Audrey Lloyd under her real name – Audrey Lopez. Well, they came back. She wasn't from Florida like she told her room-mate. She was from Michigan. Had a string of federal drug convictions. Her last stay in prison ended two years ago. She was busted again back in August last year, but the charges were dropped, suspiciously. Looks like she was an actress, Ida, just not the kind we thought.'

Ida frowned, analyzing what Feinberg was telling her. Audrey was an ex-con with federal narcotics charges dropped just in time for her to be placed in Riccardo's office.

'She was a plant,' Ida said. 'An FBN plant.'

'Yeah, that's my guess. FBN recruited and trained, and dumped with Riccardo to spy on him. We've been looking around for Karl Drazek, the guy who got Audrey the job at Ocean

Movies – maybe he's FBN as well, maybe he's working with Hennessy – but we can't find any trace of him.'

'He's probably on the run from Faron,' Ida said. 'Like everybody else.'

'Yeah, that was my thought, too.'

A uniform approached, called Feinberg away. Ida turned to see Kerry staring at her.

'This is all a dead end, isn't it?' Kerry said. 'Cooper's dead. Bud Williams is missing. No one knows where Drazek is. All our leads have dried up.'

Ida saw how upset Kerry was, but she knew there was no point trying to reach for silver linings, false hope.

'Yeah, they've all dried up.'

They shared a forlorn look. They were both stressed, tired, desperate. Even if it turned out Bud Williams was the Night-Slayer, it wouldn't feel like a victory. Not yet. He was still out there killing. And so was Faron. On top of that, Williams wasn't even the most important part of the case. The conspiracy behind him was what mattered, and that was still shrouded in mystery. And in addition to all that, Ida had promised to help Kerry find Stevie, and she'd let the girl down. With less than a day before Kerry had to fly back, they were still no closer to finding him. If there was any hope of tracking down Hennessy and Stevie before Faron got to them, Karl Drazek was it. But it seemed like no one else could find him either.

'I'm sorry,' Ida said.

'It's not your fault,' Kerry replied, not meeting her gaze.

Ida sighed and turned to look around the garden. She saw how much care had gone into its upkeep. The lawn was trimmed and watered, the borders weed free and filled with winter-blooming flowers. A confederate jasmine had been trained across the bungalow's rear wall; there was a bitter-orange tree with the grass below it cleared of fallen fruit. Ida imagined the unfortunate, lonely librarian, spending her weekends tending her garden, living a quiet life, till the Night-Slayer followed her home.

Ida looked up to see Feinberg returning.

'We just had news from the officers interviewing the library staff,' he said. 'They spotted a kid hanging around there. The officers showed them Bud Williams' mugshot. They confirmed it was him.'

Feinberg grinned.

'It's him, Ida. Everything fits. You did it. Bud Williams is the Night-Slayer.'

# PART NINETEEN

## LOUIS

# 51

Louis sat on a bench at the edge of the beach, with the city behind him and the sun setting in front of him. He lay a hand on his chest, felt the rhythm of his heart, its beats coming just a second after the pulse in his fingertips, the gap in the rhythm like a call and response, like an echo, like waves. Strange to think one day it would stop. Sooner rather than later, if what the doctor had told him that afternoon was true.

'You're approaching seventy,' the doc had said. 'It's not like you're a guitarist or a pianist, only using your hands. You're blowing on a trumpet three hundred nights a year. It puts a strain on your lungs, your heart, your chest muscles, your blood pressure. Even before the additional test results come back, Mr Armstrong, I can tell you it's too much for a man of your age.'

Louis had nodded, yes-yes-ing, but his thoughts were already elsewhere, lost in a fog. He'd wandered out of the doctor's office, wandered the streets, ended up at the beach. He wasn't sure which beach he was on, if it was one where black people were allowed, if a cop would come along and tell him not to loiter, or worse.

He watched the waves cresting onto the sand, listened to their sound, the rhythm not much different to the one under his fingertips, the echo as waves broke at different times along the length of the shoreline. Funny how that echo had reverberated for millions of years, song-like, ceaseless, timeless.

'I need to give up?' Louis had asked the doctor forlornly.

The doc had paused, shaken his head.

'Look, I don't think it's a clear-cut choice. There's a middle ground here. You can reduce your playing to a level that's safe.

Stop being such a workhorse. The way you're living now, all this time on the road, performing, it would have an impact on the health of a man years younger. You can't carry on like this, Mr Armstrong. We'll be in contact when the rest of the results come back. In the meantime, you need to start accepting the reality of your situation.'

What the doc had told him wasn't *so* bad, but why did it feel like a death sentence? Maybe because it threw into focus how few years he had left. Should he cut out playing and extend his life, or keep doing what he'd always done and die sooner? The doc had been at pains to stress it wasn't an either-or choice. But it was.

What would he do without music? Before the Waifs Home and learning to play, he was just another kid from Back o' Town, impoverished and destined to toil his entire life in obscurity, like so many millions of others. He often thought about that other life he'd escaped. That phantom life. It followed him around like a shadow. What would he have been without his talent? A railway porter? A coal-cart driver? A killer in an abattoir?

Sometimes he looked down on the other men from Back o' Town who'd made nothing of their lives. Men like his father. It was their fault for drinking too much, getting high too much, spending all their wages on liquor and women and playing dice. But he didn't look down on them for long, because deep inside he knew it was bullshit. The only difference between him and them was he'd been bestowed with talent. And talent was a privilege, like any other, so who was he to judge? When he set down the horn, he was just as unremarkable as everyone else. And maybe that was why that other path scared him so much.

Sometimes he even had nightmares about it; that he was about to play a gig but he couldn't find his trumpet, was running around an endless backstage searching for it, floundering, drowning. The nightmares came whenever he was laid up. A few years earlier the doctors had ordered him to take some rest, so Glaser had given the band eight weeks' paid leave and Lucille and Louis went on a

Caribbean cruise. After three weeks of nightmares he jumped ship, summoned the band back to New York and told them he needed to start playing again.

He watched as the sun set and night came on and the beach emptied out. He rose and looked around. He needed to get back to the Marmont, but he didn't know where he was, and it wasn't like he could just hop in a cab. He'd visited Los Angeles enough over the years to know where a colored man should and shouldn't be after dark. It wasn't just the city's many sundown towns – Glendale, Hawthorne, Burbank, Torrance – or the LAPD's Hollywood Division, where any colored person caught out after sunset was automatically a 'shake' – an interview and a warrant check. It was also the area to the west of La Brea Avenue, to the north of Beverly Boulevard. Louis knew it wasn't a great jump from a 'shake' to a something far more dangerous.

He crossed Ocean Avenue, came to an intersection, saw the cross street – Wilshire Boulevard. Of course. He'd just wandered down the same street the doctor's was on till he'd reached the beach. If he could find a payphone, he could call the hotel, have them send a car out. He headed up Wilshire, looking for one. The highline boutiques were all still open, the sidewalks busy. Well-heeled types ambled past, cast him looks. Above them, the tops of the palms swayed in a gentle wind. All was right with the world on that winter evening in Los Angeles, all was wonderful and benign, as the West declined and society tore itself apart and Louis' heart slowly gave in to time.

He saw a payphone on the corner ahead, just opposite the windows of an electrical store. He picked up the phone, dialed information, got the number for the Marmont.

'Certainly, Mr Armstrong, sir. We can have a car sent out in the next five minutes. Where are you exactly?'

Louis gave the man the cross streets.

'While you're on the line, sir. We had message from a Mr

Steve Allen. He said it was important – an address for a Mr Karl Drazek.'

Steve had come through with the address that Ida wanted.

'Just a sec,' Louis said.

He pulled his Montblanc from his inside pocket, searched for some paper to scribble down the address. He remembered he still had the envelope with the sheet music in it that Glaser had sent over – the new song he wanted Louis to record.

He copied down the address onto the back of the envelope, hung up, called Ida. It rang straight through to her answering service. He left a message asking her to call him back, then he sat on a bench just next to the payphone, hoping the car from the Marmont arrived before any cops did. He stared across the sidewalk at the electrical store. It had a wall of television sets in its windows. Each TV was covered in red and green tinsel, with fake snow sprinkled about, reminding Louis that it was Christmas Eve, and this was how he was spending it.

The TVs were all tuned to a news program – footage of anti-war protestors, of Vietnamese jungles on fire, something about wildfires in Malibu. Louis felt a vague guilt that he was thinking of bowing out with the world in such a mess. As if he was betraying the future by leaving the young to deal with a disaster that wasn't of their making.

The news cut to commercials – Pepto-Bismol, Saran Wrap, Cadillacs. Louis knew from having seen them all before that each one had a jazz tune bouncing along in the background. Gone were the days when jazz was banned from the airwaves, when it could only be heard in nightclubs, record shops, maybe a specialist radio show in the middle of the night. Now jazz was on TV as much as shows about the Mafia. The soundtrack to corporate America. An advertisement for Colgate came on, set to an approximation of a New Orleans jazz standard.

Louis shook his head and looked at the envelope of sheet music in his hand. He figured he might as well get it over with. He

374

ripped open the envelope and took the pages out. He frowned when he saw the song title – 'What A Wonderful World'. Then he skimmed his eyes over the lyrics, which had been scribbled onto the paper in pencil underneath the staves. When he looked at the sheet music itself, the music began playing in his head, just as it always did. He scanned through it all quickly and when he had the melody right, he scanned back through it again, adding the lyrics.

The syllables pulsed with his weakened heartbeat. He ran through them all the way to the end. He pondered the sentiment, how it fitted with the melody, how it fitted with the world around him, a world on fire.

Louis could see what the songwriter was trying to get across, and as always, he wondered why. It hardly seemed appropriate to what was going on in the world just then. The race hate, the arms race, the Cold War, the ever more fractious divisions in society.

Louis tried to find the greatness in it that Glaser had seen, but couldn't. The lyrics felt sickly sweet. Corny. Syrupy. Sentimental. Too optimistic and hopeful considering the current state of the world. He imagined it with the type of string arrangement Bob Thiele preferred and it just brought back memories of the nightmare elevator music he'd heard at the airport. Could Louis really bring himself to sing it? To put his weakened heart into it? While jungles were going up in flames, and every few days there was another race riot against injustice and police brutality.

Maybe it was his own morbid mood, but as Louis read the final verse, it began to feel as if these lyrics had hints of death in them, of things coming to an end. Suddenly the song felt less saccharine and more wistful. There was regret in there. Sorrow. Like it was all the thoughts of an old man looking back on his life and listing all the things he would miss when he was gone.

Suddenly the song made sense. It was a lament. A funeral march. A sunset blues. That was the point of it – that when you were faced with nothing, even this fractured world was a wonderful one. Something worth fighting for. It was a celebration, sure, but more than that it was a last plea from someone on the way out to save it all before it really did burn up.

But could he bring himself to sing the song? Did he have enough optimism left in him, let alone lung power? And most importantly, would anyone even listen?

# PART TWENTY

## DANTE

# 52

Dante and Loretta sat in the Thunderbird and waited for seven o'clock to roll around, eyes on the Burger Shack, on the dashboard clock, on the sun dipping into the ocean, casting everything into hallucinatory hues of pink and orange. They watched the cars shooting through the dusk on Pacific Coast Highway, leaving light trails of red and white through the gloom, suspended in the pollution. They listened to the radio – reports on the desert wind whipping up wildfires in Malibu, interspersed with bright, tinselly Christmas songs.

Along the strip drinkers stumbled between the bars, the kind of nightcappers who didn't stop till noon the next day. In the shadows of the stores, vagrants slumped, clutching cans of Sterno to their chests. Behind it all the oil towers loomed like an army of robots rusting in the salt air. Dante imagined them pulling up their pylons, marching off the headland, into the sea, disappearing, like that story about the Indians during a Santa Ana.

Just before seven o'clock two workers stepped out of the Burger Shack's kitchen entrance into its yard. They leaned against the van parked there, lit cigarettes, the flare of their lighters illuminating their faces.

'That's him,' Loretta said. 'That's DeVeaux.'

Dante squinted at them through the gloom, recognized the man from the photos.

'You're right,' he said.

Dante started up the Thunderbird, waiting for DeVeaux to get in a car, drive somewhere that Dante could get the drop on him. But DeVeaux didn't look as if he was going anywhere.

'Is he waiting for a ride?' Loretta asked.

Just then DeVeaux crossed the yard to the chain-link fence that separated it from the street, looked up and down. A few seconds later, a bright red Cadillac Eldorado slow-rolled past the Burger Shack, and pulled up on its far side. A chunky thug of a man got out and walked toward DeVeaux.

Dante frowned, recognizing him.

'Holy shit,' he said, sitting up.

'You know him?'

'It's Vincent Zullo,' Dante said. 'He was there at the pool party the night Licata and Roselli hired me for the job.'

Dante's mind jumped back to the mansion, Zullo standing on the terrace with his schlubby clothes and that haze of hairspray, bragging about Vegas. Of course. Vegas was the link. Zullo was based out in Vegas now, 'procuring showgirls' for the casinos. And the actresses in Riccardo's bikini movies were all Vegas showgirls, too. What if Zullo was procuring them for Riccardo, as well? And what if they were also in the coke distribution together? That's why Zullo was at the mansion that night, keeping an eye on Licata, on Roselli. That's why he came over to Dante to find out what he was doing there.

And Vegas was where Wayne Bach had come from. Zullo must have hired Bach and DeVeaux to kill Dante. But they'd fucked it up. Hence the emergency talk Zullo and DeVeaux were having now.

'Dante?' Loretta said. 'Dante! He's made you.'

Dante snapped out of it to see Zullo and DeVeaux staring straight at him from the other side of the street, in shock, in fear. Zullo pulled something from his pocket. Black metal gleaming in the moonlight.

'Shit,' Dante said.

As Zullo went to fire, DeVeaux shouted something at him. Zullo paused, realizing it was too busy for a shoot-out. There were too many witnesses, not enough escape routes. He pocketed the gun, still glaring at Dante. Then DeVeaux was running back across the Burger Shack's yard. Then Zullo was running, too, up the street, full pelt, making for his Cadillac.

'I can cut him off,' Dante said.

He yanked the Thunderbird backward, spun it around, but he got there just a second too late. Zullo lurched his Caddy into the road and fired it down the strip, heading inland, to Beach Boulevard, the freeway.

Dante fell in behind him, checked the rearview. Where had DeVeaux gone? Was he back in the Burger Shack, telling his pals what had happened? Would Dante have a hundred Harleys on his tail?

Out of nowhere, Zullo pulled a sharp left into a side street and floored it. Dante squealed round the corner after him. Houses and stores blipped past. They hit forty miles an hour. Fifty. Sixty. The Thunderbird roared, the dog howled, Loretta pressed herself into her seat. They raced past cars and people just inches from them on those busy, narrow streets. Zullo ripped his Caddy through left and right turns, fish-tailing, screeching, always following the path away from the beach, sloping upwards toward the headland. Dante checked his rearview. Still no signs of DeVeaux, or the Harleys.

They hit the high ground, and the buildings petered out. Zullo lurched through a bend, driving parallel to the ocean now, which was far below them on their right. Then the field of oil derricks came into view on their left, separated from the road by a ten-foot wire fence.

Zullo gunned his Caddy, boosting it along the dirt road. They hit seventy, eighty, ninety, swerving through the narrow bends that followed the line of the clifftops. Dante redlined the Thunderbird, the dog went crazy.

There was a bend approaching. A tight one. Zullo was nuts if he thought he could take it at that speed. But he wasn't slowing down.

'Dante . . .' Loretta said.

The bend was approaching fast.

'Dante . . .'

The bend was almost there.

'Shit,' Dante said.

He slammed on the brakes at the last moment.

The Caddy kept going, fish-tailed. Zullo braked at just the wrong point. The Caddy spun, careened off the road, hit the fence to their left, ripped straight through it, tumbled, rolled, flipped, kicked up dirt, came to halt twenty yards inside the oil field.

Dust rose, smothering everything.

Dante screeched the Thunderbird to a stop, jumped out and pulled his gun. He stalked through the broken fence into the oil field. He couldn't see anything on account of the dust, but he could smell smoke, the acrid stench of oil. Through the yellow cloud he could hear the hiss of something escaping from the Caddy's busted engine, the dog barking, the metallic wheeze of the derricks as they pumped, the howl of the wind, blowing over the headland toward the ocean. Dante saw a shape stumble off into the distance and followed it.

The dust was clearing now and he could make out Zullo hobbling along, injured, dazed, gun in hand. He was heading to the closest derrick, to the hut at its base. He reached it, disappeared inside. Dante raised his gun, trained it on the hut's doors, panicked by the thought of a shoot-out so near to where oil was being pumped.

Just as he reached the doors, he heard the dog barking behind him. He took a quick glance over his shoulder and saw Loretta and the dog approaching through the moonlight, the wind whipping Loretta's hair about.

'Stay back,' he said to her, holding out a hand.

Then he turned and reached the doors. He looked around, saw a rock on the ground, picked it up, tossed it against them. The doors rattled. Gunshots peppered them from within. Hard, slamming raps cracking into the wood. Dante counted four of them.

He threw another rock. Again the doors rattled; another two shots. Maybe Zullo was out of bullets now. Maybe not.

Dante approached and put his back to the wall just next to the doors. With the nose of his gun he pushed one of them open slowly, till he could see a sliver of the space beyond. It was shadowy, filled with machinery clanking and groaning.

Dante risked taking a step inside. He spotted Zullo slumped in the corner, staring at him, dazed, his gun in the dust just by his hand. There was blood all over his face from the car crash, dripping down onto his shirt.

Dante walked over. Zullo's eyes followed him. Dante kneeled, took Zullo's gun, slipped it into his pocket.

'Why'd you send Bach and DeVeaux to kill me?' Dante asked.

Zullo said nothing. His head rolled, his eyes tried to focus. Dante could hear how shallow his breaths were, how hard he was gasping for air.

'Vinnie, tell me what's going on and I'll help you out of here and you can hightail it before the cops arrive.'

At the mention of cops, Zullo seemed to come to. He grinned and blood dribbled from his mouth.

'Vinnie, we need to get you to the hospital.'

'I'm fine.'

There was a noise behind Dante. He turned to see Loretta standing in the hut's doorway.

'Vinnie, you give me something now,' Dante said, turning back to Zullo. 'And I'll tell my wife to go call an ambulance. She can get to a phone in five minutes, they can be here ten minutes after that. Vinnie, you can hang on till then, all you gotta do is give me something, and we can talk while they're coming.'

Zullo nodded, saying nothing.

'You sent Bach to kill me because I was looking for Riccardo?'

'Yeah.'

'Because you and Riccardo were working the coke distribution together?'

Zullo nodded again.

Dante had been right – Zullo wasn't just supplying Riccardo with girls for Ocean Movies, he was working the coke with him, too.

'Who was your coke source, Vinnie? Tell me and I send Loretta to go and get you help.'

Zullo shook his head woozily.

'What are you so scared of?' Dante said. 'I spoke to Roselli. I know it's rogue CIA agents. I just need names. Give me names and the next thing you know, the docs'll be patching you up.'

'CIA?' Zullo mumbled. 'It wasn't CIA.'

He went silent, succumbing to his concussion once more.

'Who was it?' Dante frowned.

Zullo went woozy, started coughing. He put a hand to his mouth and it came away bloody. He stared at the blood, realized he'd coughed it up, looked shocked at the thought that his injuries were worse than he'd first imagined. He looked up, as if seeing Dante for the first time.

'Vinnie, I can help you.'

Zullo finally realized it was his best chance of survival.

'It was a Narcotics Agent called Henry White,' he said. 'Now get me a fucking doctor.'

Dante frowned. He'd been certain the coke was coming from the CIA. His mind flashed back to his meeting with Johnny Roselli on the terrace of the Georgian. Roselli with his giant sunglasses, sipping his morning cognac, telling Dante that Riccardo's coke source was rogue CIA agents in Latin America, telling him how dangerous they were.

'Get me a fucking doctor,' Zullo repeated.

Dante turned to Loretta, nodded at her. She nodded back and disappeared into the moonlight to call the paramedics. Dante turned back to Zullo, who had a sinister smile on his face.

'You've been strung along this whole time,' he said. 'Roselli was throwing you off with that CIA shit. You know why? Because Roselli set the whole thing up. And he set you up too.'

Zullo grunted out a laugh, enjoying the confusion on Dante's face. It spurred him on to talk more, to brag.

'You should see this trigger White and his pals brought in from Cambodia to clean up. He doesn't fuck around, Dante. He helped White whack Riccardo and that bitch secretary of his. All these niggers from Vacaville. And now Bach and DeVeaux fucked up, they've put him on your tail, too.'

He grinned again, but woozier this time. His eyes fluttered closed.

'Shit, I need to use the john,' he said. 'I'm gonna piss myself.'

Dante frowned. He'd seen this before. Zullo was bleeding internally. His body cavities were filling with blood, and he was mistaking it for a bladder full of piss. The poor bastard didn't realize he'd be dead soon.

'What did they do with Riccardo's body?'

Zullo's eyes blinked open. He looked around, his gaze unfocussed.

'What did they do with Riccardo's body, Vinnie?'

'They dumped it over the side of the Stunt Road,' he said, breathing shallowly as he drowned in his own blood. 'Where the trail for the Rosas Overlook starts.'

Zullo's head was rolling now. He coughed up more blood. He put a hand to his mouth again, but the blood cascaded out, and even in his dazed state he finally understood that he was dying.

'Shit,' he muttered. 'Shit.'

He looked up at Dante, his eyes full of fear.

'Don't let me die here, Dante,' he pleaded. 'Not here. Take me outside.'

Dante nodded, put his arm under Zullo's shoulder and lifted him up. They stumbled out into the wind and moonlight. A work crew had arrived in a flatbed truck, were hopping off it, watching Dante and Zullo, checking out the smashed-up Caddy.

Dante laid Zullo down in the dust, turned to the workmen.

'Someone's already gone to call the paramedics,' he said. 'Maybe one of you guys should go call them, too. Just in case.'

A couple of the workmen nodded, ran back to the truck and raced off through the dust.

Dante looked down at Zullo. Zullo stared at the line of the ocean in the distance.

'I met him,' he said. 'The trigger they brought in. He's got one target left – the Night-Slayer. And he's almost found him. And then it's you. And then he's gone. And there ain't shit you can do to stop him.'

Zullo let out a long, gravelly exhalation and closed his eyes.

'You can't stop it, Dante,' he muttered. 'We've already won. Long, long time ago.'

Dante looked from Zullo to the workmen standing around. Beyond them the wind was pushing the last of the dust cloud out toward the road and the beach below. Dante could see all the way to the Thunderbird, the dog standing next to it, barking at something in the distance. Dante frowned. Why was the Thunderbird still there? Loretta should have taken it to call an ambulance. And what was the dog barking at?

Dante left Zullo slumped in his sheet of blood, surrounded by workmen. He stalked across the field, past the Caddy, through the fence. The Thunderbird's engine was still on, the driver's side door open. Dante looked down at the tracks in the freshly settled dust. Another vehicle had come while he'd been in the hut. A van by the looks of it. The van had stopped by the Thunderbird and driven off in the direction the dog was barking.

Dante thought back to the Burger Shack's yard. There'd been a van parked there. And when Zullo had run for his car, DeVeaux had run back across the yard. To get in the van.

DeVeaux had followed them. He'd grabbed Loretta. It was the only explanation.

# 53

Five minutes later Dante was back at the Burger Shack. The van was gone. It confirmed all his fears. DeVeaux had followed them, had taken Loretta. Dante stared at the Burger Shack, at the rows of Harleys lined up in front of it. He got his Colt from his pocket, looked at the dog.

'Let's go.'

He got out, left the engine running, the door open. He strode across the street and stepped inside. The place was jammed with bikers and goons. Rock music was roaring out of a music system. As Dante crossed the space to the bar, the clientele made him straight away, quietened down, Wild West saloon style. He tried not to think of how many of the men in there were violent criminals. How many were packing knives, clubs, guns. He needed to maintain focus. Don't waver, don't falter, don't show any weakness. The only advantage he had was to be quick and forceful. He approached the counter.

'Where's the manager?' he shouted over the noise of the music.

The man behind the counter was tall, broken-nosed, covered in tattoos, with burn scars all over his arms from what Dante could only assume were motorcycle pile-ups.

'Who the fuck are you?' the man hissed.

Dante pointed the Colt at the man's head.

'I'm the trouble you've all been waiting for. Where's the manager?'

The man eyed Dante, slowly turned and hit a button on the stereo behind him, and the music cut out. All was deathly quiet except for the sound of meat and eggs sizzling on the grill in the kitchen. Dante felt the stare of everyone in the room.

The man behind the counter turned back around.

'The manager?' Dante repeated.

'I'm the manager.'

'Where's DeVeaux? He was here earlier.'

The man frowned.

'I don't know. He disappeared. Jesus, put the gun down.'

'He took the van that was parked out back?' Dante asked.

The man nodded.

Dante looked about the counter, saw a pen and a pad further along.

'I want you to write down the details of the van and I want the address you got on file for DeVeaux.'

'You think I've got all that memorized? It's in the office out back. I'll go get it.'

He gestured to the bar behind him, a passageway leading to the rear. Dante debated. Let the man go and he'd come back out again with a weapon. Go with him and Dante would be trapped. He tried to figure out which of the two moves was the least stupid. In the silence he listened for footsteps behind him, looked at the chrome that ran along the back of the counter, looked for the reflected shapes of anything moving behind him. The meat and eggs on the grill continued to sizzle.

'I'm coming with you,' Dante said, waving the gun so the man turned around.

'All right, buddy.'

Dante walked round the counter, switching the gun's aim between the man and the army of killers behind him. He nodded at the man and the pair of them walked down the passageway. It was long and narrow and perfect to get trapped in. They passed the door to the kitchen, kept going, reached a second door. The man stopped.

'It's in here,' he said. 'I'm going to open up, OK? I'm going to get the keys from my pocket.'

'Sure.'

Dante watched the man closely as he took out a set of keys. He flicked his gaze between the man and the passageway they'd walked down. The dog was at his feet and he was also looking back the way they'd come, keeping watch, ready to bark if anyone came after them. Dante looked in the other direction, where the passageway continued on for a few feet, then stopped at a door with a fire escape push-bar across it, probably the exit to the yard.

The man stepped into the office, which looked like it doubled up as a storeroom.

'I'm staying here,' Dante said.

'All right.'

The man went over to his desk, rummaged through its drawers. Dante kept the Colt trained close on him, ready to pull the trigger.

'Relax,' the man said. 'I ain't going to get into a shooting match over DeVeaux. The guy's an asshole. He stole my goddamn van.'

The man hauled a box file onto the desk, flicked through it, took a card out, copied something out onto a piece of paper. He rummaged around some more in the file, copied something else out.

'There you go,' he said, crossing the room slowly, holding out the paper for Dante to take.

As he approached, Dante had a sense of someone in the passageway behind him. He flicked his gaze there, but it was empty except for the dog. Dante flicked his gaze back to the man, expecting a punch to be coming his way, a knife to the ribs. But the man was just standing there, holding out the paper. Dante took it, glanced at it. An address in Hermosa Beach, the details of the van, its license plate number.

'If you find him, tell him I want my van back.'

'If I find him, I'm going to kill him.'

'Then just try not to damage the van.'

Dante took a step back, eased toward the fire exit behind him, heart pounding. When he reached the door he slammed the push-bar, ran into the yard as fast as he could, his old bones shaking, joints screaming, lungs burning. He couldn't remember the last time he'd run like that. He never remembered it hurting so much before.

When he got out front, there were men there now, sitting on their bikes staring him out. He swung the gun at them as he raced to the Thunderbird, as he and the dog hopped in. Thank God he'd kept the engine running. He slammed on the gas and tore out of there.

But before he was even a block away, a half-dozen Harleys were after him. The wraiths of his nightmares made real. He gunned the Thunderbird, heading inland. The dog howled. The Harleys roared. The Thunderbird roared louder. Dante had the more powerful engine, but they had the acceleration. Dante needed open road, he needed a freeway.

He overtook cars, went the wrong side of the road. The Harleys fanned out, weaved. They were gaining on him. They'd be at his windows soon. They were already pulling out pistols.

'Shit,' Dante said.

As he'd almost given up hope, he heard a train whistle in the distance. The lumber yard near Talbert Avenue, where the lumber was still delivered by rail.

He lurched left, ripping through a red-light intersection, sending cars squealing, horns blaring. He looked in the rearview, the Harleys swerving through the chaos, through the skidding cars he'd left behind. He heard the train whistle again. He floored it down Talbert Avenue. He ripped a left turn, a right, another right. He came back onto Talbert just as the train was nearing. It was going slow, its cars empty, heading back up to wherever its depot was. Dante thought about all those years he'd spent riding box cars. It'd be fitting somehow if his life ended crashing into a train.

He put his foot down and prayed.

He bumped over the railroad crossing with a second to spare, hurtling past as the train blasted its horn, as the dog howled. He heard a crash, looked in the rearview. One of the Harleys had tried to follow, had been crushed. The rest of them had stopped, were on the other side of the line now, the rusting train cars trundling across.

Dante breathed a sigh of relief. He pointed the Thunderbird back toward the freeway, heart still pounding, bones still aching, adrenaline whipping through him. He'd escaped the wraiths. For now.

# PART TWENTY-ONE

## IDA & KERRY

# 54

While Kerry caught some sleep, Ida sat on the sofa in her apartment and went through Bud Williams' psychological reports, combing them for any leads she might have missed, any clues that might help her find him or Stevie or Faron. Anything at all. They made for disturbing reading. They made her even more wired.

Bud had been born in LA, to a mother who was a native Angelino and a father from Lafayette, Louisiana, who'd moved to California during the war, looking for work in the armaments factory boom. But then the war finished and the work dried up and the government started zoning the city, so Bud's father took the family back to Lafayette. When Bud was twelve, the family were involved in a car accident. The father died on impact. Bud and his mother survived. He held her as she bled out. He tried to get cars to stop and help. But they were on a stretch of country road just outside a white town. It was dark. They all drove past. She died in his arms. Bud was sent back to LA to live with his maternal grandmother. So he had a Louisiana connection, but it wasn't on any of his California paperwork, meaning when the cops did their sweep of Vacaville inmates, looking for those with a Louisianian background, they missed him.

When Bud was twenty-one he went wandering barefoot up and down the Golden State Freeway, where he caused a fatal pile-up. This was the incident which led to his incarceration in Vacaville. It made it easy enough for Ida to draw links from Bud's mother's death on the side of the road, to the pile-up on the freeway, to the crossroads sigils he left at each murder scene. Had he become enamored of Baron Samedi because his sigil was the crossroads? Or was it something else about the mythology that chimed with his psychosis? Ida had been right that the Night-Slayer was a drifter, a zombie. He'd wandered like a sleepwalker across the Golden State Freeway and killed a family in one car and a lone motorist in another. Maybe he'd been wandering ever since his parents had died.

It was also easy to draw parallels between Bud and Stevie; both orphans from Louisiana, both making their way through trauma to California, both ending up in Vacaville, checking out the same book from its library, becoming embroiled in the same dark conspiracy.

Ida sighed and put down the psychological reports, went to the kitchenette to make herself a drink, went to the phone and checked her answering service. A message from Louis asking her to call him urgently. She phoned him straight back at the Marmont.

'I've got Drazek's address for you,' he said.

Ten minutes later Ida and Kerry were in the Cadillac, Kerry driving because Ida was so dog-tired. They headed north, hit Pacific Coast Highway. The moonlit ocean stretched out to one side of them, scrubby hills on the other. On the car radio there were reports of wildfires in Malibu again, spreading rapidly on account of the desert wind. They shared a worried look; Malibu was where Drazek's hide-out was located.

Ida punched through radio pre-sets looking for something that was neither news nor Christmas tunes, found a station playing West Coast jazz, all blue notes and shadows and melancholy.

They turned off the highway and headed up into the hills, passing through an eerie landscape of isolated mansions, RV parks, empty lots that had been marked out for development with ropes and flags and realtors' signs. Something about the drive unnerved Ida, even more so than the drive to the ranch. Maybe it was because it was night, or because of the news reports about the fires, or because the clock was ticking. Or maybe it was because of the conversation she'd had with Louis just before they'd left. He'd given her Drazek's address then told her he'd got it from Steve Allen, who'd also given Louis extra info on Drazek, on Universal and the Mob lawyer, Sidney Korshak. Then Louis had told her he'd seen Korshak having lunch with the governor, how Korshak had helped the governor out on a corrupt land deal with Fox, how maybe there was something connecting them all. Ida had heard about the land deal before, but wasn't sure how it fitted with the case. Then Louis had rambled about a dark net ensnaring them all. Ida had asked him if everything was all right, and he'd come over all embarrassed, had backtracked, made an excuse to end the call. It had left Ida feeling perturbed, worried about her friend. And yet, his talk of ensnarement chimed with her own fears.

She turned her gaze from the dark landscape outside, brought her focus back onto the case.

'There's something you can help me with while we're interviewing Drazek,' she said.

'Sure,' Kerry replied.

'Keep an eye on him while I ask the questions. Watch how he responds, how he moves. The harder the question, the more likely he's going to do something that shows we've hit a sore point. He'll fidget, squirm, look away, shift in his seat, pick something up to play with, sigh. In the moments people are coming up with a lie they're so busy trying to figure out what they're gonna say, they stop trying to control what their body's up to and it gives them away.'

'I'll try,' Kerry shrugged.

Her tone suggested she wasn't sure she was up to the task. Ida wondered if it was because she was so worried about Stevie, or simply the same uncertainty she'd seen clouding the girl now and then.

'Don't be so down on yourself,' she said. 'It's like I told you before – you're good at this kind of work. You located

Hennessy's house, figured out the Vacaville connection, got that guard to talk. You tailed Brockhalt, and you realized that Ford was hiding something at the ranch. It's impressive. I'm not sure what your situation is with your military obligations, but if you want to stick around in LA, I could get you work as a trainee investigator.'

Kerry frowned, as if confused by the offer. The frown lingered a few seconds, then Kerry realized Ida was being serious, that there was a possibility of a life away from the killing fields.

'Thanks,' she said flatly.

'Take some time to think about it and let me know.'

Drazek's hide-out was an isolated house at the crest of a hill, set behind a large, tree-filled garden, and a pair of wrought-iron gates. Ida and Kerry got out of the Caddy, and Ida buzzed the intercom to the side of the entrance. As they waited, she noticed how heavily the wind was blowing, gusting over the tops of the hills, toward the coast.

'Yes?' a voice crackled through the intercom.

'Sir, we're here to speak to Mr Drazek,' Ida said.

There was a pause before the voice spoke again.

'You're mistaken. There's no one here by that name.'

Ida could hear fear in the voice, drunkenness, too.

'It's about Riccardo Licata and the death of Audrey Lloyd,' she said.

There was another pause.

'Are you police?'

'No, sir. We're private investigators. We have information that you might be at risk and, well, we're at risk, too, sir, so we wondered if we could talk to you.'

Again another pause.

'Wait there,' the voice said eventually.

A minute later Ida saw a man walking down the driveway toward them. He was tall and lean, wore a black silk dressing gown and slippers. He was in his thirties, Ida guessed, with a long face, a five-day stubble, and wiry brown hair that was all askew.

When he was just a few yards away, Ida approached the railings to speak to him, but before she could talk, the man pulled a handgun from his pocket and pointed it at them.

'Who sent you?'

'No one, sir,' Ida replied, slowly raising her hands. 'No one sent us.'

Now he was up close, Ida could see he was terrified, dangerously so.

'Then what the hell are you doing here?'

'It's like I said, we just want to talk to you about the man who killed Riccardo and Audrey. He's after us as well. And we know he might be coming after you, too. Please.'

He glared at her, confused now as well as worried.

'Sir, all we really want is to get in contact with Agent George Hennessy,' Ida said. 'You know him, don't you? You worked together.'

The man frowned, some line of logic being strung through his drunkenness.

'You don't know,' he said, his demeanor softening.

'Know what?'

'George Hennessy was murdered two nights ago.'

A couple of minutes later they were in Drazek's lounge, a vast square of a room with a sunken floor and heavy carpets and the largest television set Ida had ever seen. Mess was scattered everywhere: dirty plates, takeout boxes, overflowing ashtrays. On the coffee table, Ida noticed a hand mirror streaked with white powder.

Ida and Kerry sat on the sofas while Drazek rummaged through a mound of newspapers piled up next to his armchair.

'George was killed in the Malibu Hills. Not far from here. Someone shot his car up. Faron, I'm assuming.' He pulled a newspaper from the pile, consulted it for a second. 'There you go,' he said, passing it over.

He left Ida with the newspaper while he crossed to the wet-bar in the corner to fix them drinks. Ida scanned the details in the report. Hennessy's car had been found on a lonely stretch of the Latigo Canyon Road, his body on the shoulder just next to it, riddled with bullets. No one had been caught yet, there were no witnesses, and it had taken a while to find out who Hennessy was as the ID he had on him was fake; probably the same Sam Cole ID he'd been using for his prison visits.

Ida passed the newspaper to Kerry.

'It doesn't say anything about Stevie,' she said.

Kerry took the paper. She was still dazed, in a pit of worry. If Hennessy was dead – did that mean Stevie was, too?

Drazek returned with three tumblers half-full of whiskey, passed them around. He sat on the low sofas next to them, adjusted his dressing gown. Ida took a sip of the whiskey and it warmed the back of her throat. She saw parallels between Drazek and Ronnie Mouzon; both of them were hiding out from Faron, both of them were killing the time getting high, toting guns. But while Mouzon was underbelly, Drazek was upper crust, effete and urbane, his speech polished with a preppy, Ivy League refinement.

He fumbled about his pockets for his cigarettes, lit one up.

'I'd appreciate it if you'd let me know how you found me here,' he said.

'I can't reveal our sources,' Ida replied. 'It's a policy you'll be benefiting from, so I'd recommend you not to test it.'

He considered this, swirled the whiskey round his glass. After a few seconds, he nodded.

'You mind telling me at least why you're looking for George?' he asked. 'I hope you don't mind me calling him George and not Hennessy.'

'My partner's brother was in Vacaville,' Ida said, nodding to

Kerry. 'When he came out, he disappeared. We heard he hooked up with George to help him with his case.'

Kerry took the photo of Stevie from her bag, passed it over to Drazek.

'Ah, one of George's Vacaville boys,' he said. 'One of his precious witnesses. He'd spent months gathering them up. But I don't know where this boy is or what happened to him.'

He studied the photo some more, looked up at Kerry, as if to judge the family resemblance.

'George took good care of his informants. I doubt the boy's come to harm.'

Drazek's reassurance seemed to annoy Kerry, and Ida could tell why – it felt glib, cast off. He passed her back the photo.

'We were right about you working with George?' Ida asked. 'You helped him place Audrey Lloyd at Ocean Movies?'

As soon as she mentioned Audrey's name, something flashed in Drazek's eyes.

'Yes, I got her the job,' he said.

'She was a plant, wasn't she?'

He flinched, then raised the tumbler to his lips, using it as a prop to disburse his nervous energy.

'Why do you say that?' he asked, all fake nonchalance.

'Audrey's real name was Lopez, not Lloyd. She was charged with federal narcotics offenses back in her native Michigan. The charges were dropped before she flew out to LA. Sounds like she traded her services as an FBN informer in return for getting her charges dropped. You know she was murdered in San Pedro on Tuesday night?'

'Yes, I heard.'

He took another sip from his drink, stared into space, all glazed eyes and junkie remorse. It was supposed to play like he was upset, but he didn't pull it off. After a few seconds he sighed dramatically, as if having reached a decision.

'I suppose now that George is dead it doesn't matter if I talk about it,' he said. 'George and I went back a long way. About ten years ago I got busted on a dope-peddling charge. George helped me out, said I owed him a favor. We stayed in contact. Then we became friends. Over the years we worked busts together.'

He shrugged, took a large swallow of whiskey. This time his pain felt real. Hennessy's death genuinely grieved him. Ida wondered if there was more to their relationship than business. Hennessy had been a bachelor, just like Drazek.

'And how did you end up getting Audrey Lopez a job at Ocean Movies?'

'Riccardo used to sell drugs to the movie and TV crowd. Him and an associate of his called Vincent Zullo. They sourced the drugs, and I helped Riccardo shift them. He had the product; I had the contacts. And with him running Ocean Movies, it made our customers feel safer, like they were buying from one of their own. George came to see me a couple of years ago and said he wanted me to set up Riccardo on a bust. But I knew who Riccardo's father was. There was no way I was helping bust the son of someone like that. I'd rather do time. So we reached a compromise. I'd help George place someone in Riccardo's operation – that way if anything ever did happen, I could claim I'd been duped myself. We waited months for an opening. And then the girl that worked at Ocean Movies before Audrey quit. George told me to move in, found Audrey somewhere on the FBN's list of potential informers, flew her over, trained her, and I got her the job. With Audrey in the office, relaying information back to George, he started building his case. And then Riccardo got busted by the LAPD on a traffic stop. It pretty much destroyed the case George had spent the last few years on.'

'Is that why George went down to the jail to talk to Riccardo?'

'Yes. He thought he'd make the best of a bad situation and see if he could recruit Riccardo. He told him he was either facing the rest of his life behind bars, or if he did get out, the people he was buying his coke from would kill him. He told Riccardo they'd brought a trigger into town called Faron to clean up loose ends, and Riccardo was a loose end. Riccardo had heard of Faron, all these rumors about him. He was straight on the phone to his father, asking to be bailed out. The idiot thought if he met his suppliers face to face he could straighten things out. That day he was released, I met him at his office. Audrey was there too. He was calling them up, trying to arrange a meeting. I was telling him he was crazy, that he needed to get the hell out of town, but he wouldn't listen.'

'Were you talking about Faron that day at the office?' Ida asked.

'Yes. George had spooked Riccardo rotten with his story about Faron being in town. Riccardo hadn't believed him so George had told him there was a link there to the Night-Slayer too, the Vacaville deaths, you know, to really lay it on.'

'And was Audrey there when you spoke about all this?'

Drazek nodded.

Ida stared at him gloomily. What he'd said finally explained how Ida had come to be embroiled in the affair. Drazek and Riccardo had been talking about Faron and the Night-Slayer in front of Audrey. And Audrey knew that Ida had been looking for Faron; it was hardly a secret, not after all the feelers Ida had put out over the years. Maybe she'd been foolish, broadcasting her interest in him like that, offering rewards for information. But through a coiling chain of events, it had ended up bringing Ida to Faron, though not in the way she'd expected.

Drazek rose. 'I'll go and get us all a refill,' he said.

He headed over to the bar, returned with a crystal decanter. He topped up their glasses, lit another cigarette.

'What do you know about what happened in Vacaville?' Ida asked.

'I only know what George told me. That it was all to do with the Soviets.'

'The Soviets?'

'That's what George said. He told me there'd been these rumors that the Soviets were running experiments to see if drugs could be used to brainwash people, turn them into push-button operatives – saboteurs, assassins, revolutionaries. A fifth column of traitors that could destroy America from within. Someone in the CIA decided they needed to find out if it was possible, run their own experiments. For whatever reasons, they decided to run them in loony bins. Vacaville was one of a number of locations they used, and LSD one of a number of drugs they tested. They gave the inmates exceptionally high doses, then pumped propaganda at them. They targeted Negro inmates specifically, maybe because they thought they'd be the least patriotic in the first place, and so the easiest to turn. Maybe because they'd heard the Soviets would be targeting America's Negroes with their own program. Most likely it was just their race hysteria feeding into it. They used a few white inmates too, as controls, people like your brother.'

Drazek gestured to Kerry.

'So they'd dose up these boys, feed them all this propaganda about starting a revolution, and then they let them back out onto the streets. Released them early or let them escape. Then they tracked them, saw if the brainwashing had any effect. The whole thing was a disaster, of course. Anyone who's ever taken acid can tell you. LSD doesn't make you toe the line. It makes you unpredictable. It makes you crazy. As proved by the fact that one of the participants really lost his mind and started night-slaying his way across Los Angeles. But the agents running the tests had lost track of some of them, didn't know which one of the handful in LA was responsible. So they hired Faron to go through them all, bumping them off.'

'And it was FBN Agent Henry White who was supplying the testers with the LSD?' Ida asked.

Drazek raised his eyebrows, surprised at the extent of her knowledge.

'Yes. Exactly. George found out somehow that White was stealing the LSD from the FBN's repossession stores and passing it on to the CIA for the experiments. Apparently he'd been raiding the store for years. I'm not sure if you know, but the CIA and the FBN hate each other, they've been in a vendetta since the CIA was founded back in the forties. George had a feeling that White had been turned by the CIA, was working for them as a mole, their man in the FBN. When he found out White had been supplying drugs for the experiments, it confirmed his worst fears – that White was playing for both sides. So George decided to blow the lid on things. He started putting together a list of all the people who'd been through the program. All the people still in Vacaville and all the others still running around LA. George said it was an easy way to build a quick case against Agent White. To build leverage.'

'A quick case?' Ida frowned. 'Vacaville was a quick case?'

'Yes. It was just George's insurance against White. Vacaville was the side dish.'

'If Vacaville was only the side dish,' Ida said, trying to keep her voice level, 'what's the main course?'

'The CIA, Mrs Young. George was trying to take down the CIA.'

Ida stared at him, speechless.

Drazek smiled back.

'It was rogue CIA agents supplying Riccardo,' he said. 'The CIA's producing all the world's cocaine down there in Bolivia and Ecuador and Peru and wherever the hell else. White found some agents who were siphoning off product and together with some of his Mob friends they started sending it Riccardo's way. That's the big case George was working on the last few years. That's what obsessed him. That's why he placed Audrey with Riccardo. He was working up the chain. Me to Riccardo to White to the rogue agents to the CIA itself. George was a narcotics agent, Mrs Young, and the CIA are the biggest drug peddlers in the world.'

Drazek topped up his whiskey, took a sip.

'Vacaville and Riccardo are two sides of the same case, and White's the lynchpin that holds it all together. Bring down White and the CIA comes tumbling after. That was George's game plan anyway. George knew Vacaville wasn't enough. Do you think anyone cares if the CIA's experimenting on Negro inmates? Men who are already criminally insane? If it came out, it would barely raise a murmur. But George was convinced that if the public found out the drugs on our streets were there courtesy of the CIA, that they were endangering our precious white children in our precious white suburbs with their narcotics, all hell would break loose. And he was going mad trying to bring it about. He was going to use White and that cocaine route to take them down. That's why he went into hiding – so his status as a federal agent couldn't be revoked. Technically it could, but if he wasn't around to find out about it, it made the Bureau look incompetent, and George could plead ignorance, what the spooks like to call "plausible deniability". Anyway, George told me he only had until Christmas to get it all finished. If he hadn't built his case by then, it would all collapse.'

'Why Christmas?' Ida asked.

'I've been trying to figure that out ever since. The only thing I can come up with is that maybe we got it all wrong about Faron. Maybe he isn't in town cleaning up loose ends. Maybe he's in town to clear the way for something that hasn't happened yet. Something that's *going* to happen. At Christmas. Maybe this isn't about crimes in the past, but ones that are yet to occur. In the next twenty-four hours.'

He raised his eyebrows and Ida once more felt an imminent doom was headed their way.

'But what does it matter?' Drazek continued. 'Tomorrow it'll be Christmas and whatever flood Faron's here to shepherd in will come and then you'll have your answer. As long as we can all sit pretty till then, we'll see this through.'

Ida glared at him.

'If we just wait it out, then they've already won,' she said. 'There's still time to stop it happening.'

'But you don't even know what *it* is,' Drazek said. 'And they *have* already won. They won when they killed George.'

'He must have had evidence stashed somewhere? If he was the kind of investigator I think he was, then he was meticulous. He would have kept records. They can still be used.'

Drazek laughed, shook his head.

'He had a stash spot, Mrs Young. An off-the-books house not far from here in Malibu. Used it to store all his evidence, files, paperwork. It's because of that I got the idea to come up here myself. But that road that George was killed on, it's five minutes from the stash spot. It means Faron must have tracked him there before he killed him. Faron's not stupid. He would've gone back to the stash spot and taken all the evidence.'

'You don't know that.'

'No, but I can be pretty sure. If we know anything about Faron, it's that he's thorough.'

'What was the address?'

'You're wasting your time.'

'The address, Mr Drazek, please.'

He smiled at her patronizingly, as if indulging a child.

'It's a plot on a new housing development called the Highview Estates. Hennessy's house was the last one along the canyon. Just on the edge of that land the governor sold to Fox earlier this year.'

Ida frowned – the same real-estate sale Louis had mentioned. Her mind jumped to his talk of a shadowy net binding them all together. Maybe he'd been right. She could almost sense its presence now, encircling them, trapping them.

'But you're wasting your time, Mrs Young,' Drazek continued.

'Faron must have got there days ago. Ransacked it. It's already over. George was the best agent in the whole FBN. He was whip smart, dedicated, tough. He'd followed every angle, gathered all the evidence, and still that wasn't enough to stop them. He'd even found out where Faron was based, but that didn't stop Faron from getting the better of him. All we can do now is lie low and ride out the storm.'

Ida stared at him, her heart racing.

'George knew where Faron was?' she asked. 'Did he tell you?'

'Not exactly. He said he was holed up in some abandoned part of town somewhere.'

'An abandoned part of town?'

Drazek nodded, knocked back his whiskey.

Ida stared at him, trying to fit what he'd said into everything she'd already learned. Suddenly her thoughts jumped to Pete Cooper's car at the ranch, what the policeman had told them about it.

A few seconds passed then she turned to Kerry.

'We need to go,' she said. 'I know where Faron is.'

# 55

Kerry pulled into a Gulf joint perched on the rocks overlooking the ocean on Pacific Coast Highway. She filled up the Caddy while Ida crossed the vast emptiness of the lot to use the payphone by the store. Kerry considered what they'd learned from Drazek, the possibility of finding Stevie, Ida's suggestion that she could find work if she stayed in LA. Maybe Kerry was succumbing to the city already, the way it turned people into dreamers, but the thought of staying appealed to her.

When she was done she hopped in the car and drove it over to the payphone, waited till Ida had finished her calls.

'Well?' she asked.

'Seems like Feinberg's between the Glass House and his home. I left messages at both. I also left a message for a pal of mine who works as a fixer too. The one who's looking into Riccardo Licata's death. You fill up the car?'

Kerry nodded.

'I'm going to use the restroom,' Ida said. 'Then I'll get us some coffees and then we'll carry on — we've got a long night ahead of us.'

Kerry nodded, sat on a bench just by the payphones. She stared out at the ocean, at the waves rolling through the dark, crashing against the rocks below. She took the Dilaudid bottle from her pocket. It was almost empty. She'd taken a couple before sleeping that afternoon but they'd worn off and the scars were burning again. She debated popping another couple, weighing up the pain against the drowsiness, but she returned the bottle to her pocket, turned to look at the cars rushing up and down the highway, the dark mass of the hills looming above. Beyond them a light was flickering, like a will-o'-the-wisp, dancing faintly across the peaks.

'It's a brushfire,' Ida said.

Kerry turned to see Ida standing next to her, watching the lights glimmering through the murky sky.

'Wind must have pushed them this way,' Ida said. 'Let's hope it changes direction soon. Here . . .'

Ida passed Kerry one of the two coffee cups she had in hand. Kerry took it and they walked back to the car. When they got inside it, they watched the eerie glow atop the hills a moment, then Kerry turned to Ida.

'Can I ask you a question before we get started?'

'Sure.'

'When you came to my motel room that first day, you asked me for info and I turned you down and you just walked out of the cabin. Why didn't you press me to tell you what I knew? I've got this feeling now you knew I'd call you back.'

'You're worried you're predictable?'

Kerry frowned. She hadn't thought of it in those terms.

'I guess.'

'You weren't being predictable. I just had a feeling you'd come around.'

'Why?'

'Because you're smart. And alone. And you've got a righteous fire in your eyes that I've only ever seen in one other person.'

'Who?'

'Someone who passed away a few years back. My detective partner. A long, long time ago. Someone who always did the right thing.'

She stared out across the asphalt and the dark ocean beyond. Then she turned to look at Kerry.

'Why are you asking?'

'Because you did the same thing when you offered me

investigative work if I stayed in LA,' Kerry said. 'You didn't press, try to persuade me. Like you knew I'd say yes.'

'And will you?'

Kerry nodded.

'Yeah,' she said. 'I think I'd like to stay in LA.'

An hour later they were cruising the length of the abandoned area in the path of the freeway extension: four miles long, two blocks across, like someone had sliced a knife through the middle of LA. Some stretches had been cleared already, with great cement pillars rising into the sky, on top of which the elevated sections would be built. Most of it, however, was still full of houses, standing empty and forsaken, waiting for the wrecking crews that would put them out of their misery.

'Remember what I said about Faron's MO when he comes to a city?' Ida asked.

'He likes run-down, empty neighborhoods.'

'There's nowhere more run-down and empty than here. Mouzon said Cooper had gone crazy trying to track down Faron. And at the ranch, the detective said Cooper's car had been seen at a bunch of break-ins of derelict houses in the path of the freeway extension. But the detective got it wrong. Cooper wasn't driving around breaking into these houses. He was driving around searching for Faron, just like Mouzon told us he was. It was only when Drazek said Faron was hiding out in an abandoned part of town that it clicked. Cooper and Hennessy were both hunting for Faron, and they both realized he was hiding out here. But I guess neither of them managed to find out which house exactly.'

'This whole strip's miles long.'

'Yup. It'd be a lot easier if we had the cops helping us. That's why I said it's going to be a long night.'

As they drove they spotted a few houses occupied by squatters and vagrants, others where thieves had been at work, ripping out copper. Further on were stretches where houses had been extracted already, and stood a few feet in the air on giant metal rollers, awaiting the trucks that would relocate them. In other places, houses had already been taken away, leaving behind great craters in which rainwater and desert sand had accumulated. Scratch the asphalt veneer that had been painted on the land and the wilderness underneath came through.

It spooked Kerry. There was something eerie about this abandoned strip of suburbia, the absence of any life. She was chilled by the thought that if there ever was an apocalypse, if those missiles Lockheed were designing over in Burbank ever did their work, this neighborhood was what the aftermath might look like.

It wasn't until almost midnight that Ida spotted something.

'Hold up,' she said.

Kerry stopped the car and Ida stared at the house just opposite them. It looked as abandoned as all the others. But even though there was no car in the driveway, there was a pair of muddy tire tracks between the garage and the road.

Ida stepped out of the Caddy, kneeled in the road and examined them. Kerry followed her out.

'These mud tracks are coming from the driveway onto the road,' Ida said. 'But no set coming the other way. Last time it rained was just before we spoke to Mouzon.'

'Yeah, I remember. I got drenched on the drive over there.'

'It's been dry since then. One set of tracks means there was a car on the driveway while it was raining, and then, when the ground was still wet, it drove out, and hasn't come back. Let's check the rear of the house.'

Kerry drove them round. They were in luck. The houses on the row directly behind the suspect house had all been pulled up, making it look like a line of bombed-out football fields, a vast darkness, studded by craters filled with the rain of days ago. Although the houses had gone, rows of trees were still in place, delineating the outlines of the old plots. Here and there water pipes and electrical wires stuck up out of the ground where houses had been removed.

They found a spot for the Caddy behind the garage of a house further along. They walked back to the suspect house, crossing the muddy battlefield into the backyard. They peeked in windows. The place was empty.

Ida opened her bag, took out a plastic Master Charge card from her purse. She slipped it along the top of one of the rear windows. The card unlatched the latch. They slid open the window. They dropped into a bedroom. They wiped the dirt from their shoes. They pulled guns and checked the place quickly, Kerry's heart beating against her ribcage the entire time with the thought that this was Faron's hide-out.

It had been abandoned long ago, with the furniture gone and what was left covered in dust and mold, water-stained and crumbling. But there were signs of more recent occupation, too. In the kitchen was a garbage can full of food wrappers. In the bathroom was soap and a towel. In one of the bedrooms were bloodstains. Splatters all over the walls, the carpet a giant brown mess. It smelled heady, the deathly scent of curdled blood.

'This is his place, right?' Kerry asked.

She looked through the gloom at Ida, and could tell by Ida's worried expression that this was where Faron lived and killed. In an abandoned house in a condemned neighborhood where no one could hear the screams.

In the last bedroom was a sleeping bag and a rolled-up, lightweight camping mattress. Next to it was a box, and a pair of bulky green canvas bags. In one bag was money and clothes, in another knives and guns – an M16 assault rifle, an MP5 submachine gun. In the box was a collection of maps. Ida took them out and studied them. Road maps of LA and the surrounding areas, one for southern California, but the topmost was of Santa Monica and Malibu, the same hills where Drazek was hiding out, where Hennessy had been killed.

Ida returned everything to the box, looked around.

'Have you noticed what's missing?' she asked.

'There's nothing much of anything.'

'Exactly. No books, no magazines, no radio, no beer cans, no wine bottles, no ashtrays. Nothing to suggest enjoyment, relaxation, humanity. Nothing beyond the means of survival and killing. This is his place all right.'

'So what do we do?'

'We get the hell out of here before he comes back, then we call the cops.'

# 56

They put another call through to Feinberg and he arrived thirty minutes later, in an unmarked cruiser with two colleagues. Ida pointed out the house. Feinberg and his pals slipped in via the back window to see for themselves. When they came out, Feinberg went over to the cruiser, radioed something in, came back to Ida.

'I called it in as top priority,' he said. 'We're going to get a SWAT team down here, station men around the houses. Set a trap. We're going to catch him right here. Good work, Ida.'

He went back to speak to his men. Ida watched him go, worried by what he'd just told her.

'What the hell's a SWAT team?' Kerry asked.

'Special Weapons and Tactics,' Ida said. 'It's a new unit the LAPD just set up in response to the race riots a couple of years back. They've got special training and military-grade weapons, sniper rifles, machine guns, tear-gas grenades, their own tanks, armored cars and helicopters. It's like the Police Department just got a paramilitary wing.'

After Feinberg called it in things moved quickly. Cars sped in. Cars dropped off cops. Spotters were placed at intersections. Snipers nestled. A ring of men encircled the neighborhood, hidden so well amongst the surrounding houses that even though the whole area was teeming with them, it still looked deserted.

Ida and Kerry were moved to a derelict bungalow diagonally opposite Faron's, where Feinberg and the heads of the SWAT unit had assembled a mobile command post.

415

'We're all set,' Feinberg said when they'd settled in. 'As soon as he comes back, we'll wait for him to get out of his car, and grab him on the driveway.'

Ida nodded, but she had an awful feeling it wouldn't be so easy.

About an hour later, the voice of a spotter crackled across the police radios.

'We've got a blue Chevrolet Corvair heading west along Hill-crest at Cedar.'

A minute later another message came through.

'The Corvair just passed us at Oak Street. Still heading west. Could be our guy.'

A few seconds later Ida could see headlights.

'We've got a visual of the Corvair approaching the suspect house,' Feinberg said into his radio.

The lights loomed, swept the empty room. The car eased up to the suspect house, stopped, waited, then drove off.

'What the hell?' Feinberg muttered.

The car crept down the road to the next house along, stopped again. No one got out of it. It just stayed there by the curb, waiting.

'What the hell's he doing?' one of the other cops asked. 'Is it him? Why's he at the wrong house?'

A few seconds passed, then the car's engine cut out. Its lights, too. A silhouette of a giant got out, a bulky holdall in one hand.

'Is that him?' Feinberg asked, turning to look at Ida.

She didn't respond, she just stared at the figure as though fixed in place by a nightmare.

'Ida, is that him?' Feinberg repeated. 'You're the only one who knows what he looks like.'

She couldn't see his face, but the silhouette of his body hadn't changed in the twenty years since New York. He was still tall and upright and big. Still athletic, still powerful. How old was he now?

How old had he been then? The nightmare from her past was in front of her and the intervening twenty years collapsed, vanished like a magic trick. And all that was left was the same fear and panic she'd experienced back then, the same helplessness in the presence of evil.

She turned to Feinberg, struggling to wake from the trance, but he'd already decided he couldn't wait for her.

'Go. Just go,' he was saying to the SWAT unit leader, who was barking orders into his radio. They'd capture the man now and figure out who he was later.

Ida turned to look back at Faron, realized only then that he hadn't moved from the car, that he was scanning the neighborhood. Then there was the slightest trace of awareness in his expression, and Ida realized why he'd driven past his house, why he was studying the surroundings. He'd seen something, a stray cop, a sniper, a unit somewhere. He knew they were on to him.

She went to say something to Feinberg, but before she could, Faron was running, away from the car, bolting over the sidewalk. But he didn't run toward the suspect house, he ran toward the next one along, the one he'd parked in front of.

The teams surrounding the suspect house were in the wrong place. Faron had wrong-footed them, had bought himself a few seconds. As the teams ran down the street to catch up with him, Faron burst into the neighboring house, slamming the front door behind him.

When the teams reached the house, they bounded up the porch steps, and smashed through the front door. But instead of them charging into the house, there was a loud click, and the street was painted with light.

Everything seemed to stop. Go silent.

Then there was a deafening boom. The door flew outwards, knocking the cops backwards, sending them tumbling across the lawn in flames.

It took Ida few seconds to realize what had happened. He'd

booby-trapped the house. The front door. That's why he'd run into the other house. He'd set it up as a way of escape in case he was ever followed.

Feinberg and his buddies were already rushing out, across the street, toward the house, where gunfire was lighting up the windows, the muzzle flash of what felt like a hundred guns. Bullets skittered off the road, shredding the wooden walls like tissue paper. Faron must have had a submachine gun stashed inside the other house, too.

Feinberg and his buddies were rushing across the sidewalk, into range of the gun.

'No!' Ida shouted.

But it was too late.

They were barely onto the front lawn before they jerked. A red mist ripped out of their chests that floated in the dark. Then they fell down in a line.

Before she knew it, Ida was up and running as best she could, out into the street, the ground pounding into her joints, sending spikes of pain through her old woman's bones.

By the time she was on the sidewalk the gunfire had cut out. She ran over, praying they hadn't been caught too badly.

But Feinberg was dead, half his chest blown away. Next to him two of his men moaned. Paramedics from the SWAT team rushed over, but Ida could see they didn't stand a chance. She turned back to look at Feinberg. He didn't deserve it. His wife and children didn't deserve it. It should have been Ida who died at Faron's hand. That was what she'd envisaged. A great, guilt-ridden sadness swirled about inside her just as the gunfire started up again. She dropped to the ground along with everyone else. After a few seconds she lifted her head, glanced around, saw someone further on who looked like Kerry, pressed against a fence.

The gunfire continued, moving toward the back of the house. When Ida looked up again, she couldn't see Kerry. Had she been caught in the firefight?

Ida rose. As she trotted past the paramedics she could make out the chatter over their radios – *men down . . . medical assistance . . . suspect moving east.* The same direction Kerry had gone.

Ida ran over to the next house along, bumped her back against its side wall, readied her gun, listened. Through the darkness she could hear distant sirens, the shouts of men closer by, her own heavy, labored breathing. She felt her legs aching, her lungs aching, realized it was from running across to Feinberg, and then into this hiding spot. She couldn't remember the last time she'd run. When had it become so painful? So fraught?

Suddenly flashlights were swooping through the darkness. It couldn't have been the SWAT team being so stupid, giving away their location.

She stepped around the side of the house, into the backyard. More flashlights, more cops, marching toward the row of palms that separated the backyard from the muddy, crater-strewn emptiness further on.

A scream rose up from the other side of the palms. Kerry? The cops raced toward it, through the tree line, flashlight beams bouncing in the dark.

Ida ran after them, through the pain once more. She made it past the palms, out into the battlefield-like space beyond. She squinted into the darkness, couldn't make out anything except the strange terrain. In the distance a few houses were still standing, a few trucks were parked.

Suddenly there were gunshots. One of the police flashlights pirouetted, its beam turning red as its owner's blood splashed across it. Then it fell to the ground, along with its owner, and its crimson light shone across the mud.

More gunshots. Toward the trucks. Two sets this time. A handgun and the submachine gun. Kerry and Faron. It had to be.

The cops ran. Ida followed. Down across the field to the trucks, where houses had already been loaded onto their flatbeds. Ida stopped. The cops ran on. They hadn't smelled it. The gun smoke. It was stronger around these houses, these trucks. This was where Faron had been.

Ida backed up against the nearest wall for protection. Looked around. She tried to listen for movement. Couldn't on account of the sirens getting louder. The police were flooding the neighborhood with cars. One zoomed right past, red and blue beams lighting up the space. Ida used the light to scan her surroundings, but she couldn't make out much.

Then she saw movement near a house further along. A silhouette. Big. Faron. The cops had missed him. They'd moved on. Where was Kerry? Had he already killed her?

The car passed and took its feeble light with it and all was darkness again. Ida tried hard to listen once more, straining her ears over the sound of her own breathing. She heard a buzzing noise in the air. A police helicopter, its giant spotlight beaming down onto the neighborhood. The noise got louder, drowned out everything. The light flicked about. It was being directed by men on the ground, but it was in completely the wrong location. Faron was just near Ida. Close by in the darkness.

Then she saw him, heading over to the far side of the field, trying to get to the suburbs beyond, where there were people, phones, cars. And then she saw Kerry, right in Faron's path, unaware of him. He'd see the girl in a moment and kill her.

'Kerry!' Ida screamed over the roar of the helicopter.

Faron stopped and turned toward Ida, squinted in the darkness.

Red and blue lights flashed past and illuminated the field and they stared at each other. There was a look of surprise on his face. The same thin face, the same tiny eyes, but his brown hair had been bleached by the years, his skin was wrinkled, his features softened. Recognition stirred. He remembered her. Even though it had been two decades and they'd only met for the smallest of moments, he remembered her.

Ida raised her gun. Faron did likewise. They fired at the same moment, just as the police lights disappeared. Ida flattened herself against the mud as everything went dark. The helicopter light flickered toward them on account of the muzzle flashes. Its spotlight lit up the rows of houses on their stilts, the trucks, the craters, the forlorn-looking palms. The light reflected off the rainwater puddles filling the craters.

Ida saw Faron rise from the ground. He looked in her direction, then he ran toward the spot where she had last seen Kerry. Beyond him a shape was speeding down the road, approaching, a car with its lights off. Where the hell was Kerry?

Ida ran over the crater-filled ground, praying the light from the helicopter didn't fall on her and reveal her location. She tripped on something and fell, her gun flew from her hand. She landed in a puddle up to her elbows. Shockwaves rattled up her arms, but the water and mud had softened the fall, protected her from the worst of it. She looked behind her, saw plumbing pipes sticking up out of the water. She scrabbled around for her gun. Grabbed it, rose, limped on.

She saw Faron's hulking shadow far ahead, almost at the edge of the field. The speeding car screeched to a halt. It wasn't a police cruiser. It was a Dodge, and it still had its lights off. Accomplices. How had Faron alerted them?

Faron crossed the last few yards to the car. A moving target. Aim for the driver, Ida thought, static target. Shoot him and Faron couldn't get away. She stopped running, aimed again, fired.

The bullet shattered the side window but she couldn't see if she'd hit the driver.

Faron jumped into the backseat and the car sped away, door still open, lights still off.

'Dammit,' she said, her heart pounding.

Faron had gone, but the danger wasn't over; she was still at risk of being accidentally shot by the cops. And so was Kerry.

She looked about the field.

'Kerry,' she screamed.

She stumbled off in the direction where she thought she'd last seen her. The helicopter was over her now, alerted once more by the muzzle flash. It should have been following the car, but the car had its lights off. Ida was probably the only one who had noticed it.

She reached the spot she'd last seen Kerry, and there, further on, a body was lying in a crater.

'Oh, no,' Ida cried.

She ran over, stumbled into the crater, waded across it. The body further on was Kerry, curled up on her side, unmoving.

'Kerry?' she said.

She approached the body, stretched out a hand.

The body moved. Kerry looked up at her.

'Are you all right?' Ida asked. 'Are you hurt?'

Kerry didn't answer for a long time, then she shook her head. Ida tried to figure out what had happened, but couldn't make sense of it. And it was only then that she realized why the girl was so scared. The muddy field studded with bombed-out craters and palms trees, the gunfight, the smoke in the air, the helicopter strafing everything with light. It was just like being back in Vietnam.

# 57

Ida and Kerry sat on the porch of the bungalow where they'd waited for Faron. Across the street the house next to his was still smoking from the explosion, the place where the front door had been now just a jagged black chasm through which men were coming and going, the lawn littered with charred debris. Ida took in the crime-scene buzz, the three bodies on the sidewalk, the men combing the neighborhood for evidence, the LAPD top brass who'd been arriving in a steady stream.

Ida was desperate for info, updates, praying that maybe they'd caught up with Faron already. But everyone around her looked too overwrought to answer her questions, too wired. A botched operation for the new SWAT team, three dead cops, a killer on the loose, explosions in the middle of the city. It was a surprise the news crews hadn't turned up yet. Maybe the cordons that were supposed to ensnare Faron were now being used to keep out the journalists. Above it all the helicopter still hovered, had been joined by a second, their beams sweeping the neighborhood.

Ida took her cigarettes out, offered one to Kerry, who didn't respond, just stared into the distance. The anxiety attack the girl had experienced in the field was clearly still affecting her. Ida had held her up all the way back to the bungalow. When they'd arrived, she'd laid Kerry on the porch and had gone to tell some of the officers about the Dodge she'd seen picking up Faron. They said they'd send the information up the chain of command, get an APB put out.

A paramedic approached, asked if they needed anything. Ida was covered in mud from when she'd fallen, but she hadn't broken anything. She explained to the paramedic what had happened to Kerry, and the paramedic suggested an injection of Nembutal to get her through the shock. Kerry refused with a shake of the head and the paramedic moved on.

Ida watched her go, looked back at the bodies still on the sidewalk. Maybe she shouldn't have given in to her fear and called the cops. Maybe if she'd had more courage she could have hidden in Faron's house, ambushed him, killed him in cold blood when he walked through the door. Or maybe when Faron's car had arrived and Feinberg was asking her if it was him she could have responded quicker, not fallen victim to her fear again, and they could have grabbed him before he'd run into the house.

Ida finished her cigarette and spotted a few of the men who'd been with Feinberg before the raid.

'I'm just going to try and get some info,' she said.

Kerry nodded a fraction of an inch, but didn't break off staring at whatever personal hell she was staring at.

Ida went over and introduced herself to the men.

'Have there been any updates?' she asked.

They shook their heads.

'He got clean away,' one of them said, still not quite believing it.

Ida shared his sense of stunned defeat. An entire army of policemen and still he'd got away. She was certain now that whatever deadline Faron was working to, he'd beat it, even though he had the whole of the LAPD after him now. It was already Christmas Eve night; in a few more hours he'd be gone.

She was about to return to Kerry when she heard her name being called. She turned and saw a harried-looking, youthful cop approaching her.

'Mrs Young? My name's Frank Towne. I worked the Night-Slayer case with Detective Feinberg.'

He held out his hand and Ida shook it.

'We're going to get the bastard,' he said.

'Good. Feinberg was a friend of mine. Has his wife been informed yet?'

'Someone's on their way to let her know.'

Ida nodded, imagined the pain the woman was about to go through.

'We know it was you that tipped Feinberg off about the location,' Towne said. 'He mentioned you had previous dealings with the suspect. We were hoping you could give us a rundown on him. There's nothing in our files and . . . well, we've all heard the rumors and we're not sure what to believe.'

Ida noticed how shell-shocked Towne looked. All the other officers standing around, including the top brass, had heard what Towne had said and were staring at her now, like she was the expert suddenly, the one to lead them out of this mess.

'Sure,' she said. 'I'd be happy to help. Like I said, Feinberg was my friend.'

Towne nodded his thanks.

'Before we do that, there's something else. The forensics found a body in the trunk of Faron's car. We're not sure who it is, but since you were tracking him, maybe you could have a look? See if you can ID him?'

Panic swirled up in Ida as she wondered who it might be.

She nodded and Towne walked her over the road.

'We only found it just now,' he said, gesturing to the car's trunk. 'We're going slow with the evidence search in case there's anything else he booby-trapped.'

They reached the car. Wrapped up fetally in a tarp inside the trunk was the unmistakable shape of a body.

Towne gestured to one of the forensics and he pulled back the tarp to reveal the body. She stared at it a moment and then realized who it was and a wave of fearful sadness passed through her so heavily it almost made her stumble.

'Mrs Young? Are you OK?'

'No,' Ida muttered. 'Oh, God, no.'

Instinctively she turned back to look across the road to the bungalow. Kerry was still sitting on the porch steps, but she was looking up now, right at Ida. Even from a distance, in the darkness, Ida could see recognition on her face.

Kerry rose, started running toward them, all fear and adrenaline.

'Close the tarp up,' Ida said to the forensic. 'Close the damn tarp.'

But he didn't move, just frowned.

And by then it was too late. Kerry was already there, staring in shock at the body.

'No,' Kerry said. 'No.'

Ida tried to hug her, but Kerry pushed her away, refusing to let anything get between her and the sight of her brother lying dead in the trunk.

Ida tried to hug her again, and this time she held Kerry tight, felt the scream as it passed through the girl. Ida knew that scream. It was the same one she had screamed when Jacob's father had died, when her first husband had died. It was the same scream she'd heard for years afterwards, its echo reverberating through her life. It was the scream of something breaking inside Kerry, something that could never be made right again.

# PART TWENTY-TWO

## WILDFIRES

# 58

The first thing Dante did was drive over to Kyle DeVeaux's — a shithole studio apartment in Hermosa Beach, full of garbage and reefer smoke. There was an unmade Murphy bed, a giant swastika flag, mice on sticky traps in the corners, a blonde girl strung out on something stronger than just pot. The girl said she hadn't seen DeVeaux for a couple of days. In exchange for fifty bucks, she gave up a little black book he had left at the apartment.

Dante found a payphone and called O'Shaughnessy, told him that a man named DeVeaux had taken Loretta, gave him the details of the van DeVeaux had stolen.

'Shit,' O'Shaughnessy said. 'I'll get an APB out.'

He pulled DeVeaux's rap sheet, looking for known associates, more names and addresses to add to those in the man's little black book.

Dante mentioned the White angle.

'You know him from when you were at the FBN?' Dante asked.

'White,' O'Shaughnessy said, startled. 'Agent Henry White?'

'You know him?'

'Yeah, I know him. White's the asshole who forced me out of the FBN. Him and his goons tried to have me killed.' O'Shaughnessy paused. 'He's crazy, Dante. Sadistic. You ever meet someone and the moment you lay eyes on them a chill goes through you? That's White. The fucker had a photo on the wall of his office of a Jap he'd bayoneted during the war. He used to give a lecture on it to all the new recruits. You need to be careful with him, Dante. Especially if he offers you a deal. If you want,

I can speak to some old pals back at the FBN. See if I can broker something? Maybe track down DeVeaux?'

'Thanks.'

Next Dante called his answering service, thinking DeVeaux or White might have left a message for him, to discuss terms of negotiation, or surrender. But there was nothing except a message from Ida, asking him to call her urgently, leaving him a phone number which Dante didn't recognize. When he called it, though, it rang off.

Next he drove over to Roselli's, but the concierge told him Roselli had gone on vacation. Of course he had. Roselli always over-wintered at some resort or other – Palm Springs, Lake Tahoe, Boca Raton. And this year he had an extra reason to leave town.

Dante drove to his apartment in Venice. He parked, scoped the area, went in, removed floorboards, pulled out a canvas bag he kept ready with money in it, a .38, a shotgun, ammunition. He stepped back out onto the street, looked around. The moon was high in the sky and it was the night before Christmas. He had a Santa bag of guns, money and ammo. He had a list of people to visit. He had a dog and a muscle car.

He got into the Thunderbird and criss-crossed LA with his anxiety gnawing him up. Desperate. Not thinking straight. Rattled by the realization that Loretta's warning was coming true – his luck was finally running out. He was losing his family all over again. Now that his nightmare was becoming real, he saw that Loretta had been right about his flaws and motivations. All those years he put everything on the line because he felt guilty, unworthy, because deep down he thought it should have been him who died in Chicago. He'd put everything in jeopardy just to prove something to himself which could never be proved.

The horror of it spurred him on to find Loretta.

So he chased names, pressured them, daisy-chaining his way through the LA underworld, from a crash pad in Westwood to a nightclub in Florence to a cage hotel in Boyle Heights to a de-luxe family home in Highland Park where a father had up till then well hidden his criminal connections from loved ones and neighbors.

At gone three in the morning, Dante was still knocking on doors. It gave him the element of surprise. People were scared of him, this wild-eyed, sleep-deprived old man, waving a gun about, shouting his wife's name. They gave up info, leads, lines of enquiry, in the mist of the moment. Then ten minutes later wondered what the fuck they'd done.

Four a.m. passed. Dante followed all the leads. Helicopters flitted through a night sky wiped of its stars by light pollution, by smoke billowing in from Malibu, by Dante's angst. On the freeways there seemed to be nothing but wraiths and shadows and the blips of cop cars. Now and then Dante looked north, expecting to see the lights of the brushfires glowing in the sky above the Santa Monica Mountains, but there was just that pall of smoke, taillights drifting up through the hills.

None of the names panned out, none of them got him closer to Loretta's whereabouts. The leads just emptied out into yet more leads, like the freeways pouring into one another.

He hit the hospitals in case maybe Loretta had fought back, maybe DeVeaux had crashed the van. But it was the night before Christmas and the Emergency Rooms were full of drunks and domestic-abuse victims, people who'd attempted suicide, people on the wrong end of DUIs, muggings, barroom brawls. No one could confirm Loretta had been admitted.

He called his answering service. Nothing. He called the number Ida had given. Also nothing.

Dante realized time was running out, and he was getting nowhere. Maybe he'd have to stop searching for DeVeaux and instead find the man's boss – Agent White. Negotiate with him. See if O'Shaughnessy could broker a deal. But still Dante had a sense that the wind was calling him that night, that something was afoot out there in LA's great swimming-pool plains, something lurking in the darkness.

As dawn came, he got back to the names, carried on through the morning.

Still no joy, still no breaks.

When the hunger pangs were making him delirious, he pulled into a Flying A, refilled the Thunderbird, ordered a coffee and a sandwich for himself, a couple of franks for the dog. He caught an hour's sleep with the seat tilted back. When he woke he went to a payphone to check his answering service. As he was waiting for the call to connect, he peered through the window next to him, into the gas station's store, where the attendant was watching a TV on the counter. Dante caught a glimpse of helicopters and assumed it was a report on the wildfires, but they weren't firefighting choppers, they were LAPD, and they looked like they were hovering over the city.

When the operator told him he had no messages he hung up, entered the store almost in a daze.

'Everything OK, sir?' the attendant asked.

'Sure,' Dante said. He nodded to the TV. 'What happened?'

'A shoot-out. Some crazy bastard booby-trapped his own house, killed three cops, and got clean away. LAPD's running all over town looking for him.'

Dante frowned. The helicopters and cops cars he'd seen rushing along the freeways all night, the ones he'd paid no heed to.

Three photos flashed up on the screen, the three dead cops. Dante recognized the first of them: Detective Feinberg, Ida's pal who was working the Night-Slayer case. Was it the Night-Slayer who'd set that booby trap? Who'd killed three cops and escaped a cordon? It didn't seem likely. And then Dante remembered what Zullo had said, about a contract killer being brought to town from Cambodia. An Agency man. Dante's mind drew a line between himself and Ida, the Night-Slayer, the CIA, the FBN. That mystery from right at the start of the case, that feeling that something big was going down, big enough for both Dante and Ida to get pulled into its wake. There was only one name that could explain it all.

'Faron,' Dante muttered.

# 59

Kerry sat slumped on the sofa in Ida's apartment, spending her Christmas Day watching the manhunt unfold on the TV. The story had bumped the wildfires and the Night-Slayer off the top of the bill. A stand-off in the path of the freeway extension, a booby-trapped house, three cops dead after a home-made bomb had gone off, the perpetrator still at large, the LAPD's new SWAT team messing up one of their first-ever missions. The news anchors had already come up with a name for it – *Bloody Christmas*. It was newshound heaven interspersed with advertising breaks brimming with corporations wishing America a Merry Christmas.

She watched it all in a daze, the Nembutal casting her off into a wooziness that wasn't quite sleep. The paramedics had given her a shot of it after all, to stop her screaming, and she'd been in a stupor ever since. It was a nice place from which the horrors of the previous night didn't seem quite as horrific, where the burns on her body didn't burn, where the fact that she'd missed her flight back to Vietnam and would be declared AWOL seemed like nothing more than a bureaucratic inconvenience. But she knew this was just temporary, that as the Nembutal wore off, the pain, the grief, the anguish, would come.

She'd failed to find Stevie. Failed to save him. She was certain that Faron had killed him that night, maybe right before he'd driven back to the abandoned house. Meaning she'd been just a few hours too late. She thought back to that muddy field, the fire-fight. She couldn't remember much of it, but she could picture Faron staring at her, gunshots distracting him. She had a vague sense that Ida had saved her life. But maybe it would have been better if she had died, killed by the man who'd killed Stevie, lost down the barrel of the same gun. The way it was now, all Kerry had to look forward to was an emptiness that would be numbing at best. She had lost. Faron and White had won. She thought back to her meeting with White, when he'd grabbed her by the throat and told her she was out of her depth. She hated to admit it, but he'd been right. The bad guys had won. They always did.

'I guess this means Faron's gonna leave town,' Kerry said, turning to look at Ida.

Ida frowned. Kerry got the sense she was thinking about lying, but then she seemed to decide against it.

'He'll only leave when his mission's done.'

'He killed three cops,' Kerry said. 'He's got the whole LAPD after him.'

'This is all he lives for,' Ida said, gesturing to the carnage on the TV. 'Men like Faron don't run away from the fires they start, they run into them.'

Throughout their investigation, Ida had exuded a calming sense that she was in control. Kerry had never once felt scared, because Ida was around. The only time Ida had faltered was when Mouzon had first mentioned Faron's name. Before that she had seemed in her element even there at Mouzon's hide-out, at night, in the middle of Glendale, trapped in a room with two armed and dangerous men. But Ida didn't look like that woman anymore. Something had broken inside her, just like it had in Kerry.

They carried on watching the news. During an ad break there was a trailer for the *Steve Allen Show* that night, promising appearances by Louis Armstrong and a special mystery musical guest. The trailer seemed to make Ida even more anxious. She rose and called her son in San Francisco, her husband in Germany. Kerry barely registered the conversations through her daze. She considered calling someone in the Air Force to explain what had happened, why she'd be late reporting back to duty. She wasn't sure of the process, but she was certain there must be an exemption for someone in her situation, some bereavement-related consideration that would stop her being disciplined. The worst part wouldn't be talking to the authorities, it would be telling Ida that she wouldn't be staying in LA after all, that she'd be leaving.

'I'm going to make some coffee,' Ida said when she'd finished the calls. 'You want some?'

'Sure.'

Ida went into the kitchen. Kerry tried to sit up and managed it. Then she stood, walked over to the window, stared out over the ruins of what used to be Bunker Hill. Everything in the street below was eerie and still. From the bar across the street Christmas music seeped out, Eartha Kitt singing 'Santa Baby', the bar's patrons joining in raucously. Just below its red and green tinseled windows, two drunks were slumped on the sidewalk.

Kerry felt herself swooning, her head going woozy. She reached out a hand and steadied herself on the windowsill. She closed her eyes, and for the first time in weeks it wasn't fire that appeared in the darkness behind her eyelids. It was Stevie, curled up in the trunk of that car.

On the news she heard them cut to a segment on the Christmas Day ceasefire over in Vietnam, instigated just a day after President Johnson had flown over there to visit the troops, dishing out turkeys and Purple Hearts, speechifying at Cam Ranh Bay, the same Air Force base from which Kerry flew her missions. She opened her eyes and turned to look at the TV. She hadn't seen Cam Ranh Bay since the day of the fireball, the napalm day. It unsettled her to see it there, in that room in Bunker Hill, like two worlds folding over onto each other, causing not a dislocation in space, but somehow, a dislocation in time.

The images on the TV cut from the Air Force base to shots of Marines stalking through the jungles of Kerry's nightmares, making her recall the day she'd driven out to the jungle, the acid she'd dropped, how the darkness took on form, that sense of a great evil enveloping the world, a serpent tightening its clasp. The next day she was back at work in the C-130 with the acid yet to leave her system, enplaning, triaging, debriding, suturing, applying tourniquets, transfusing blood, comforting scared boys into the great beyond as they cried for their mothers. Because they *were* boys; their average age nineteen, while the nurses averaged out at twenty-two. So it was their little brothers they were watching die, the boys a few years below them in high school.

Kerry had assumed that when she got back home, she'd feel a sense of rightness again, that once more the world would have order to it, decency, that it wasn't all just chaos. But now she was back she realized that wartime feeling wasn't specific to Vietnam. It was everywhere. On the streets of LA, in Vacaville, at the ranch, at Faron's, in those empty, muddy lots. The chaos was everywhere, and it always had been. It just took the war for her to notice it. She'd brought the serpent back from Vietnam, and now it was inside her, following her wherever she went.

With Stevie dead, she knew now what she had to do: go back to Vietnam, go back to the bloodshed, go back to the combat climbs and enemy fire, the malaria and cholera and hundred other diseases most nurses only read about in textbooks. This was what she deserved.

Ida returned from the kitchen, handed her a cup of coffee and sat. Kerry steeled herself, knowing she'd be giving Ida yet more bad news.

'I thought I should let you know,' Kerry said. 'I've been thinking. I'm gonna leave, after all. As soon as I can. Tomorrow probably.'

Ida frowned.

'You can stay here as long as you want,' she said. 'There's no rush.'

'Thanks, but I'll just be taking up space. I'm going to call my superiors. Book another flight. Finish my tour.'

Ida looked stung. She stared at Kerry inscrutably, so Kerry wasn't sure if she was processing her disappointment, or planning a way to get her to change her mind.

'There's the funeral to consider,' Ida said.

'Funeral?'

'Stevie's funeral.'

Kerry paused, a feeling of stupidity rising through her. She hadn't even considered that there'd be funeral arrangements, the legal mundanities that come in the wake of a death.

'You're his next-of-kin, Kerry,' Ida said. 'His *only* next-of-kin. You should be involved. Maybe you should stay for that, at least. Get your head straight, fix all the things that need fixing.'

'I'm already late reporting back,' Kerry said. 'Come midnight I'll officially be AWOL.'

'I think under the circumstances the Air Force'll grant you a few extra days' leave for bereavement. You can stay in the apartment. And if you want to stay longer and resign your commission, I can probably find you a job, like I told you.'

Kerry considered this, felt warmed once more by the possibilities of Ida's offer. But along with the warmth came a deep queasiness. She shook her head.

'I'm not sticking around. I only came here to find my brother. And now he's dead, I've got nothing to stay for.'

They stared at each other gloomily; then suddenly the phone rang, making them both jump.

'I thought no one had this number,' Kerry said.

'I only gave it to two people.'

'Who?'

'Feinberg and Dante,' Ida said, crossing the room to pick up the call.

# 60

Half an hour later Dante was stepping into the apartment and Ida was shocked by his appearance – red-eyed, wired, his clothes rumpled.

'What the hell happened?'

'Someone took Loretta.'

They sat in the lounge and he told Ida all about it and she tried to console him.

'I've been searching for DeVeaux the hard way but it hasn't panned out,' Dante explained. 'I'm going to have to go begging to White.'

Ida filled him in on Kerry's encounter with the man as Kerry was back slumped on the sofa, floating in and out of her Nembutal daze. When Ida had introduced them, Kerry had smiled and croaked out a 'glad to meet you', but had passed out again not long after. Ida told Dante what she'd learned about White. He told her about Roselli and Zullo. They shared all their info, leads, developments, put it all together to see where their cases dovetailed, where they didn't. Everything rested on White, the person who connected Ida's investigation into Vacaville with Dante's investigation into Riccardo.

'Makes sense that White's the CIA's mole in the Narcotics Bureau,' Dante said after Ida had told him what she'd learned. 'White was helping the CIA run their drug test in Vacaville. When Riccardo compromised their cocaine route, they gave White a CIA safe house to kill Riccardo in, brought in Faron from Cambodia to help clean up.'

439

'Faron was in Cambodia?' Ida asked.

'That's what Zullo said.'

She sighed. Her theory about Faron being out in Southeast Asia had been right. He went wherever the killing was, progressing from a Mafia boogeyman to a CIA boogeyman.

'But then Zullo didn't know the whole story,' Dante said. 'He didn't know White was hooked up with the CIA. They kept him in the dark on that. One thing he did say, though, is that Faron just had the Night-Slayer left to kill and then he was leaving town. And that he'd almost caught up with him.'

Ida nodded, tried not to let her spirits sink even further – Faron was as good as gone, Bud Williams as good as dead. Her failure was complete. She thought about the Christmas deadline that Bud Williams had mentioned to his grandmother, that Mouzon and Drazek had mentioned, too. Ida filled Dante in on it.

'Drazek told us he thought Faron wasn't really here cleaning up *after* something, but cleaning up to *make way* for something, clearing a path for something that was going to happen now. At Christmas.'

'Clearing the way for what?'

'I've got no idea.'

'If the deadline's today, then I'm running out of time,' Dante said. 'Maybe once it passes they won't need to keep Loretta alive.' He looked up at her, distraught. 'I need to contact White right away.'

'You're going to call him?'

'It's already Christmas, Ida. What choice have I got? Maybe I can bluff him into letting Loretta go. Maybe I can use all this Hennessy and Drazek stuff to fool him into thinking I've got some leverage.'

'Dante, you're not thinking straight. You don't know for sure that the deadline's going to affect what they do with Loretta.'

'I can't take that chance.'

'You go and meet White and you'll end up the same as Riccardo.'

'What choice do I have? Let them keep Loretta? Maybe I can swap her for me.'

'I can't let you do that. Let's figure something out first. Don't go rushing into a trap because you're desperate and your emotions are going crazy. I'll help you. And worst comes to worst, I'll go with you to meet White.'

He shook his head.

'I'd never ask you to do that.'

'So I'm just supposed to let you walk out of here and kill yourself? That's not how I do things, Dante.'

'You need to stay here and protect the kid.' He gestured to Kerry, who was still sleeping on the sofa.

'She'll be fine here for a few hours. You said it yourself, Faron's just got Bud Williams left to kill, and then he'll be leaving town.'

'Then you stay here and finish your side of the investigation,' he said.

'There's nothing left on my side. I found out what happened to Audrey, and we were too late to save Kerry's brother. It's over. Faron'll kill Bud Williams and leave, Hennessy's case'll turn to dust, no one'll ever know the truth about Williams or Vacaville. And that'll be it.'

They shared a forlorn, defeated look, acknowledging that they had run out of time and options.

'The cops might still catch Williams,' Dante suggested.

'The whole LAPD's running around looking for Faron now. Three dead policemen. Tempers are high. You think they're gonna muster up the resources to go after Williams in the middle of all this? And even if they did, whoever was behind those tests'll make damn sure the Vacaville origin won't leak out. It's over, Dante. It's all over. The least you can do is let me help you come out of it alive. Maybe between the pair of us we can pressure White, get Loretta back and get him to leave us both alone.'

She stared at him. It felt like Dante wanted to make a counter-argument, but couldn't muster one up. He was tired, overwrought, out of whack.

He sighed, he rubbed his temples. Eventually, he nodded.

'Thanks, Ida,' he said.

They smiled at each other.

'Gimme two minutes to get ready,' she said. 'Then I'll wake Kerry and let her know what's going on.'

Dante looked over at the sofa.

'She seems like a good kid,' he said. 'And she reminds me of someone – your old pal from Chicago. The scars. That look in her eye.'

'Yeah, I know. I thought that, too.'

They looked at her a moment longer, then Ida went into the bathroom, washed her face and hands, hoping the cold water would wake her up. As she dried her hands she thought of Danielle Landry lying in her bathtub of money, how her family would probably never know the truth of what happened.

She walked back into the lounge and froze.

Dante was gone.

# 61

As Dante sped away from Ida's he hoped she'd understand, that she'd realize if the situations were reversed, she'd most likely do the same thing. But still he felt he'd betrayed her. And since he'd probably never be seeing her again, it meant their last meeting would always be tinged now by Dante's lie, by a cheap trick. He'd also kept from her one of the most important things Zullo had said – that when Faron was finished with the Night-Slayer, he was coming after Dante. He knew if he'd told Ida that, she'd definitely be putting her life on the line to save him, and he'd already caused enough deaths.

He pulled up outside the courthouse on Spring Street. Got out, looked around. The entire area was deserted, with the eeriness of an empty film set, as if at any moment trucks and stagehands might arrive and dismantle everything, drive it all away.

He walked to the courthouse entrance, stepped into the main hall. Two security guards on either side of the doors rose from their slumber.

'Can we help you, sir?' the one closest to Dante asked.

'I'm looking for the FBN office.'

'It's a federal holiday, sir. The offices are closed.'

'The FBN never closes. If it did, I wouldn't have an appointment.'

The guard eyed him.

'Who's your appointment with? We'll need to call through for them to come and get you.'

'Agent Henry White.'

'And what's your name?'

'Tell him I'm the ghost of Riccardo Licata.'

The security guard scrutinized Dante again. Dante gave him that crazy, wild-eyed old-man look he'd perfected over the last twenty-four hours. The guard walked over to a phone, put a call through, walked back over.

'Someone'll be down to see you.'

Dante nodded.

The guard returned to his seat, but he didn't slump onto it like before. He sat bolt upright, hands on his hips, inches from his holster.

A few seconds later, the lights above one of the elevators started pinging down to the first floor. The doors opened and two men stepped out. They were dressed like Feds, but neither matched Agent White's description. They were both in their thirties, one was tall and thin, the other shorter, with a blond mustache.

They walked over to Dante, eying him the entire time.

'You here to see Agent White?' the tall one asked.

Dante nodded. Up close he could see that their eyes were bloodshot, their pupils dilated. Their complexions ashen. They were both juiced up on something.

'White's not available,' the tall one said, alcohol on his breath. 'I'm Agent Phillip Schodt. This is Agent Mark McKinney. Maybe we can help you?'

'I want to see White.'

'White's not available. I told you. He's out of town. Tell us what you want.' Schodt's words were laced with menace now as well as whiskey.

Dante looked them both over. He'd had a feeling that White wouldn't be at work on Christmas Day, but to hear that he was out of town threw him off.

'You work with White?' Dante asked.

'Sure.'

'No, I mean, do you *work* with him?'

Dante stressed the word, stressed the fact that he was asking if they were involved in White's off-the-books activities.

Schodt's eyes narrowed.

'Yeah, we *work* with him.'

'I'm Dante Sanfelippo. I was there yesterday when Vincent Zullo died in that oil field over on Huntington Beach.'

The two Feds exchanged looks, then cast glances at the two security guards who were watching everything from their perch just by the doors.

'Outside,' Schodt said.

They exited the building onto the steps of the courthouse.

'What do you want?' Schodt said.

'DeVeaux kidnapped my wife while I Florence Nightingaled Zullo into the great beyond. What the fuck do you think I want? I want her back.'

The two men frowned, shared a look again, surprised by the news that DeVeaux had taken Loretta.

'We don't know what DeVeaux's been up to,' Schodt said. 'If he took her, it wasn't sanctioned. White's not even here. He's in Washington.'

'Then give me a number for him. Tell him to call off DeVeaux. Or I take what I know to the cops, the press. To Nick Licata.'

Again the men conferred with just a look. Then they nodded. Both of them were smart enough not to call his bluff right away.

'White's at the Statler Hilton in DC. Room three four six. You can call him there or you can wait. He'll be back in town tomorrow morning.'

Dante nodded, turned and walked back to the Thunderbird. As he sped off, he looked in his rearview: the two men were still standing on the steps, watching him, memorizing the Thunderbird's license plate.

A few minutes later he found a bar on North Main Street, yanked the Thunderbird to the curb. The place was as depressing as he expected a bar to be in downtown LA on Christmas Day.

Barflies and juicers hunched over their drinks. A TV was on low. Just by the cash register was a miniature plastic Christmas tree with rainbow-colored lights blinking away; the only concession to Yuletide apart from a man in a Santa suit slumped in a corner, eyes closed, mumbling to himself.

Dante ordered a beer. Spent fifteen minutes drinking it before he called White. He didn't want to catch White off guard, he wanted him forewarned, his threat exaggerated. He wanted to be sure White's colleagues had warned him first, told him that Dante looked unhinged, dangerous.

He finished his beer, walked over to the payphone at the back of the bar. He called the operator, asked for long distance, gave the name of the hotel. When he was put through, they connected him to White's room. Dante's heart pounded in time to the ringing.

'Sanfelippo?' White asked when he picked up.

'Yup.'

'My men at the office said you'd be calling. What do you want?'

'I want my wife back.'

'I think we can arrange that. DeVeaux's a hothead. He shouldn't have done what he did. It was unsanctioned. I'm flying back tomorrow. Let's meet. Hash things out.'

Dante frowned. It couldn't be this easy. He recalled what O'Shaughnessy had said – not to trust White, especially if he was offering a deal.

'When and where?' Dante asked.

'There's a place up in the Palisades. It's nice and quiet. We can talk, do the exchange.'

'What's the address?'

'We'll give it to you tomorrow. I'm flying back early in the morning. Call my men at nine a.m. and they'll tell you where to be.'

White gave him a number and hung up. Dante put the receiver

back into its cradle and stared at the phone's metal dial. Tomorrow he'd have to meet White at a location that White had prepped, a location where White had all the advantages. Dante would be following in Riccardo's footsteps, marching to his own death, but what choice did he have? He was past the point of saving himself, but maybe through a miracle he might be able to save Loretta. Or maybe it was like Ida had said, he just wasn't thinking straight.

He walked back to the bar and ordered another beer. For some reason his thoughts jumped to Napa Valley, the vineyard, those rolling green hills, that boundless sky. He realized now why he'd always felt somehow that it was a pipe dream – because just like his family, he felt he wasn't worthy of it. It was only now that circumstances were forcing him to give it all up that he truly realized what a fool he'd been.

The barman put Dante's beer on the bar. Dante took a sip, looked at the dog.

'Merry Christmas,' he said.

# 62

Ida walked north along Olive Street, west on 3rd, her legs still aching from the running she'd done the night before, her wrists still sore from when she'd tripped. But the pain seemed fitting, justified. She'd let Dante trick her and now he was heading into a trap from which he probably wouldn't escape. When she'd realized he'd run out on her, she'd felt a surge of anger, then foolishness, then a needling agitation that she couldn't contain. She'd needed to go outside and clear her head, so she'd woken Kerry and told her she was going to get them some food. It was a risk, but a small one; Faron didn't know where they were holed up, and even if he did, he was busy tracking down Bud Williams, evading the cops, or maybe he'd left town already. Ida could risk a trip to a local deli, at least.

As she walked she savored Bunker Hill's shabbiness, its honesty, how its ramshackle looks matched her own inner turmoil. The more she walked, however, the more she saw how little of the old neighborhood remained, how many of the flophouses and bars had been bulldozed for office buildings and vast barren parking lots. The places where poor people had lived, destroyed so rich people could have places to park.

Despite the Christmas decorations dotted about, everything felt lifeless and empty. Walter had once remarked how the emptiness in LA was because it was a city of dreams, and dreams, by definition immaterial, could only ever exist in a void. Ida felt that void now, the space where a dream should be, missing from the world around her, and from inside her too.

She found a deli, went in, ordered sandwiches for herself and

Kerry. As the counter man made them up, Ida thought back to her conversation with Louis, about legacies. Maybe it was only natural that alternatives came and went. If they weren't viable they died; if they were too viable they joined the mainstream and so, also died. Maybe the point was for there to *be* an alternative. Always. But the way things were going, Ida wondered if they were all slowly dying out – jazz, detective agencies, communities like Bunker Hill. Maybe that's what all the social and political revolutions around them were: the last vain attempts to stop an inevitable process of homogenization.

'Ma'am,' she heard a voice say.

She looked up to see the counter man holding out her food.

On the walk back, her thoughts swirled around Dante, hoping still he might make it through. Then she thought about Faron, out there somewhere, eluding the police. Maybe he'd already completed his mission and was flying back to Cambodia to continue his work for the government over there.

When Ida had first encountered him all that time ago in New York, the CIA was just being set up, arising from the ashes of World War Two. Ida had been offered a job with the fledgling Agency and she'd seriously considered taking it. Twenty years later it turned out it was Faron they'd given a job to. Not Ida, the conscientious investigator, but Faron, the psychopathic killer. How had the Agency's mission been corrupted so badly in just a couple of decades? On some levels, Faron and the CIA were the better match, the way they both worked in the shadows, instilled fear, like a kind of voodoo, the same magnetic voodoo that had shadowed Ida for most of her life. She was certain now there'd be no justice for Stevie, Feinberg, Hennessy, the Night-Slayer's various victims.

She'd been a fool to think she could come back from retirement. At every step of the investigation she'd messed up, made the wrong choices, been beaten to the evidence and witnesses.

Then she'd been tricked at the last by Dante. She'd always prided herself on being sharp. But that had all slowed down now, and just like Louis accepting that he could no longer play the horn, maybe she had to accept these limitations too.

Tomorrow she'd drive Kerry to the airport and she'd fly back to Vietnam and contrive a way to wind up dead, because Ida was certain now that was what Kerry wanted, whether she knew it or not. Just like Ida had made the bad decision to sell the agency after Sebastián had died, Kerry would use Stevie's death as an excuse to return to Vietnam, to lie in the grave of a family already dead, giving up the chance to build a new one here in LA.

Ida would attend to Stevie's funeral, and maybe Dante's too. And then, in total failure, everything would return to normal. She'd watch over her shoulder for the next few months, but what did she have to be scared of now? She had nothing to threaten them with. By losing so comprehensively, she'd ensured her own safety. And the world would carry on being run by cheats and bullies. How could anyone fighting against self-interest ever win? Clarke had sold out her agency to the Pinkertons. White had sold out the FBN. The authorities at Vacaville had sold out their inmates. The CIA had sold out its own country. But then Ida realized with some bitterness that she too had sold out – it wasn't entirely Clarke's fault that her agency had ended up with the Pinkertons.

When she got back to the apartment she saw Kerry had fallen asleep again, still clutching her coffee, the TV still playing the news. Ida slipped the cup out of Kerry's hand, watched the news reports for a moment. Faron's name still wasn't being mentioned, and no one had linked the shoot-out to the Night-Slayer. She wondered what would be worse for the cops – having two violent circuses playing across the city simultaneously, or people finding out it was actually all the same circus.

Ida went into the kitchen and poured herself a whiskey, too

glum to eat the food she'd bought, perturbed by Faron, saddened by Kerry, anxious about Dante. She came back into the lounge, flicked through the TV channels, stopped on NBC, Steve Allen horsing around on his *Christmas Special*, reminding the viewers that Louis Armstrong and a mystery guest would be performing later.

Ida sat and watched the show, sipped her whiskey, turned to look at Kerry, at the scars running down her face. She thought of how the girl had looked when they'd first met, standing in the doorway of her cabin, fearful and unsure. Just like Ida had been fifty years earlier, in Chicago, on the day she'd met Michael and he'd taken her on as his protégé. Snow had been falling, and Ida had shivered in her Southern coat, ill-equipped for her new Northern home.

'Well, Ida, let's see what you're made of,' Michael had said, and his words had warmed her under those cold, white skies.

How she missed Michael, even after all these years. Why had she never trained up another detective like he had? She'd been given the torch by Michael, who in turn had been given it by his own mentor, Luca. Why hadn't Ida continued the chain, conveying the light on through the darkness? That was the big regret she had about her career, and it was only now she realized it. Michael had given Ida gifts which she'd failed to pass on, and now they'd be lost to the world. And that was the failure which hurt the most.

# 63

Louis sat in a backstage dressing room in the Steve Allen Playhouse, killing time till the show started. He thought of all the hours he'd spent in empty rooms like this, waiting to perform, all the nights spent on buses, trains and planes, the long-haul loneliness of a jazzman's life. Had it been worth it?

The door opened and Steve Allen stepped in with another figure: a tall, skeletal white man that Louis vaguely recognized. He had a stooped, hangdog posture, his hair was straggly, his eyes glazed, his skin disconcertingly pale. Whoever it was, he looked half-dead and out of his mind on dope.

'Louis, you know Chet,' Steve said, gesturing to the figure behind him.

And then it clicked. Chet Baker. The trumpet player and singer. The biggest jazz star on the planet back in the '50s. The perfect mix of talent, looks and whiteness, until he'd succumbed to drugs, money and legal problems. There'd been rumors he'd died. But here he was, alive, though scarcely recognizable.

Louis rose and hooked a smile onto his face.

'Yeah, sure. Chet. How's it going?'

Louis held out his hand and Chet shook it, cold and clammy, barely making eye contact.

'Chet's performing tonight,' Steve explained. 'He's the mystery musical guest.'

Louis tried his hardest not to balk. Chet didn't look as if he was in any fit state to be playing. He needed a bed, some soup, a doctor to ween him off the dope.

'Chet Baker and Louis Armstrong on the same show,' Louis

said, turning to Steve. 'You're gonna give the audience trumpet poisoning.'

Steve laughed. Chet chuckled.

'When was the last time we met?' Chet asked in his characteristic mumble.

'Some jazz festival years ago,' Louis replied. 'France, maybe. Or Canada?'

However long ago it had been, Chet had aged at triple speed. Louis' eyes darted across the room. Just like the lobby, the walls here were covered in a gray-tone sea of headshots. Sure enough, there was Chet, in a photo that was probably only ten years old, but looked like it could have been a different person. Glossy brown hair, deep brown eyes, the cheekbones angled so high you could jump to your death from them. That beauty was still there on the man now, but it was tainted, harrowed. Like Chet was the best-looking skeleton Louis had ever seen.

'I think it was in Italy, back in the fifties,' Chet said. 'Before I got deported.'

Louis nodded, recalling news stories about Chet doing time in Italy, a scandal involving an heiress, or a princess.

They made more small talk, Steve cracked a couple of jokes, then he slapped them both on the back and stepped out of the room. Louis' mind wandered to his attaché case in the corner.

'Got a while till the show starts,' he said. 'Wanna get some fresh air?'

Ten minutes later they were standing on the playhouse roof, Louis sparking a joint. Night had turned the city a smoky blue. Tiny lights twinkled all across it, like LA was a lake strewn with fallen stars.

'I didn't think you were still playing,' Louis said.

'I wasn't. I dropped out for a while there, did some other stuff, odd jobs, pumping gas. I'm on the comeback trail now, though. Been doing some session work with some Mariachi bands.'

'Jesus, Chet.'

'Yeah, I know. But it pays the bills.'

Louis wondered if he should offer Chet the joint. If he was one of those musicians who used pot to steady themselves before a gig, or if it made his playing worse. The decision was taken out of Louis' hands when Chet pulled out a pack of Luckies and lit one up instead.

Chet smoked and told Louis how a couple of years earlier his mouth had been smashed in during a dope buy gone wrong in San Francisco's Fillmore District. It was the last straw for teeth already weakened by years of heroin abuse. Now he was trying to relaunch his career with dentures and a methadone prescription, trying to play through false teeth and searing pain.

Louis wondered how much of the redemption tale was true. One thing he knew about junkies was they were expert guilt-trippers, but he could tell the part about Chet's pain was real. It was etched all over his ravaged face.

'Shit, Chet,' Louis said. 'That's rough. That's real rough.'

Chet nodded. Louis thought of Bunk Johnson, one of jazz music's pioneers, ending up on a sugar wagon back in Louisiana, sending Louis a letter begging for money to get his teeth fixed, to get his career back on track.

They both fell silent and stared out over the view. The streets looked eerie in the darkness. Lights blipped through the murky sky above, heading toward Malibu. The giant clock on top of the Hollywood Ranch Market spun backwards through time. Louis felt the desert wind on his face.

'Santa Ana night,' Chet said. 'You can taste it. Whole of Malibu's burning up. They said on the radio three firefighters died already.'

Louis nodded. He'd seen the footage on the TV while he'd been eating his Christmas dinner back at the Marmont: walls of flame, helicopters, airplanes dropping pink fire retardant over the hills.

'Poor bastards,' Louis said.

'At least they died fighting for something,' Chet shrugged. 'It's a beautiful world, man. Glad there's people fighting to save it, you know.'

He took a last drag on his cigarette and flicked it over the edge of the building. Louis watched its light sail through the blackness.

Twenty minutes later Louis stepped into the roar of the studio, bright lights blazing in a woozy heat. The set had been decorated with a giant Christmas tree, tinsel and sugar canes stapled all over the walls. On Steve's desk was a bowl of suspicious-looking eggnog. Steve himself was sitting behind his desk, holding up a few of Chet's more recent albums that had sunk without a trace. Steve assured the audience they should pick up copies and then he introduced Chet and the cameras swung around to where Chet was seated on a high stool with the Donn Trenner Orchestra behind him.

Louis watched from the wings, praying Chet didn't embarrass himself. He looked glassy-eyed and listless. But you couldn't go on looks alone. Louis had seen many a jazzman in a drug-induced stupor, in a liquor haze, in the depths of madness, step up on stage and play the most inspired music. Maybe Chet was one of them.

Chet mumbled something and then the band struck up the opening bars of 'My Funny Valentine'. It was his signature tune, but an odd choice for a Christmas special. Chet lifted his horn to his lips and Louis felt a shudder of concern. The first few notes came out fine, and Chet seemed to get better as he went along. But the look on his face told a different story; how much it was costing him in pain to be up there.

It was killing him.

Why didn't he just put the trumpet down? Why didn't he just sing? Surely he could still sing? Why was he so obsessed with playing the trumpet at the expense of everything else?

And then a painful epiphany burned through Louis as he realized he should be asking himself all those same questions.

The song ended, and the audience clapped, and Chet rose wearily and headed to the wings.

'How'd I do?' he asked Louis.

'Good, Chet. Real good.'

Chet seemed to search Louis' face for some trace that he was lying. But eventually he gave it up. Louis put his arm over his shoulder.

'Your chops hurting you?'

Chet nodded.

'But you're still playing,' Louis said.

'I'll keep playing till I drop. What else am I going to do?'

Louis nodded and Chet stumbled off. Louis watched him go, something about the encounter nagging at him, something about Chet up on stage, playing through the onslaught. Something about it made him feel guilty, but he couldn't figure out what.

About a quarter of an hour later Louis was still in a daze when one of the production assistants told him he'd be on soon. He grabbed his trumpet from the dressing room and returned to the wings. As he waited for Steve to introduce him, he suddenly realized why he'd been feeling guilty. It wasn't just Chet on stage, it was their conversation on the roof, the thought of those firefighters dying. While Louis was smoking joints and playing tunes on the TV, the world was on fire, and people were laying down their lives to save it. And not just firefighters, people like Ida too.

Steve said something, and the cameras swung in Louis' direction and the audience turned, bursting into rapturous applause. Louis walked out onto the stage, into the glaring lights. He took his place in front of the band. They waited for him to give the nod so they could launch into the opening of 'Mack the Knife'. Louis had played the song a million times in more countries than he could care to remember, but it still pulsed for him. The music, the lights, the air, reverberated and shone with time.

He knew what he had to do now. If he – the eternal optimist – had fallen victim to the pessimism, how many others had, too? If hope was lost, so was the will to fight, and then where would the world be? All Louis had to offer now was one last hopeful song. Who was he to refuse the call? He'd go on for as long as he had breath in his lungs. Not for himself, but for everyone. It was a beautiful world, despite everything, and it sure as hell was worth fighting for.

Louis nodded at the band and they launched into the tune.

He raised his trumpet to his lips and blew.

# 64

Dante ordered another beer and a double whiskey. He wanted to get out of the bar as quickly as possible – it was a hell of a place to spend his last night on earth – but he also wanted to get drunk as quickly as possible. He turned to the TV at the end of the bar, which was tuned to NBC, the *Steve Allen Christmas Special*. Louis Armstrong was blasting his way through 'Mack the Knife', beaming with a joy and optimism that Dante envied. The barman brought him his drinks and they both watched the performance, Dante sipping his beer, the barman chewing a toothpick. Armstrong brought the song to a close and the audience roared. Steve Allen applauded and segued to one of his absurdist comedy skits – footage of himself standing in his garden in Royal Oaks.

'It's a nice part of LA,' Allen said to camera. 'Except for the neighbors.' He lifted a rifle and fired across his lawn. There was a hasty cut to stock footage from an old Western: Apache warriors being shot from their charging horses. There was another quick cut back to Allen on his patio, lowering his rifle, his wife handing him a cocktail.

The barman grunted a laugh. Dante downed his whiskey and ordered another.

On the TV Allen was back in the studio now to reintroduce his special musical guest. The audience clapped, and the cameras swung around to the stage, revealing a gaunt man perched up on a stool, trumpet in hand. The man mumbled that for his second song that night, he'd be performing 'Alone Together'. Dante realized who the man was – Chet Baker. It solved a minor mystery from the first night of Dante's case, when he'd heard the same song on the radio and wondered if Baker was still alive, if he'd made it through his addictions.

Dante toasted Baker in his head, sipped his whiskey, listened to him blowing his lonely, haunted trumpet, sounding as soul-weary as Dante felt. The perfect song to drink to in a seedy downtown bar the night before a reckoning. If only there was a way Dante could bluff White at the meeting the next morning, bargain with him. But he couldn't think how. He'd been outmaneuvered by the Feds, just like Riccardo had been. Outmaneuvered and beaten.

The politicians had remodeled themselves in the image of gangsters, taking up the Mafia's tactics so ruthlessly they were outsmarting the Mob itself, as if it was nothing but a carcass to be stepped around now. In the golden era, the Mob had infiltrated politics and remade it in their image. Now the politicians had completed the circle. Con men and crooks had assumed positions of authority and they made better criminals than the mobsters ever did. Men like Roselli had accidentally created a monster in the government, just like the government had accidentally created a monster in Vacaville.

On the TV, 'Alone Together' ended, and the audience clapped and the show cut to commercials. The barman switched channels, landed on the news and its bloody roster of current affairs – Vietnam, the manhunt for Faron. The Night-Slayer didn't even cop a mention. Disasters moved fast, news moved faster. And then, a report came on from Washington about the FBN.

Dante was so wrapped up in his gloom he didn't realize what the anchor was talking about at first. When he did realize, he asked the barman to turn up the volume.

'. . . *confirmed by the Justice Department late yesterday afternoon in Attorney General Ramsey Clark's final weekly press conference before Christmas. Before the FBN is wound down in the New Year, it will be removed from the jurisdiction of the Treasury to the Justice Department. Mr Clark said agency staff have been informed of the decision, and have been assured that their jobs would be retained for the foreseeable future, until either a replacement agency was set up, or the FBN was merged with either FDA's Bureau of Drug Abuse Control, or US Customs; all possible plans the White House and the Justice Department are currently considering.'*

Dante stared at the TV.

The FBN was being closed down, the announcement buried in a Christmas-time press conference.

Was this why White was in Washington? For the closure of the FBN? O'Shaughnessy had said it was on the cards, and now it was actually happening.

And suddenly it all made sense.

This was the Christmas deadline.

Drazek had been right – it wasn't about covering up the past, it was about clearing the way for the future, for what would come in the FBN's place. Dante realized now why White had done everything he could to cover up Vacaville and the cocaine routes. Why Hennessy had gone underground to take on White. This was why White was in Washington.

Dante laughed, shook his head. And then he realized something else. If he was right, then maybe he did have leverage after all. He could still scupper White's plans. He could save Loretta and himself. All he needed was Riccardo's body. If he could find it in what little time he had left.

# PART TWENTY-THREE

## INFERNOS

# 𝕷𝖔𝖘 𝕬𝖓𝖌𝖊𝖑𝖊𝖘 𝕿𝖎𝖒𝖊𝖘

LARGEST CIRCULATION IN THE WEST

## Tuesday Final

TUESDAY MORNING, DECEMBER 26, 1967

80 PAGES, DAILY, 10c

~

## LOCAL NEWS

~

# HOMES EVACUATED IN FACE OF FIRE PERIL

*By John Fradkin*
*Times Staff Writer*

LOS ANGELES County – Stubborn brushfires spread across large swathes of the Santa Monicas yesterday, prompting U.S. Forest Service and county Fire Department officials to issue warnings and evacuation notices. Fast-moving Santa Ana winds have spurred on the fires, which have been burning for several days, leading to evacuations in Calabasas and Monte Nido.

An aerial tanker dumped 20,000 gallons of fire-retardant solution on flames to the east of Malibu Creek, while over 100 U.S. Forest Service and county firefighters attempted to cut a line around the hot spot of the blaze.

While several smaller fires have been brought under control to the north, larger blazes continue to move southeast at the time of writing, raging unchecked through the brush-covered canyons and hillsides closer to the Malibu coastline.

A Forest Service spokesman urged residents to stay in contact with local officials and to prepare for further evacuations.

Please turn to Page B, Col. 3

# 65

Dante sat at the top of the Stunt Road with the dog and watched the sunrise gilding the landscape in pink and gold. To the south the mountains tumbled into the ocean, to the west brushfires flickered over the brows of distant hills; black plumes of smoke rose into the sky, slanted by the desert wind.

Dante had already found the body, which was the easy part. Now he had to convince the cops he had nothing to do with its appearance in the ravine, that the papers he'd planted on it were genuine, that he could get the corpse into the legal system without White realizing what he was up to. And he had to do it all quickly. The court date was for that afternoon. The meeting with White would be earlier. It had been hours since Dante had called the cops to report the body, and still they hadn't turned up.

He'd found the body where Zullo had told him it had been dumped – *over the side of the Stunt Road. Where the trail for the Rosas Overlook starts*. It was a good spot to get rid of a corpse. High in the mountains, on the corner of a hairpin bend. Just on the edge of the hairpin, where the trail branched off, a wide space had been cemented over on the shoulder for cars to park. You could pull up in the parking spots, throw a body over the side, watch it tumble through the brush into the ravine below, and be on your way in under a minute.

Dante heard the approach of cars behind him. He turned and rose. Two LA County Sheriffs cruisers. The doors opened and two cops got out of each car. Three of them were regular deputies, but one had rank insignia on his sleeve. They all looked sleepless and annoyed, just an hour or two from the end of their night shift. The one with the insignia approached Dante, looked him up and down.

'I'm Deputy William Harris,' he said. 'You the one who called in the body?'

Dante nodded. Harris looked him up and down again.

'Where is it?' he asked.

Dante pointed to the ravine. 'Down there. About a hundred yards. I can lead you to it.'

Harris peered down the ravine. Turned back to Dante.

'Dispatch said you made the call at just after five a.m.'

'That's correct.'

'You mind me asking what you were doing down in a ravine at that time of night?'

'Taking the dog for a walk.'

'At five a.m.?'

'He's got insomnia.'

Two of the deputies sniggered, which only riled Harris further. He turned, glared at them, turned back.

'All right, wise-ass. Let's get down there.'

Dante led them over to the path, down the steep slope, all the way to the ditch bordered by cottonwood trees where Riccardo's body lay. It was at least a hundred yards below the road. No way Faron and White could have tossed it there – they'd dumped it further up the ravine and coyotes or cougars had dragged it further down. It was covered in animal bites, half the face had been ripped off, the eyes were missing, the entrails had spilled.

The deputies stood in a ring around the body and examined it. The last sorry remains of Riccardo Licata.

'He's been here a good long while,' one of deputies said.

Harris went through Riccardo's clothes, pulled out a wallet. It was Dante's own wallet, cleaned and made to look like Riccardo's. Dante had driven over to Riccardo's office the night before, had helped himself to objects he could plant on Riccardo's body: business cards, credit cards, receipts, photos, anything that would help with a quick identification, anything that could incriminate White. Then Dante had floored it to Santa Monica, to a twenty-four-hour supermarket to pick up a flashlight, batteries, a Polaroid camera, a copy of the *Times*, a trail map.

'Riccardo Licata,' Harris said, reading the business cards. 'Well, that was an easy identification.'

He looked up at Dante accusingly. Dante shrugged.

'So, this is where you take your dog for a walk in the middle of the night, hunh?'

'I was taking him along that trail up there.' Dante gestured to a trail on the far side of the ravine. 'The dog ran off down here, barking, I guess he caught the smell of the body. I followed him. Found it. Called it in. I'm a conscientious citizen.'

Harris glared at him again. The story was ridiculous, but it would buy Dante some time. The truth was, Dante had spent hours searching the area immediately below the parking spots. Being out there in the ravine for so long he started to see things, the jagged darkness flaking away, rainbow colors streaking through the night. He had a sense of the wilderness around him. Its vastness. The life it contained. The animals watching him. Or maybe something else, a presence, shimmering in the night, in the air piled up in that timeless place, a dark reservoir of something whose nature Dante couldn't get a handle on, not even if he had a few lifetimes to ponder it.

When the beam of his flashlight finally landed on Riccardo's body, at just after four a.m., Dante checked that it really was Riccardo, then he planted the wallet, laid the copy of the *Times* next to Riccardo's face and took a few Polaroids. Then he'd made a note of the location, climbed out of the ravine and driven back down the road to call the cops.

'All right,' Harris said, turning to his men. 'Y'all go back up to the prowlers and call it in. I'll stay here with Mr . . .'

'Sanfelippo,' Dante said.

Harris's men frowned, finding the orders strange, but they

nodded, headed back up the slope. Harris eyed them as they went, and Dante had a sense of where this was going.

When the other deputies were out of earshot, Harris turned to Dante.

'All right, cowboy. Start talking. I know who the Licatas are, and I noticed you got an Italian name, too. So don't give me no shit about taking your dog for a walk. You a bounty hunter?'

Dante considered lying, but the fact that Harris had sent his men away to discuss the matter suggested he'd be amenable to a bribe, and he wanted Dante to know it.

'Something like that,' Dante said.

'Well, you wanna fill me in on the details or do I need to hook you and book you?'

'The body's Nick Licata's kid. He was out on a half-million bail paid for by Nick. The kid disappeared. Nick asked me to find him.'

'And you're a bail recovery agent?'

'No, I'm a family friend. But I'm getting a finder's fee. Problem is the kid's supposed to be in court today and I know I won't be getting a death certificate soon enough. But if someone in law enforcement could give me a document to pass on to the judge stating a body's turned up that's most likely the defendant's, the judge should postpone the court date, and I'll be getting the finder's fee. It's a substantial finder's fee.'

Harris eyed him, then grinned.

'And how much of this finder's fee are you willing to share?'

# 66

Ida sat on a bench outside the airport's Hertz concession while Kerry went inside to return the Cutlass she'd rented. After they'd woken up that morning Ida had tried once more to talk the girl out of returning to Vietnam, but she hadn't succeeded. What did Ida have to persuade her to stay? The offer of work? A new start? Stevie's funeral? Kerry had decided it wasn't enough. The best way for her to prove she loved her dead brother was to go back to Vietnam to die.

So Kerry had called the Los Angeles Air Force Station, then Travis Air Force Base, trying to get a message through to her captain in Vietnam, to explain why she was late returning, to see if she could arrange a way back. Then she'd called up Braniff and booked a flight up to Sacramento. From there to Travis and Vietnam. Kerry had asked Ida to take care of the two guns she'd bought while in the city and then had tried to give back the copy of Ida's manual.

'I didn't manage to read much of it,' Kerry had said. 'But it was good. Interesting.'

'Keep it,' Ida had said. 'I meant what I said about you making a good investigator. Consider the offer an open one. Anytime you want to come back, I'll see how I can help you out.'

'Thanks, but I know what I've got to do.'

Ida mulled it over as she waited on the bench outside the Hertz concession. She watched the planes flying by overhead, wondered if Faron might be on any of them. She watched the cars coming and going in the endless parking lots that surrounded the airport. On the road leading out onto Century Boulevard there was a giant billboard welcoming people to the city, the same advertisement that hung over the grounds of the Wigwam Motel, showing carefully curated images of LA and underneath the municipal slogan: *It All Comes Together in Los Angeles!*

Ida stared at it, eyes narrow. It didn't come together in Los Angeles. It never had. It was a city designed to afford you every opportunity to keep apart. Ida studied the images arrayed across the billboard – orange groves, beaches, the Hollywood sign, Grauman's Chinese Theatre, a couple horse-riding, someone surfing, some dainty-looking oil derricks in the background.

The images seemed like a code for LA, the city self-mythologizing, and through the myth, becoming real, then falling into myth once more. Like a serpent eating its tail.

Kerry walked out of the Hertz concession.

'Assholes charged me twenty bucks for the broken window.'

Ida nodded, not really listening, her eyes still fixed on the billboard, something about it snagging, calling out to her.

'You OK?' Kerry asked.

'Something about that billboard.'

'It's the same one that was over my motel.'

'Yeah, I know.'

Ida continued to stare at it. She got the feeling that the images related to the case somehow, that if she cracked their code she might solve it, but she couldn't quite see how. She realized it was the couple riding horses that bugged her. It seemed even more phony than the rest of the billboard. That old California of cowboy movies. That same fake pioneer myth that Governor Reagan had used to get himself elected. She thought of her conversation with Louis, his talk of the governor and the corrupt deal he'd been involved in for his horse-riding ranch, his links to organized crime, Louis' contention that they were all ensnared in the same net.

She shook her head. It was just her old mind rambling. She

rose from the bench and she and Kerry headed toward the airport buildings.

But they'd only taken a couple of steps before Ida stopped again, turned back to look at the billboard once more.

The horse-riders.

The ranch.

Realization flooded through her, like a dam had burst.

'What is it?' Kerry asked.

'Bud Williams told his grandmother he was hiding out on a ranch,' Ida said.

'Sure,' Kerry shrugged. 'The same ranch where Faron killed Cooper.'

Ida shook her head.

'Bud told his grandmother it was a horse-riding ranch.'

'So?'

'You saw Cooper's ranch. There weren't any horses there. The stables collapsed years ago. We just assumed it was the same ranch.'

'So Bud made it up.'

'No. He was staying somewhere there were horse-riders, and I know where. Hennessy's place in Malibu.'

'His hide-out?'

Ida nodded.

'Drazek said it was next to the governor's old horse-riding ranch,' she explained. 'That Hennessy stashed evidence there. Well, what if some of that evidence was a person?'

'Bud Williams,' Kerry muttered, understanding now.

'Hennessy took Stevie in as a witness,' Ida said. 'Why not Bud Williams, too? It'd explain why Bud told his grandmother he was staying at the ranch with friends from prison. Stevie and Hennessy.'

They stared at each other.

'He's there,' Ida said. 'Hennessy's dead. The place is empty. He must have gone back there to hide out after he killed the librarian. I'm sure of it. Where else could he have gone with the cops looking for him? Maybe this isn't all over. Maybe we can still find him. If you want to come with me, that is. Instead of getting on that plane.'

'You want to go to Malibu?' Kerry asked. 'Now?'

'Sure, why not?'

'You saw the news, Ida. The whole place is burning up. They're evacuating.'

In the rush of the breakthrough, Ida hadn't considered the wildfires. A shiver of fear ran through her, the same fear that had caused her to make so many mistakes recently, the same fear she now knew she had to face down. What better way than by stepping into an inferno?

'Good,' she said. 'Traffic'll be light.'

# 67

When Dante was done with the sheriffs he called Nick Licata and gave him the news. If Nick was upset to find out that his son was dead, he didn't show it. He brushed it off, talked business. Dante relayed the details, the info for his lawyer to pass on to the court, the size of the bribe for the sheriff's deputy. Licata told Dante to swing by later for a debrief. Dante agreed, pretending like he might actually still be alive by then. He hung up and called the number White had given him.

'We found DeVeaux,' a voice said at the other end. 'We got your wife for you. Come over.'

The voice gave Dante an address. Dante scribbled it down and hung up. He called O'Shaughnessy and put his backup plan into action. It was only when Dante was giving O'Shaughnessy the address that he realized it was the same place where this had all started – the mansion in Pacific Palisades where the pool party had been, where Dante had spoken to Licata and Roselli. His mind flashed back to Zullo on the terrace, telling Dante it was a pop star's house, Zullo gloating that he was extorting the man. And now Zullo was dead, White had inherited the extortion, and Dante would be coming full circle.

An hour later he pulled up to the mansion's gates, which were already open. Everything was peaceful and still. The mansion was enormous, far from its neighbors, isolated. A good spot to kill someone and cover it up. A good spot for things to go wrong and a bloodbath to ensue.

A bomber flew past and shattered the eerie quiet, clattering toward the brushfires in Malibu. Dante watched it go. He checked his watch. He drove up the driveway.

When he got to the house he saw two men standing by the doors. The same two Feds he'd met at the FBN headquarters the day before – Schodt and McKinney.

Dante killed the Thunderbird's engine, stroked the dog.

'So long, pal,' he said.

He got out, walked across to the men, saw they had the same glazed eyes as the day before, the same sheen of cold sweat. Once more they were boosted on the very narcotics they were supposed to be eradicating. Dante wondered if they were ever sober.

Schodt made a gesture. Dante raised his arms and McKinney frisked him. Dante had left his Colt and the shotgun in the Thunderbird, knowing there was no point trying to take weapons with him. When McKinney finished, Schodt opened the door and gestured for Dante to enter.

'He's out back,' Schodt said.

They stepped into the hallway. With no people in it this time, the place seemed even bigger, and deathly silent apart from the echo of their footsteps. They walked through to the lounge, through the open doors onto the terrace with the pool and the million-dollar views; there was the city, the ocean, the smoke blowing in from Malibu, turning the sky sepia brown. And there, sitting on a wrought-iron garden chair just in front of the pool house, was the giant figure of Agent Henry White. Well over six foot, completely bald, broad-shouldered, hulking, his body fat spooling over the sides of the chair.

He grinned when he saw Dante.

'Mr Sanfelippo. Take a seat.'

Dante sat in a chair across from White, while Schodt and McKinney sat behind him, hemming him in. Dante studied White. He had the same glazed eyes as the two men, the same sense that he was out of it on booze and drugs, but also terrifyingly in control at the same time.

'I've heard a lot about you,' White said. 'Dante the Gent, isn't it? You've got quite the reputation.'

'I haven't had a reputation for years. Where's my wife?'

'She's here. She's safe.'

'I want to see her.'

'Not just yet.'

'I want to see her.'

White raised his wispy eyebrows.

'Let's do this cordially, shall we? Like I told you on the phone yesterday, this wasn't supposed to happen. What DeVeaux did was wrong. We caught up with him, we got your wife back. Now we just need to discuss the implications and you're free to go.'

White raised his hands, like it was all so simple. Dante frowned. White was stalling. His men could have slipped a garrote over Dante's neck already by now. They could have dragged him to the pool and drowned him. They could have put a bullet in his head. There was only one reason they hadn't − White wanted info. He wanted to know how much Dante had uncovered, who he'd told, how much they'd been compromised. It meant he had some time still. Time for things to turn to his advantage. Time for O'Shaughnessy to show up. Dante flicked his gaze to the pool house, to the terrace wall beyond, the drop down to the road below. Nothing moved. No sign of O'Shaughnessy. Maybe he'd been delayed. Maybe he wouldn't be coming. Maybe if Dante's primary plan failed, there'd be no backup.

'You were there when Zullo died?' White asked.

Dante turned to look at him. This was what he was stalling for − he wanted info on Zullo, how much he'd revealed before he'd died, the size of the leak.

'I was there,' Dante said.

'What did he tell you?'

'Not much. He was dying. I figured out most of it myself when I saw the announcement about the FBN being closed down.

475

That's when it all clicked into place. That's when I realized what you'd been up to.'

'Oh? And what was that?' White said, raising his eyebrows again.

The gesture was meant to be nonchalant, expressing surprise, a pleasing turn of events. But Dante saw it hid some disquiet underneath. He could use that disquiet, that fear, to keep White talking. Maybe whatever White was high on might help with that, too.

'You've been trying to bring down the FBN,' Dante said. 'Something about this all never made sense – I thought it was rogue CIA agents supplying Riccardo, siphoning off coke from the triangle of death. But it never sat right. And then when I saw that announcement about the FBN closing, I realized why – I'd got it all wrong. It wasn't rogue agents. It was official CIA policy. The Agency was bringing in the coke deliberately.'

'That's a bold statement,' White said.

'But it makes sense. Especially when you think about the triangle, how inefficient it is. Cocaine goes from Latin America to Europe, from there heroin goes to the States, from there guns go back to Latin America. It's a perfect cycle. It's beautiful. But, like I said, it's inefficient.'

'Because?'

'Because you could just ship the cocaine from Latin America direct to the states. Cut out the European leg. Cut out the heroin swap. It could just be a straight trade – South American coke for North American guns. The only problem is, there's not a market for cocaine in the States. There hasn't been since the nineteen thirties, so how would you sell it here?'

Dante thought back to the coke in Riccardo's car, the kids doing coke at the pool party, Zullo and his running nose, the quip about the whole music industry being on the drug, O'Shaughnessy saying they were busting more and more coke dealers.

'But you can *develop* a market here in the States,' Dante said.

'Just like a market was developed in the nineteen thirties for heroin. You *create* the market, and suddenly it's so much easier. No going to Europe to swap heroin for cocaine. The triangle becomes a simple straight line. It's more elegant, robust, and cheaper.'

Dante looked at White and White couldn't help but smile. He'd been involved in a huge con, a giant con, the biggest one going. Bigger than the Mob using Jimmy Hoffa to wring out the Teamsters pension fund. Bigger than them using Vegas to dupe Howard Hughes out of his fortune. Bigger even than them trying to whack Castro so they could get their Cuban casinos back. But what good was running the biggest con in the world if you couldn't brag about it? Dante could tell that White was a narcissist. That he needed an audience. That he needed Dante sitting here telling him how smart it all was. He needed outsiders to figure it out, to marvel at the audacity, so that he could revel in it.

'There's only one problem,' Dante continued. 'The FBN. While the CIA's running round the globe setting up drug routes, the FBN's running around trying to stop them. Two arms of the US government with directly clashing remits, fighting each other like they're Mafia families in a vendetta. What's the CIA to do? Except put its rival out of business. Infiltrate the FBN, turn some of its men into double agents. Men like you. Let them rip it down from the inside. Mire it in scandals and regulations, declare it not fit for its job, and then replace it with a brand new agency that's controlled top-to-bottom by CIA men, so they can continue going around the world doing what they do. Which is exactly what's happening.

'The FBN's going to die, and in its place a new narcotics enforcement agency will come into being, one staffed only by CIA-compromised agents who'll look the other way, a stooge agency that'll let the CIA smuggle whatever they want, wherever they want. So much easier for them to have total control of narcotics enforcement, than to be in a constant battle with the FBN.'

Dante shrugged his shoulders, eyed White. This was what Drazek had meant about Faron being in town to clear the way for something. They were clearing the way for this new agency to be born. They were cleaning up the skeletons in White's closet – Riccardo, Vacaville, the Night-Slayer. They were making sure White was bulletproof before the FBN's closure was announced and the new agency came into being. Hence the Christmas deadline – the date the announcement was to be made. There was only one reason why they'd go to such lengths.

'What did they offer you for your part in it?' Dante asked. 'All the trouble they went through to clean up after you, it must be for the head role. They offered to put you in charge of the new agency, didn't they? You'll get to run the whole of federal narcotics enforcement, national and international, and the only stipulation is, you turn a blind eye to whatever the CIA's up to.'

White's smile turned into a grin, broad, beaming, lighting up the terrace. Dante wondered if he was the first outsider to have figured out the size of the con, if this was the first time White had got to bask in the glory.

'It's been going on for years,' White said. 'All this infighting. Every time the FBN went after some drug traffickers across the globe, the State Department would step in and tell us to back off, because the drug traffickers were CIA assets. Thailand, Cambodia, Morocco, Monaco, Lebanon, Turkey, Greece, pretty much every country in South America. The FBN had its hands tied behind its back. Think of all the waste. All the money down the drain. The CIA spending millions on its plans and the FBN spending millions to counteract them. It made no sense. When the CIA approached me, their plan made sense. It's better for the government and the taxpayer. Everyone wins. We get rid of the FBN. We get rid of the triangle of death. We get rid of all the infighting. It's the future. There's going to be a cocaine influx into the country and it'll all go to helping our friends in Latin America, to fighting communism, to ensuring America's security. We've got the producers in Ecuador, Peru, Bolivia. We've got the cartels in Mexico to bring it over, and we've got our Italian friends Stateside to distribute it. The nineteen seventies becomes the cocaine era. The country goes sledging through a snowstorm of it. And the beautiful irony is, all those drug users, all those liberals and communists and dropouts using the stuff, the ones who are all so anti-American, they won't have a clue that while they're snorting that white powder up their nose, they're funding the very people they despise.'

White's grin broadened even further, distorting the features of his face, turning those red-glazed eyes into thin slashes. For some reason he found this irony, of people opposed to American expansionism helping to fund it, the cherry on the cake.

Dante flicked his gaze around the terrace once more. Everything was unmoving, serene. His gaze landed on the windows of the pool house; in their reflection he could just about make out the shapes of Schodt and McKinney sitting behind him. If they moved, Dante might just have a couple of seconds' warning.

'There's one thing I don't get,' he said. 'Why'd you partner with Riccardo? You could have gone with power players. Instead you went with the idiot son of the idiot boss of the Mickey Mouse Mafia.'

'Riccardo was a test run,' White shrugged. 'Roselli's choice. Someone small we could use to see how things would work. He was expendable. Just like Zullo. And the pair of them were cheap. Their cut was nominal.' White smiled. 'Riccardo didn't have a clue who he was really buying from. Not till Hennessy went to the jail and told him. After that we had no choice.'

White shrugged. Dante looked him over. The man was a crook, but worse than Riccardo or Roselli or even Zullo, because at least they never pretended to be public servants. White and his handlers had taken down a federal law enforcement agency, to replace it with a corrupt stooge organization. It made Dante's Mob look parochial in comparison. Once more he had that sense that the Mob wasn't dying, it was simply being replicated in government, moved from the margins into the mainstream. The con men and crooks were so ubiquitous now, you couldn't even see them.

'So you'll understand,' White said, 'with so much at stake, why we can't let you and your wife go. There's been so much spilled blood already to set this up, it'd be like all those people died for nothing.'

This was the moment Dante had been preparing for, where White upped the stakes to find out how exposed he was.

'My wife doesn't know anything about any of this. Let her go and we can talk about things.'

'What have we got to talk about?'

'Riccardo Licata's body.'

White raised his eyebrows again. Dante was starting to recognize the tic, what it was designed to mask.

'I found his corpse earlier today at the bottom of a ravine underneath the Stunt Road. It's where you and Faron dumped it. You killed Riccardo in that safe house the Agency loaned you over in the Hills, let him bleed out in the bathtub, and then you drove him to the Stunt Road and tossed him off the side. I planted evidence on Riccardo's corpse to link it back to the safe house, back to you. Then I moved his body somewhere secure. For a hundred and forty pounds of rotting flesh, that body's quite valuable. It's worth at least half a million in bail money to Nick Licata. He said he'd cut me in, by the way. And I guess when the cops find it and you're linked to his murder, this scheme of putting you in charge of the new agency goes up in smoke. Which won't make you too popular with the CIA. You'll be killed in a jailhouse hit before this ever goes to trial. It's a shame, all those people who died to set it up, all that money spent. All for nothing.'

White glared at Dante through his drug haze.

'Bullshit.'

Dante shrugged. He pulled a half-dozen Polaroid photos of

Riccardo Licata's corpse from his jacket pocket, tossed them onto the table. White frowned, leaned forward, inspected them. Dante had framed them with the copy of the *Times* in shot, so White would know they were recent. Dante had even turned the newspaper to the headline announcing the closure of the FBN. At the time he'd thought it was a nice touch; now he was wondering if it was overkill.

'Let my wife go and I'll tell you where I dumped the body and you can get rid of it properly this time. Your whole scheme is back on track and we can talk about cutting me in.'

'Cutting you in?'

'Sure. I'm the best fixer in LA, Agent White. You want to set up drugs routes here, I'm the guy you call. I know everyone and everyone trusts me. Ask Roselli. We can move product out of my distribution company once it's up and running again. You won't have to worry about Nick Licata or no-hopers like Riccardo and Zullo. You cut me and in return I give you LA.' Dante threw his hands up in the air, like it was so simple. 'Or you kill me and my pal tells the cops where the body is. Your choice, Agent White. Los Angeles. Or dying in jail.'

Dante shrugged.

'Oh, and one other thing,' he said. 'You let me kill DeVeaux for what he did to my wife.'

This last request made White laugh. Dante had judged right that he'd be receptive to audacity. White eyed Dante, then he nodded at Schodt and McKinney. They rose, went into the house. Dante surveyed the terrace once more.

A few seconds passed and White's men came back out with Loretta walking in front of them. She looked worried and tired, but physically fine.

They sat her in a chair next to Dante. He studied her and she nodded that she was OK.

'Now,' White said. 'You tell us where you stashed Riccardo's body, or your wife dies.'

# 68

Ida and Kerry hooked north in Ida's car, the radio tuned to a local station which was broadcasting non-stop info on the fires.

*'Officials think the blazes are moving southwest . . . high winds have pushed the fires . . . residents are being evacuated . . .'*

As they drove along the freeway, Kerry could see the mountains in the distance, looming ever larger. In front of them countless miles of smoke hung in the sky like a shroud, tinting everything pale brown.

They hit Pacific Coast Highway, and the mountains veered closer. Kerry saw through the smoke, to where the inferno had taken hold. Pearls of orange fire were strung like necklaces along the ridges, their flames illuminating the tracery of the mountains.

By the time they reached Topanga Beach they could smell the smoke. From that point on there were traffic jams at the on-ramps all along the highway, people fleeing, trucks and cars piled high. At Latigo Canyon men from the Highway Patrol were trying to impose some order on the evacuation, which left them too pre-occupied to stop Ida and Kerry from turning off the highway and heading in the opposite direction to everyone else, inland, into the heart of it.

Ida passed Kerry a road map. Kerry traced the path to the housing development Drazek had told them about: *The Highview Estates*. They'd had to call information from the airport to get the name of the road it was situated on, had marked it on the map.

'We just need to climb up the ridge and follow the road along its top,' Kerry said.

The road wound ever upwards, bending around the contours

of the incline. When they reached the brow of the ridge, the scene beyond hove into view. In the middle ground were the houses of the Highview Estates, perched on top of the ridge. Beyond them, further along the hilltops, was the inferno; spurred on by the wind it was speeding toward the development from the far side, almost touching it. It looked like the earth itself was on fire. The sky above black as a stove.

'Looks like the entrance to hell,' Kerry said.

They carried on driving. On the slopes below them they saw bulldozers moving back and forth, gouging lines in the earth, creating a firebreak in the chaparral. They saw men in Forest Service fire jackets and hard hats standing by their jeeps, talking into radios, consulting maps. They looked up when they saw Ida and Kerry driving past in the wrong direction. They frowned or shook their heads. They got back to work.

In the Caddy, the radio reception was intermittent now.

'. . . *The flames have climbed the lower slopes . . . are now heading toward . . . helicopter and plane support has been diverted . . .*'

Kerry heard a roaring noise behind her and turned to look, worried a tree or house was about to collapse onto the road. But through the smoke she saw it was a firefighting plane. A repurposed bomber from the war, lumbering through the sky. It traced the path of the ridge, flew over the houses. When it was above the fire further on, it rolled, its tanks opened, and a pink trail of fire retardant uncoiled from its underbelly, drifted toward the flames.

As they neared the Highview Estates, the heat got worse, the wind bouncing sparks across the asphalt in front of them. On the sides of the road the chaparral was already singeing – yucca, deer weed, manzanita, all of them curling and turning black.

Within a couple of minutes they reached a pair of gateposts with signs announcing they were now entering a housing development: *The Highview Estates*. Houses appeared on either side of the road. All of them were large, luxurious, each one spaced generously apart from its neighbors, set in extensive gardens. But it was a scene of chaos, of impending catastrophe. Outside the houses, children sat in cars as parents rushed in and out, carrying their prized possessions. Other homeowners were staying put, watering down their yards with hoses, spraying the wooden walls of their buildings. On a couple of roofs, men were spraying the tiles.

'These have only just been built,' Ida said. 'This is brushfire country. The Indians used to burn this land every few years to get rid of the brush, stop fires breaking out. When the Spanish came they didn't understand why, so they outlawed it. Now there's fires every couple of years. And with all the trees and chaparral removed, landslides too. And in the middle of all that someone in City Hall let people build houses here.'

She shook her head and they drove on, looking for a turning that descended the ridge, into the canyon, where Drazek had told them Hennessy's house was – *the last one along*. They reached the end of the development, where the largest, most opulent houses were perched on the very edge of the ridge. Just past these last houses the road turned, headed down the southern slope. Ida took the turning and just as they were descending, Kerry caught a glimpse in the gap between two houses of what was happening beyond the estate, in the distance. It looked like chaos. Firefighters were trying to build a break along the road. Cops and Forest Service men were hustling evacuees into their cars. Above them bubble helicopters droned and circled in the glowing orange sky. Further on, Kerry could see blackened sections of hills that the fire had already consumed.

They carried on driving and the scene disappeared. They journeyed further into the canyon. The houses petered out until they reached the very last one. It was smaller than the others, had the feel of a holiday home to it. And it was perfectly situated as a hide-out, right at the edge of the development, near a road that ran up the side of the next ridge along, meaning whoever lived there could come and go without being noticed by the other residents.

'It must be that one,' Ida said.

She stopped the car. Everything was eerily still. The only movement the smoke in the distance, the only noise the helicopters and flames on the other side of the ridge.

'Our guns are in the glovebox,' Ida said.

Kerry nodded and took them out, passed Ida hers.

They got out of the car and were blasted by the heat.

They crossed to the house. Ida approached the door, knocked. There was no answer. She tried the handle, and it was open. They stepped inside.

'Hello?' Ida said, fanning the hallway with her gun. 'This area's being evacuated.'

No response.

They walked through the hall, checked doors as they went. In the lounge the TV was on, tuned to the news. They checked the kitchen, then took the stairs. They could hear a radio or another TV, coming from one of the bedrooms. Ida approached it, Kerry just behind her.

'Hello?' Ida said again as they reached the door.

She eased it back with the nose of her gun. The bedroom beyond looked empty at first glance. The bed was unmade, the radio on the dresser switched on, nothing stirred, no movement except the ashes and sparks flying past the window outside.

But there was another noise underneath that of the radio – sobbing. Squashed up into the corner, between the bed and the wall, curled into a ball, was the sorry figure of Bud Williams, crying to himself. He looked like the photo his grandmother had given the cops – average height, chubby, his hair unkempt, dressed in jeans and a shirt.

Here was the Night-Slayer. Here was the man they'd been searching for. A man who'd butchered four innocent people, terrorized an entire city, curled up now, sobbing like a child.

Ida approached him and he looked up. His hollow-eyed expression reminded Kerry of the soldiers she used to evacuate in Vietnam, the ones who'd been living in jungle foxholes for months on end, surviving on canned food and rats, the ones for whom they stocked up the plane with baloney sandwiches and milk before every flight. There was an extinguished look in their eyes, like they'd lost the ability to be human. Bud Williams had the same expression. Kerry could imagine him slinking through the city, quietly, pitiably, avoiding contact with other people, then some random trigger causing him to lurch out of his foxhole and into horrific violence.

Ida kneeled in front of him, spoke to him in a whisper so gentle Kerry couldn't make out what she was saying. Kerry waited, splitting her gaze between the scene in the bedroom, and the view out of the window, the ashes floating past it like ripped paper, like someone had shredded the forest and cast the pieces into the wind. Beyond the ashes, trees were on fire like matches stood upright along the slope.

They needed to move fast, they needed to get out of there. But Kerry knew Williams needed coaxing, that if they rushed him, it might take even longer.

She tried to keep her breathing steady, her heart rate in check. Suddenly she felt like she was on the edge of things, not just the edge of the super-city, but something much more dangerous. This brand new house built in a firetrap canyon seemed so wrong, promising so much false security against the chaos.

In the distance, the insect-like helicopters droned on tinnily. On the radio, the news announcers tried to mediate the horror. By the wall, Ida tried to coax a murderer back to reality. None of it made sense and Kerry had that same dispiriting feeling again that it never would.

She heard a noise and turned to see that Ida had got Williams onto his feet, was leading him toward the door. They made their way back down the corridor.

As they reached the stairs, Kerry happened to glance into one of the other bedrooms. She caught a glimpse of a dresser, a gray square stuck to its mirror. Something about the image called to her. She left Ida and Bud in the corridor, and walked into the bedroom. The gray square stuck to the mirror was a photo, of her and Stevie dressed up as a cowboy and an Indian, standing in their yard in Gueydan. It was Stevie's copy of the same one Kerry had. She realized this must have been his room while he'd been staying here, and just like her, he'd placed the same photo onto his mirror.

'Kerry,' Ida called.

Kerry took the picture and slipped it into her pocket. She scanned the room for any more of Stevie's possessions, but couldn't see any. She rejoined Ida and Bud in the corridor.

'Everything OK?' Ida asked.

Kerry nodded, stifling her emotions.

They descended the stairs to the front door. As they stepped out onto the porch, Kerry spotted something further up the road that hadn't been there before – stopped behind a thicket of lilac bushes was a black Dodge she vaguely recognized. It took her a second to realize where she'd seen it before. It was the Dodge that had picked up Faron that night at the abandoned houses.

Panic stabbed through her.

But before she could warn Ida, the bullets were already ripping through the porch.

# 69

'Where did you stash the body?' White asked.

He glared at Dante, any pretence of being open to negotiation gone now.

'I take it that means you don't want to cut me in?' Dante said.

White swung a punch that caught him on the chin, sent him rolling, collapsing onto the paving stones that led to the pool. Loretta screamed, was up out of her chair. Dante was shocked by how fast White was, despite all that weight, despite all the drugs.

Next thing Dante knew, he was being lifted up by Schodt, while McKinney was restraining Loretta. He was thrown back into his chair. He wiped the blood off his lips.

'The next time you don't answer,' White said, 'it's your wife that gets punched.'

Dante turned to look at her. There were tears in her eyes that she was trying to keep back. She knew as much as he did that they'd both be killed. All Dante could do was delay the inevitable, hold out as long as possible while he maybe came up with a plan, because he was convinced now that O'Shaughnessy had left him in the lurch.

'You need to be careful with me,' he said. 'You kill me and the cops get sent straight to that body.'

White nodded at Schodt. He swung a punch. It connected with Dante's jaw, sent him sprawling again, sent his chair skittering onto the lawn. White hadn't followed through on his threat to punch Loretta, but still she was screaming.

Schodt picked up Dante again, locking his arms behind his back, pushing him over to the pool, pushing him down so Dante was on his knees, right at the edge. Then Schodt grabbed Dante's head and dunked it in the water. Cold. Biting. Dante held his breath, his lungs burning.

Schodt yanked his head back up. The world hove into view. Sunlight smeared. Dante gasped.

Schodt dunked him once more. Left him longer this time. Dante opened his eyes, and the chlorine stung. He could make out shapes in the blue, the shadows of the men behind him, the shadows of leaves floating on the surface further on. He desperately wanted to breathe. He realized it wasn't the men that he was fighting now. It was his own body. They were letting his body do the work for them.

He was pulled up out of the water again. He gasped again, sucked in air.

'Where did you put the body?' White hissed. 'This is the last time I ask before we start on your wife.'

White nodded at McKinney, who lifted Loretta up, manhandled her over to the side of the pool, dumped her next to Dante, her knees on the very edge. White pulled out a revolver, held it to Loretta's temple. She was shaking with fear. She turned to look at Dante. He shook his head minutely, to let her know he couldn't give White what he wanted, that they were both too old and out of options to survive this.

She nodded, trying to reconcile herself to it.

'Not the worst place to die,' she said.

Dante frowned. He looked around at the million-dollar view spread out before them – the whole of LA, the mountains still majestic, the sun glowing, the ocean sparkling, endless, a taste of what was to come. Maybe she was right. It wasn't the worst place to die.

Dante looked up at White, who still had the gun at her head, still waiting for an answer, still high and unpredictable. Maybe Dante should make another wisecrack, let him shoot Loretta and then get himself shot. It would be quick. Then it would all be over.

Suddenly there was the sound of barking. The dog was on the terrace, probably alerted by Loretta's screams. His nose up, his muscles tense, his body leaned back, ready to pounce. Dante stared at the dog, confused by his presence, but also reassured – by his defiance, by the fact he couldn't care less that the odds weren't in his favor. Delay, Dante thought. Don't lose hope. He looked up at White.

'I dumped the body at the same safe house you killed Riccardo in,' he lied. 'In the backyard, under those fruit trees by the retaining wall. I figured it made sense keeping everything at the same crime scene.'

White's eyes narrowed as he considered this. He turned to Schodt.

'Call Mitchell,' White said. 'Tell him to go over there and check and call us back.'

Schodt nodded, let Dante go and headed inside. Dante slumped onto the tiles. White lowered the gun from Loretta's head, held it by his side. Dante looked at her. He looked at the dog, barking still. He frowned, realized it wasn't just White and McKinney the dog was barking at. From its position further along the terrace, there was another possibility.

Which meant this was it. This was the moment.

Dante and Loretta were kneeling, White and McKinney were standing, Schodt was walking inside to make the call. The positioning was as good as it could be, and it had to happen now, because if Schodt made that call, the clean-up would be so much trickier.

'Take a deep breath,' Dante whispered to Loretta.

She frowned, not getting it. Dante's heart thumped.

'Breathe!' he said.

The same moment McKinney realized what the dog was barking at.

'Shit,' he said, raising his gun.

Now, Dante thought.

He barreled into Loretta, arm over her shoulder, pitching them both forwards, into the pool, crashing through its surface, Loretta flailing, the cold hitting them, cold enough to stop their hearts, to suck the air from their lungs.

He thought of the Indians from the myth, jumping into the Pacific. He thought of the oil derricks at Huntington Beach, marching into the water, disappearing beneath the waves.

He felt Loretta trying to push upwards, to the surface, and he pulled her down. She opened her eyes and through the blue chlorine sting they stared at each other, gazes blurred and burning. She was bewildered, scared. He tried to calm her with his expression, kept her down.

Then the roar of guns started up. Even under the water they could hear it, a firefight above their heads, out on the terrace. Screams, thumps, shattering glass, the howls and barks of the dog.

They looked up instinctively. They could see muzzle flare now, bursts of it in time with the roars. Submachine guns. Like the tommy guns of Dante's Chicago days, but more accurate, more deadly.

Silver dots whispered into the water around them, tracing lines of air like wires. By the time Dante realized they were stray bullets, something larger had splashed into the pool, scaring them both. They turned to see a huge black shape rotating, swirling, releasing a mist of blood into the water. It rotated some more. It was White. Cherry spots on the cotton of his shirt. A look fixed onto his face that Dante couldn't fathom. A dead man's stare.

Loretta jerked in shock. Dante held her tighter.

There were more roars from the terrace.

Then the noise died out.

Dante's lungs were burning. He wanted to break out of the water, breathe again. But he gave it a few more seconds, just in case.

There were no more shots.

He nodded at Loretta. They both rose, burst up into the daylight. Gasped for air.

They looked around. It was a bloodbath. Schodt and McKinney were both dead, lying in puddles of blood by the side of the pool. The glass doors at the back of the house had been shattered. There was the smell of gunpowder. The dog was trotting over to them. O'Shaughnessy was standing at the edge of the pool, holding an MP5. There were another four men with him, all likewise armed, roaming the terrace, stepping through into the house to look for accomplices.

O'Shaughnessy held out his free hand, pulled Loretta out of the pool, then Dante.

'You both OK?' he asked.

They nodded. Dante turned to Loretta and they hugged. He felt her body against his, its warmth, its solidity. They let go of each other. The dog was yapping about them now. Dante turned and looked down into the water where White's body floated across the pool's surface, a trail of blood turning it a rusty brown.

'Sorry it took us so long,' O'Shaughnessy said. 'First clear shots we had we took 'em.'

'Sorry you had to do it the hard way.'

O'Shaughnessy shook his head. 'It was payback. You and Loretta get out of here. We'll start with the clean-up.'

Dante nodded. They'd arranged on the phone beforehand to make it look like a bust gone wrong. Like White and his goons had been killed by drug smugglers they were trying to arrest, like they should all get hero's funerals.

Dante and Loretta made their way back across the terrace, the lawn, the shattered glass. As they stepped through into the house, Dante turned and took a last look at the million-dollar view behind him. From his perspective it seemed like the blood-tinted pool was touching the smoke-tinted sky, that they'd merged into a single body, that water, air, smoke and blood had become one – beauty and destruction intertwined, drifting over the city, trailing a fiery redemption that Dante felt was burning just for him.

# 70

Bullets smashed into the house, skittering into the wood. Ida yanked Williams back, knocking into Kerry, tumbling into the hallway as the walls and floorboards were ripped apart under the onslaught. They scrambled backwards, out of range, ran into the kitchen at the back of the house.

'You both OK?' Ida asked.

'I'm all right,' Kerry nodded.

'Bud, you doing OK?'

Williams mumbled a response.

Ida looked back down the hallway to the open front door. The barrage had stopped, all was quiet.

'You think he's still there?' Kerry asked.

'Could be. Or maybe he's coming round the back.'

They turned to look through the windows, studied the empty ground at the rear of the house. Further on was a wooded area that sloped down into the valley, beyond which was the fire. Ida felt a dizzy claustrophobia, trapped between Faron out front, and the inferno behind.

'What do we do?' Kerry asked.

'I don't know. Let me think.'

As she tried to figure it out, she noticed Williams staring out of the windows, talking to himself, muttering, panicked.

'He's here,' he said. 'The Devil's here.'

Had he seen Faron? Was he flanking them?

'Where, Bud?' Ida asked. 'Where is he?'

'*So do not fear, for I am with you; do not be dismayed, for I am your God.*'

'Bud!'

But he didn't answer, he just carried on staring out of the window, reciting Bible verses.

Ida scanned the surroundings, trying to spot Faron. But she couldn't see anything. She turned back to look at Williams.

'Bud, where did you see him? Bud?'

Again he didn't answer. He finished his verses and steeled himself. Then he ran to the back door out into the dust.

'No,' Ida shouted.

She watched him disappearing over the edge of the slope, down into the woods, toward the inferno.

'Look,' Kerry said, gesturing further along the tree line.

Faron. He was already after Williams. He must have been walking in an arc around the house to flank them when he'd seen Williams running into the woods.

'What do we do?' Kerry asked.

'I don't know.'

'They're getting away. We've got to do something.'

'They're running into an inferno.'

Kerry looked at Ida with an expression that was hard to fathom – disappointment, hurt – and something else that Ida hadn't seen so clearly on the girl before – bloodlust. Kerry had seen Stevie's murderer run off into the distance and it had awakened her anger.

'We need to go after him,' Kerry said.

'Who? Faron or Williams?'

Kerry glared, her anger all too clear. The death drive was still in the girl. Even after everything they'd been through, she was still choosing death.

And then she broke off glaring, turned and ran out of the house after Faron and Williams.

'Dammit,' Ida muttered.

She steeled herself and ran after Kerry as best she could. With every step her lungs burned, her heart pounded, shockwaves rattled through the aging armature of her body. She stumbled down the slope, past oaks, sycamores, walnuts, past thickets of ceanothus, sagebrush, chamise. The smoke got worse. Ash poured through the sky. The leaves underfoot were so parched they crackled like ice as she ran. Now and then she thought she heard gunshots only to realize it was a tree splitting and crashing.

Eventually the slope eased off into the canyon bed, a flat clearing. Ida stopped, tried to catch her breath, felt the pain sear through her body. On the other side of the clearing was the slope of the next hill along, the fire already at its peak. She could see the flames swooping between the trees, a curtain of monstrous torches as tall as the largest oak. Plumes of black and gray smoke marbled into the sky, choking the light. Ida used the smoke to check the wind direction. It had changed, was sending the fire toward her, down the slope, into the clearing. She had even less time than before.

A scream reverberated along the canyon. Kerry. Ida looked down the canyon bed in the direction it had come from. Further along was a firebreak, dozens of yards across, gouged out of the earth, and next to it, a high stone wall.

As Ida turned to run toward it, she heard a scuttling, shifting, braying sound. It took her a second to realize what it was – countless animals running through the oaks and eucalyptus on the hill opposite, away from the flames, into the clearing. A surge of quails, skunks, rabbits, bobcats. As if the carpet of the woods had risen up in a wave. And then a larger rustling, a deer and its calf bursting through the trees, both of them covered in soot, the doe searching for a path through the flames to get her baby to safety.

For the first time since Ida had left the road it wasn't fear that gripped her heart, but a deep, painful sadness. There'd be others burning in this inferno: wild birds and domestic animals. And people, too. The woods were littered with cabins and shacks where vagrants and dropouts and runaways lived. How many had been left behind in the evacuation?

As the last of the animals rushed past, something knocked Ida off balance. She tripped and fell, smashed her head on a rock and a kaleidoscope of dark colors swirled around her. Ash flecked her vision. The sunlight dimmed and disappeared.

How long had she been lying on her bed of leaves and ash? Her throat stung, her lungs burned. There was a fierce heat all around. Like a furnace. Like a cremation.

She opened her eyes and saw the fire had crept up on her while she'd been knocked out. The slope on the far side of the clearing was already ablaze; the flames racing down it with eerie speed. Firebrands fell from the trees, rolled along the ground. Everything moved in the roiling flames, danced in hypnotic orange flickers. In the distance she heard a crashing sound like mortars going off, like the roar of hell.

Around her, black ashes smothered everything. Her clothes and hands were smeared with them. The darkness had become real, heavy, was bundling her up, suffocating her. She tried to rise but couldn't. Too breathless in the heat, her lungs searing. There was no oxygen now; it had been sucked out of the air to feed the fire, leaving just a thick chemical stench.

There was no way out of this.

She knew what the easiest course of action was – to lie back down, to let the smoke fill her lungs, knock her out, so when the flames crossed the clearing and reached her, she would already be asleep.

Lie down. Breathe. Drift into nothingness.

She coughed and turned onto her side, closed her eyes. Everything was dark and peaceful now. She could feel herself falling away.

But just as she was about to succumb, her mind snagged on something – the merest grain of a thought – the thought of the others out there in the inferno, of Kerry left to fight Faron alone. An all-consuming sadness poured through her. A barbed sadness. It needled her, dragged her back from the edge, woke her up, made it impossible for her to just lie there.

She couldn't do the easy thing. She had to keep fighting. Right to the very end. Even if she couldn't save Kerry, at least she'd die standing on her feet. The idea of it spurred her on, filled her with a last burst of strength.

She opened her eyes. And just as she did so, a gust of wind blasted past, and she heard a rumbling noise, buzzing and sharp. A bomber. Roaring across the canyon from the east, opening up its tanks, dropping a pink cloud of flame retardant. The dark sky above shimmered in a haze, warped. Droplets fell through the blackness, sparkling, hissing, evaporating, dissipating the smoke.

The plane moved off, having dampened the flames enough for Ida to breathe again.

She tried rising once more. And managed it.

She set off scrambling along the canyon bed, toward the firebreak and the stone wall from where Kerry's scream had arisen.

When Ida reached the stone wall, she skirted around it and stopped, awed by the sight in front of her. On the other side of the wall was a man-made plateau on which another housing development had been constructed. Just a few large houses set behind the stone wall. If the firebreak had been created to save them, it hadn't worked. The fire had passed through here days ago and turned them all to cinders, their wooden frames collapsed and lying in heaps. Here and there stubs of plumbing poked up out of the ground. In one spot a house had completely burned away except for its stone fireplace and chimney, which rose into the air like a totem pole, like an altar. Elsewhere blackened lumps suggested destroyed cars and outbuildings.

Ida stumbled through this scene of destruction, unnerved by how empty and quiet it was, even though the fire was just further down the canyon. She came to a perfect square in the soot in front of her and stopped. It took her a second to realize what it was – a swimming pool, its surface so covered with ash it was almost indistinguishable from its surroundings. She stared at it a moment. The oily slicks on its surface undulated, revealing what was underneath – mink coats, jewelry boxes, diamonds, gold chains. Glistening like Jean Lafitte's pirate treasure. The owners of the house had stashed their valuables in the pool, hoping they didn't burn.

She heard a noise and looked up. Shapes appeared through the ash beyond the wall, skimming through the sky. Half a dozen birds, their wings on fire. Ida watched them pass. Heard their dire squawking. Wondered if, when they finally fell to earth, they would spread the fire to new parts of the forest, cutting off her path back to safety, trapping her.

Something moved on the far side of the pool. Ida raised her gun, aimed, waited. From behind the melted wreck of a car, something separated itself from the ash carpeting the ground. Kerry, dragging herself forwards, face and clothes smothered in soot, one arm clasped over her abdomen. She was moving away from Faron, who Ida could see now standing further in the distance. He stomped toward Kerry, raised his shotgun. He hadn't noticed Ida.

She saw it all playing out. Faron shooting Kerry then turning his gun on Ida, killing her finally, after all these years.

'Hey,' she screamed. Thinking of no other way to distract him from firing the shot that would set it all in motion.

He looked up at her. Their eyes met. Before any expression formed in them, Ida fired. Again and again. So scared she'd miss that she was wasting rounds, emptying her gun. And he was firing back, off balance. And everything felt like it was frozen, the lines of the bullets connecting them, their interlocked gazes, all of it in a place beyond time.

And then one of the bullets caught him. In the shoulder. He jerked, fell into the black dust. And time resumed with a thump.

Ida's heart was beating again, the world recommenced its motion. Fear flooded into her like a tide. Terrified he'd rise, she aimed for him once more as he lay scrabbling on the ground. She squeezed the trigger. Her gun clicked empty.

She ran around the pool, through the pain, grabbed Kerry by the shoulder, tried to sit her up.

'Are you all right?'

Kerry nodded that she was OK.

'Where's your gun?' Ida asked.

'I dropped it back there.' Kerry gestured behind her, toward Faron. Ida saw the gun lying halfway between them. Faron was still writhing about on the ground, his blood bright red on the black earth. But he was turning now, a hand on the ash, scrabbling more shells from his pocket, reloading the pump.

Ida didn't have time to think. She ran toward Kerry's gun, toward Faron. The distance seemed to stretch, like she was in a nightmare. Faron was already rising, already swinging the shotgun toward her. And she was nowhere near Kerry's gun yet. She'd get there too late.

Faron fired. Both barrels.

But his aim was off, the wound in his shoulder sending his shots wide.

Ida reached Kerry's gun, collapsed into the ash, lifted it as Faron was reloading.

She fired.

They looked at each other through the muzzle flare.

He grinned even as Ida's bullet burrowed into his forehead, as his body was knocked back onto the ground, as his blood began to pump out of the wound.

Ida let out a sob, a woozy exhalation of adrenaline and relief. But even though she knew he was dead, she kept her gaze fixed on him, waiting for him to twitch, to rise up, to continue the fight. After all these years of fearing him, it felt impossible that he could no longer be a threat.

As she stared, she heard something over the distant roar beyond – Kerry shuffling toward her. She was saying something, pointing beyond Faron to Williams, who was stumbling back toward them through the smoke, dazed, agitated, confused, but physically fine. He looked at Faron's body, then at Ida, with surprise.

'Come on,' Kerry said. 'We need to go.'

Ida nodded. The wind could change direction at any moment, sending the fire between them and the road, cutting off their path. But Williams continued to amble toward them as if he had all the time in the world.

Ida rose, grabbed him by the wrist and together with Kerry they pulled him back the way they'd come. Kerry was still unsteady on her feet, dazed, like she'd been hit, concussed.

'What happened to you?' Ida asked.

'I don't know. The smoke, maybe. I kept on blacking out.'

They stumbled on. They left the development, reached the slope which led back to the road. Another bomber roared overhead, dropping another pink cloud all around them. It made the rocks slippery, made them hiss and steam, made them crack open in explosive booms.

They clambered up the slope, Ida's limbs straining, her muscles feeling like they were being ripped apart. They made it to the higher ground. Ida stopped and turned to look at the canyon below them, to make sure once more that Faron was dead. She waited a few seconds for the smoke to shift, and then she saw him lying prostrate in a pool of saturated red, surrounded by a sea of black ash. Lifeless. Finally. The flames were catching up with him, were already licking at his boots. Soon he would be nothing but ash, like he'd never even existed.

They carried on up to the road. They reached Ida's car. Ida pushed Williams into the backseat, and she and Kerry got into the front. Ida prayed that Faron hadn't tampered with the engine.

She turned the key, and it started.

Ida drove up the incline. They passed Faron's car on the side of the road, half-hidden behind a clump of ceanothus bushes. Kerry watched it as they went, frowning.

'Stop!' she shouted.

'What is it?'

'Stop,' Kerry repeated. 'I saw something on the backseat. Bags. Folders. Maybe he found Hennessy's evidence. We need to go back.'

Ida stopped the car. Turned to look back down the slope at Faron's Dodge. It was already being engulfed in flames, along with the two houses either side of it, the shingles of their cedar shake roofs popping in the heat.

'No, Kerry. We don't have time. We've got Williams. We need to go.'

Kerry stared at her and Ida was worried she'd jump out again and run to Faron's car. But something passed through Kerry's eyes; something inside her had broken. She nodded, tears streaming down the soot on her face.

Ida eased off the brake, and they carried on. As they reached the brow of the ridge, and she turned the bend, they glanced back down the road.

'Look,' Kerry said.

Ash was swirling up from Faron's car, yellow fragments of legal paper, whole folders, blowing across the road, catching alight, glowing, sparking, tumbling across the scorched earth – the last evidence of the grand conspiracy, disappearing in the wind.

# PART TWENTY-FOUR

## IT ALL COMES TOGETHER
## IN LOS ANGELES!

January 1968

# Los Angeles Times

LARGEST CIRCULATION IN THE WEST

## Monday Final

MONDAY MORNING, JANUARY 1, 1968

80 PAGES, DAILY, 10c

~

## LOCAL NEWS

~

# 17 DEAD AND THOUSANDS LEFT HOMELESS AS FLAMES BURN 180,000 ACRES

*By John Torgerson*
*Times Staff Writer*

MALIBU – The worst series of brushfires in Southern California history were finally brought under control yesterday, leaving shocked residents and county officials to count the damage. Since the fires started just over a week ago, seventeen fatalities have been confirmed, twelve of them firefighters, almost 300 homes have been destroyed, and almost 200,000 acres of land, in an arc from Thousand Oaks to Topanga, have been left blackened and scarred. Uncounted thousands were forced to flee their homes in areas where official evacuation orders were imposed.

During the worst of the fires, the coastal plain resembled a war zone, with smoke rising over two miles into the sky, swept along by hot, dry Santa Ana

winds. Residents across the Southland, sitting on
porches, yards and beaches, watched the conflagration as if watching a fireworks display.

### Unusually Fierce Winds

Firefighters and Forest Service Officials blamed
fierce Santa Ana conditions for the fires; the fiercest
in recent memory, unseasonably late, unusually
strong, completely devoid of mercy. The winds
reached up to 85 miles per hour and swept sparks
through canyons, all the way to the ocean, causing
fires to spread rapidly along multiple routes at once.

At the height of the blaze, a single conflagration
stretched from Agoura Hills to Malibu Beach, where
movie stars' houses burned, and the asphalt of
Pacific Coast Highway melted. Evacuees watched the
hellish scenes from the beaches, on which unlucky
horses that had been caught in the blaze and were
still aflame, were put out of their misery by the bullets of Sheriff's Deputies' guns.

### Pages of pictures: Page 14, Section A, and Section C, Page 1

'It's only just the start,' one Malibu resident complained. 'Now the brush has been burned, the rain'll
come and the mudslides. Whole subdivisions'll go
down. The government needs to spend more money
on protecting us.'

Perhaps the calls for such fixes will be heeded;
among the homesteads destroyed was that of Governor Ronald Reagan, who briefed the press on
rescue and reconstruction efforts over the weekend.

Please turn to Page B, Col. 1

# Los Angeles Times

LARGEST CIRCULATION IN THE WEST

## Thursday Final

THURSDAY MORNING, JANUARY 18, 1968

80 PAGES, DAILY, 10c

~

## NATIONAL NEWS

~

# NEW DRUG ENFORCEMENT AGENCY ANNOUNCED

*By Stephen Newark*
*Washington Correspondent*

WASHINGTON – The Justice Department announced yesterday that the Federal Bureau of Narcotics is to be merged into the FDA's Bureau of Drug Abuse Control (BDAC) to form a new 'super-agency' to oversee narcotics control.

Attorney General Ramsey Clark announced the move at his weekly press briefing, following on from a pre-Christmas announcement that the FBN was to be moved from the Treasury's control to the Justice Department's, before being wound down. Mr. Clark cited jurisdictional overlap between the FBN and BDAC, and the need for stricter budget controls as reasons for the merger. Though talk among those close to the decision say another major factor was the FBN's recent run of corruption scandals.

The new organization, provisionally entitled the Drug Enforcement Administration, will be headed up by Thomas Mitchell, the former Deputy Director of the CIA's Crime and Narcotics group. The choice of head came as a surprise to many as it had been expected someone from within either the FBN or BDAC would fill the post. Factions within both organizations had been maneuvering in recent weeks to get one of their candidates installed at the top.

Briefing off the record, staffers in the Attorney General's office suggested the choice of someone unaffiliated to either of the two predecessor agencies may have been a means for the new organization to maintain neutrality and start with a clean slate.

# 71

*Thursday, January 18th*

Kerry had set off early that morning, under a bright sky, the smell of orange blossom in the air. She'd had to take the Ventura Freeway as the melted asphalt of Pacific Coast Highway was still being re-laid after the fires. Skirting along the northern edge of Malibu she could see the hills close by blazing yellow with wild mustard. Beyond them, higher up, were the charred, blackened hills and mountains where the fires had burned. The air was so dry and clear she could make out all the details – the bluffs, the ridges, the roads, the scorch marks, the firebreaks gouged into the earth.

The sight of them made her shudder with revulsion, her emotions jumping back to the inferno. In the nights since, dreams of fire had terrified her once more. As if the same flames that had burned her in Vietnam had followed her here to finish the job, but through blind luck, and Ida's help, she'd survived.

She and Ida had been buying the papers every day, searching for news on Faron's body being discovered, news on the FBN and the CIA, on the conspiracy with Vacaville and the cocaine routes. But there'd been nothing. The FBN had been closed down and its successor – the DEA – was already being set up. The successor which would bust the small fish, while letting the CIA-connected big fish move whatever narcotics they liked around the world. There was no talk either of the drug tests in Vacaville, or of their connection to Bud Williams.

After Ida and Kerry had left Hennessy's, they'd stopped at a

Forest Service checkpoint and called Detective Towne, who'd come and taken Bud into custody. As a way of keeping Ida and Kerry out of it, they'd concocted a story with Towne that Bud had been wandering about in the forest and a passer-by had found him, handed him over to the authorities, then disappeared.

Within a day *Night-Slayer Caught!* headlines were splashed all over the papers. Journalists were swarming over Bud's backstory, his time in Vacaville. But no mention was ever made of the drug tests that had sent him over the edge. Public anger was reserved for the authorities who'd clearly released Williams from the Medical Facility too early. After a quick psychological check he was sent straight back to Vacaville to await a more comprehensive medical competency evaluation, which would decide whether he was fit to stand trial.

And that was it.

The narrative of the Night-Slayer's origins would be one of governmental incompetence, of the Department of Corrections assessing his risk incorrectly when they released him. Vacaville had already been cleared of anything incriminating long ago. Hennessy's evidence had burned in the wildfires. The rest of the inmates who'd taken part in the program had dispersed or been killed or were smart enough to keep their mouths shut. And who'd believe them, anyway? They'd all been certified as criminally insane. Maybe a few of the guards might turn whistle-blower, but they were probably smart enough to keep quiet, too. The only real shred of evidence remaining was Williams, and no one had heard from him since he'd been reincarcerated. And even if he could get word out, would anyone believe him either?

In a way, it had worked out well for Ida and Kerry. The cover-up benefited them as much as it did the CIA. With Faron and White dead, and Bud Williams safely locked up in a secure facility, there was now no reason for the Agency to send anyone after them. Faron's charred remains, if they were ever found, would be too burned up to be identified; he'd go down as just another anonymous victim of the wildfires, not a CIA operative tasked with killing innocent Americans. Hennessy's files, and the evidence they contained, were all gone. The fire had done its work, and Ida and Kerry could go on with their lives.

For Kerry that meant making the arrangements for Stevie's funeral. She'd thought about burying him near their family home. But was it really a family home? Was there anything left in Louisiana apart from disappointment and painful memories? Kerry thought that maybe laying Stevie to rest in LA could be a statement of intent, a way of reassuring herself that she'd stay, build a life in the city. She'd had enough of running toward death. She and Stevie had promised each other they'd start a new life in California and Kerry could keep up her end of the pact at least.

There were only a handful of people at the funeral: Kerry, Ida, Ida's husband who'd returned from Germany, her friend Dante and his wife Loretta, Tom from the hostel. It was pitiful, but then why wouldn't it be? It was the funeral of a teenaged runaway.

After the ceremony they'd gone back to Ida's in Fox Hills and as everyone stood about talking in the lounge Kerry had a sense of people coming together. She'd traveled to LA to find the last remaining part of her family and now there was nothing left of it. But in this gathering she sensed the possibility of finding a new family. Not the one she'd come here to find, but a family nonetheless.

So she took up Ida's offer to stay, had called her captain at Cam Ranh Bay, asked for sick leave for bereavement, requested a discharge on medical grounds. Her captain had told her he'd help her out in any way he could, would initiate the process. Now all that was left was for her to travel to an Air Force base and go through the formalities. She could have gone to Los Angeles Air Force Station in El Segundo but chose instead to drive all the way up to Travis, because it was just a stone's throw from Vacaville, and she had unfinished business there.

\*

When she got to Travis she was directed to a small building somewhere at the edge of the base. She parked outside it, killed the engine, turned to get her bag from the backseat and the burns on her neck pulsed. The heat of the wildfire had set back her recuperation, but not by much. In a few weeks the worst of it would subside. In the meantime she was tackling the pain with aspirin, having decided not to buy any more Dilaudid when her original supply had run out. No point picking up an addiction just to see her through a few more weeks.

She stepped into the building, was directed to a tiny office where a bored-looking administrator ran her through the formalities. She signed a form stating she agreed with the assessment that she was no longer capable of remaining on active duty, she was given a card to read out acknowledging she understood the GI Bill of Rights, she was made to sign a paper declaring the same, then she was asked if she had any military equipment to return.

'I brought my dress uniform. And my battle fatigues.'

'Clothes aren't equipment.'

He handed Kerry copies of the papers she'd signed, and an envelope.

'It's got your last paycheck inside,' he said. 'Have a nice day now.'

'That's it?' Kerry frowned.

'That's it. You're a civilian again.'

She felt disappointed by the lack of ceremony, how mundane the whole thing had been.

When she stepped outside, she looked at the bundle of clothes she'd brought with her. The battle fatigues were almost completely faded, a sign back in Vietnam that Kerry was experienced, that newcomers needed to pay her respect. All that was gone now. She ran her thumb over the fabric. Maybe she should keep the clothes, store them in a box somewhere, show them to her kids if she ever had any.

She looked around, found a garbage can and tossed them in.

\*

Ten minutes later she was at Vacaville. She signed in, was led through into a reception area, where she sat on a bench and waited for the guard. She'd called him days earlier to arrange the visit, discovered his name was Luke. He'd sounded surprised to hear from her, told her they were fielding multiple calls from journalists every day trying to interview Bud Williams, but the authorities were making sure no one got close to him, vetting all visitors, keeping him in solitary confinement, sedated with barbiturates. Between them, Luke, Kerry and Ida had come up with a fake name for her and a cover story – she was posing as a worker from a charity connected to the church Bud Williams' grandmother attended, there to do a wellness check and deliver religious literature.

She looked up and saw Luke approaching across the reception area.

'Miss Harrison?' he said, using the fake name.

Kerry smiled, rose from the bench. They shook hands.

'May I?' He gestured to Kerry's bag, made like he was looking through it, then he led her down a series of corridors.

'I'm not sure how much sense you're going to get out of him,' he said.

'Yeah, I know. I read the psychological reports. It's worth a try, though.'

They kept going, turned a corner, down another corridor, and then they approached a door. Luke pulled keys from his belt and unlocked the door. They stepped through into a tiny visiting room where Bud was sitting at a metal table, his hands and feet cuffed. Chains connected the cuffs to the table legs, which were bolted into the floor.

'Bud, your visitor's here,' Luke said.

Bud looked up at them, his face blank. Luke had been right – he was doped to the eyeballs.

'I'll wait outside,' Luke said.

Kerry sat, placed the bag on the table, studied Bud. Here was the Night-Slayer, the man who'd gruesomely butchered four Angelinos, who'd terrorized the city. Here was Bud Williams, a frightened-looking, confused, sedated kid, not much older than herself. She felt it would have been right to sit in moral judgment of him. It was what his crimes demanded, and his victims. But he cut such a pitiable figure she found it hard. He barely seemed connected to this world. It was almost like trying to assign blame to the actions of a sleepwalker. How could someone be evil and not evil at the same time? How could he be so unique and also so unremarkable?

'You're the lady from the fire,' Bud said. His voice was soft and childlike, almost comically so, with a slight Louisiana lilt even after all his years in California.

'Yeah, you remembered,' Kerry replied.

'They said you were from Grandma's church.'

'That too, Bud. Look, I brought you some stuff.'

Kerry gestured to the bag, but he just carried on staring at her.

'Bud, I wanted to talk to you about the time you spent at that house in the hills. Agent Hennessy's house.'

He came over all fearful. His eyes went wide.

'They told me not to talk about it.'

Kerry wondered who 'they' were – the doctors, or the people involved in the cover-up? Had they coached him? Threatened him?

She raised her hands, trying to calm him.

'I'm not interested in Agent Hennessy,' she said. 'I just want to know if there was someone else staying at the house while you were there?'

Kerry took out the photo of Stevie, slid it across the table.

Bud looked at it, nodded.

'He was Hennessy's friend,' he said. 'He stayed there with me sometimes. He was nice. Is he OK?'

Kerry paused.

'Sure, Bud. He's doing good. Listen. This is where it gets

complicated. This guy, Hennessy's friend, did you and him talk while you were staying at the house?'

'Sure, we talked. All the time.'

'Did he ever mention his family? His sister? Did he ever say anything about her?'

Even as she asked the questions, she felt stupid. Why had she thought this was a good idea? What did she hope she could learn? Ever since Ida had moved back to Fox Hills, and Kerry had been staying on alone in the Bunker Hill apartment, she'd found herself fixating on Stevie's last days. Then at some point she'd realized Bud might be able to fill her in on them, that he might tell her something that would lessen the pain. She'd become determined to speak to him, grabbing that final straw which might help her get closer to her brother. But now she was here, she just felt foolish for thinking it would help her if she learned more about Stevie's last days.

'He never said anything about a sister,' Bud said. 'We talked about Louisiana, though. That's where we're both from.'

'What did he say about Louisiana?'

'He talked about a house, a medicine tree in the garden. How beautiful it all was. He showed me a photo. Him and a girl dressed up like cowboys and Indians.'

'He say anything about the girl?' Kerry asked, tears in her eyes.

Bud shook his head.

'What about with Hennessy? You ever hear him talking with Hennessy?'

'Yeah, they talked about Louisiana, too. They talked about the bayou. About a dead man floating in a bayou.'

Kerry's breath caught.

'What dead man, Bud?'

Bud shrugged at her through his sedative daze.

'A dead man floating in the bayou.'

'Was it his father?'

'I don't know, miss. All I remember is them talking.' He looked at her, shook his head. 'Lot of dead people in the world, miss. Lot of dead people.'

She stared at him.

'Is that why you're so interested in folklore? In voodoo?'

He shook his head.

'Then why?' she asked.

He smiled.

'Because voodoo's what makes the world go round.'

Kerry frowned, continued to stare at him. Then she nodded, pretending she understood. She brought the conversation back to Stevie and Hennessy, asking Bud the same question she'd asked previously, but phrasing it differently. Again the answer was too vague. Again she knew she couldn't press him too hard for fear he'd clam up.

She persisted for another twenty minutes, but got nowhere. Whatever it was she came here to find, she hadn't found it. The visit hadn't helped heal her wounds, it had opened them up even further.

A half-hour after leaving Vacaville she was parked off the side of the road leading back to the freeway, just opposite one of those signs: *Warning! Hitch-hikers may be escaped lunatics.* It made her think of Bud and his talk about dead people and voodoo. Ever since they'd first tracked him down, she'd had questions about his crimes. Probably the same ones the journalists and psychiatrists had – why had he done what he'd done? Was he killing for pleasure? Was it a compulsion? Was he trying to fix the broken part of his psyche with the murders? Was it all just a ritual? Sacrifices to a voodoo God he'd fallen into worshipping?

But as he'd sat in front of her, forlorn and pathetic, she realized all such speculation was pointless. He didn't have the self-awareness or the lucidity to know why he'd done anything. He was a zombie, a sleepwalker, a man drifting through a dream world, never realizing that his actions had consequences in the real world that he could barely perceive. There'd be no answers. Just the depressing lesson that bad things happened for no reason. That Bud was just a part of the chaos, strife and violence that underpinned life.

Luke's beaten-up Oldsmobile appeared further down the road, turned off, pulled in next to her. He got out, crossed to her car, got in. He had two paper packages with him.

'Sandwiches,' he said. 'Cheese or ham?'

Kerry took the cheese one, and they ate, watching the dust swirling about on the road, the sign on the other side shaking in the wind.

'You get anything useful out of him?' Luke asked.

Kerry shook her head.

'Yeah, he's pretty strung out,' he said. 'And he never made much sense in the first place.'

'If anything it made things worse.'

'How so?'

'It just made me realize how stupid I was for coming up here.'

'It wasn't stupid. It was a chance, and you took it.'

'Sure.'

It felt as if Luke was being honest, not just trying to make her feel better. But she still felt stupid, like she'd been fooling herself. There were no simple solutions. Kerry was damaged, physically, emotionally, psychologically. It would take years to work her way through everything. The road to where she wanted to go would be long and difficult; there'd be setbacks. First of all she needed to figure out *how* to fix herself, *how* to get better. Because if her trip here had proved anything, it was that Bud Williams was not the answer. And the idea that Stevie and Hennessy had discussed her father's death just muddied the waters further. She thought back to that Army Corps nurse who she'd flown out to Vietnam with that first time, what she'd said about the ones who accepted they needed help being the ones who made it through.

'What's going to happen to Bud?' she asked.

Luke shrugged.

'It's supposed to be up to the doctors and the judge. If they decide he's fit to stand trial, he'll either end up tied and fried or the people in charge of the cover-up will have him killed before he ever sets foot in a courthouse. A faked suicide, an overdose, a fall. I'm surprised they haven't tried it already. Maybe he'll get lucky and they'll let him spend the rest of his life in the prison system, doped up and in solitary.'

He shrugged again, wearily.

They talked a while longer, till he said his break time was almost done. Kerry handed him a scrap of paper with her number on it.

'If you're ever in LA,' she said.

He smiled, tipped an imaginary hat, then got out of the car. Kerry watched him drive off through the dust.

She needed a cigarette. She fumbled around the dash, found her pack, lit a smoke. In the lighter's flame she saw the napalm blaze of Vietnam, the brushfires of Malibu, Faron's body consumed, the stash of evidence burned, Stevie curled up in that trunk.

She had to believe that one day she'd stop seeing all these things, that she'd stop looking for a family that was no longer there, that she hadn't really left pieces of her soul in Vietnam, in Louisiana, that one day she'd be whole again. It might not happen, but she knew the best place to try. The place where it all came together.

She started up the car and headed back to LA.

# 72

Dante sat on a bench with his back to the seafront, watching the terrace of the Georgian Hotel, its well-heeled guests, its perfectly attired staff. On Ocean Avenue crowds headed for the sand or the shops, passing by the red poinsettias adorning the windows and doorways of pretty much every building. From the seamless blue sky above, light bounded down so clear and pure and sharp, it could have been movie-stage lighting. Dante basked in it, aware he didn't have long to enjoy it. He and Loretta would be leaving soon. There was only one piece of business left, one last hurdle to jump before they could leave with their safety assured. Everything else was already wrapped up.

Dante had been forced to sell the distribution company at a huge discount with the warehouse and stock gone, really only selling the name and the goodwill and the existing contracts. But he'd offset most of the shortfall with the finder's fee he'd got from Licata, enough to keep the bankers' fears assuaged, so the deal went through. The buyer had even offered jobs to the company's current employees when a new warehouse was found.

And then the fire investigator's report came back. Due to the large volume of alcohol in the warehouse, it was impossible to tell if any accelerant had been used to start the fire, if it was arson. Bach's body had been recovered, but it was so badly burned they couldn't identify him. So with most of the evidence and the crime scene incinerated, the prosecutors didn't think it was worth pursuing as homicide.

The only thing that didn't look like it was going Dante's way was the insurance report. The company was stalling, saying it would take months to complete. Dante got the sense they were trying to wear him down, or were looking for loopholes. If what he knew about insurance companies was right, they'd find a way not to pay out. But he didn't care. He'd scraped enough together to salvage the vineyard deal, and it had gone through. Hoping the insurance paid out almost seemed greedy.

He'd gone to see Licata a couple of times over the last few weeks. The first time to explain how he'd found Riccardo's body. Dante had concocted a story that Zullo had killed Riccardo, that Zullo was the coke source, that he was getting it from someone out in Vegas. Probably. Blaming it all on the unfortunate Zullo meant Licata would never learn about the CIA link. Dante had even kept Roselli's betrayal a secret, how Roselli had only suggested Dante as the man to find Riccardo because he wanted the search to fail, figuring Dante wasn't up to much anymore. Even though it must have been Roselli who'd tipped off White when Dante started making progress, causing him to send Bach and DeVeaux round to the warehouse to kill him. By keeping quiet, Dante had saved Roselli's life, which meant he had leverage against Roselli to safeguard his own future.

As for the two men who'd been following Dante in the black sedan, he still wasn't certain who they were, though he had a feeling they were probably CIA. Hence his sitting on a bench in Santa Monica in the winter sun.

At a little after ten an old man shuffled along the avenue, sat at a prime table on the Georgian's terrace. Dante waited till the waiter had gone over to take his order, till the man had lit a cigarette. Then he rose and headed over. Roselli spotted him before he'd even stepped onto the terrace. Dante took a seat opposite him without saying a word.

'Dante,' Roselli said, trying to stifle his discomfort. 'This is unexpected.'

'I was banking on it. You have a nice break in Palm Springs?'

'It was Lake Tahoe. But, yeah, it was nice.'

'A lot quieter than LA, I bet.'

'Sure.'

They eyed each other. Dante lit a Lucky, happy to draw things out, to let the tension play, to see if Roselli folded first and was the one to break the silence.

'I heard you were there when Zullo died,' Roselli said.

'I was there when White died, too.'

Roselli looked surprised.

The waiter approached. He laid Roselli's morning coffee and cognac on the table.

'Anything for you, sir?' he asked Dante.

Dante shook his head. The waiter nodded and left them. Dante looked across the vista in front of him, the swaying palms, the yellow sand, the endless blue ocean dotted with surfers waiting for the big one, the glint of a plane soaring through the air.

'You know,' he said, 'one thing I could never figure out was why you'd use Zullo and Riccardo for something this big. But White cleared that up for me. He joked about how he'd put the squeeze on the margin. You figured the only way to make it worth your while was to pass on the squeeze to a couple of two-bit bums like Zullo and Riccardo because you knew the bosses would laugh in your face at the deal they were forcing you into. You got out-muscled and outmaneuvered by the Agency, Johnny. You should be fucking embarrassed.'

Roselli said nothing. He just stared at Dante through those giant round sunglasses of his. Took a sip of cognac.

'So what do you want?' he asked eventually. 'You came here to gloat? To laugh at me? You already won, Dante. You came out on top. Zullo's dead. White's dead. Licata thinks it was Zullo who killed his son. The Agency's set up their new coke routes elsewhere. What are you coming to me for?'

'Insurance,' Dante said. 'Despite my warehouse burning down, I pulled through the vineyard deal. I'm leaving LA. Today.

Right after we stop talking. I'm driving off into the sunset, Johnny, and I don't want the stink of this following me.'

'How's that?'

'If I let anyone know what you've been doing – Licata, any of the other bosses – you're screwed. Setting up drug routes without cutting in the Commission? Looking the other way while Riccardo tried to topple his pops? Letting Riccardo get whacked? Licata might be weak but he's still a made man. Anyone finds out what I know, you're dead. I've made arrangements. Anything happens to me, everyone finds out.'

Even with the sunglasses hiding his eyes, Dante could sense the change in Roselli's attitude, an acceptance of the fact that Dante had outsmarted him.

'You think I'm going to talk?' Roselli said, offended. 'How long do we go back, Dante? Come on.'

'It's not you I'm worried about. Our side of this is wrapped up. The only people who might see me as a loose end are your handlers in the Agency. So if my name ever comes up as a loose end, you set them straight. I'm just a drink distributor who retired to Napa Valley. I've got no proof of anything, and I don't know anything, and even if I did, I'm a stand-up old-school guy who keeps his mouth shut because he ain't a rat. No need for any spooks to come after me. 'Cos if they do, it all comes out, and you're a dead man, too.'

Dante raised his eyebrows, waited for Roselli to respond.

Roselli took his time, but only for the sake of his dignity.

'The Agency's way above my pay grade. You said it yourself, they outmaneuvered me. No one calls off their attack dogs.'

'You'll find a way. You're Johnny Roselli. You brought us Hollywood on a plate. You set up the skim in Vegas. You set up the hit on Castro. On Kennedy. You helped the Agency set up their offshore slush funds. You're in the middle of bilking Howard Hughes out of a few hundred mill. You'll find a way. Your life depends on it.'

Roselli considered this, sighed.

'I didn't want it to shake out this way.'

'But it did. And it's all your fault for bringing in the Agency in the first place. This used to be our thing, Johnny. Our thing. It used to be that *we* paid *them*. That *we* controlled *them*. Now they're using us like hired help. All these deals you've been cutting all these years, they've made us weak and them strong. They remodeled their whole operation on ours, and now we got nothing. This new world they've built, we got no place in it anymore.'

'You don't think I know that already?' Roselli said. 'You don't think I know they've taken over? That we're too old now? You don't think I'm jealous you're getting out while you can?'

'You can think whatever you want,' Dante said, rising. 'Just remember what I told you. My fate is your fate now.'

When Dante returned to the Thunderbird, Loretta was waiting for him in the passenger seat, the dog in her lap. Dante got in, lit another cigarette.

'Well?' she asked.

'Roselli's a smart guy. We'll be fine.'

'So that's it? We're going?'

'Yeah, we're going.'

They smiled at each other and Dante felt a boundless gratitude for what he had, for the life he'd been blessed with.

He started up the car and sidled through Santa Monica, heading for the 405, moving out of the city after all these years. Dante would return to the same wine-growing, Mediterranean lifestyle that his grandparents had sought to leave behind when they'd emigrated from Italy almost a century before. It was funny how things shook out.

As he drove, he basked in the sun, felt its warmth on his face. He watched the traffic zooming past, felt the hum of the city. He thought about the life he'd spent in amongst its streets and alleys, its nightclubs and hotels, its mountains and beaches. LA really was heroin country. A hit to the veins. For forty years it had kept Dante and Loretta in a beautiful embrace, but now it was time to move on.

He reached out to Loretta, and she clasped his hand. They hit the freeway, and the Thunderbird soared.

# 73

Ida stood at her desk in the office and ripped open the brown paper of the package that had just been delivered. She'd received a few bouquets since she'd started the new agency, but no parcels. She pulled the last of the paper away to reveal a small attaché case. She frowned, opened it up, realized it was actually a carry case for a tape player, with a tape already loaded into it. Stuck to the top of it was a note:

*Something for the new office. I'm glad you didn't give up, Ida. The world needs every hero it can get. Louis*

She frowned again. It was probably an early version of the song he'd flown to Las Vegas to record. It surprised her. He never normally sent her copies of his records, and certainly not on something like a tape player. The last time she'd seen him was at LAX when he was flying off to the recording session. Ida had told him about the new agency. Louis had told her he was going to continue performing, safely, under doctor's orders. They'd laughed at each other. They'd hugged. He'd waltzed off toward his gate.

Ida put the tape player onto the desk, plugged it into the wall socket, tried to figure out how it worked. She tilted it into the sunshine coming in from the windows so she could read the symbols on the buttons.

She heard the outer door open and close, someone stepping through the reception area, where hopefully soon there'd actually be a receptionist. The office was as small as the one Ida had rented when she'd first moved to the city; just this room for her and Kerry, and the room out front for the receptionist. The building was one of the few old ones left on the edge of Bunker Hill that had not been zoned for demolition, partly why the rent was so cheap. Ida would be back in old Los Angeles, in the heart of things. Even as that heart changed beyond recognition. She knew she was a little old to be starting up again, but she only needed a few years to train up her protégé, could take a backseat once she was up to speed.

Kerry stepped through into the office.

'How'd it go?' Ida asked.

Kerry had made the trip upstate the day before. To the Air Force base, and then to see Bud Williams.

'He couldn't tell me much,' she shrugged.

Ida nodded. She'd expected that to be the case. They'd gone to great lengths to arrange the visit, to see if Bud might tell Kerry something about Stevie that would fill in the details of those last missing weeks, that would soothe her bereavement. Ida had felt all along that any consolation the girl might gain would come from the act of going down there, from exhausting her possibilities, rather than from anything Bud might have actually revealed. It was all part of the process.

Kerry perched herself on the windowsill, gestured to the tape player. 'What's that?'

'It's a present from a pal of mine. I think it's a recording of a song he made. I'm just trying to figure out how it works, but first . . .'

Ida went to her bag and opened it up. She passed Kerry her silver cigarette case.

'It was given to me by my mentor, Michael Talbot. He got it from his mentor. A detective named Luca D'Andrea, back in New Orleans. Decades ago now.'

'You're giving it to me?' Kerry asked.

'I guess it's a tradition.' Ida smiled.

She thought about what the case had been through: hurricanes and floods in Louisiana, explosions in Chicago, snowstorms in

New York, firestorms in LA. She wondered what it would go through yet. Whatever that was, Ida knew Kerry would make a good successor, and today, the first official business day for the new agency, was the right time to pass it on.

'Thanks,' Kerry said, with an earnestness that showed she appreciated the gift's importance. Kerry opened up the case and read the inscription on the inside. Closed the case. Brushed her fingers over its engraved design and slipped it into her pocket.

In that moment Ida felt something more than the promise of a new adventure; she felt the certainty of something eternal, an unbroken chain stretching through the darkness. From Luca to Michael to Ida to Kerry, and on into the future. No matter how times changed, how life ebbed and flowed, how cities transformed, there would always be detectives, or people like them, fighting for what they believed in, helping others, trusting in the irresistible power of hope.

Through the window behind Kerry, a plane soared through the air. Ida watched as it banked and turned an angle, glinting like a needle, threading itself eastwards through the endless blue vault of the sky. She imagined it was Louis in that plane, heading off for new horizons, for his own new adventures.

She studied the tape player once more. Found the on switch. Hit the play button. It emitted a mechanical hissing sound, like the crackling of a record before it begins to play, and then the song started up. As they sat there listening to it, Ida in her chair, Kerry perched on the windowsill, smiles rose up on their faces. The song was like a blues and a hymn all at once. A celebration and a lament. The one only possible because of the other. She thought of all the pain her friend had been through over the course of his life, all his more recent woes. And this was how he'd responded. It was as if he'd absorbed all the violence and hatred around him so as to leave the world freer of them, to produce an antidote.

Ida could see now why Louis had sent her the song. Despite the chaos, or maybe even because of it, it was a wonderful world.

If you gave it a chance. The pair of them had been ready to give in to the pessimism, but both of them had realized, through their own traumas, that they couldn't ever quit. They had to keep on. Right the way to the end. Ida looked again at the note:

*I'm glad you didn't give up, Ida. The world needs every hero it can get.*

The song came to an end and left something in the room. A warmth. A glow. A mist in the air. Kerry and Ida looked at each other, acknowledged something that couldn't be said. It was as if the song had been written for just that moment, for just that place, for just that particular color of hope.

'Your pal's Louis Armstrong?' Kerry asked.

Ida smiled, nodded.

Kerry nodded back, surprised.

'Play it again,' she said. 'It's good.'

Ida figured out how to rewind the tape and they listened to it another two times and again it left that golden mist in the room.

They could have stayed like that for hours on that bright winter morning, but their reverie was broken by a knock at the door, the sound of someone approaching through the empty reception.

'Sounds like our first customer,' Ida said, turning to Kerry.

Kerry nodded and straightened her back.

Ida smiled.

'Well, kid,' she said. 'Let's see what you're made of.'

*'Some of you young folks been saying to me "Hey Pops, what you mean 'what a wonderful world'? How about all them wars all over the place? You call them wonderful? And how about hunger and pollution? That ain't so wonderful either."*

*Well, seems to me it ain't the world that's so bad but what we're doing to it. And all I'm saying is what a wonderful world it would be if only we'd give it a chance. Love, baby, love. That's the secret. If lots more of us loved each other we'd solve more problems. And this world would be a gasser. That's what old Pops keeps saying.'*

LOUIS ARMSTRONG

# AFTERWORD

Writing this book was often an exercise in reality being stranger than fiction. I'll start with the most bizarre – LSD mind control experiments really were conducted at the California Medical Facility in Vacaville. They began in 1967 and were run by CIA operative Dr James Hamilton as part of the CIA's notorious 'MK-Ultra' program, in which drugs were given to human test subjects – often illegally – to determine their effectiveness for interrogation, brainwashing and psychological torture. Agents in the FBN had been covertly supplying the CIA with drugs for these experiments since 1951.

It is estimated up to a thousand Vacaville inmates were experimented on over the life of the program. One interesting conspiracy theory is that Donald DeFreeze, the founder of the terrorist group the Symbionese Liberation Army (who infamously kidnapped the heiress Patty Hearst in 1974), was one of the test subjects, having been sent to Vacaville after a gun battle with police in November 1969.

The 'Triangle of Death' was established in the 1960s by 'Group France', a Corsican drug smuggling ring that included ex-Nazi collaborator Auguste Joseph Ricord. Headquartered in a Buenos Aires restaurant, the group sent cocaine from Latin America to Europe, and heroin from Europe to the States, where the Mafia distributed it. That the cocaine originated from Latin American regimes backed by the CIA has led to speculation that the CIA at best knew of the smuggling, and at worst, was actively involved in it.

This latter view was certainly shared by many FBN agents who attempted to investigate these drugs routes. FBN Agent John G. Evans expressed the sentiment thus: 'Other things came to my attention, that proved that the CIA contributed to drug use in this country. We were in constant conflict with the CIA because it was hiding its budget in ours, and because CIA people were smuggling drugs into the US. But Cusack [FBN Chief of Foreign Operations] allowed them to do it, and we weren't allowed to tell. And that fostered corruption in the Bureau.'

Numerous FBN Agents were 'turned' by the CIA. There is also plenty of evidence to suggest the CIA not only had a hand in the FBN's demise, but also in the creation of its eventual successor – the DEA. The extent to which the DEA is a 'stooge organization' for the CIA is a matter of debate, but it makes a nice conspiracy on which to hang the plot of a crime thriller. I did have to compress the time frame, however; the FBN was merged with BDAC in 1968, as per the book, but it wasn't until 1973 that the newly amalgamated organization was itself dissolved and replaced by the DEA.

Special Agent George White was an actual person, and probably the most famous of all the FBN operatives. A sadist and double agent for the FBN and the CIA, White managed the CIA's MK-Ultra safe house in New York in for a time in the 1950s, which was used as a location for the poisoning of unsuspecting members of the public with LSD. The activities in the New York safe house are explored in the Errol Morris documentary *Wormwood* (2017, Netflix), and form part of Jon Ronson's non-fiction book *The Men Who Stare at Goats* (2004), subsequently adapted into a feature film in 2009.

After New York, White took over several CIA safe houses in San Francisco, all whilst continuing to work for the FBN as a 'supervisor at large'. He retired in 1965, but he makes such a perfect villain, I centered the story around him. Here he is in a letter to his MK-Ultra boss, the chemist and CIA spymaster, Sidney Gottlieb: 'I was a very minor missionary, actually a heretic, but I toiled wholeheartedly in the vineyards because it was fun, fun, fun. Where else could a red-blooded American boy lie, kill, cheat, steal and pillage with the sanction and blessing of the All-Highest.'

The information on the FBN detailed above, and in the novel, is drawn from Douglas Valentine's definitive histories of the organization and its successors, *The Strength of the Wolf* (2004), and *The Strength of the Pack* (2009).

Ronald Reagan's extensive links to organized crime have been written about in many books and articles. His corruption as governor of California, and in particular the land deal mentioned in the novel, is based on evidence detailed in Dan Moldea's *Dark Victory: Ronald Reagan, MCA, and the Mob* (1986). The ranch at the centre of the land deal is now part of the Malibu Creek State Park, and open to visitors. In the book the ranch is in the wrong place – I had to 'move' it about seven kilometres to make it adjoin Hennessy's hide-out, which I'd placed further west along the Santa Monica Mountains. (For a detailed map of the locations mentioned in the book, please visit my website: www.raycelestin. com, where there are also research photos, a bibliography and other bits and pieces.)

The descriptions of the ranch that Ida and Kerry visit (where the bodies are discovered) are based on those of Spahn Ranch, home to Charles Manson and his 'family'. The details of the fire at the end of the book are mostly based on the giant wildfires of September 1970. The same fires that destroyed Spahn Ranch, leaving Manson's 'family' homeless.

The details of the killing in the airport parking lot are based on the murder of Julius Petro by the Mafia hitman Ray Ferritto in LAX in 1969.

The statistics on the number of African-Americans killed by the Los Angeles police during the mid-sixties come from Kevin Starr's *Golden Dreams: California in an Age of Abundance* (2009). Written in a glittering prose that most novelists would be proud of, it was my favourite of all the California histories I read.

Kerry's experience of the Vietnam War is a composite made up from the accounts of nurses who served in the conflict, most of them taken from Elizabeth Norman's excellent *Women at War* (1990).

Gangster and CIA go-between 'Handsome Johnny' Roselli disappeared in 1976, shortly before he was recalled to the U.S. Senate Select Committee on Intelligence to give evidence on the assassination of President Kennedy. His body was found a few months later inside a steel drum floating in Dumfoundling Bay, Florida. He'd been asphyxiated. His killers were never caught. Also killed shortly before he was due to give evidence to the same committee was the boss of the Chicago Outfit, Sam Giancana – shot in his own house while under police guard.

The young agent who gives Louis the sheet music is Jerry Heller who worked for Joe Glaser's management agency at the time. Heller went on to found Ruthless Records in the 1980s, and became one of the most seminal, and controversial, figures in West Coast rap, thereby providing a direct link between the gangsters of the Capone era, and the gangster rappers of more recent times.

The extension of the 405 Freeway actually happened a few years earlier than it does in the book. It's a conceit I shamelessly stole from Alison Lurie's *The Nowhere City* (1965), one of the great LA novels.

Another event slightly off in its timing is the Hollywood collapse which provides the backdrop for the novel. Although the first signs of the coming sea-change were being felt in 1967, it wasn't until a couple of years later that the studios found themselves in the dire financial straits detailed in the book. MGM's infamous auction of movie memorabilia actually happened a little while later still, in 1970.

The last major element I changed was in the genesis of the song 'What A Wonderful Word'. All through the series, I've tried to keep Louis Armstrong's history as accurate as possible, but I didn't manage to keep that up here. Bob Thiele actually approached Armstrong with the idea for the song directly, playing him a demo of the composition while Armstrong was on tour in Washington, DC. Armstrong liked it and agreed on the spot to record the song. Tying the song into the pessimism Armstrong was probably experiencing at the time was my invention. The song was released in September 1967, so a few months before the book takes place.

Despite Armstrong's worsening health, he outlived his manager, Joe Glaser, who passed away in June 1969. Some years after Glaser's death, it was revealed that the Mob lawyer, Sidney Korshak (who appears in the book having lunch with Reagan), was not only the legal counsel for Glaser's management company, but also the owner of most of the company's stock as well. The management company Armstrong helped build was even more of an underworld entity than he could have imagined. Reagan's long-lasting connection to Korshak, and the mobsters Korshak worked with is detailed in Gus Russo's *Supermob* (2006). It's no surprise that the FBI labelled Korshak 'the most powerful lawyer in the world'.

Armstrong passed away in his sleep, at home in Queens, a month before his seventieth birthday in July 1971. He lay in state at the 7th Regiment Armory on Park Avenue, where 25,000 people filed past the coffin. At the funeral, which was televised, honorary pallbearers included Duke Ellington, Ella Fitzgerald, Frank Sinatra, Bing Crosby, Dizzy Gillespie, Count Basie, Guy Lombardo, Nelson Rockefeller, David Frost, Ed Sullivan and Johnny Carson.

'It's been hard goddam work, man. Feel like I spent twenty thousand years on planes and railroads, like I blowed my chops off . . . I never tried to prove nothing, just always wanted to give a good show. My life has been my music, it's always come first,' Armstrong said not long before his death.

But perhaps the best way to leave things is with the words of an unknown mourner who was interviewed by CBS whilst waiting in line at Armstrong's laying in state – Louis Armstrong had been 'a friend to all people, all colors, all nations. When they say that he was the ambassador, that's what he was – the ambassador of love.'

RAY CELESTIN
*London, July 2021*

*Acknowledgements*

Since my last book was published two critics who always gave my work enthusiastic reviews have passed away – Sarah Hughes of the *Guardian* and the *Independent*, and Marcel Berlins of *The Times*. Their reviews always buoyed up my ever-low confidence in my writing, for which I'm incredibly thankful. Rest in peace. I'd also like thank for all their help Mariam Pourshoushtari, Shemuel Bulgin, Chris Branson, Stephen Reynolds, Chantal Lyons, Adam Shelby, Julia Pye, Lucinda Smyth, Ben Heather, John Gaffney, Ed Meckle, Thonie Hevron, Douglas Valentine, Stephanie Jones, Sam Armour, Jane Finigan, Francesca Davies, Susannah Godman, Maria Rejt and Alice Gray. Everyone at L&R, Mantle and Macmillan. As usual, special thanks to Ben Maguire, Cedric Sekweyama and Nana Wilson.

The City Blues series begins with

# THE AXEMAN'S JAZZ

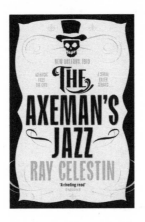

*New Orleans, 1919.*
*As a dark serial killer — the Axeman — stalks the city, three*
*individuals set out to unmask him . . .*

Detective Lieutenant Michael Talbot — heading up the
official investigation, but struggling to find leads, and
harbouring a grave secret of his own.

Former detective Luca d'Andrea — now working for the
Mafia; his need to solve the mystery of the Axeman is
every bit as urgent as that of the authorities.

And Ida Davis — a secretary at the Pinkerton Detective Agency.
Obsessed with Sherlock Holmes and dreaming of a better life, she
stumbles across a clue which lures her and her musician friend,
Louis Armstrong, to the case — and into terrible danger . . .

As Michael, Luca and Ida each draw closer to discovering the
killer's identity, the Axeman himself will issue a challenge to the
people of New Orleans: play jazz or risk becoming the next victim.

## OUT NOW IN PAPERBACK.

Discover the second book in the City Blues series,

# DEAD MAN'S BLUES

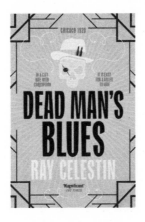

*Chicago, 1928.*
*In the stifling summer heat three investigations begin . . .*

Pinkerton detectives Michael Talbot and Ida Davis are
hired to locate a missing heiress. But it proves harder than
expected to find a woman known across the city.

After being called to a gruesome murder in Chicago's
violent Black Belt, crime-scene photographer, Jacob Russo,
can't get the dead man's image out of his head, and decides
to track down the culprit himself.

And with a group of city leaders poisoned at the Ritz, Dante
Sanfelippo – rum-runner and fixer – is called in by Al Capone to
discover whether someone is trying to bring down his empire.

As the three parties edge closer to the truth, their paths will cross
and their lives will be threatened. But will any of them find the
answers they need in the city of blues, booze and brutality?

**OUT NOW IN PAPERBACK.**

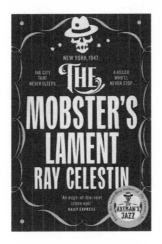